The REBELS *of*

The draug heaved itself out
ragged, and in some places bone showed through gaps. Slimy bits of it fell away to patter on the deck along with the seawater dripping from its limbs. Where the head and neck should have been, rising from a ragged hole in the torso, was a clump of seaweed, the lamina stirring as though still floating in some phantom current.

Beholding the bizarre sight, Heimdall faltered. Strings of rotted flesh flopping around its upraised half-skeletal hands, the draug pounced like an arrow flying from a bow.

Only Heimdall's years of training and battle experience saved him. His two-handed sword caught the dead man in the chest, cracked exposed ribs, and halted its charge. But the draug showed no signs of being hindered by the new wound. Taking a deep, steadying breath of salt air, Heimdall insisted to himself that was no reason for panic…

ALSO AVAILABLE

MARVEL CRISIS PROTOCOL
Target: Kree by Stuart Moore

MARVEL HEROINES
Domino: Strays by Tristan Palmgren
Rogue: Untouched by Alisa Kwitney
Elsa Bloodstone: Bequest by Cath Lauria
Outlaw: Relentless by Tristan Palmgren

LEGENDS OF ASGARD
The Head of Mimir by Richard Lee Byers
The Sword of Surtur by C L Werner
The Serpent and the Dead by Anna Stephens

MARVEL UNTOLD
The Harrowing of Doom by David Annandale
Dark Avengers: The Patriot List by David Guymer
Witches Unleashed by Carrie Harris

XAVIER'S INSTITUTE
Liberty & Justice for All by Carrie Harris
First Team by Robbie MacNiven
Triptych by Jaleigh Johnson
School of X edited by Gwendolyn Nix

MARVEL LEGENDS OF ASGARD

The Rebels of Vanaheim

Richard Lee Byers

ACONYTE

FOR MARVEL PUBLISHING

VP Production & Special Projects: Jeff Youngquist
Associate Editor, Special Projects: Caitlin O'Connell
Manager, Licensed Publishing: Jeremy West
VP, Licensed Publishing: Sven Larsen
SVP Print, Sales & Marketing: David Gabriel
Editor in Chief: C B Cebulski

Special Thanks to Wil Moss

MARVEL
© 2021 MARVEL

First published by Aconyte Books in 2021
ISBN 978 1 83908 078 4
Ebook ISBN 978 1 83908 079 1

This novel is entirely a work of fiction. Names, characters, places, and incidents are the products of the author's imagination or are used fictitiously. Any resemblance to actual events, locales, organizations or persons, living or dead, is entirely coincidental.
Sales of this book without a front cover may be unauthorized. If this book is coverless, it may have been reported to the publisher as "unsold and destroyed" and neither the author nor the publisher may have received payment for it.
Cover art by Tomasz Jedruszek

Distributed in North America by Simon & Schuster Inc, New York, USA
Printed in the United States of America
9 8 7 6 5 4 3 2 1

ACONYTE BOOKS

An imprint of Asmodee Entertainment Ltd

Mercury House, Shipstones Business Centre

North Gate, Nottingham NG7 7FN, UK

aconytebooks.com // twitter.com/aconytebooks

*For all my friends in the
Gen Con Writer's Symposium*

PROLOGUE

The house was built of vertical planks, had a thatched roof, and was supported on the outside by sloping posts. It was one of many such homes that had grown up beyond the towering walls of the royal city of Asgard. Odin's capital had grown since its founding, and there was no longer room for new homes within. Hogun waited for Gunhild on the gravel path lined with purple rosebay flowers that ran up to the door.

Gunhild was a skinny little girl with narrow, thoughtful blue eyes, a snub nose, and her pale blonde hair done up in braids. When she saw the stranger awaiting her on the path, she faltered.

That, Hogun supposed, was understandable. He knew he cut an intimidating figure with his dangling black mustachios, dark clothing, and the heavy mace in his hand. His appearance was part of the reason people named him "Hogun the Grim".

"It's all right," he said. "I'm a friend. Your mother's brother was hurt in a hunting accident. A wild boar gored him. Your parents had to run off to see him, and I volunteered to watch you after you came home from your lessons." He tried to smile, and as was often the case, the expression felt unnatural on his face.

In fact, his account wasn't quite accurate. He'd been inspecting a section of Asgard's fortifications with Gunhild's stonemason father when the man's wife came scurrying up all in a panic. Once she made it clear she wanted to rush off to see the injured brother forthwith, Hogun had offered to find someone suitable to mind the child.

It should have been easy enough, but somehow wasn't. If he'd had the household full of personal servants to which his status as one of the Realm Eternal's finest warriors entitled him, he could have sent one of them. But he preferred to live simply, alone with his thoughts when he retired to his utilitarian quarters, and now he was suffering the consequences. With the end of the school day rapidly approaching, he'd had to come to look after Gunhild himself.

He consoled himself with the reflection that it was only for one night. Surely he could foist off the task on somebody else come morning.

Gunhild eyed him for another moment, and then something, his explanation of his presence or perhaps even his attempt to force a smile, seemed to persuade her of his bona fides. "Is Uncle Varick going to be all right?" she asked.

"Yes," Hogun said, reckoning that if the man hadn't died on the spot, it was probably so. Asgardians were resilient, and their healers were skilled. "Come inside." He tramped to the door, and she trudged after him.

The long structure had twin rows of posts holding up the ceiling, benches along the walls, and chests tucked under the benches for storage. The front half was all one open space, but partitioning provided a measure of privacy toward the back. Hogun took a glance around and then considered the little girl glumly peering up at him.

"Did you bring work home from school?" he asked.

"No," she said.

"Do you have chores to do?"

"No."

Inwardly, Hogun winced. For a moment, he wondered if he could send Gunhild to bed, but of course that was preposterous. It wasn't even suppertime yet, let alone bedtime. He was going to have to try to entertain the child, a task for which he felt ill-suited due to both temperament and lack of experience.

"Do you have a ball?" he asked. "We could go back outside and throw it back and forth."

She shook her head. "I mean, I don't feel like it."

"Well, how about a hnefatafl set? Or dice?"

"I don't feel like that, either."

"We could play the question game. What am I thinking of?"

Gunhild sighed. "Is it a mace?"

Hogun gaped at her. "How could you guess it right away?"

"You glanced at the one in your hand as you were talking."

"Well… very clever. All right, it's your turn to pick something and mine to guess."

"Do we have to?"

Hogun scowled in vexation, but after a moment that feeling gave way to puzzlement. As he and Gunhild's father inspected the royal city's ramparts, the builder had often chattered about his family. The merry, lively daughter he'd described bore little resemblance to the dour child before him.

"I truly do believe your uncle will be all right," Hogun said, "and your mother and father will come home as soon as they can." He paused and continued tentatively, "I think it wise to stay home, in case your parents do return with news."

"I know," Gunhild said, but her demeanor remained as cheerless as before.

Hogun's impatience came surging back, and he took a long, steadying breath in an effort to keep it from showing. "Then what ails you? Tell me, and I'll help you if I can."

His words made the child look a bit guilty. "I'm sorry. I just have something on my mind."

"If it's not your uncle, then what?" Hogun realized that, despite his attempt to seem otherwise, he still sounded annoyed. He felt his own flicker of guilt for that and tried again to soften his voice. "If you tell me what's wrong," he reiterated, "maybe I can help you sort it out."

She looked him up and down all over again, sizing him up anew. Eventually she said, "You'd have to swear not to tell *anyone*."

"I swear it on my honor as a warrior of Asgard," he replied. "I swear it by Gungnir, the spear of the All-Father himself. Now, come sit down and tell me what's the matter." He sat on a bench. She flopped down beside him and frowned as she put her thoughts in order.

"I have these friends," she said at length.

"Of course," he said, to encourage her to continue. Even he, as irascible and taciturn a man as he knew himself to be, had friends, and good ones, too: Volstagg, Fandral the Dashing, and even Thor the God of Thunder among them.

"Girls and boys I know from school," Gunhild said. "There's

also this man named Yonas. He's grumpy and mean. He won't let anybody come on his land."

Well, it is *his* land, Hogun thought, but what he said aloud was, "Why not?"

"He says it's because his land borders the edge of the world and he doesn't want anybody falling off. But we think it's because he doesn't want anybody else eating the sloe berries and cloudberries that grow near the edge. Even though we only ever took a few!"

"Well," Hogun said, "whatever the man is actually worried about, it *is* dangerous to go too near the edge."

The Realm Eternal was a vast expanse of land perched on one limb of Yggdrasil the World Tree. It was both flat and finite. It was thus quite possible for unfortunate souls to fall off the edge. Then they would either smash themselves to pieces on a rocky outcropping protruding from what amounted to a prodigious cliff face or tumble forever through the cosmic void.

Gunhild grunted in a way that somehow conveyed her impatience with yet another adult belaboring the obvious. "Anyway, my friends. There's this boy, Leos. He's a year or two older than most of us, and he's sort of like the leader."

Hogun thought he had an inkling of where the story was going. "And Leos is angry that Yonas chased you all away? He wants to get back at him somehow?"

The girl nodded. "Kind of. If you're in Yonas's wood and you look over the edge, there's a ledge. It's pretty far down, but it's there. It has a lot of berries growing on it, and Leos said we could climb down to it and make it our special hideout."

"And since it's on Yonas's land, give or take, that would make it even more fun."

"Yes. Nobody could find us when we didn't want to be found."

In a way, Hogun approved. It sounded as if this Leos had the fearless spirit of a true Asgardian warrior. He and his brothers had undertaken comparable reckless adventures before his siblings and father died and the world seemed a darker place. Still, he knew it was the job of adults to restrain children when the latter's notions became too harebrained.

"You and your friends mustn't do that," he said. "It's much too dangerous to clamber around over the edge."

"I *know* that," Gunhild said. "But like I told you, Leos is the leader, and he says that anybody who won't climb down to the ledge is a coward. Nobody wants to be a coward."

"If you can't convince the others to give up the scheme," Hogun said, "then you have to tell someone – their parents, your teacher, maybe even this man Yonas – who can prevent what they mean to do."

"But that would make me a tattletale! My friends would hate me, and I couldn't blame them."

He drew breath to tell her she was wrong and then realized that, according to his own code of honor, she was absolutely right. A person didn't betray his or her true companions. He could never have found it within himself to betray Volstagg, Fandral, or Thor, no matter what the circumstances.

For a second, he imagined that he himself could inform some responsible party, then recalled Gunhild had sworn him to silence.

Scowling, he pondered, seeking a solution that proved elusive. He was no fool, but he was used to straightforward problems where one side was his own and the other the enemy, and a fellow could drive at the objective without concern for the incidental consequences. In comparison, Gunhild's dilemma was a muddle.

She watched him for several moments as he sought after the answer, and then the hope in her expression wilted into disappointment. "It's all right," she said. "You tried to figure it out."

Perhaps it was her somber acceptance of the idea he couldn't help her, couldn't even help a little girl with a schoolyard problem, that finally shook something loose in his head. If it wasn't the answer she needed, maybe it *contained* the answer.

"Don't give up on me yet," he said. "You've heard of Heimdall?"

"Uh huh."

"Well, long before the building of the Rainbow Bridge, he was a young thane in service to Odin, and he had a problem like yours. It appeared that the only way to do his duty and stop something awful from happening was to betray people he cared about. Would you like to know what he did and how it all worked out?"

"Yes."

"Then show me the larder, help me get started making our supper, and I'll tell you the story."

O·NE

Heimdall caught his breath as Golden Mane, his winged steed, carried him from the sky of Asgard into the transcendent reality where Yggdrasil, the World Tree, towered in a star-bedizened and nebula-smeared vastness with the Nine Worlds perched up and down its length. He no longer had reason to fear being here. The preternaturally keen senses he'd acquired by smashing the head of Mimir armored him against the mind-withering influence of the void, and his augmented sight revealed the glimmering pathways that kept him from losing his way. But the vista before him still inspired awe even though it wasn't inordinately perilous anymore.

"I could fly around out here for a long time," he called to his companion, "just to enjoy the view!"

"Fine by me," Uschi replied. "I'm in no hurry to get where we're going."

Long-legged and with a face that currently wore an expression of grim resignation, Uschi commanded a company of Valkyries. Her training and the rituals of her sisterhood enabled her to endure the space beyond the Worlds as easily as Heimdall did. Save for his color, white to Golden Mane's black, her stallion Avalanche, with his beating pinions, resembled his own.

Her status as a thane of the Valkyries had been immediately apparent when Heimdall met her during the war with the Jotuns. It had taken years longer, however, to discover she hailed from Vanaheim and had grown up not far from his own childhood home, for unlike him, she rarely spoke of her family. Evidently, they were estranged.

Heimdall considered that a pity, and when his duties allowed him time for a visit home, he'd wheedled until Uschi grudgingly agreed to accompany him. It was, he fancied, a concession she would have given to few, if any, others. They'd become staunch friends in the years since the war with the frost giants, facing extraordinary perils together and saving one another's lives on more than one occasion.

He had no misgivings about pressuring her into the homecoming, for surely, he thought, if she and her parents saw one another again, they'd reconcile. His friend was such a valiant warrior, had done such mighty deeds in the service of the Realm Eternal, that her kin could only be proud of her.

"It will be all right," he said. "You'll see." He pointed. "And there's the path to Vanaheim."

The path twisted and shimmered like the lightest silvery dusting of frost on the ground except that there was no ground underneath. Despite the apparent lack of solid footing, the stallions' legs worked as steadily as their wings. As Heimdall and Uschi rode along the way, a stag, colossal almost beyond comprehension, nibbled at Yggdrasil's leaves. The creature was as ghostly as it was huge, and the stars and nebulae glowed through it. It paid the travelers no mind, and after another moment even Heimdall's eyes couldn't see it anymore. Several heartbeats later, the riders passed from the void into the sky of Vanaheim, and he spotted the first sign that the world of his birth had changed in his absence.

Thanks to the All-Father's magic, Asgard was a land of perpetual summer. Vanaheim, however, ruled by Frey, God of the Harvest, subject to Odin's ultimate authority, had always been an even more verdant and bountiful realm, an expanse of endless green forests of birch, goat willow, and pine, along with foaming, murmuring rivers and blue seas. Mostly, it still was, but there were also patches of woodland where leaves and pine needles had turned brown and fallen, where branches had twisted as if in agony, and cankers on the tree trunks oozed sap.

Heimdall frowned in puzzlement and a bit of dismay and then dismissed the matter from his mind. The blight was troubling, he thought, but surely someone was attending to it, and those people were likely foresters and mages. It was unlikely one of Odin's warriors, even one possessed of astonishingly keen sight and hearing, had anything to contribute, so he might as well get on with his holiday as planned.

To his relief, the blight hadn't touched his father's lands. The woodlands where he'd learned to hunt, the apple orchards, and the rye and barley ripening in the fields all appeared unaffected. Not far beyond the castle, an imposing gray fortress stood as well maintained as it was ancient, the land sloping downward to the sea and the huts of the fisherfolk. He was surprised, however, that no one was trawling or pulling up wicker fish traps to remove the catch within. On the contrary, all the boats were drawn up on the shore, and he wondered if today was some festival, wedding, or other celebration. Unfortunately, when he and Uschi flew close enough to see down into the castle courtyard, he realized it wasn't that at all.

Half a dozen pallid corpses lay in the center of the space. By the look of them, something had battered and smashed at them until broken bones pierced vital organs, or those organs were simply pulverized, and life left them. A crowd had assembled to inspect the dead: Heimdall's parents and a number of their household warriors among them.

As always, Heimdall's heart lifted to see his mother and father. At the same time, though, he was mindful that he was reuniting with them in the aftermath of a tragedy. It now seemed likely there was work for him here after all.

Such being the case, he might have expected the arrival of reinforcements would elicit some show of enthusiasm from the folk below. Valkyries like Uschi were renowned warriors, and in the years since he and his sister Sif had played a pivotal role in defeating the frost giants, he'd acquired a comparable reputation. But people were peering up uncertainly. If he hadn't known better, he might almost have imagined it was in consternation.

"This," Uschi said, "is the kind of welcome I'll get when I show up at *my* parents' stronghold."

"They're happy to see us," Heimdall replied, meanwhile thinking that surely there was no reason why it wouldn't be so. "It's just that we've surprised them at a sad moment. As soon as we're on the ground, you'll see."

He waved his arm, signaling for the crowd in the courtyard to clear a space big enough for the winged steeds to land, and they understood and complied. Once Golden Mane furled his wings, touched down, and trotted the few extra steps required to shed his remaining momentum, there was no doubt that everyone could see who Heimdall was, but there were still no shouts of welcome. Everyone just watched. He marked it down to the mournful nature of the occasion he'd interrupted.

He swung himself down from the saddle, and the Gjallarhorn, a long, curved ox horn with a mouthpiece and a brass ring around the wide end, bumped at his hip. Like his heightened senses, he'd acquired the enchanted trumpet in the course of fighting the Jotuns and had held onto it ever since. It was useful for signaling on the battlefield and for damaging certain types of foe. Uschi dismounted after him and followed him toward his parents.

"Mother! Father!" Heimdall called.

His mother Estrid, a dainty-looking apple-cheeked woman with a fondness for red garments, returned his smile. His father, Rodric, a burly, square-faced warrior whose fringe of beard, despite the longevity of the Vanir and Aesir, was beginning to go gray, apparently wasn't quite ready to do the same. "Do you bring a message from Odin?" he asked.

Heimdall blinked in surprise. "No. I came home for a few days because I had the chance. Are you expecting a message?"

"No!" Rodric said. He dredged up a smile. "It's good to see you, my son." He gestured in the direction of the corpses. "But as you can see, this isn't a good time for a visit."

"Unless it's the best time," Heimdall replied, surprised at the implication that his father would prefer him to turn around and go back to Asgard. Was Rodric still seeing him as a little boy who ought to be shielded from danger? "This is Uschi, a captain of the Valkyries. If you need another warrior, you won't find a better one. And, Father, I still remember the swordsmanship you taught me."

"Thank you," Rodric said. "Thank you both. But we don't need any more help. We know how to handle... the situation."

"What *is* the situation, Lord Rodric?" Uschi asked, a hint of impatience in her tone.

After a moment's hesitation, Rodric said, "A draug attacked one of the fishing boats."

Heimdall frowned. Draugr were dead men returned from the grave. Sometimes they were folk who'd been spiteful and greedy in life and who appeared to be pursuing their wicked ways even after their demise. In other cases, the trigger for the reanimation seemed less apparent. Perhaps hostile magic woke them, or, wise folk had speculated, it was some evil influence seeping along Yggdrasil from Realms like Niffleheim where malignant forces held more sway. However they came to be, draugr often craved the blood and flesh of the living but were also known to kill out of sheer viciousness.

Heimdall was surprised because draugr, though not unheard of, had always been rare in Vanaheim and the other worlds perched high in Yggdrasil's branches. They were a more common affliction in Midgard and other realms lower down. But he supposed wickedness could bubble up anywhere. He and Sif had even unmasked such in the royal court of Asgard itself, with the result that the All-Father had sent the treacherous Lady Amora into exile.

"Plainly," his father continued, "we must destroy the draug before it comes again to attack another boat or even the homes along the shore. But you needn't concern yourself, my son, nor need you, Captain Uschi. My warriors and I have the situation in hand."

"I know you do," Heimdall said. He didn't want to offend his father's pride. "But I'm still one of your warriors even if I've gone on to be other things, too. What kind of son would I be if I let my father go into battle without me?"

Uschi smiled a crooked smile. "I'm not your blood, my lord, but since I landed in this courtyard, I've been your guest, and I'd consider it poor hospitality indeed if you kept me out of this fight."

Heimdall's father and mother exchanged glances. Then Rodric said, "If you're both resolved to help, then of course I welcome it."

"Good," Heimdall said. "Now that that's out of the way, what's the battle plan?"

"Well," Rodric said, "we can't very well swim to the bottom of the sea and seek out the draug in its lair. So, we'll go out in ships and lure it up to attack us."

"That makes sense," Heimdall said, his mind whirring with possibilities, "but may I make a suggestion? As I understand it, draugr are as intelligent in death as they were in life. The creature might hesitate to attack a longship with folk who are plainly warriors aboard. We should go forth on fishing boats disguised as fisherfolk, without armor and with weapons and shields stowed but ready to hand."

His father nodded. "Good idea." He gave Heimdall the warmest, most open smile he'd offered yet. "You always were clever. Your mother and I could tell even when you were small."

"We'll need to set out in the morning," Uschi said, "spend

the day out on the water, and pretend we're coming back into port late, after nightfall. The draug won't attack before the sun goes down." Heimdall noticed her glumness had fallen away. In his experience, she was always keen to put down threats to the people of Asgard, but in this instance, he suspected she was also glad for an excuse to delay returning to her own childhood home.

Rodric grunted, his momentary cheer falling away. "Now that, Valkyrie, is where you're wrong."

Two

The hot sun beat down as Heimdall and Uschi, both sweaty and disheveled in the garb of fisherfolk, struggled inexpertly to haul the net aboard. Heimdall was glad that at least he still had his sea legs. His various missions on behalf of King Odin and Queen Frigga had put him aboard ships and boats often enough that his body still remembered what it was to have a rocking, creaking deck beneath it. Uschi, whose duties generally had her either flying on her winged steed or standing on solid ground, was having a bit more trouble keeping her balance. Skarde, the barefoot, shirtless, tattooed mariner whose vessel this was, who'd put to sea with the warriors to help them impersonate fisherfolk successfully, looked on with a sigh and a slight shake of his head.

The decision to embark in smaller fishing boats instead of longships meant there were perforce fewer warriors per vessel. Rodric's fighters were strung out across the entire fishing fleet, two or three to a boat, with one or two of the bravest fisherfolk aboard as well. It wasn't a situation that troubled Heimdall. He and Uschi had defeated Jotuns and ice giants.

Though he'd never before encountered one, he thought a draug was no great matter after that. Indeed, he hoped that when the dead thing came up out of the water, it would attack the boat they were aboard and not another.

Uschi noticed Skarde's reaction to her landlubberly performance and answered it with a scowl. Heimdall chuckled.

"You truly didn't have to come out here," he said to her. "But you were eager to seize any excuse to delay going home to see your parents."

The Valkyrie grunted. "You're right. I would have gone to Jotunheim if you'd suggested it. I doubt the welcome would have been any colder. Let's get this cursed net up." A final heave brought the coarse mesh with gleaming, flopping fish caught in the weave onto the deck. Uschi then glowered at the raw scrapes on her hands, and with that discomfort, Heimdall sympathized. Over the course of several hours, he'd discovered that a person could spend years hardening his palms and fingers by gripping a sword hilt and the reins of a horse, but somehow, the hard work aboard a fishing boat would punish them nonetheless.

He wiped his hands on his wool tunic in the hope that would ease the stinging, and then the tossing surface of the blue sea began to darken. It was as if clouds had covered the sun even though the sky was clear and it shone as brightly as before.

"The draug is coming," Heimdall said.

Uschi looked out across the waves. "Are you sure?" she asked, whereupon he realized that what he'd observed was as yet imperceptible to others.

Such was often the case. He'd learned to rouse his preternatural sight and hearing when he needed them and quell them when he didn't. Life would have been unendurable had they been bombarding him with a thousand details and impressions every moment. But his gifts were never *entirely* quiescent, and thus he was apt to spot things other people missed.

"I'm sure," he replied, and he didn't have to wait long before the process was evident to everyone. The sea darkened as if some colossus had spilled a prodigious quantity of ink into it, and when it was completely black, the blackness leaked on upward into the air. Over the course of a minute or two, what had been a sunny day curdled into the equivalent of a moonless, starless night.

As had been reported, the hunters' quarry was a draug that brought its own darkness with it. Heimdall contemplated the mystical power required to produce such an effect over such a wide area and for the first time felt a twinge of trepidation. Was it possible a draug was a more formidable foe than he'd imagined? He took a deep breath, let it out slowly, and the anxiety mostly subsided.

"Weapons?" Skarde asked. He was a steady man who'd done some fighting in his time. Otherwise, he wouldn't be out here on the water. Nonetheless, his baritone voice came out higher than normal, a sign that he, too, had felt a pang of fear.

"Not yet," Uschi said. "We still have to lure the draug into the snare. Heimdall will tell us when it's time."

Heimdall reckoned that he might be the only person who could judge when it was the optimal moment for that, because the world continued to darken until even he could barely see from the bow of the modest craft to the stern. Despite his lingering uneasiness, it made him hope even more strongly that luck would send the draug to this boat and not another whose warriors were all but blind. He summoned the full measure of his preternatural sight, peered across the waves, and gasped at what he saw there.

He and his fellow warriors had expected a single draug to clamber aboard a single boat. Once the attack was under way, the other vessels would converge on that one and their warriors would board it and join the fray. Or, if the creature sprang back overboard and sought to swim away, they'd throw spears and loose arrows. If it tried to dive deep, they'd attempt to catch it in the fishing nets.

In other words, they'd laid their plans in anticipation of battling a lone draug, and why not? All the tales and sagas described heroes combatting one such abomination. But now, concealed in the unnatural darkness from every eye but Heimdall's, at least one creature was swimming toward *every* boat.

Waiting until the perfect moment for the warriors to reveal themselves now seemed like a guarantee of disaster. "The weapons!" Heimdall shouted. "Now!"

He, Uschi, and Skarde all scrambled for the boat's little cabin, jamming in the low doorway for a moment as everyone tried to enter at once. The Valkyrie buckled on her sword belt and took up her round pine shield with its iron boss. Skarde grabbed a spear a head taller than he was with a long, leaf-shaped point suitable for thrusting or slashing. Heimdall drew his two-handed sword from its scabbard.

He also snatched up the Gjallarhorn. The fishing boats weren't especially close to one another because bunching up might have given the trap away, and the trumpet's voice was louder than any shout that he could manage.

Back on deck, he drew a deep breath, brought the Gjallarhorn's brass mouthpiece to his lips, and blew. A long note blared across the water and served to draw the attention of everyone aboard the other vessels. "Draugr!" he bellowed. "Swimming toward *every* boat! Arm yourselves now!"

A slight splashing sounded at his back. He realized that as he'd shouted out his warning, calling out over the starboard side of the vessel to the other boats, draugr had reached the port side. Turning, he dropped the Gjallarhorn to dangle on its leather cord and gripped his sword with both hands.

"They're here!" Skarde yelped, his voice now positively shrill.

"Steady!" Uschi snapped. Pale hands gripped the ankle-high gunwale.

"I've got the prow," Heimdall said. "You two, hold the stern!" Hampered by the darkness as he was not, Uschi and Skarde edged toward the back of the boat with their weapons probing before them.

Heimdall stepped to the gunwale with some of the fish in the net still flopping feebly around his calfskin shoes. He cut downward expecting to sever one of the draug's hands or at least maim and cripple it before the living corpse could pull itself onto the deck.

The two-handed sword did indeed cut but only superficially. To his startled dismay, Heimdall felt a jolt as though he'd struck sturdy mail or a tree trunk rather than the spongy, fish-gnawed flesh of a drowned thing that had been underwater for weeks or even longer.

The draug heaved itself out of the sea. Heimdall scrambled backward to keep away from it. He needed to open up the distance so that he could reach it with his sword, but the creature would be unable to strike or grapple with its empty hands.

The draug's flesh was ragged, and in some places bone showed through gaps. Slimy bits of it fell away to patter on the deck along with the seawater dripping from its limbs. From the shoulders down it was horrific, but also the foe Heimdall had steeled himself to confront. What he hadn't anticipated was the lack of any remaining semblance of a human head. Where the head and neck should have been, rising from a ragged hole in the torso, was a clump of seaweed, the lamina stirring as though still floating in some phantom current.

Beholding the bizarre sight, Heimdall faltered. Seeking to take advantage of the lapse, the draug rushed him. It didn't move in the lurching, halting manner he might have expected of a reanimated corpse, either. Strings of rotted flesh flopping around its upraised half-skeletal hands, it pounced like an arrow flying from a bow.

Only Heimdall's years of training and battle experience saved him. Startled though he was, he reflexively swung his blade in a stop cut. The two-handed sword caught the dead man in the chest, cracked exposed ribs, and halted its charge.

But the draug showed no signs of being any more hindered by the new wound than it was by the first one, or by its lack of eyes, or general decay for that matter. Taking a deep, steadying breath of salt air that had grown cold now that shadow tainted it, Heimdall insisted to himself that was no reason for panic. Apparently he'd have to dismember the unnatural creature to stop it, but he could do that despite the unnatural hardness of its substance. He just needed to strike with all his skill and every iota of his Vanir strength.

He and the draug circled one another. The confines of the prow provided scant room to maneuver and avoid the creature's attacks. It kept rushing him, and he only barely managed to dodge it. The rocking of the boat and the slippery fish under his soles made the footing treacherous, and once, he caught his foot in the net, tripped, and nearly fell. Meanwhile, Uschi's occasional curses and Skarde's wordless cries revealed that they were fighting dead things in the stern.

Heimdall's foe faked a shift to his right, and, pretending to be deceived, he turned with it. At once it lunged in toward his exposed left. He pivoted and cut.

The stroke sheared deep into the draug's shoulder, all but severing one arm and slamming it to its knees. The injured limb flopped down, useless. Heimdall grinned, but his momentary satisfaction turned to shock when, before he could yank his weapon free, the dead thing, heedless of any damage it might thereby be inflicting on its own fingers, gripped the blade of the sword with its good hand. Heimdall then found himself playing tug of war for possession of the weapon.

For a few heartbeats, with his teeth gritted, he thought he might win. Then he heard more splashing. Another pair of oozing ragged hands rose out of the sea to grasp the gunwale, and a new draug pulled itself onto the deck.

The newcomer was even more rotted by time and immersion than its predecessor, much of its fleshless bone encrusted with barnacles or host to dangling sea anemones. It had no head at all, not even a clump of seaweed to substitute for one, but for all that it lacked, it moved with the same agility as its companion and oriented on Heimdall immediately.

He feared letting go of his sword hilt even with one hand lest his first adversary succeed in wresting the blade away, but he didn't dare let the second creature close in on him. It would rip him apart or carry him over the side to drown. He kept hold with his right hand, grabbed the Gjallarhorn with his left, and sounded it as he'd learned to do when using it as a weapon.

The second draug's outstretched hands were almost within grabbing distance when the tone caught it. The note didn't break it into a scatter of bones as it had once shattered the frozen forms of ice giants. But the sound did slam it like a battering ram and hurl it back over the side to splash down in the sea.

Meanwhile, though, just as he'd feared, the first draug was pulling the sword from his right hand. Heimdall dropped the Gjallarhorn, gripped the sword hilt with both hands, and discovered to his dismay that even that was not enough. The reanimated corpse was still pulling harder than he was, still relentlessly drawing the weapon in its direction.

For a helpless instant he couldn't think of anything to do, but then a desperate notion came to him. He stopped resisting the pull and pushed with all his strength, lunging forward as he did so.

The reversal caught the draug by surprise, and it failed to compensate in time. Acting in concert with Heimdall's, its own strength helped to turn the forward motion of the blade into a forceful slicing action. Its gripping hand came apart, and the fingers fell to the deck. So, too, did the maimed arm, entirely severed at last, and the sword sprang free.

Still undeterred, the draug scrambled up off its knees. Heimdall feinted high, cut low, and severed its lead leg partway up the thigh. The dead thing pitched forward onto its face, and he hacked it to keep it there.

Even after he'd dismembered it completely, the pieces kept flopping like the newly netted fish. At least, he thought, the draug could do no more harm that way, whereupon his imagination conjured a ghastly picture of the severed limbs crawling around on their own like serpents. The Vanir would trip over them, and the arm that still had a working hand would grip their ankles and crush them. Heimdall flipped the pieces overboard with the point of his sword.

The second draug clambered back into the bow.

The oozing, rotting creatures sickened Heimdall and he'd learned almost at the cost of his life to be wary of their capabilities. He felt tempted to fling this draug back over the side with another blast from the Gjallarhorn. But even if that discouraged it from attacking yet again, he was here to destroy the draugr, not merely send them into retreat, and the trumpet's magic seemed unable to dispatch them. He gripped the two-handed sword anew.

The best tactic, he judged, was still to control the distance so that he could strike while remaining out of the draug's reach. Sidestepping, he dodged one lunge and sprang after another, cutting with all his might the instant he was clear. It still wasn't easy to hack through the dead thing's astonishingly tough substance, but eventually he had it twitching on the deck in writhing pieces like the first one.

With the prow cleared, he turned his attention to the stern, the low little cabin fortunately not blocking the view. Each of his companions was fighting one of the draugr. Like the ones he'd dispatched, the two dead things had waving strands of seaweed in place of a head. Slashing broadsword in one hand, shield in the other, Uschi was thus far holding her own. The rocking of the boat still had her unsteady on her feet, however, and her foe had smashed or torn away pieces of the shield. Skarde appeared to be in even greater peril. He'd driven his spear into a dead thing's chest, and the leaf-shaped iron point was sticking all the way out of its back. As aggressive as before, however, the draug pushed its way up the ash-wood shaft, and its raking hands would soon be within reach of the fisherman. Screaming, Skarde struggled to shove the reanimated corpse over the side, but his panicky effort was only serving to slide the spear farther through the creature's torso and so bring the combatants closer together.

Much as he would have liked another moment to catch his breath and steady himself, Heimdall had to intervene without delay. He maneuvered around behind the draug and hacked its legs out from under it. That put an end to it working its way closer to Skarde, who then did his best to immobilize it with the spear and hinder its frantic efforts to bash and snatch at its opponents. Meanwhile, Heimdall landed cut after cut to its forearms and shoulders.

By the time the arms dropped away, he was breathing heavily from hacking apart three unnaturally tough horrors in quick succession. But there was at least one left, and so he immediately turned in Uschi's direction.

Uschi didn't need his help. Since he'd last looked her way, her draug had finished smashing her shield to splinters, but despite the rocking deck, she succeeded in inflicting considerable harm on it. It was now missing an arm and prone on the deck with her foot planted in the center of its back to keep it that way. Bellowing "Asgard!" with every stroke, her cries full of mingled loathing and fury, her broadsword rising and falling, she finished the task of dismembering it. When she'd finished, she took a deep breath of composure and asked, "What now?"

Heimdall looked, listened, and could detect no sign that any more draugr were about to assail Skarde's vessel. "Now," he panted, "we follow the original plan, give or take. We find a boat in need of help, and we give it." As formidable as the draugr had proven to be, he had a grim sense that such a boat would be easy enough to locate.

When he exerted his senses to the fullest and gazed to starboard, however, he discovered to his surprise that his father's warriors were faring better than expected. A couple had fallen, and draugr were pressing some others hard, but fighters who'd cleared their own boats of foes were coming to the latter's aid, relying on the clamor of battle rather than the sight of it to scull their craft to the proper locations.

Heimdall suspected that the living were prevailing in no small part because of magic. When he used his sight to the fullest, he could see supernatural energies. Not being a warlock himself, he lacked the knowledge to interpret what he beheld, but it was at least always clear to him when such forces were at work. And at this moment, they were. A number of the warriors scattered across the boats cut and thrust with broadswords that had runes etched along the blades. Now that they'd drawn the weapons from their scabbards and the draugr were at hand, the symbols shimmered with a blood-red phosphorescence.

Heimdall's father bore such a sword. Clad in the simple garb of a fisherman just like his followers, Rodric caught a headless draug's blow on his shield and riposted with a stab to the belly. As Heimdall's recent experiences had demonstrated, the attack should have been useless against one of the living corpses, and in fact, the creature didn't fall down. But it froze with the shock and pain of the wound, and in that moment of paralysis, Rodric yanked the blade free and hacked at its outstretched arm. Seemingly bypassing the draug's supernatural toughness, the sword stroke lopped off the thing's hand at the wrist as easily as if it were a living man. Rodric finished dispatching it and rushed to the aid of a beleaguered comrade.

"Our side is winning," Heimdall said, "but there's still work for us."

He turned to Skarde, who was white-faced and shivering but appeared to be doing his best to shake off the terror engendered by fighting his draug.

"We need to go that way." Heimdall pointed to the nearest boat where things were going poorly, maybe because no one aboard had a sword with glowing runes. "I can see to guide us through the dark."

Three

As the Vanir destroyed one draug after another, the darkness the creatures had engendered gradually brightened until, when the fight was through, the sunlight revealed a litter of torsos and severed limbs that, unlike Heimdall, others hadn't bothered to flip overboard. When the victors returned to shore and to the acclaim of the fisherfolk who remained behind in their village, they built a bonfire to consume the dead things' remains. The creatures' body parts burned slowly and gave off a black malodorous smoke. Heimdall and Uschi found Rodric watching the conflagration on the side of the pyre from which the breeze carried the smoke.

The older man clapped his son on the shoulder. "Only four men lost," he said. "If not for your warning, we might have fared far worse."

Heimdall smiled, no less pleased by his father's praise than when he was a little boy. The initial strangeness between them seemed to have passed. Perhaps it had simply been due to the older man's preoccupation with the menace lurking under the waves. Either way, he felt settled that all was well. "I told you Uschi and I would be useful."

"And so you were." Rodric's expression and tone became more somber. "I've sent a rider to the castle to say we've won, and we'll bury our dead when we get back there ourselves. We'll give the two fishermen the same honors as my two guards. They showed the same courage."

Heimdall glanced over at Skarde, now grinning and holding his youngest daughter in his arms while the rest of his family clustered around him. "They did."

His father's face brightened again. "And then tonight we feast. Silver arm rings for everyone who came out on the boats."

"That will be a fine reward," Uschi said, "but I confess, I'm more curious about the swords you and a few others carry. I couldn't really see for myself in the dark, but Heimdall tells me they destroy draugr far more readily than my blade or his."

Rodric glanced down at the hilt of his weapon. Sheathed, the runes and any residual glow hidden by the scabbard, it looked like an ordinary well-made broadsword even to Heimdall's eyes. "Yes. So it seems." Rodric hesitated. "I apologize for not giving one to either of you, but it didn't seem so important at the time. I thought we were only dealing with one draug and the two of you might never end up facing it at all. The fight is over now, but maybe I can find a pair for you, if you'd like."

"Thank you, my lord," the Valkyrie said, "but if that would mean taking a sword away from one of the warriors who fought bravely today, please don't. I managed well enough with what I have."

"As did I," Heimdall said.

Rodric smiled. "I remember a two-hand sword always suited you best even when I started teaching you and you were barely big enough to hold even a wooden pared-down version."

Heimdall felt the warmth of the fond memory. He recalled his father carefully trimming the practice sword down to the proper size and the excitement of holding it in his hands for the first time. He drew breath to ask Rodric if the wooden blade was still to be found, but Uschi spoke before he could.

"One draug-slaying sword would be a treasure. You have what, a dozen? Were they simply gathering dust in your armory? I've never heard Heimdall speak of them."

Rodric frowned at what he might have considered an impertinent question, and his son felt a flicker of annoyance on the older man's behalf. It did seem a little odd that Heimdall had never heard of these particular enchanted weapons before, but then again, his family was an old and wealthy one. Who knew what precious things were tucked away inside the castle vaults? In any case, the private affairs of his kin were none of Uschi's concern.

But Rodric chose to answer anyway, perhaps because his sense of courtesy demanded no less. "There have been reports of draugr troubling Vanaheim in recent weeks. Just a few here and there, you understand, but nonetheless I deemed it prudent to lay hands on the proper tools to deal with the problem in case it happened here. Fortunately, there's a clan of dwarves down in Nidavellir who know the runes for slaying the dead, and I was able to acquire some of their handiwork."

The Valkyrie started to ask another question, but the Vanir lord cut her off. "I see it's time to carry our slain fighters up to the fortress. I mean to ride along. That will show them honor, too." He gave Uschi and Heimdall a nod and strode away. "Bring me my horse!" he called.

Once Rodric was out of earshot, Heimdall turned to Uschi and said, "I'm not so sure he liked your manner."

"I didn't mean to offend," Uschi replied smoothly. "He's made me welcome, and I've now seen firsthand that he's a brave warrior and an able leader. He deserves my respect, and he has it. Still, don't you have the feeling there are things he's not telling us? Don't you think it's odd that he didn't see fit to mention the rune swords at all? Or that other draugr had turned up in other parts of Vanaheim?"

For an instant, her questions made Heimdall wonder, but the flicker of doubt was no match for the countless happy memories that made it seem absurd. "You're only asking that because you don't know him the way I do. He's as forthright and honest a man as any jarl can be. Certainly, he's never kept secrets from me."

"If you say so," Uschi said.

"I do, so let it rest. There were draugr, we slew them, and now it's time to relax and enjoy the victory."

"You realize this isn't like you. Ordinarily, you're the one always pulling away masks to discover the truth beneath."

"Only when there *are* masks and hidden truths. Trust me, this time there aren't. So don't you go chasing shadows because it gives you another excuse to put off seeing your family."

Uschi glowered. "Fine. I'll fly out to visit them first thing in the morning."

Heimdall paused, wrestling with the knowledge that he'd sounded a bit harsh to one of his best friends. "Would you like me to accompany you? To visit your parents, I mean." Uschi hadn't asked and he hadn't offered, but it seemed as if he should be there if she wanted him. Especially after all she'd done for his family. After all she'd done for him.

Uschi went quiet, as if considering. "No. Thank you, but I would rather do this alone."

Four

Most members of Rodric's household had little inclination to rise with the sun after the feasting and the many toasts the night before. Still, her new silver arm ring glinting red in the dawn light, Uschi found a yawning groom ready to assist her in preparing Avalanche for flight. The fellow was willing enough but had no experience with the tack of winged horses, and after watching him fumble for a few moments, she told him to stand aside and saddled her stallion herself.

She then mounted up, walked Avalanche out of the barn, and urged him into a trot once they were in the courtyard. The stallion unfurled his wings, lashed them, and then they were off the ground. Rising, he cleared the castle wall and she guided him east, on a course roughly parallel to the shoreline that was the northern limit of Heimdall's father's holdings.

At first her journey took her over the lands of other lords scarcely less prosperous, all of them likely owing at least a part of that wealth to an alliance with Rodric's house. Her mouth twisted with an unaccustomed, resentful envy as she thought of all the families eager to establish a connection to such a house and not, say, a lesser one that would value such a bond far more. She realized her bitter disdain was unfair – it was simply sound judgment that would prompt a jarl to seek a tie with a rich and powerful neighbor – but still couldn't quell the feeling entirely. It diminished the pleasure she would otherwise have taken in soaring high above verdant woodlands and fields on a bright, clear morning.

Eventually, the holdings of greater lords gave way to those of humbler ones, and to stretches of forest remote from any visible human habitation. Soon, she knew, she'd reach her own family's domain, and the knowledge was like a stone in her belly.

Why, she wondered, had she let Heimdall talk her into this? Part of the answer was that in the years since the war with the frost giants, he'd become her dearest friend, closer even than any of her sisters among the Valkyries. She supposed, moreover, that deep down, some weak part of her still desired reconciliation with her parents. That part must have taken control in the moment when she'd agreed to accompany Heimdall to Vanaheim, and afterward she would have felt ridiculous if she'd reneged on her promise. There was nothing to do but make the visit and get it over with. Afterward, she expected she'd at least enjoy the satisfaction of telling her know-it-all comrade he'd been wrong for once.

When her family's lands came into view around noontime, they seemed sad and rundown even in comparison with her final memories of them. Catkins and other scrub claimed fields that were once cultivated, possibly because there were no longer farmers enough to work them. Some of the thatch-roofed farmhouses looked abandoned, with no smoke rising from the smoke holes and no children running and shouting or chickens pecking and strutting in the overgrown yards outside.

At first glance, her parents' stronghold showed less obvious signs of decline than the fields and farming villages. With its circular wooden wall enclosing the wooden longhouses within, it had never been as grand as Rodric's stone fortress, but it still stood intact, the palisade of tree trunks unbroken. But no wind blew, and the banners hung limp, defeated in the attempt to display their devices. When Avalanche flew low enough, Uschi could see a place where the walkway behind the top of the palisade sagged dangerously and was going unrepaired. Only a single sentry patrolled the ramparts to shout and advise the citadel of her approach.

Experiencing a pang of guilt, she insisted to herself that her family's misfortunes were *not* her fault.

She set Avalanche down in the open center of the ringed fortress. By then, people were emerging from the buildings to take a look at the newcomer. A couple who evidently remembered her fondly called out her name. A few who were strangers goggled at the spectacle of a Valkyrie on her winged steed, a rare sight hereabouts. The majority, however, stared in a manner reminiscent of the moment when she and Heimdall arrived at his family's stronghold. This time there were no mangled corpses in evidence, but they likely assumed her return would put her parents in a foul humor, and about that, she expected they were correct.

She swung herself out of the saddle and handed the winged stallion's reins to an awestruck servant. "For your purposes," she said, "he's just like any other warhorse. Treat him that way and you'll get along fine."

A guard emerged from the doorway of the largest longhouse, the one housing the master and mistress of the stronghold. "Lady Uschi–"

"*Captain* Uschi," she said, spurning the title that was her birthright for the one she valued and had earned.

"Captain Uschi, Lord Peadar and Lady Juliska will receive you in the hall."

"Lead the way," she said, meanwhile sardonically thinking, of course. Why would they rush out of doors just to greet their only daughter? They have their dignity to think of. Odin forbid that Peadar should show her the same sort of warmth that Rodric, a far more important jarl, had shown to his child.

The hall was a high-ceilinged room with a long fire, allowed to burn down to embers for the moment, in the center between the side platforms, benches, and tables for the diners. Uschi's parents sat atop the dais at the far end. Her footsteps echoing, Uschi had to march all the way down the length of the hall before her father and mother acknowledged her. She made sure to do so with head held high.

The father Uschi preferred to remember had often found a smile for her even when most preoccupied with his worries. The stooped, gaunt man on the high seat glowered as if he'd set softer emotions aside. "Captain," he growled.

Was this, Uschi thought, really how it was going to be? *Fine, then.* At least this way, she'd feel free to make her visit as brief as possible. She inclined her head. "My lord. My lady."

"By the Tree!" Juliska exploded. She was a plump woman whose coiled braided hair stuck up above her head in a way that made her look like she was wearing a beehive for a hat. "Can't we say 'Daughter' and 'Father' and 'Mother'? Can't we at least do that?"

Uschi felt another twinge of guilt. Even Peadar's face might have betrayed the slightest flush of remorse, but if so, it was only for an instant. "If Uschi brings a message from Odin," he said, "I will address her as befits the king's messenger."

Uschi frowned in puzzlement. First Lord Rodric and now her own father. Why did every Vanir jarl, even their own kin, assume she and Heimdall bore tidings or commands from the All-Father? And why did they seem to take that as reason for trepidation? "It's nothing like that," she said. "I just wanted to see you." Although, she reflected, *wanted* was the wrong word for it, and the awkwardness presently unfolding was making her regret the decision more and more.

Peadar stared at her as though trying to decide whether she was telling the truth. Finally, he said, "I doubt you returned to do your duty at last. So, was it to gloat over the ruin your selfishness inflicted?"

Juliska put her hand over her husband's, perhaps in an effort to urge him to curb his anger. "Your father doesn't mean that," she said to Uschi. But Uschi suspected he did.

By and large, her childhood had been a happy one, but she'd nonetheless been aware of her father's frustrations as his influence and wealth began to slip away. More prosperous jarls had offered alliances, offices, and trading partnerships to other men. Warriors and other karls had left his lands and his service in search of greater opportunities. Meanwhile, he'd pursued one scheme after another to reverse his fortunes, plans that, for whatever reason, never quite worked out.

Though she'd understood what Peadar was doggedly attempting to do, it had still come as a shock when his last great scheme centered on her. Uschi's arranged marriage with the scion of a family on the rise, one rich in gold but hungry for the prestige that association with what was still an honored lineage might bring, could restore his house's fortunes. When she'd realized there was no hope of dissuading her parents, she'd run away and found a sorcerer to transport her to Asgard. The mage had been a drunken bumbler and the shift from world to world had nearly killed her, but afterward she made her way to the royal city and in time won a place as a Valkyrie apprentice.

"Father," she said, "even if I wanted to, there's nothing to gloat over. You still hold these lands and this stronghold. You're still a respected jarl."

He waved his hand as though brushing away a fly.

She felt it was futile to continue speaking but couldn't quite bring herself to stop. "The life you planned for me wasn't the life I wanted. I'd told you I meant to be a Valkyrie ever since I was very small."

"But it didn't matter!" he replied. "You were our only child. After the miscarriage, the healers said your mother couldn't have any more. It was your duty to do what was best for your family! You're our legacy!"

Uschi turned to Juliska. "Mother," she said, "you know that in the end, I just couldn't." Her mother had always felt more sympathy for her than her father and made some effort to broker peace between the two. What Uschi had momentarily forgotten, though, was that ultimately Juliska always came down on her husband's side.

"I know you don't have a... great interest in the love of men," she said. "But you wouldn't have been the first married couple to make accommodations. You could have given your husband an heir or two, and except for that, you could both have sought companionship elsewhere."

"That wouldn't have worked for me."

"Well," Juliska said, "it's even possible we could have worked out some sort of formal affiliation with the daughter of another house. Such things are rare, but not absolutely unheard of. We'll never know now because you ran away."

"You don't understand," Uschi said.

It was true that she wanted only other women for her bedmates and that contributed to her rejection of her parents' plans for her, but it wasn't the only reason. Carnal desire didn't burn as hot in her as it did in many others. She was happy to indulge it when it manifested, but it was a small thing compared to the joys of being a warrior and a leader of warriors, of soaring across the sky on a winged steed and seeing other lands and other worlds, of debating, carousing, and laughing with Heimdall and other comrades – all satisfactions she would never have known had she followed the path her father had chosen for her.

"Stop trying to reason with her," Peadar said to Juliska. "She wouldn't listen to us before she left, and it's plain nothing's changed. She hasn't even apologized for stealing the Brightblade."

"I didn't steal it!" Uschi said. "It's the right of our family's firstborn child to bear it. It always has been." Her fingers reflexively closed around the hilt of the broadsword hanging by her side as if some part of her feared her father might try to take it back.

Possibly noticing the action, he sneered. "Oh, don't worry. As I understand it, it's too late to undo that bit of mischief, either. You lost the fire magic, and now what was a treasure is just a common sword."

"I exhausted the enchantment in a good cause." Saving Heimdall's life and helping vanquish the giants, to be precise.

"Spare me your excuses. If you didn't come back either to repent or to mock, why are you here?"

"I told you already," Uschi said. "Just to see your faces and hear your voices. Just to see how you were faring."

"Well," said Peadar, "now you have."

That, she understood, was a dismissal. Juliska winced but said nothing in protest. Uschi saluted the lord and lady on the dais, turned, and stalked back out into the courtyard.

Afterward she reflected with an edge of bitter humor that the reunion had gone exactly as she'd expected. "Curse you, Heimdall," she murmured. "I don't care if you have keen wits, the eyes of a falcon, and the ears of a hare. You don't *always* know best."

And as he didn't, she wasn't inclined to prolong her stay even a moment longer. She took three strides toward the stables before realizing there *was* a reason, nonetheless.

Avalanche had made a long flight from Lord Rodric's hold to this one. She now regretted undertaking the journey, but that was no reason to mistreat the stallion by making him carry her back immediately. Tomorrow would be time enough. Meanwhile, she was still her parents' child no matter how estranged. She assumed she could prevail on the servants to find her a chamber in which to spend the night.

She passed the afternoon seeking out the few folk who'd

seemed gladdened by her return. Those conversations were more pleasant than the one with her parents, but even they had a furtiveness and a reserve that saddened her. Her old friends truly must be afraid of incurring Peadar's displeasure.

Then, when the sun was sinking, the sentry on the wall called out that a longship was approaching. Curious, she climbed up onto the wall-walk and peered out over the sea. Though she lacked Heimdall's preternaturally keen eyes, she was nonetheless the first to discern the golden boar emblem emblazoned on the sail and the matching carved, gilded boar's head adorning the prow.

Having made them out, she grunted in surprise. Her family's fortunes might be in decline, but it appeared that Frey, God of the Harvest and lord of all Vanaheim, was paying a visit anyway.

Five

Heimdall smiled as he turned the pages of one of the many books he'd pored over as a child. He'd blown dust off the volume before opening it. It appeared that some of the drier and more esoteric books in the household collection had seen little use since he'd departed for Asgard. Even the scholar currently employed to teach the karls' children their letters and numbers evidently saw no reason to consult them.

That, Heimdall thought, was only to be expected. As a boy, his enthusiasm for books and school had always made him seem peculiar to his fellows. Fortunately, he'd been good at his warrior training and vigorous outdoor games, and that went a fair distance toward winning him acceptance. So did the protective attitude of his sister. From the cradle, Sif was a shield maiden through and through and ready to try her hand at thrashing any bully, no matter how much older and bigger that child was.

Even with all that working for him, though, Heimdall might have felt strange about his more intellectual interests, might even have felt tempted to abandon them to better fit the common image of a young Vanir warrior, if his parents hadn't encouraged him to pursue them. A bit paradoxically, perhaps, it was that very attitude that decided him he did want to be a thoroughgoing warrior exactly as Rodric had been in his youth, whereupon he traveled to Asgard to enlist in Odin's service.

At first, he'd felt awkward and out of place and wondered if he'd made a mistake. During the war with the frost giants, though, he'd found his calling, and at the end of it all, Queen Frigga had assigned him duties well suited to his nature. As an agent of the Crown, he traveled the Nine Realms, solved problems, learned fascinating things, and for the most part only led troops when there was an enemy to lead them against, thus escaping the tedium of presiding over a company in peacetime. All in all, Heimdall was content.

He read a few more lines about the fish-catching behavior of diving ducks and loons. Then a scream shrilled through the window of the tower chamber housing the schoolroom and library. Startled, he rose, strode to the window, and thrust his head out. Meanwhile, the shriek wailed again. No one going about his or her business in the courtyard below reacted, and he realized that only with his keen hearing had he caught the noise.

He found it somewhat reassuring that the screams plainly weren't coming from anywhere inside the fortress, but that didn't mean they weren't cause for concern. He sharpened his senses to the fullest, ignored the thousand noises that immediately became audible within the castle, and listened. When the next cry sounded, he was relieved again to discern it was the cry of a horse and not a human being.

But even if he was only hearing a horse, he still wanted to render aid. The poor animal was clearly in urgent need of one sort of help or another. He peered beyond the castle walls to locate it.

In that, he failed. Even the sight he'd inherited from Mimir couldn't see through solid objects, and there was a thick stand of ancient rowans and lindens blocking his view. Still, the screams were plainly coming from the direction of the castle's pasturelands, and it made sense that the horse was to be found there. He grabbed the two-handed sword and scabbard he'd left hanging on the back of a chair and slung them over his shoulder. His footsteps thumping, he trotted down the tower's spiral staircase and on out the castle gate, allowed to stand open now that the threat of the draugr was over.

As he neared the source of the screams, the sound naturally shrilled louder. He encountered two adolescents, one boy and one girl, who evidently bore some responsibility for looking after the herds and who were likewise hurrying to find out what was the matter. Heimdall waved away their time-wasting attempt to greet the son of Lord Rodric and Lady Estrid with fitting deference, and they all jogged on to the pasturelands together. Meanwhile, the whinnying cries became less frequent, as though the horse was running out of strength to call or despairing that anyone would ever come in response. When he and his new companions finally laid eyes on the beast, Heimdall realized with a pang of regret that despair was an appropriate reaction to the animal's plight.

The roan stallion lay alone in a field bordered by gray alders and bird-cherry bushes growing in a patch of boggy ground. If it had been grazing with others from the herd, those others had fled lest the calamity that had overtaken it befall them as well. Now the animal writhed and squirmed with its ears and tail torn away. Raw bloody wounds appeared as darker spots on its reddish coat, and it had an unnatural crook in its back. Periodically, between screams, it struggled to stand, but its legs only twitched and shivered uselessly. Heimdall judged that its spine was broken, and that was an injury even the most skillful tender of animals couldn't heal.

"Oh, no," said the girl, "that's Honeyboy. Lady Estrid loves that horse."

"I know," said the boy, "and there's nothing we can do for him except end his suffering." He drew his belt knife from its sheath. "Wynne and I will do it, sir. Honeyboy knows us. It'll be easier for us, and the horse, too."

"All right," Heimdall said, "but stay back for another moment." He scrutinized the stand of trees and brush on the far side of the meadow, peering and listening for any sign that the creature that had maimed and crippled the stallion was still lurking hereabouts. There was nothing: not the gleam of an eye, the curve of a mostly hidden animal shape, nor a soft, padding footfall as the predator skulked along. Not the thumping of a beast's heart nor the whisper of breath in and out of its nostrils.

"All right," he said. "You can go to Honeyboy. It's safe."

The girl – Wynne – and her fellow herder eased forward crooning soothing words as they came. Tears ran down Wynne's face, but she didn't let her voice break lest her distress frighten the injured stallion more than he was already. Meanwhile, Heimdall worried he'd just made a ghastly mistake and sent the two young karls into danger.

He told himself that surely wasn't the case. If the beast that had maimed Honeyboy was still anywhere nearby, he would have seen and heard it. It was simply the viciousness of the injuries inflicted on the stallion coming just a day after he'd fought the draugr that was unsettling him.

Well, that and the peculiar nature of the present situation. After all, what sort of beast would bring down a horse, break its back, rip away the ears and tail, and then just go away without finishing off its crippled prey and eating a portion of its flesh? Heimdall conjectured that some depraved human being might have done it instead, but to his warrior's eye, it didn't look as if the stallion's attacker had used weapons as a person likely would. There were no gashes from sword cuts or puncture wounds from spear thrusts. If the assailant was manlike at all, he or she had relied on naked hands and brute strength – like the lifeless things that had clambered onto the fishing boats.

Of course, even if Heimdall and his comrades hadn't ended the menace of the draugr, that didn't mean such a creature was still in the immediate vicinity. He drew his two-handed sword from its scabbard and scrutinized the patch of woods – the only possible hiding place – a second time. As before, there was no sign of any danger. Meanwhile, the young herders crept closer to the injured horse and thus that much farther from whatever protection his blade afforded. They were just a pace or two from their objective when he spotted what had escaped him hitherto.

In that instant, he felt, along with alarm, a pang of anger at himself for previously missing what he now observed. But it seemed that even the sight and hearing of Mimir could overlook something when their possessor was intent on detecting something else entirely. Heimdall had been looking for a menacing creature standing or creeping on four legs or two, not a motionless lump largely concealed by a low place in the boggy ground.

Something lay buried there under black mud and fallen branches, but not quite completely. Heimdall could make out roan hair through one small hole in the covering as well as a tiny smear of blood on the ground in front of it.

He wasn't immediately certain what his discovery meant, but his instincts howled that Wynne and her companion were indeed in peril. "Get back!" he shouted, sprinting forward. "Behind me!"

By then, the girl was stooping to stroke the fallen Honeyboy on the side of the head. Showing far more control over his movements than he'd revealed before, the roan stallion rolled toward her and changed.

Heimdall had watched sculptors working in clay. The transformation was similar had the sculptor's hands been invisible and the material – Honeyboy's body – taken on an entirely new shape in the time it took a person to draw a breath. At the end of the change, he was still as massive as a horse, but his form was that of a bloated human being, his swollen torso and limbs splitting his shirt and trousers at the seams. His skin was a dull blue. His sunken eyes glared, his mouth snarled, and even Heimdall, still several strides distant, could smell the stench of decay that rose from the creature's body.

This, he realized, was a different sort of draug, one that could shapeshift. It had killed the real Honeyboy, hidden the body, and assumed the form of a horribly injured counterpart to lure the prey it truly desired: the herders who'd come running in due course. It was pure good luck that Heimdall had shown up, too, and maybe not so good at that if he failed to close with the hideous thing in time.

Now on one knee, the draug grabbed for Wynne's head with a hand that looked swollen big enough to envelop it completely. The girl was quick and *almost* recoiled in time. The fingers missed her head but caught hold of one of her dangling copper-colored pigtails. The dead thing hauled her toward its gaping mouth.

Shrieking with rage, fear, or a mixture of the two, Wynne's friend stabbed at the pulling hand with his knife. The point, however, only inflicted a scratch before glancing away. In a number of respects, this draug differed from the drowned men Heimdall had encountered yesterday, but it was just as difficult to hurt.

It was also just a moment away from plunging its teeth into Wynne's flesh. Instead of attacking the draug, Heimdall made his first cut at the length of pigtail linking captor and captive. The long blade severed the braid and, suddenly released, Wynne reeled backward and fell on her rump. The boy dropped the knife, freeing up both hands, scrambled to her, pulled her back to her feet and away from the reeking hulk. Heimdall planted himself between the adolescents and the unnatural thing that had meant to kill them.

"Run!" he said without taking his eyes off the draug. "To the castle! Go!"

The rapid thump of their footsteps revealed they'd heeded him. Meanwhile, the draug sprang to its feet and charged him. Bloat and decay weren't slowing it down any more than the deterioration due to drifting drowned and dead underwater had hindered its aquatic kindred.

As Heimdall sidestepped that first lunge, he judged that his tactics should likewise be the same as he'd employed on the boats: stay out of the draug's reach while cutting it to pieces. It was more difficult when his adversary was a head taller than even a tall man like himself, when its arms were accordingly longer, but at least he had more room to maneuver.

His heart pounding, he soon decided he needed the space, for some mystical property armored this draug's body even better than the protection the sea-dead had possessed. He cut repeatedly with all his strength but only inflicted shallow gashes. The one perceptible effect was to thicken the cloud of stench that surrounded the thing until his eyes burned and watered and he feared he might vomit even though that would surely give the creature the opening it needed to smash him senseless or seize him and wring his body like a washcloth. As he struggled to ignore the smell, the sunlight dimmed as if the welling vileness were poisoning it.

He needed a better tactic before weariness or nausea slowed him or he simply made a fatal mistake. As he tried to think what that might be, it occurred to him that, unlike the draug from the sea, his current foe had an actual head as opposed to a mass of waving weed or nothing above the shoulders at all. If he couldn't cut off the limbs, maybe the head would prove more vulnerable.

Unfortunately, even with a two-handed sword, the neck of such an enormous foe was a more difficult target than the extended arms or legs. But Heimdall retreated a couple of steps, panted, and let his blade droop and his guard become sloppy. Evidently taken in by his attempt to feign exhaustion, the draug rushed him with arms extended. He dodged the all-out attack and made a high cut.

An instant later, he felt the familiar jolt. The draug's neck was dense like its limbs. But perhaps not *as* dense. The sword sliced through rotting flesh and grated on bone.

Its head now askew, flopping on its damaged neck, the draug started turning to threaten him anew. Heimdall stayed where he was and cut again. The sword finished its work, and the head, now entirely severed, tumbled through the air to thud down in the grass. The massive body fell also. As Heimdall had gambled, decapitation had rendered this particular horror inert.

Still watching the remains, just in case the draug was merely feigning a second death, Heimdall backed out of the worst of the stench. A moment later, running footsteps thumped, leather creaked, and mail clinked behind him. "Heimdall!" Rodric called.

Neither piece of the draug was moving, so Heimdall risked a glance over his shoulder. His father had grabbed a sword and shield and collected a couple of fully equipped warriors on his way to the pasture. Wynne and the boy had come back too, to lead the fighters straight to Heimdall's aid. After what the young herders had seen, that had taken courage, and he made a mental note that their bravery should be rewarded.

That was a matter for later, though. "I think it's all right," Heimdall called back to his father, pleased Rodric would throw himself into battle to protect his people. "The draug seems to be truly dead now."

Rodric came forward and gripped his son's shoulder. "Good work. Let's hope this is the last of the draugr."

"I do hope it," Heimdall replied, "but we'd better not assume it is."

"Meaning?"

"Come take a closer look at this." Heimdall led his father to where the draug's severed head lay in the grass. "The skin is blue now, the flesh beneath bloated, the expression demented and bestial. But he's still recognizable."

"Nuri!" Rodric exclaimed. Nuri, one of the two warriors who perished aboard the fishing boats. Nuri, whom they'd buried yesterday.

"Yes," Heimdall said, "and you realize what this means."

"The sea draugr passed their curse onto him," Rodric said grimly. "That means they may have passed it on to our other dead as well. We'll need to dig them up and see."

SIX

Uschi watched from the top of the stronghold wall as Frey's warriors beached the longship, and her parents and their own finest guards greeted the newcomers. She thought it odd that the lord of all Vanaheim had arrived without additional vessels to provide an escort, but perhaps he was considerate of Peadar's dwindling fortunes and limited resources to provide hospitality for a large number of guests.

In any case, even with only a single ship at his disposal, Frey didn't lack for splendor. His personal guards were plainly an elite, and the silver and gold decorating their trappings flashed in the afternoon sun. So, too, did the huge metal boar Gullinbursti, Frey's war-steed and one of the masterworks of the dwarves. Currently standing motionless toward the stern of the vessel, Gullinbursti resembled a statue except for the articulation of his joints, but Uschi had seen the automaton run as fast as any wingless horse and slash with its tusks to deadly effect as it carried its master into battle.

Frey's importance was likewise manifest in Peadar and Juliska's deferential attitude as they waited for their overlord to spring down from the longship, and Uschi knew there was a reason beyond the formal relationship of ruler and subordinate jarl to account for that. In the loose parlance of mortals, dwarves, giants, and what have you, all the Aesir and Vanir were "gods." Only a handful, however, truly were deities, powerful beings either innately possessed of mastery over particular natural or supernatural forces or invested by Odin with the ability to exert such mastery. Frey, God of the Harvest, was one such.

By rights, Uschi, Peadar's only child even if she'd spurned the birthright that normally would have accompanied that station, should have been down at the shore to welcome Frey along with her parents. When her father had been assembling those who would greet the god, however – and she'd hesitantly approached to offer to join the delegation – he'd shot her a glare that plainly indicated he wanted her to stay away. She had too much pride to plead otherwise.

So here she was, watching resentfully from afar as Peadar and Juliska saluted Frey. It was difficult to make out details at a distance, but the God of the Harvest seemed mostly the same. She'd occasionally observed him going about his business in the royal city of Asgard or fighting on a battlefield or two. He was tall and thin with his long hair gathered behind him, an extravagantly curling mustache, and a pointed beard, all of that so blond it was nearly white. One thing was different, however.

Frey famously possessed Laevateinn, the Sword of Destiny, an enchanted weapon said to make its master invincible, in part because it flew and fought entirely on its own. He still wore that weapon on his hip – the golden, ruby-eyed boar's head pommel was unmistakable – but he also bore a different broadsword in a scabbard hanging down his back.

When the greetings were through, Frey waved his hand, and two warriors carried a coffer made of gray metal off the boat. In the center of the lid was a raised emblem, a hammer made of a darker substance or stained black. The men removed the lid to reveal a number of broadswords, each of them, it appeared to Uschi, a twin to the one her father himself was wearing. Frey lifted out three of the blades and presented them to Peadar. His manner was that of one bestowing a precious gift, and Peadar received them reverently. He then presented them to three senior members of his guard.

It appeared to Uschi that the swords from the box were also identical to the one hanging over Frey's back. Her mouth pursed in thought. They might also be identical to the enchanted draugr-slaying blades Rodric and several of his men had used aboard the fishing boats, but she wasn't sure.

She squinted in an attempt to see the distant scene more clearly. It didn't help. Of course, even if she'd been able to make out faraway sights as easily as Heimdall, she still couldn't have seen any runes while the swords were in their scabbards.

With the presentations completed, Frey and her parents talked on. While again she couldn't be certain, she had a sense that the warlord of all Vanaheim was less pleased with what he was hearing than he'd been before. He frowned up at the fortress, and Uschi felt a pang of wholly irrational trepidation, as if he was specifically scowling at her peering down from the ramparts.

After some more conversation, the folk on the strand formed a column for the short trip up to the stronghold. Surging into motion, Gullinbursti leaped off the longship as nimbly as a cat and presented itself for its master to ride.

As the column drew nearer, Uschi shook off her momentary uneasiness. In its place grew the angry feeling that she should greet Frey when he rode into the courtyard whether her father liked it or not. She was, after all, the thane of a company of Valkyries, and it was only fitting that she should hear whatever Lord Peadar thought about it.

If she was being honest, it also occurred to her that Heimdall had said her deeds in the service of Asgard would make her parents proud and reconcile them to the path she'd chosen. The Fates knew, her friend hadn't turned out to be right about any of her family difficulties so far, but it was also true that she hadn't had the chance to regale Peadar with tales of her exploits. Frey surely knew something of them, and, when she presented herself, might well allude to them in laudatory terms. Maybe then her father's heart would soften.

More likely not, but even if it didn't, she might at least be able to satisfy her curiosity about the gift of the swords and Frey's visit in general. In any case, she would have made her point that a Valkyrie wouldn't hang meekly back in the shadows, and afterward, she'd be able to tell Heimdall that she'd done everything possible to reconcile with her parents. She hurried down the steep creaking stairs that connected the wall-walk to the courtyard and positioned herself where Frey couldn't help but see her when he and her parents rode in through the gate.

They, and the warriors and other retainers riding or marching in the column behind them, stopped short when they did. Peadar glared, and Juliska winced. That was more or less to be expected, but it surprised Uschi when Frey stared at her with recognition but without warmth; almost, she might have imagined, with suspicion. Audhumla's milk, she thought, what terrible things had her father said about her?

She rather wished she'd kept her distance as Peadar and Juliska had wanted her to, but it was too late now. She was standing right in front of Frey astride his shining magical boar of a steed, and she had to offer him the respect due from a thane to a superior. She inclined her head and said, "My lord."

Frey just stared for another heartbeat. Uschi wondered if he wasn't even going to acknowledge her, or if he expected her to simply turn away, clear the way for Gullinbursti, and afterward keep her distance and lament her mysterious fall from favor. That, she thought, steeling herself for whatever was to come, was *not* going to happen. Finally, he said, "Captain Uschi."

"Yes, my lord."

"Your father tells me that, like Lord Rodric's son, you've returned home purely to enjoy the company of your family."

Well, she thought sourly, that's one way of putting it. "Yes, my lord."

"Then you'll understand that Lord Peadar and I won't require your presence at our private deliberations."

"But of course, you're welcome at the feast!" Juliska said. The glance she gave her husband was half-insistence and half-anxiety that he'd hold the insistence against her.

"Thank you," Uschi said, meanwhile bitterly thinking she could imagine few prospects less inviting than sharing a meal with folk who would at best treat her with cold, grudging formality. Better to secure her own little feast from the kitchen before the servers carried forth the platters and stay out of her mother and father's hall. She inclined her head a second time and stepped out of the way of the procession.

On the other side of the courtyard, removed from everyone's disdain, she watched her parents and Frey swing themselves off their mounts. Frey then conferred with one of his followers, a sharp-featured woman with three carved-bone medallions hanging around her neck. Judging from her lack of weapons and armor, she wasn't a shield maiden. She was some other sort of functionary. Possibly even a witch.

SEVEN

The sun was setting by the time Heimdall's parents had prepared a party of warriors and workers equipped with spades to open the graves. Though the jarl had instructed everyone involved in the venture to keep quiet about it, word had nonetheless reached the castle population at large and many of those who lived outside the walls as well, even fisherfolk in their village by the shore. As a result, about three dozen spectators had congregated to view the proceedings.

As Heimdall watched the diggers shovel, he heard the murmured conversations of the onlookers and realized they weren't all of the same mind. Some thought this a pointless endeavor and resented what they regarded as the needless desecration of the burial places of those laid to rest just a day before. He hoped they were right, that the dead man he'd beheaded in the pasture was the only one who'd contracted the draugr curse.

Other spectators suspected there were indeed draugr in the remaining graves, and in many cases they feared meddling with the things as night approached, the world grew dark, and evil gathered strength. A trepidation that, Heimdall wryly reflected, hadn't prevented them from turning out to watch whatever horrors might ensue. Not for the first time, it seemed to him that in a goodly number of cases, people were a strange, irrational lot.

To give those wary onlookers their due, though, he and his parents had likewise worried that it might be reckless to open the graves as the light fell. They'd decided, however, that delay would give any remaining draugr the chance to rise and prey on the living and was accordingly even riskier.

He very much hoped that when he'd slain the draug in the pasture, that had been the end of the trouble. His dry mouth and edginess, however, revealed that deep down, he suspected the truth was otherwise. The dead things that came out of the sea had possessed one set of abilities, and the creature that had killed his mother's favorite horse another. Despite his learning, for once he felt out of his depth.

"This should be just about deep enough," one of the gravediggers said. He and his partner started shoveling more gingerly, tossing less dirt out of the hole with each scraping scoop of the shovel so as to avoid inflicting damage on the corpse they were uncovering. Spectators craned to see what lay at the bottom of the hole. His fingers tight on the hilt, Heimdall gripped his two-handed sword and other warriors their spears lest the dead man rear up and attack.

That didn't happen, though, and once revealed, the motionless body wasn't any bluer, any more swollen, or any more foul-smelling than any corpse that had lain buried for a day. Heimdall sighed with relief.

One of the spectators said, "Burn it anyway, just to be sure!"

"No," Rodric said. "There are no signs he's going to rise as a draug. We won't disturb his rest any more than we've done already." As before, the muttering that ensued revealed that the spectators disagreed on the wisdom of their jarl's decision. Some thought it proper, but the more frightened wanted the corpse chopped up and burned, never mind showing respect for the honored dead. Heimdall supposed his father was right but still resolved to keep a wary eye on the grave.

The diggers left the first grave open while they started excavating the second. There'd be time enough to fill the holes back in after Rodric and his guards had checked all three.

Once revealed, the next body, that of one of the slaughtered fishermen, appeared as harmless, as free of the taint of unnatural forces, as the previous one. Maybe, Heimdall thought with a first tentative stirring of relief, the trouble really was over.

That hope died when the gravediggers opened the third grave. Heimdall caught a whiff of the thick, stomach-churning stench seeping up from it. "This one is a draug!" he shouted. "Get out of the hole!"

The diggers dropped their spades and tried, but they were too slow. The slain fisherman, now slate-blue and bloated, burst up through the last of the earth and reached for one staggering karl who'd been working as a digger.

Fortunately, the warriors who were standing around the grave were ready for a moment like this. With their frenzied battle cries shrill with revulsion, they thrust downward with their spears. From past experience, Heimdall doubted the weapons did the corpse-thing much actual harm, but they hindered and distracted it enough for the other men to grab the diggers and haul them up to safety.

Afterward the fighters shoved with their spears to pin the

snarling, thrashing, reeking creature down in the hole. The draug tore one lance out of his chest and snapped the ashwood shaft of another. By that time, however, little as he'd wanted to venture closer, Heimdall had figured out precisely how he was going to make his sword cut. Now, the opening appeared. Bellowing "Asgard!" he swung his blade, and the dead fisherman's head tumbled away from his shoulders to thud down in the grave. The decapitated body ceased its frenzied struggles.

"All right," Rodric said, "this one we will burn."

Workers had previously built a pyre of white birch logs and birchbark tinder, the whole doused with wool oil, and set the pieces of the draug Heimdall had slain in the pasture in the middle of the pile. Lifting them with reluctance and grunts and gasps of disgust, they placed the head and body of the new corpse-thing there as well. Heimdall joined in as he had with the slaying. His rank would have excused him, but he would have felt vaguely guilty to let others deal with the foulness while he stood idly by. At least, he thought grimly, he was gaining more experience with it, however much he might have wished it otherwise.

Once everyone was clear, a warrior set the pyre alight by striking sparks from a curved fire-steel. He recited a brief invocation to Thor as he set about his task, and in theory, the Thunder God, wherever he might be, aided the effort with a flicker of his lightning.

The fire blazed up and spread quickly. The conflagration gave rise to the same black, stinking smoke as the flames that had consumed the remains of the sea draugr, but as before, it proved possible to avoid the worst of it by standing upwind of the pyre.

And stand most everyone did, while daylight bled out of the world and shadows lengthened. Heimdall suspected his companions wanted the reassurance of seeing the draugr reduced to embers and ash, and in fact, he felt something of the sort himself.

By the time the last curved sliver of the sun sank below the western horizon, the disintegration was nearly complete. Some folk, deciding they'd witnessed all that was required to set their minds at ease, had already wandered off. Then, however, shortly after night took full possession of the world, the headless body of the newly slain draug sat up. Heimdall cried out and recoiled in startled alarm, and the other people gathered before the pyre did the same.

Heimdall feared that unless someone intervened, the draug was about to demonstrate yet another ghastly new power. At this point, there was scarcely anything left of the creature, just a rickety-looking structure of bones with the last few scraps of charred flesh flaking away. Nonetheless, he suspected it might still be as resistant to harm as other draugr had proved to be. He drew his two-handed sword anew and readied himself to smite with all his strength as soon as the thing came out of the fire.

But it didn't do that. Instead, it groped about itself in a manner that might almost have been comical in less horrifying circumstances, found the severed head that was now little more than a skull, and set it on the broken top of its spinal column. It then turned the head from left to right, raking the living with the gaze of empty sockets out of which the eyes had burned and melted away.

People wailed, cringed, fainted when the skeletal thing looked directly at them. To Heimdall's right, his mother whimpered. He felt a shock of horror that she'd been touched by the draug's sight. Then the draug looked at him. His temples throbbed, the strength went out of him, and his knees buckled. For a terrifying instant, he believed he was dying. Then the skull continued turning, and his vigor flooded back.

Aghast and furious at what had just befallen his mother, relieved to still be alive, no longer caring that he'd have to enter the flames to do it, he gathered himself to attack. But before he could charge, the skeletal draug completed its malignant surveying of the crowd and fell apart into a litter of burning sticks.

At once, Heimdall turned to his mother. "Are you all right?"

Estrid shakily rubbed her head, sweeping a stray lock of hair back from her brow as she did so. "I… think so." She glanced around at the rest of the throng. "I think everyone is." And in fact, the others appeared to be shedding their momentary affliction, those who had remained upright helping neighbors who'd fallen back onto their feet.

Rodric turned to address his wife and son. "Was that what people call the evil eye?" he asked, keeping his voice low.

"Possibly," Heimdall said. "The people of Midgard have one or two sagas where the draug can cast curses by gaze alone, just as some sorcerers are said to do. If that one could do it too, maybe we're lucky it was already crumbling to ash when it tried."

He hoped what they'd experienced was the last impotent manifestation of the draugr evil but was grimly aware how that same hope had been dashed before.

EIGHT

Once she'd wolfed down the roast duck, stewed peas, and oat flatbread spread with soft skyr cheese she'd taken from the kitchen, Uschi was restless and wandered the fortress wall-walk and courtyard. Meanwhile, toasts, laughter, and songs sung to the accompaniment of lyres, flutes, goat horns, and drums rang out from the hall.

Plainly, Uschi thought sourly, her absence wasn't preventing anyone from enjoying the feast. Well, maybe her mother missed her, but certainly no one else.

Why, she wondered for the thousandth time, had she allowed Heimdall to talk her into coming back here? She knew some foolish part of her had hoped her shrewd friend was right that a reconciliation with her family was possible. Now, however, she knew what that hope had been worth. She promised herself that when she had the chance, she'd tell Heimdall forcefully that there were occasions when even the best of friends should keep their noses out of their comrades' affairs.

Much later that night, the celebration that so wore on her nerves finally began to break up. Calling their farewells, tipsy men and women stumbled forth to seek their beds. Other folk with even less head for drink snored on or beneath their benches. Uschi could still hear some diehards carousing, but the noise of the revels was softer than before.

Maybe, Uschi thought, she'd finally be able to sleep. But edginess was still gnawing at her nerves.

In a last effort to wear herself out and so make it possible to slumber, careful on that portion of the wall-walk that sagged and creaked alarmingly under her boots, she made a final circuit in the moonlight. Upon descending, she headed for the stables. She wanted to check on Avalanche before she retired.

She often did that even when back home in the royal city of Asgard, where the grooms in the Valkyrie stables were thoroughly versed in the proper care of winged stallions. Avalanche, after all, was her *other* best friend. He'd been her steed since she apprenticed to her warrior sisterhood and had carried her through countless journeys and battles. He, moreover, never led her astray with importunate wheedling and bad advice.

Upon arriving at her parents' stables, she reached for the handle to one of the doors, and an unanticipated reluctance seized her. Just because she was restless, she thought, was no reason to risk waking her steed and any other slumbering horses. It would be sensible to seek her bed forthwith, and she almost did. Except that it felt peculiar that the impulse had so abruptly sprung to life inside her head, and that it was so contrary to her usual custom of looking in on Avalanche before she sought her rest.

Possibly that meant nothing. Still, war and other perilous missions on Odin's behalf had convinced her to be cautious when instinct suggested she should. She eased the door open until the gap was wide enough for her to slip through.

The interior smelled of straw and leather tack. In the darkness, she could discern the center aisle running the length of the stables with stalls to either side. Except for the vague forms of the two nearest, she couldn't make out the horses at all. She could hear them, though. Some grunted in their sleep. Others, wakeful, snorted and maybe hoped her visitation meant a feeding was at hand.

It belatedly occurred to her that to check on Avalanche properly, she would have to grope around, find a lantern and the means to light it, and as all was tranquil, the process truly wasn't worth the bother. Just go to bed, Uschi, she thought, and was turning to do so when she glimpsed a flicker of faint green phosphorescence from the corner of her eye.

She spun back around. The green light was gone, leaving her to wonder if she'd truly seen anything at all. Manifest in her accelerated heartbeat, instinct insisted she had.

Now all but blind once more, she listened. Perhaps, nearly masked by the soft shuffling noises the horses made, there was a sound softer still. Maybe, deeper in the stable, someone was whispering.

Uschi crept forward, and as she did so, the light came again. This time, it persisted and crawled from one small adjacent spot to another, and then to another after that. Gradually, the three spots glowed brighter all at once.

Once that occurred, there was enough light for Uschi to discern that the phosphorescence emanated from the bone pendants hanging around the neck of the sharp-featured woman she'd noticed conferring with Frey that afternoon. The witch –

for surely she must be so – was whispering her incantation directly in front of Avalanche's stall. If the brightening light and a cold crawling feeling in the air were any indication, the magic was nearing its completion. Uschi's rage mingled with fear that the sorceress might be trying to harm the steed. For an instant, she remembered Amora the Enchantress, likewise a witch and, during the war with the Jotuns, her bitter foe.

"You there!" Uschi shouted. "Stop that!"

Startled, the sorceress jerked around. She thrust out both arms as if she were shoving someone, and although Uschi was still several paces away, she felt the impact of hands on her shoulders. The force sent her reeling backward to fall on the straw-strewn earthen floor.

She jumped up, drew her sword, and gave chase, but the witch was running too, and made it through the door at the other end of the aisle ahead of her. Uschi would have continued the pursuit except that fear impelled her to check on Avalanche immediately. She *thought* she'd interrupted the spell short of its culmination, but she didn't *know*. Perhaps magic had harmed the stallion already.

She hurried back to Avalanche's stall and threw open the door. Possibly to give him room to spread his wings a bit, the groom had put the Valkyrie's horse in one of the wider spaces, and now he was lying on his side. Despite his whiteness, he was an all but indistinguishable mass in the gloom. Dreading the worst, she cried out his name, knelt beside him, and ran her hands over him seeking wounds or other signs of injury.

To her profound relief, there were none. Instead, it seemed Avalanche was simply sleeping the deepest slumber of which horses were capable, the sleep in which they lay down. Her voice and touch roused the stallion, and he grunted and clambered to his feet.

At the same instant, yellow torchlight shone through the exit the sorceress had taken, and two of Peadar's warriors tramped in with swords in hand and the witch following along behind. For a moment, Uschi believed she was going to have to fight them. The fracas would have felt like a proper continuation of all the coldness and recriminations that had gone before.

But when the torchlight revealed her clearly, the guards faltered. "Captain Uschi!" the shorter, stouter one exclaimed. He then looked around to address the sorceress. "This is Lord Peadar's daughter."

The witch laughed a relieved, rueful sort of laugh. Uschi suspected she was feigning her reaction, but if so, she was doing a convincing job of it. "I know who she is. I just couldn't tell in the dark. I only saw a shadow shouting at me and then coming at me with a sword."

"Why were you putting a spell on my steed?" Uschi said.

"I was placing a blessing on *all* the horses," the sorceress said. "Yours just happened to be the one I was standing in front of. You'll notice his stall is more or less in the middle of the stables. That helped the magic spread out to touch all the animals. Or would have, if our misunderstanding hadn't interrupted it."

"I don't believe you," Uschi said.

The witch sighed. "That grieves me, captain. Truly. But if you're accusing me of some sort of mischief, perhaps we'd better find Lord Frey and your father and let them sort it out."

Evidently, Uschi thought sourly, she was going to end up spending more time in the hall after all.

When they all arrived, though, they discovered that both

the God of the Harvest and Uschi's parents had already departed the dregs of the feast. They had to wait while those important folk were fetched. Meanwhile, the remaining feasters whispered to one another wondering what was afoot.

After a brief time that felt far longer to Uschi in her impatience, those who could adjudicate the dispute arrived. Though he'd presumably been summoned out of bed, Frey looked as fussily dressed and impeccably groomed as ever, not a hair in the white-blond curling mustache, pointed beard, or even his eyebrows out of place. In contrast, Juliska and Peadar had clearly pulled on their clothes in haste, and it didn't appear that either had bothered with a brush or comb. The latter, in particular, looked disheveled and agitated although he'd had the presence of mind to buckle on the sword his overlord had given him. He remained paler than Uschi was accustomed to seeing him, but Peadar pulled himself together as he, Juliska, and Frey took their seats on the dais. "Come forward," he said, "and tell us what in the name of the Tree is going on."

"This woman – Ysolt – found us and said someone accosted her in the stables and threatened her with a sword," said the shorter warrior. "When Daividh and I went to look, we found Captain Uschi." He sounded nervous, as though regretting the ill fortune that had involved him and his comrade in what might escalate into a serious quarrel between his own lord and lady and the master of all Vanaheim.

Uschi was nervous as well. It wasn't lost on her that she was about to denounce one of Frey's trusted servants without actual proof, and this after the God of the Harvest had seemed cold to her earlier that day. Still, hiding any signs of trepidation, she stepped forward past the guard. "What this warrior omits, no doubt because he and his friend didn't see it, was that Ysolt was casting a spell on my horse Avalanche. Perhaps on all the horses, but I'm certain she targeted mine."

"A *benign* spell," the sorceress replied. "A charm of health and good fortune."

"I don't believe you," Uschi said. "Why would you lay any spell on my steed without consulting me first?"

Ysolt spread her hands. "Lord Frey bade me perform the blessing. I didn't then deem it necessary to talk to the rider of every horse in the stables even if that rider was a Valkyrie. If I overstepped, I apologize."

Uschi turned to the god seated on the dais. "My lord, is this true?"

Frey nodded. "In fact, it is. Your father is a fine jarl and a gracious host. I wanted to repay his hospitality with such benefactions as it is within my power to bestow."

Things were going every bit as badly as Uschi had worried they might, and a satisfactory outcome seemed increasingly unlikely. Still, the explanation didn't make sense to her. "Starting with the horses?" she said. "In the middle of the night?"

"Certain enchantments," Ysolt replied, "are more efficacious if cast at certain daymarks, often the daymarks that fall at night."

Uschi glanced at her parents in the hope of some sort of support, if only because the other mounts in the stables belonged to them. Peadar, however, simply scowled at her impatiently. Juliska looked upset but showed no signs of speaking up, perhaps because she didn't know what to say in her daughter's defense, perhaps because she assumed no one would heed her anyway.

Instead, Frey spoke again. "Captain, did your horse suffer any harm from Ysolt's spellcasting?"

"No," Uschi said, "but I interrupted her before she could finish."

"Was the stallion in fear, as if he felt evil forces gathering around him?"

"No," Uschi said reluctantly, "he was asleep. But that was strange in and of itself! He's a magical creature and a trained warhorse. He *should* have been agitated that a stranger was casting a spell on him. Unless the witch began with some enchantment that put him to sleep."

"Or," said Frey, "he was slumbering peacefully because no one and nothing posed a threat. Think about it, captain. If Ysolt truly wished the horse harm and succeeded in putting him to sleep, it would then have been quick and easy simply to slip a dagger into him."

"I don't know exactly what she intended," Uschi said, "but–"

"Enough!" Peadar snapped. "We've heard you out, and the only result has been to embarrass your family. You owe Lord Frey and Ysolt an apology."

"No need for that," said Frey, his voice kindly but with a note of condescension. "Years ago, Captain Uschi helped unmask the treachery of Lady Amora. Since then, it's perhaps natural that she views witches with suspicion. But, captain, I would say that, now that we've all looked into this matter, you'd do well to go to bed. I have no doubt events will seem less sinister after a good night's rest."

Plainly, further argument was futile, especially since Uschi's parents weren't going to support her. Her face hot with anger and frustration, she inclined her head and said, "My lords.

My lady." She then turned and strode alongside the crackling long fire down the hall. Some of the onlookers on the benches whispered to one another as she passed or sniggered at her discomfiture.

Before stalking out the door, she turned. Partly, it was to show the occupants of the hall that she was neither shamed nor cowed by their amusement. Despite any excuses or arguments to the contrary, she still trusted the intuition that said Ysolt had indeed been engaged in something "sinister". Partly, she supposed that despite her better judgment, she was also seeking *any* sign of regret or contrition from her father.

In that, she was disappointed if not surprised. His manner agitated once again, one hand clutching the hilt of his new sword, Peadar was speaking urgently to Frey. Uschi couldn't make out the words down the length of the hall in any case, but she observed that her father, upset though he was, going by his flushed cheeks, was whispering, nonetheless.

After a moment, Frey raised his hand to halt the flood of words, as if the hall was too public a place for this conversation even if they kept their voices low. He murmured a few words of his own, and then he, Peadar, and Juliska exited the room through the doorway behind the dais.

What, Uschi wondered, had *that* been about? Peadar had said she should apologize. Was he doing so quietly on her behalf? While bemoaning what a disappointment of a daughter she was? Or was it something else entirely?

She had no way of knowing. But she did know she was going to spend the rest of the night watching in the barn, not lying in her bed. If Ysolt or anyone else came back to hurt her beloved Avalanche, she'd be there to prevent it.

Then, at first light, she'd saddle the winged stallion and fly back to Lord Rodric's castle. Maybe Heimdall could make sense of all this. She knew she was no fool but also that her friend had a mind that lent itself to solving puzzles, when he wasn't interfering in other people's family affairs. In any case, she'd had about as much of this family reunion as she could stomach.

Nine

Heimdall and his mother slipped away for an interlude when it was just the two of them together. The hideous moment at the burial site, when the burning draug rose from the pyre and attempted to cast its curse upon them, had left them shaken. He hoped the attempt to recapture one of the happy experiences they'd shared when he was small would help them recover their equilibrium.

They climbed to the top of one of the castle towers and then on to the round, flat roof bordered by crenellations. It had been a favorite retreat of theirs when he was growing up. The stars of Vanaheim blazed in the night sky, and when he looked north, even without invoking the vision of Mimir, he could see the pale glimmer of surf breaking on the shore. The world hereabouts looked beautiful, untroubled, and unsullied, and he told himself that surely, *surely*, it must finally be so.

He and Estrid enjoyed the view in silence for a time. Then she said, "It's a shame Sif wasn't here to help deal with the draugr. She would have liked it."

Though he would have much preferred talking about something other than the living dead, Heimdall chuckled. "I'll wager she would at that. You know she would have come if she could. Her duties wouldn't let her get away. She'll visit when she has a chance."

"I do know," Estrid said. "My children are such... personages now. I don't imagine you can stay much longer."

Heimdall cocked his head. "I told Queen Frigga I'd be away from Asgard until the new moon. You aren't trying to get rid of me sooner than that, are you?"

"You know better than that!" his mother said. "It's just... this can't be the visit you were hoping for."

"All the more reason to enjoy the rest of it." And if, despite his efforts to believe otherwise, the trouble *wasn't* over, he should be here to help his parents deal with it.

"Well, your father and I love having you," Estrid said. She smiled in a way that almost made it look as if she were trying to push some sort of worry out of her head. Maybe she wasn't absolutely certain the draugr were gone, either.

Perhaps he could ease her fretting. "Mother, you know I'll always come if you need me. Sif will too." He hesitated. "Honestly, you could have sent for us the moment the sea draugr appeared. Odin and Frigga would have let us come. They might even have sent a company of warriors along with us."

For a moment, his mother seemed flustered as she said, "That's not... I mean, there was scarcely any time before the fishermen died and you appeared. And you see, we've now rid ourselves of the evil."

"Fair enough," he said. "Just please know I'm here for you." He was loath to press the matter further when she didn't seem to want to discuss it and they were enjoying the sort of reunion he'd envisioned at last.

"Should we go down to the kitchen?" she asked. "There are some blackberry patty leftovers from supper. I should check on the bakers. They're making raspberry kissel for tomorrow, and they never put in enough honey."

The castle was grand enough that the kitchen occupied a building all its own, where the heat and the smoke wouldn't trouble the rest of the fortress. The cooks and scullions could go about their work without interference, except for that provided by the lady of the stronghold. Now that the evening meal was done and the round wooden bowls, trenchers, steatite cups, and drinking horns had been washed and put away, the space was less busy than it would have been earlier. Still, two cooks remained to get a head start on tomorrow's labors.

As Heimdall searched the larder for the remaining blackberry patties, Estrid located the baker simmering cider and honey in a pan atop one of the open hearths. She'd always liked overseeing the baking, occasionally trying the patience of servants, and apparently that hadn't changed. He smiled fondly, glad she was still the mother he remembered even when times were dark.

"Good evening, Lieven," Estrid said, making a show of conviviality while eyeing the pot. "May I ask, how much honey did you use?"

Lieven was a florid, balding fellow with a belly that suggested he was fond of his own baking. "About this much," he said, holding his finger and thumb apart, a hint of resignation in his voice.

"Don't you think it could do with a little more?" Estrid

turned to look for the earthenware honey jar where it sat atop the nearest table. Across the room, Heimdall grinned and, having located the blackberry patties, took a first sweet bite of the one he'd selected. A bit of the filling leaked out to stain his fingers.

"Whatever my lady wishes," Lieven said with a sigh. "I can–" And with that, the karl doubled over coughing blood, the discharge spattering his goatskin shoes and the beaten earth floor beneath.

"Lieven!" Estrid said. "What's wrong?"

Still coughing, he tried to straighten up and then collapsed, banging his head on the edge of the table on his way down. The honey jar and other items on the tabletop jumped and rattled.

Estrid kneeled beside Lieven and rolled him over onto his back. Heimdall dropped the blackberry patty and hurried over to crouch down beside her. The baker's ruddy face had gone pale, and his eyes had rolled up in his head. He wasn't coughing anymore, but bloody foam and mucus smeared his mouth and nostrils and bubbled in time with his labored breathing. A gurgling sound issued from his throat, and intermittent spasms or tremors shook his limbs.

"Lieven!" Estrid repeated. "Lieven!" If the karl heard, he was incapable of showing it.

"Let me try something," Heimdall said. Concerned that the baker was choking, he pulled down on the baker's chin and forced his mouth open, then reached inside with two fingers. He scooped out sludge composed of blood, mucus, and saliva, but whether he'd cleared Lieven's airway sufficiently for the stricken man to breathe easily, he couldn't say, any more than he could guess why the sludge was present in the first place. He looked over his shoulder at the remaining cook, who'd come forward to stare down aghast at the tableau he, Lieven, and Estrid presented. "Go fetch the healer! Fast!"

The karl gave a jerky nod and bolted.

The castle healer was Fleta, a woman Heimdall remembered well from his childhood. The scar running down the left side of her face was a souvenir of her youth as a warrior, before she'd decided to devote herself to bandages and splints, poultices and elixirs. She had a stern manner that became positively grim when tending children who'd injured themselves attempting some reckless dare. It had taken him a while to realize her disapproval masked a caring heart.

When Fleta hurried in, the cook who'd run to fetch her stayed outside, maybe because it had occurred to him to fear contagion. Not bothering with salutations, she said, "Move back and give me room to examine him." Heimdall and Estrid complied, and the healer knelt by Lieven, laid her palm on his forehead, touched her fingers to the side of his neck and counted to herself, and bent down to press her ear to his chest. Straightening up again, she asked, "Do you have any idea what might have brought this on?"

Estrid shook her head. "He seemed fine one moment, and then he was coughing up blood the next."

For an instant, Heimdall wished he could profess the same lack of insight. It would be more comfortable not to have the thought that now occurred to him, to dismiss it instead of speaking it aloud. But that was impossible because everyone must be prepared for the possibility. "I noticed this man Lieven in the crowd that watched the burning of the last two draugr."

Estrid frowned. "That means the thing in the flames gave

him the evil eye. Cursed him with a look as certain wicked mages and some other creatures can. Him and forty other people."

Including us, Heimdall thought. He'd wanted to believe he, his parents, and all the others present had resisted the effect, but it was now impossible to be certain. For all he truly knew, maybe *no one* had withstood it.

Fleta's habitual frown deepened. "It's good you told me, but let's not jump to conclusions. It might just be a coincidence. In any case, we can't leave Lieven on the floor. Can one of you find a couple of men to carry him to my quarters?"

"We only need one man," Heimdall said. "I can help carry him myself." He wouldn't relish doing so but thought it only made sense that he should. If Lieven was contagious, he'd already been in close proximity to him.

The castle stores yielded a litter, and Estrid prevailed on a sentry to carry one end of it. As they crossed the courtyard, Heimdall was glad it was already dark. Fewer people were about to see what was happening. Still, he was sure someone noticed, and he didn't like to think of the possible reaction when word spread.

The Vanir were well familiar with wounds, injuries, and even the death that might result from them. Serious sickness, however, was a more mysterious matter. As a general rule, they were simply too hardy for illness to pose much of a threat, and if matters now were otherwise, the situation might well alarm them to the point of panic. All the more so if they too suspected a connection to the draugr.

Estrid and the sentry waited outside the door, but Heimdall followed Fleta inside. While she examined Lieven more thoroughly, he endeavored to do the same, probing the sick man's body with his heightened senses.

The effort availed him nothing. He heard the baker's labored, congested breathing and irregular heartbeat, but he had no doubt Fleta had too, and the gifts of Mimir notwithstanding, he couldn't actually look inside the afflicted man's body.

Fleta had evidently heard of Heimdall's special talents and surmised what he was attempting. "Anything?" she asked.

"No," he said. The admission made him feel useless.

"Then go back outside and give me room to work."

Heimdall did so and then heard Fleta muttering symptoms and possible remedies to herself, preparing a drug to coax down the sick man's throat, and reciting an incantation. As the healer worked, Estrid ordered a passing servant to summon her husband, and in due course Rodric came tramping up. After being apprised of the situation, he stood awaiting developments with the rest of them.

Scowling, the older man looked as angry as he was concerned. His fingers clenched repeatedly on the hilt of the runic broadsword hanging at his side. "Curse him," he muttered. "Curse him!"

"Curse who?" Heimdall asked. "The draug in the fire?"

The older man blinked. "Yes. Of course. That thing." Just as he finished speaking, the door opened. When Fleta beheld her lord, she bobbed her head slightly, as much of a show of deference as Heimdall could remember her according anyone.

"How is he?" Estrid asked.

Fleta sighed. "I've done what I can. I'll go on doing it, but I doubt it's going to be enough. I've never seen anything like this sickness before."

"Did the draug put the evil eye on him?" Rodric asked.

"I said I've never seen anything like this before," the healer snapped. Then her manner softened. "It's possible."

"Is everyone who stood at the pyre going to get sick?" Estrid asked.

"Will anyone who didn't?" Rodric asked, his question overlapping hers.

"I *told* you–" Fleta began, and then another karl came rushing up to the group.

"My lord," he gasped, "my lady. My son's taken ill. I came for the healer."

"Go," Rodric said to Fleta. "Do what you can."

"Meanwhile, I'll go to the tower library and consult the old books," Heimdall said. "Maybe a remedy's in there." And maybe, if he found it, he wouldn't feel so helpless and fearful for the future.

"Right." Fleta turned to the sentry. "Guard the door. Don't let anybody in." She ducked back inside long enough to pick up a wooden drinking bowl containing, Heimdall assumed, the portion of the elixir she'd prepared that she hadn't managed to induce Lieven to drink. With that cradled protectively against her chest, she followed the frantic karl off to minister to his son.

Heimdall hastened to the library and, the musty smell of old parchment tickling his nose, started poring over the appropriate tomes. At first, he didn't bother lighting one of the iron fish-oil lamps. When he used the sight of Mimir, he had no trouble reading by the meager light entering through the window. His gifts were good for that much, anyway, he thought with a tinge of bitterness.

He couldn't summon the sight without invoking the hearing as well, however, and repeated explosive bouts of coughing and cries of consternation rising from elsewhere in the fortress jabbed at his nerves. After a while, he quelled his heightened senses, kindled the lamp on the table, and squinted to make out the runic text thereafter.

Finally, frustrated, he closed the last book that seemed even vaguely relevant, rechecked the shelves in case he'd missed any others, and then heaved a sigh of defeat. Assuming they were trustworthy, reports from Midgard had taught him a bit more about draugr than he'd known before, but nothing that seemed germane to healing the victims of an incipient plague the corpse-things had created.

That frightened, helpless feeling rose in him again. Struggling against it, he told himself that Fleta, with her healer's lore, would find significance where it had eluded him. He rose, stretched, and headed for her chambers. She might not be there if she was hurrying around the stronghold tending those who had fallen ill, but she'd presumably return periodically to check on Lieven's condition and to make more of the potion she was using as needed.

He faltered in shock when he rounded a corner and came within sight of the entrance to Fleta's chamber. The sentry she'd left there lay on the floor with his throat torn out in a pool of the blood that had spilled from the wound.

It seemed an impossible nightmare that such a thing could happen in the castle itself. For an instant, his childhood home didn't even feel like the same place anymore, but rather a maze of secrets and horrors.

He had to thrust his dismay aside, though. However strange

and ominous it seemed, this *was* his family home, and the people herein were in need of whatever protection he could give.

The door behind the murdered sentry stood ajar. Heimdall sharpened his senses once more. He still couldn't see much of the healer's quarters beyond the narrow gap of open doorway, but he could hear countless noises rising from the castle and beyond. He ignored all that didn't interest him to focus on any sound in Fleta's room.

Beyond the threshold, all was silent. Somewhat reassured that he wasn't likely to be fighting for his life in the next few moments, he was nonetheless keenly, unpleasantly aware that his two-handed sword was still back in his own chamber. At the start of the evening, he'd seen no reason to carry it around in his own family's fortress, and since Lieven's collapse he'd been too busy to go back for it.

He stalked cautiously up to the fallen guard. The dead man's throat looked like it had been slashed open repeatedly, and a sickening stink of corruption hung in the air around him. Particles of decayed, oozing flesh lay atop his body and around it on the floor. Heimdall stooped, appropriated the warrior's butted spruce shield and broadsword – not one of the ones with runes, unfortunately – before pushing the door all the way open.

As he'd expected, the extra bed Fleta had installed for patients so grievously wounded, injured, or ill that she wanted to be able to minister to them in an instant at any hour was empty except for the bits of decay and smears of ooze Lieven had left behind. What he'd fervently hoped he wouldn't see was that Fleta *was* here, but in that he was disappointed. The healer sprawled in much the same mangled, bloody condition as the dead warrior outside, staring sightlessly up at the ceiling. It looked as if she'd been seated at her worktable making more of her medicine with mortar and pestle when the thing that had been Lieven rose, crept up behind her, and attacked.

It didn't appear that pieces of flesh were missing or had been eaten, but maybe the new draug was guzzling blood. Or maybe it was killing out of pure malice.

With an effort, he thrust such grisly speculations aside as irrelevant. What mattered was that the corpse-thing was loose in the castle and, having slaughtered two people in quick succession, seemed likely to go on killing until it was stopped.

He listened before moving back into the corridor just in case the draug had come back and was lying in wait beside the door. Even with the hearing of Mimir, he heard nothing to indicate such was the case, but, his heart thumping, he still lunged into the hall with borrowed sword and shield at the ready. He pivoted to check in all directions... and found no one but the dead warrior still slumped on the floor.

He'd have to track the draug, then. He told himself that should be easy enough when it was leaving a trail of flecks of rotten flesh and eye-searing stench behind, but after a few paces, there were no more bits of oozing decay even when he peered with the eyes of Mimir. Several steps after that, the foul odor faded from the air.

Heimdall frowned in puzzled dismay. Apparently catching the dead thing was going to be far more difficult than anticipated. After the fight in the pasture, he had some notion of how the draug might have covered its trail, but he couldn't see a ready method for countering the trick. Still, he told himself, it was essential that he try. He drew a deep breath and shouted, "Guards! Karls! Anyone, to me! There's a draug loose in the stronghold!"

Distressed by the outbreak of sickness, the household was already wakeful, and perhaps for that reason, it wasn't long before a dozen folk, some warriors, some not, some properly dressed and others still adjusting their tunics and belts, assembled to gape at the slain warrior. Meanwhile, Heimdall studied them for any sign that one was a shapeshifting horror in disguise. If the creature stood before him, he couldn't tell it. Such being the case, he supposed he had no choice but to assume they were all what they appeared to be and hope that by convening a search party, he hadn't simply made it easier for the draug to claim more victims.

Doing his best to be the confident leader the others needed him to be, he waved his hand to indicate the butchered guard. "You see how it is. Lieven died and came back as a draug. We need to find the creature before it kills more of us. It won't be easy. I suspect it can disguise itself to look like something else, but we have to do it anyway. Spread out in pairs and search the stronghold. Warn anyone you meet. If people seem able, tell them to search as well."

"*I'm* not able!" said a scrawny man with a wispy beard. He'd pulled on a white linen undertunic but not bothered to don the tunic that normally would have gone over it. "I'm a carpenter, not a warrior! I couldn't do anything to a draug if I did find it."

Heimdall felt a surge of anger. Recognizing that, in large measure, it was because the fellow's fear and feelings of helplessness mirrored his own, he tried to keep that reaction off his face and voice. "What's your name?" he asked.

The carpenter hesitated. "Callum."

"Well, Callum, no one is asking you to fight the draug. You're with me. You'll help me look for the thing, and if we find it, you'll go for reinforcements while I engage it and keep it from slipping away. In fact, that's how everyone will pair up. One warrior and one karl who's something else."

The pairs dispersed in various directions to search the entirety of the castle, the keep, the secondary buildings, and the grounds. Heimdall was one of the warriors who remained in the massive central building. Though still keenly aware of all that he didn't know, he thought it likely the draug was still inside. Why should it go elsewhere when there was an abundance of prey right here?

As he and Callum crept along, he exercised the senses of Mimir. After nearly failing to spot the dead horse at the edge of the pasture, he was all too aware that even with his preternaturally keen sight and hearing he could miss something if he wasn't looking for it, so he sifted through all the impressions that came to him for *anything* that seemed ominous or that he couldn't immediately identify.

Eventually he caught a slurping noise coming from one of the upper levels of the keep. It could have been something as innocuous as a person eating turnip soup or barley porridge. But then again, how likely was it that anyone had procured hot soup from the kitchen at this late hour, especially in the wake of Lieven's collapse? Heimdall's imagination conjured up a gruesome picture of the thing that had been the baker sucking at the torn throat of a third victim.

Refusing to let that daunting image balk him, he headed for the nearest staircase. "Follow me," he told Callum. "Quietly."

Just as he reached what his hearing told him was the proper level, the slurping stopped. The door to the chambers occupied by the steward who kept Rodric's accounts was standing open – open like the door to poor Fleta's chamber, his frightened thoughts whispered – and after a moment, a black cat padded out. It turned and gazed at the men on the steps.

Heimdall peered back. At the far end of the shadowy length of hallway, the cat's forepaw had left a slight smear of blood on the floor, and it had another such on its mouth, which its pink tongue licked away an instant later.

This, Heimdall decided with a thrill of dread, must be the draug. Unnatural toughness, infecting their victims with their curse, using the evil eye to spread sickness... by the Tree, was there any limit to their abilities? How was he or any warrior short of Odin himself supposed to guess what was coming next, let alone contend with it?

He thrust that defeatist attitude aside. He'd contend with the draug because it was necessary, and he was the one here to do it.

The question was how. The creature was still well out of striking distance, and in the guise of a black cat, it was small and quick enough to vanish if it suspected it was in danger.

The goal, then, was to prevent that. "That's it," he whispered without turning his head toward Callum. He hoped the draug's hearing wasn't as sharp as his own. "Keep climbing the steps. Once you're on the next floor, find some guards."

The carpenter obeyed without questioning. Maybe he was eager to put distance between himself and the draug. If so, Heimdall scarcely blamed him. If not for his responsibilities, he would have gladly done the same.

Meanwhile, the cat's yellow eyes stared down the corridor, and Heimdall worried that it still might lose itself in the dark if he approached it with obvious hostile intent. He was, after all, an armed warrior, and thus far, the draug had shown a preference for easier prey. True, it had killed the sentry, but it might have judged that necessary to gain access to the rest of the castle, and it had seemingly taken the man by surprise from behind.

Heimdall decided he needed to look helpless, then, in order to lure the thing that had been Lieven close enough that evasion was no longer possible. Sauntering, trying to look as if he took no notice of the cat, he started down the hallway. After a few paces, he faltered, doubled over coughing, and fell to his knees, where he kept up the charade.

The cat continued to stare.

Come on! Heimdall thought, though there was a timid or possibly merely sensible part of him that desired anything but. I'm obviously defenseless! I've fallen victim to the evil eye the same as you did! True, he wasn't retching up blood like a real victim of the sickness, but with luck, the shield in front of him prevented that difference from being apparent.

The cat hesitated. Heimdall feared it had sensed something was amiss, but then it stalked forward once more. As it approached, it changed, the transformation as fast and fluid as when the supposed Honeyboy resumed its true form. One moment, the cat was on four legs, and the next, on two. Feline smallness and sleekness became a massive, swollen, manlike form, and black fur melted into bruised-looking blue skin mottled with patches of putrescence. The stink of rot flooded the air.

Still kneeling, head lowered, eyeing the approaching draug over the rim of the shield, Heimdall felt as afraid as ever in his life. He yearned to spring to his feet and assume a fighting stance without another instant of delay. But, he thought, if he acted too soon, the corpse-thing would still have a chance to return to cat form and elude him. He kept on coughing and feigning helplessness as the creature came closer and closer.

Soon, it was only a pace away. Reinforcements had yet to appear, but, heart pounding, pulse racing, he judged it would be suicide to delay any longer. He scrambled to his feet and swung his sword at the draug's neck.

With a quickness that belied its swollen, rotting condition, the corpse-thing threw up an arm to block the sword. Heimdall felt the familiar shock, as if he'd attempted to cleave something as hard and dense as stone. The blade made only a shallow gash before he pulled it back. As he did, the draug slashed at his weapon arm with jagged nails grown as long as the fingers that sprouted them, and the claws missed by a hair. He now knew how the creature had cut open Fleta's neck to drink her blood.

Heimdall feinted to the flank and made the true cut at the draug's head. Undeceived, the reeking horror caught the broadsword in one hand and pulled. The weapon nearly popped out of Heimdall's fingers before he tightened his grip and jerked it back. It came free in a spill of slime but to his disappointment failed to saw off any of his adversary's taloned fingers.

The draug lunged at him with both hands clawing. He caught the frenzied attacks on his shield, and the thing's nails, driving deep into the spruce boards, stripped pieces of wood away. Drops of dark spit or putrescence flying from its mouth, the dead thing snarled, laughed, or perhaps did both together.

Heimdall ducked and tried to hack the draug's lead foot out from underneath it but once again failed to cut deeply enough. Now that it was too late, he wished he'd taken the time to retrieve his two-handed sword. He was competent with broadsword and shield but more capable still with the larger weapon, and he feared that in this instance, this might be the difference between life and death.

As the draug threw itself at him repeatedly, and he caught the attacks on his rapidly disintegrating shield, the violence of the creature's assault and the sheer weight of it threatened to knock him reeling. As he cut at its neck, its head, its limbs, he also struggled to keep his feet underneath him.

The effort only helped for a few more heartbeats. Then the talons of both the draug's hands hooked the top of the shield, and he realized the creature was about to wrest what little was left of the armor away. He let go of the grip lest holding on deprive him of his balance and, just as importantly, hoping the corpse-thing's guard would be open in the instant it was still preoccupied with depriving him of his means of protection. He stepped to the side and cut at its neck with all his strength.

The broadsword bit deep, but not deep enough to remove the draug's head from its shoulders. The dead man flailed, and the back of one decayed, reeking hand smashed Heimdall in the face. The blow threw him backward. He banged his head against the corridor wall.

The two impacts in quick succession stunned him. He realized they had and sought to shake off the effect, tried to drop back into a fighting stance, to interpose the broadsword between the draug and himself, but saw the corpse-thing was moving faster than he was, poising its claws to tear into his flesh. Despairing, he silently implored the Fates to at least grant him a clean death. At least keep him from rising as a putrescent horror to menace his own parents and their followers.

Before the draug could strike, though, a pair of warriors came running up behind it. The one armed with a battle-axe arrived an instant before the other and struck down at the top of the draug's head. The stroke didn't split the creature's skull as the guard likely expected, but it tore away rotting flesh and an ear before, its force spent, skipping off the creature's shoulder.

Seemingly surprised, the draug lurched around toward the man with the battle-axe. By that time, though, the second warrior had rushed into striking distance, and he had one of the enchanted blades that had proved so effective in the fight aboard the fishing boats. The runes shining red as he swung the weapon, the sword completed the work that Heimdall's repeated cuts to the neck had begun. The draug's head tumbled away from its body, and the rest of it collapsed.

The warrior with the axe regarded Heimdall. "Are you all right, sir?"

Heimdall drew a long, steadying breath. He had the feeling that had he not, he would have babbled or maybe even wept in gratitude for his narrow escape. "Thanks to you and your friend here."

"And the carpenter," said the other warrior. He made a disgusted face as he looked at the slime now fouling the rune blade. He then glanced around, likely looking for a cloth to wipe it clean before returning it to its scabbard. "He was afraid to come back here, but he sent us."

"I never heard or saw you coming," Heimdall said. The gifts of Mimir notwithstanding, all his attention had been fixed on the draug. It seemed to him that time and again since the dead things started appearing, he'd been coming up against the limitations of his abilities. It almost felt like he was being mocked. He was grateful that at least so far, his mistakes and inadequacies hadn't cost him or anyone else their lives.

"Was this the only one?" asked the swordsman with the rune blade.

"So far as I know," Heimdall said. "But there's no telling what will happen if other people die of the sickness. It may be a long night."

And somehow, despite what seemed like hopelessly long odds, they had to ensure that no one else was dead at the end of it.

Ten

Once Uschi reached Lord Rodric's lands, she was surprised and also relieved to spot Heimdall and Golden Mane flying northward toward the sea. After the cold strangeness she'd encountered in her parents' stronghold, what a pleasure it would be to share the company of a friend. She might not even complain about him sending her on her miserable visit home. She did hope, though, that he could help her make sense of all that had puzzled her.

Heimdall *didn't* look surprised to see her, and she realized that with his heightened sight he'd likely seen her long before she'd noticed him. Maybe he'd even heard Avalanche's white feathered wings beating at the wind.

Heimdall beckoned for her to join him in his flight toward the water. She caught up with him just shy of the fishing village on the shore. To her surprise, he wore his mail and helmet and a frown to go with them.

"Is there more trouble?" she called.

"More draugr," he replied, and now that she was closer, she

marked how careworn her friend had begun to look in her brief time away. It filled her with concern and the desire to help him.

"That's bad," she said, "but nothing we can't sort out together."

He dredged up a smile for her. "By the Tree, it's good to have you back."

In the settlement ahead, the fishing boats sat drawn up on the rocky beach. Plainly, none of the fisherfolk had chosen to put out to sea to pursue their livelihoods. Rather, a goodly number of them had congregated in an open space among the huts, and one fellow was haranguing them. Nearby, a freshly made driftwood pyre like the one that had burned the sea draugr awaited lighting.

Heimdall frowned. "Swoop in over their heads before we set down," he called to her. "Look intimidating."

"Why?" she asked. Surely her friend had no quarrel with his own parents' followers?

"Can you hear what the speaker is telling them?"

"No."

"Well, I can, and they need a scare thrown into them." Heimdall urged Golden Mane into a dive. Uschi and Avalanche followed. Startled fisherfolk looked up and clamored as the winged stallions' hooves hammered the empty air just a stone's toss over their heads. A number reflexively crouched as if there was an actual possibility of the steeds trampling them.

The riders set their horses down at the edge of the village, where there was no need for the mounts to be careful lest the end of a pinion catch on the edge of a thatched roof. Heimdall swung himself off his black steed with its golden eyes and mane and turned toward the crowd. As she dismounted, Uschi noticed her friend left his two-handed sword on his back and the Gjallarhorn, a formidable weapon in its own right, dangling at his hip.

"If there's really trouble," she asked, "should we go in with weapons drawn?"

He shook his head. "These are my parents' loyal karls. I hoped a moment of awe might make them more willing to listen to reason, but now we'll approach them as friends, not enemies."

"Why would they ever doubt that's what we are?"

"There's no time to explain. It only takes an instant to wield a dagger."

The observation reminded Uschi of Frey and the unsatisfactory response to the accusation she'd leveled at Ysolt. Her mouth twisted. "Somebody else told me that last night."

Heimdall's gray eyes narrowed, a sign, she'd learned, that something had stirred his curiosity. Still, he said, "I hope you'll explain that later as well. But for now, just follow my lead."

"Fine." She left the Brightblade in its scabbard, left her shield hanging from her saddle as well, and she and Heimdall strode into the village together.

The crowd of fisherfolk watched their approach. She noticed that a couple of the karls looked sheepish if not guilty or ashamed, and a couple of others appeared angry, as if she and Heimdall were butting in where they had no business or had failed or wronged the village in some way. Others smiled a welcome that, to her eye, seemed forced and feigned.

"Would you care to explain yourselves?" Heimdall said.

The fellow who'd been haranguing his companions had a

square, commanding face and bare brawny arms sleeved in faded tattooed patterns. Above one elbow, he wore a gleaming silver ring, a sign, Uschi knew, that he'd been brave enough to accompany Rodric's warriors when they fought the sea draugr. "We're just waiting to see if the sick ones get better," he said, "and if there's anything we can do for them."

Heimdall sighed. "You're a good man, Geary. Too good to lie, especially when there's no point. I could hear what you were saying when I was still up in the sky and what you were all whispering to one another as my friend and I entered the village."

Geary scowled. "Well, then, what of it? We know the two who are lying sick inside." He gestured to the hut behind him. "They're our kin. Our neighbors. And they wouldn't want to come back as draugr to hurt the rest of us. If they could still talk, they'd beg us to stop that from happening."

Uschi's eyes narrowed. *Come back as draugr?* That was new and all she needed to convince her that Lord Rodric's people were still in dire trouble.

Other fisherfolk muttered their agreement with Geary.

"And so," Heimdall said, "you'd murder your own folk on their sickbeds."

"It makes sense, doesn't it?" Geary replied. "If they die by the knife, then they *didn't* die of the sickness. If they didn't die of the sickness, they won't rise as draugr."

"Especially if we cut off the heads and burn the bodies!" said a woman to Geary's left.

"You can't just butcher the sick," Heimdall said. "They may recover. Many of those who fell ill are still hanging on."

"For the time being," Geary said. "How are they supposed

to get better with no healer to tend them? The word is, a draug killed Fleta in the night."

"Nile who teaches the children their letters has learning enough to make medicine based on Fleta's books and read out the charms she recited."

"So what?" Geary said. "I respected Fleta, but the best she could do didn't keep one of the sick from dying, rising again, and tearing out her throat."

"Lieven the cook died and turned into a draug when her back was turned," Heimdall said with great patience. "That would have kept her from taking the precautions to ensure the corpse didn't come back to life even if she knew them. But *I* know them. I found them in books in the castle library. I'll share them with you. That way, if the worst happens and your sick friends do die, you won't have to worry about them returning in the dark."

Uschi felt a flicker of affectionate admiration. If there was a solution to a problem, or at least a partial solution, to be found in some dusty old book, you could count on Heimdall to ferret it out.

"Tell us the precautions, then," Geary said, skepticism in his voice.

"There are various methods," Heimdall said. "Given the seriousness of the situation, I advise using as many as you can. Put a pair of open iron scissors on the dead man's chest and twigs or pieces of straw inside his clothing. Tie the big toes together, and stick needles into the soles of the feet. Turn the body in three different directions before you carry it out into the open air, and then, yes, burn it. Any questions?"

"One," Geary said. "How do we know you and your friend

aren't draugr come to persuade us to do useless things that will only let more of your kind rise from the dead to kill us?"

The unexpected question startled Uschi. Heimdall, too, looked momentarily taken aback but recovered quickly. "We're standing in the sunlight. For the most part, the dead things come at night or conjure up their own darkness to cloak them."

"Only for 'the most part'. We don't know that they will from here on out. And if they can change shape, why not put on the forms of the people they were when they were alive? How better to trick us?"

"We've only seen them take on animal forms," Heimdall said. "A maimed horse and a black cat."

"So far," Geary said. His skepticism made Uschi wonder if they were going to have to fight after all. She resisted the urge to reach for her sword lest that be seen as a provocation.

"Think about it," Heimdall said. "Am I attacking you? No. I'm talking to you like any ordinary person. And how did Uschi and I arrive here? On Valkyrie horses. The steeds are magical and wise as well. Do you think we could fool them into thinking we were their usual riders if we were really abominations in disguise?"

A number of the fisherfolk looked to Geary to see if any of this was persuading him. A bald man with an intricately carved ivory ring in his left ear said, "When Rodric's boy puts it like that, it doesn't seem likely." Other villagers murmured similar sentiments.

"All right," Geary growled. "We'll try it your way for now."

"Good," Heimdall said. "Thank you. Call on the castle for anything you need, Nile to come minister to the sick, or warriors to deal with another draug should one appear. But do *not* kill people who are still alive no matter how sick and close to death they seem. That's murder, and your jarl will treat it as such and as an act of rebellion as well. Now, Captain Uschi and I will take our leave." He turned and walked away with never a glance back at people who had mere moments before surely been considering attacking him for a shape-changed horror. Uschi followed his example.

When they reached Avalanche and Golden Mane without anyone chasing after them, she let out a breath and said, "You handled that well."

He gave her a wry look. "Did I?"

She shrugged. "I thought so."

"You'll have gathered," he said, "that the problem with the draugr keeps taking on new dimensions. First we had the sea draugr, with seaweed for heads or no heads at all. Then there was a dead thing on land that walked by day and changed shape. Then one that rose on its pyre to give people the evil eye. The curse made some of the spectators ill, and one of those who died then became a draug himself."

Uschi frowned. "Were *you* there watching the creature burn?"

Heimdall waved his hand, brushing her concern away. "I seem to be all right. Apparently, the curse didn't fall on everyone. Not right away, anyhow. If I should fall ill, I'll count on you to do what's necessary."

"I'm not going to do what you just ordered Geary not to do." Certainly not to her best friend.

"I understand," Heimdall said, "but if you're there ready at the moment I turn…"

"That's not going to happen!"

"Let's hope not. What worries me currently is that I

can't define the limits of the problem when the draugr keep displaying new capabilities, and that makes it difficult to come up with solutions. I don't *know* that the corpse-things won't start taking on the forms of living people. I don't know whether poor Fleta's remedies will keep any of the sick from dying, or that the illness won't turn out to be contagious even without a draug's evil eye helping it along. I don't know that the precautions I found in the lore from Midgard will keep the dead from rising."

"You sounded sure when you recommended them to the fisherfolk."

Heimdall smiled a crooked, rueful smile. "I had to give them something. Because there's one thing I *do* know. We can't afford a panic. First, people will murder those who are truly sick. Then, those who simply cough or look as if they might be sick. Then, anyone they fear is a shapeshifting draug in disguise. It could turn into a slaughter worse than anything so far. And maybe the sages of Midgard knew what they were talking about, and their safeguards *will* keep the dead from walking."

"I hope so. It's past time your bookishness was finally good for something."

He snorted. "My parents are managing things at the castle. I'm flying around to the outlying steadings looking for signs of draugr and offering counsel and reassurance. Will you join me?"

She gave him a nod. "Of course."

As Heimdall swung himself onto Golden Mane's back, and the horse unfurled his wings and gave them a preparatory rustling shake, he said, "You didn't spend much time with your own family. Didn't the visit go well?"

The question reminded her that she'd meant to tell him of all her frustrations and amorphous suspicions and see what he made of them, but she hesitated to bother him with them while he was trying to handle a genuine crisis, so she simply answered, "No."

He sat quietly for a moment, giving her the chance to say more. When she didn't, he replied, "I'm sorry to hear that." He kicked his heels back into Golden Mane's flanks and set the black steed into motion.

The winged horses found an updraft that flung them and their riders high into the air. Moments later, Heimdall pointed out to sea. "Look there!" he called, excitement in his voice.

Uschi peered and made out a speck amid the waves. A leaden weight of apprehension congealed in her belly.

"Can you make out the device on the sail?" Heimdall asked.

"No," she replied, but her instincts told her it was a golden boar. No ordinary longship could have made the trip from her father's holdings to Lord Rodric's in scarcely more time than it had taken Avalanche to fly there, but presumably a true god and the overlord of all Vanaheim could acquire an enchanted vessel if he cared to.

"It's Frey's ship," called Heimdall, confirming her guess. "I don't know why he's coming at this particular time, but maybe he can help us."

Maybe, Uschi thought, but maybe, too, the ship is here because Frey is chasing me. She didn't know why he would be, but feared it nonetheless.

ELEVEN

The sun was setting by the time Heimdall and Uschi set their winged steeds down in the castle courtyard. As he dismounted, his stomach rumbled.

Uschi grinned. "Hungry?"

"Yes," he replied, "and you know what we used to say. If you have to go without sleep, it's good to at least have a full belly."

"Why wouldn't you be able to sleep? We've been patrolling your father's lands all day."

"Yes, but if more draugr appear in the night, the gifts of Mimir make me the sentry best able to spot them." He smiled. "Truly, it will be all right. We're Asgardian warriors. It takes more than a bit of lost rest to lay us low."

After he and Uschi gave their steeds into the keeping of the grooms, he spoke to a karl hurrying from the kitchen to the keep with a platter of pork boiled in beer in his hands. Heimdall appropriated a handful of meat, and the Valkyrie did the same. "I take it," he said, "my parents and Lord Frey are still eating in the hall."

The kitchen worker hesitated. "People are eating in the hall, captain, and of course we'll be happy to serve you. But Lord Rodric, Lady Estrid, Lord Frey, Lord Peadar, and a handful of others are in the council chamber meant for private business. We were told to set up a table with food, ale, and wine before they went in and that no one was to disturb them after." From his expression, he feared that his jarl's son would take offense at what he'd said.

Heimdall *was* annoyed, but not at the server. He mustered a smile, said, "Thank you," and sent the fellow on his way. He then stood munching the meat in his fingers but too irritated to take much note of the garlicky taste.

Uschi saw his frown. "Your thoughts?" she asked.

"At first, I was glad to see Lord Frey coming. It meant we'd have help. But things didn't go as expected. Nothing against them, but why did he bring your parents along? While we flew over his lands, he, the jarls, and others strategized. Obviously, we on our Valkyrie steeds make good scouts, but we're also thanes of Asgard. We could contribute something of value to the planning."

Uschi nodded. "I agree."

"Well, as the council of war is still happening, I don't intend to be kept out any longer. A day in the saddle has given me time to think, and I have one or two notions the others really ought to hear. You should come, too. We both belong there."

Uschi grunted. "Before you barge in there – *if* you do – there's more you should know. I wanted to tell you before, but when I arrived, you were already in the thick of things, and it isn't a conversation for shouting back and forth across the sky."

"Let's hear it, then."

Uschi glanced from side to side and then said, "Over here." She led him to a portion of the courtyard that was currently unoccupied. It put them in the shadow of the west wall, where the air was cooler, cut off from the last rays of the setting sun. Heimdall noticed that the location also placed them about as far as they could get from any of Frey's retinue in their splendid gold and silver trappings.

Keeping her voice low, Uschi related all that had befallen her when she returned to her parents' stronghold. When she finished, Heimdall said, "And still, Avalanche shows no ill effect from Ysolt's spellcasting?"

"No," the Valkyrie replied.

Heimdall could see why Uschi had been suspicious. He would have been furious if he suspected anyone was trying to hurt Golden Mane. But in this case, maybe his friend, already disgruntled by the frigid reception she'd received, was letting her predispositions get the better of her. That seemed particularly likely given that Avalanche was fine.

"Then maybe it was just a blessing," he said. "Why would it be anything else?"

Uschi shot him a dark look. "I don't know. But consider this. Between your parents' lands and mine, a number of jarls have holdings that border on the sea. If Frey had simply been making a progress, he would have stopped to pay a visit to each of them. He didn't. He came straight here."

"Because he was chasing you?" That seemed even more unlikely than someone attempting to harm Avalanche.

"I think so."

"Why?"

Uschi spread her hands in frustration. "I don't know!

Because he was worried what I might say? Or do? I want you to help me figure it out!"

"I will. I promise. I trust you, and if you think there are secrets that need uncovering, then there truly are. But can you see why I think we need to focus on the immediate crisis first?"

Uschi sighed. "I do. But maybe it's all part of the same thing. Lord Rodric said he decided to lay hands on the rune blades when he worried draugr might come to trouble his lands. But that's not the way it happened. It's Frey who has the swords and is giving them to the jarls. He gave three to my father. So why didn't your father tell us that?"

Heimdall strained to recall Rodric's exact words. He couldn't. He'd heard them only two days ago, but much had happened since then and little of it pleasant. However, he did remember his father drawing his blade to combat the draugr and save the two children in the field, and how his father would do anything for his people. "I don't know. It's possible my father simply spoke imprecisely. Truly, if you knew him as I do, you'd find that easier to believe than that he intentionally lied. At any rate, wherever the draugr-slaying blades came from, it's hard for me to see it as a bad thing. A warrior used one to save my life last night."

"I'm glad of that – of course I am – but it's still a discrepancy. Doesn't everything seem off to you? Like our families are keeping secrets?"

Her words tugged at him because he couldn't deny that things *did* seem subtly wrong. But even so, he was as certain of his parents' love and worthy character as of anything in his life. It seemed inconceivable that they meant him ill or were engaged in anything dishonorable.

"If people seem different," he said, "maybe it's simply because the draugr and the disease have them all on edge. If not, I promise you again that we'll look into that and into everything troubling you once the crisis is over."

She grimaced. "All right. I suppose that will have to do."

"Thank you. The Fates know, I need your help. Right now, I'm going to go help Lord Frey and the others make a plan. Please, come with me."

She hesitated. "I'll stand with you in the fights to come, Heimdall. You know that. But I don't care to see Lord Frey and my father just yet and endure yet another chilly conversation. I imagine that anything I'd think of, you'll think of as well, and you'll find Frey more receptive to your suggestions if I'm *not* there backing you up."

Heimdall sighed. "I truly am sorry I urged you to pay a visit that went so badly."

"You meant well. Go now. You don't want the council of war to continue deliberating without you."

"If you're sure." He paused, giving her the opportunity to change her mind, and then entered the keep. He prowled by the hall where the growl of conversation and the clink of utensils revealed supper was still in progress. The scents of pork and baked fish in bread wafted out to inspire a fresh pang of hunger and another gurgle from his belly. Clearly, the one fistful of meat hadn't been enough to sate him, but eating more could wait until the present business was through.

The council chamber was on the floor above the hall. Two spearmen wearing gold and silver were flanking the door and crossed their weapons in front of it to deny him entry.

"You're Lord Frey's warriors," Heimdall said. "If you were

my father's, you'd know I'm Lord Rodric's son. I belong in this meeting."

"Everyone who belongs is inside already," said the spearman on the right, a warrior with startling amber eyes looking out from under shaggy brows and a slab of forehead. "Our orders are to keep everyone else out."

Heimdall fought to quash a surge of annoyance, or, failing that, to keep the feeling off his face and out of his tone. "Do me a kindness. Stick your head inside and ask."

"No need. We have our orders," the tawny-eyed spearman said.

"Have it your way." Heimdall walked a few paces back the way he'd come, turned back around, raised the Gjallarhorn to his lips, and blew.

The resulting blare flung Frey's warriors stumbling a few steps down the hall. One fell, and the other tripped over him and dropped on top of him. Their features clenched in shock and pain, they let go of their spears and shields to cover their ears.

After he'd first used the Gjallarhorn as a weapon, it had belatedly occurred to Heimdall that he, with his enhanced hearing, might have suffered its debilitating effects no less than his targets. He never had, though. Apparently, the one who sounded the trumpet was impervious to its magic. With the corridor still echoing with the wail of the instrument, he returned to the door to the council chamber and opened it. Stunned, the guards Frey had posted there were no longer in any condition to stop him.

Within, he found the god, his own parents, Uschi's father, a sharp-featured woman wearing carved bone medallions, who from the Valkyrie's story must be Ysolt the witch, and several warriors, four of the god's and three of the household's. All the fighters had draugr-slaying rune blades either still worn at their sides or hanging from the backs of their chairs by their sword belts for comfort's sake.

Everyone was staring at the door and thus at Heimdall's entrance. The blast from the Gjallarhorn hadn't slammed them as it had the sentries, but the loud note had plainly startled them and riveted their attention.

Estrid gave Heimdall a small, surreptitious shake of her head that he took to mean she thought he shouldn't be here. He hoped the look he gave her in response conveyed confidence that everything would be all right. He placed himself before Frey and inclined his head in respect.

"Good evening, my lord. The guards outside didn't understand that I should be in this meeting. I had to sound my horn to get past them, but I assure you they'll be all right."

"Heimdall," Rodric said. "I ordered you to patrol the lands beyond the castle."

"That's what I have been doing," Heimdall said. "But even Valkyrie horses need food and rest occasionally. For that matter, so do I. So, I thought that before I flew back out into the night, I'd attend this council." He offered his listeners what he hoped was a winning smile. "You never know, I may have something worthwhile to contribute."

His father's scowl didn't waver. "If Lord Frey wanted you here–"

The God of the Harvest raised his hand to stop Rodric in midsentence. "It's all right, my friend. I'm actually interested in hearing what Odin's trusted agent has to say."

"Thank you, my lord." Heimdall took a breath and ordered his thoughts. He'd come a way since the day when he, a callow new recruit to the legions of Asgard, had dared to approach the queen with his thoughts on the All-Father's strangely protracted Odinsleep. To a degree, he'd grown accustomed to discussing weighty matters with august "personages", to use his mother's word. But hitherto he'd rarely spoken to Frey, and never more than a few words. He didn't want to ramble or blather and so try the patience of the lord of all Vanaheim.

"I've been reading accounts of the draugr that come to us from Midgard," he began. "As you may know, the corpse-things trouble the mortals of that Realm far more than they normally bother us."

"I'm aware," said Frey, watching Heimdall with cold appraisal in his pale blue eyes.

"But that being said," Heimdall continued, "I can find no tales of any of the warriors of Midgard having to deal with more than one draug at a time. One draug with one set of uncanny powers. In contrast, Vanaheim appears to have as many of the creatures as a stray dog has fleas, and new ones keep revealing new abilities to confound us. You clearly know this, Lord Frey. It's why you're giving draugr-destroying weapons to your jarls, to stem the tide."

"I'm waiting," said the god, "for you to tell me something I *don't* know."

"I don't know that I can do that," Heimdall said, "but I do have a suggestion. If all Vanaheim is facing a crisis, let's inform King Odin and ask him for help. Uschi or I could be in Asgard tomorrow."

Estrid winced. Frey and the others received Heimdall's

suggestion with a stony silence that surprised him. Why, he wondered, did his proposal seem so unpalatable? Had he offended by implying the Vanir lacked the strength and wisdom to handle the draugr on their own?

After a moment, Frey said, "No such journey will be necessary. I've already apprised the All-Father of the situation here."

Heimdall had the feeling it would be pointless if not imprudent to speak more on the subject, but, not for the first time, the belief that he saw what others did not prompted him to press on. "Yet so far as I know, we have no Aesir troops augmenting our own forces. We have no sorcerers of the royal court weaving spells alongside Madam Ysolt. Odin himself, the mightiest warlock of all, isn't working any magic to aid us. With respect, Lord Frey, is it at all possible the All-Father didn't understand the extent of the crisis?"

The god scowled. "No. It is not."

"Perhaps someone should speak to Queen Frigga. After all, my lord, she's your own daughter. She was born and raised in Vanaheim, and the land and the people still hold a special place in her heart."

"I said no!" snapped Frey. "You will *not* return to Asgard!" He took a deep breath, and the mottled redness faded from his normally fair complexion. "If you truly wish to help your parents and your people, you'll stay here and do as you're told." He looked to Rodric. "Isn't that so?"

"Yes," Rodric said, "please, stay and continue what you're doing."

"If you and Lord Frey will it," Heimdall said, disappointed by his father's lack of support, "then of course I'll stay. But maybe there's still a way for me to be more useful than I would be simply flying up and down the length and breadth of our family's domain."

"And what might that be?" the God of the Harvest asked.

"I'm no warlock," Heimdall said, "but I've learned a little about magic, what can be learned simply by reading books and listening to practitioners. From what I understand, it's likely that if some evil power is afflicting all Vanaheim, the curse is centered somewhere, and the malignancy radiates from there to affect the Realm. If we can destroy that point of origination, we'll end our problems. The first step in destroying it is to find it."

"Ysolt has said as much," Frey replied, "but thus far, she hasn't located it."

"With all respect to her powers, my lord, maybe I can do better."

For the first time, Frey seemed to be considering Heimdall with a trace of warmth, as a potential resource rather than an irritant. "Do you truly believe you can find it?"

"I hope so, my lord. You're surely aware of the patches of blight staining what until recently was a green Realm from one end to the other. It's likely they're a manifestation of the same evil that's spawning the draugr, and perhaps the source is lurking in one or another. It's surely worth a look, and my winged steed Golden Mane can carry me swiftly from one to the next."

"And are you sure you'll recognize the source if you do fly over it?"

"Once again, I hope so. One of the tales from Midgard speaks of a light like foxfire shining from a draug's lair, and you've likely heard of my powers of sight. If there's any unnatural glow coming from the source of the curse, I should be able to spot it even in daylight."

Frey turned to Heimdall's parents. "In my place, would you entrust him with this mission?"

"Yes!" Estrid said. Heimdall was grateful that, in contrast to his father, she at least was willing to support his ideas. "If my son says he'll do it, he won't rest until it's done, and it's exactly what needs doing. You know it is, my lord!"

Frey turned back to Heimdall. "So be it, then, captain. Rest and refresh yourself tonight and begin your search in the morning."

That, Heimdall realized, was a dismissal, and he once again felt the stubborn urge to insist he had a rightful place in the meeting. But he'd raised the points he meant to raise, obtained as much satisfaction as he was likely to get, and finally convinced Lord Frey to regard him as a genuine asset. Such being the case, he decided not to overstay his welcome and risk annoying the god and causing him to revert to his previous opinion.

He inclined his head and walked through the door. On the other side, the two spearmen had reclaimed their posts and regarded him with poisonous dislike. Beholding them, he felt a twinge of guilt that he'd resorted to violence to get past them even though there hadn't seemed to be a ready alternative.

"I'm sorry I had to use the horn," he said.

"What?" replied the one with the yellow eyes.

Heimdall raised his voice. "Sorry for blowing the horn. I promise, your hearing will return, and any headaches or nosebleeds will go away." He gave the warriors a nod and continued on his way.

He thought that despite their disagreement, he should apprise Uschi of recent developments. Maybe his report would allay her misgivings. After some casting about, he found her in the stables watching Avalanche, free of bridle and saddle for the moment, munching oats in a stall.

"I take it they let you into the meeting," Uschi said.

"More or less."

"And what came of it?"

"Well," Heimdall said, "I went in to accomplish two things. The first was to recommend that we advise Odin of the situation here and ask for help."

Uschi nodded. "Sensible."

"But also, as it turns out, unnecessary. Frey has already communicated with the All-Father."

"Then where's the help?"

"I don't know, exactly. Maybe the king judges that we Vanir are capable of handling the situation by ourselves. Or maybe he's already cast a spell to aid us, and people like you and me just can't tell it."

The Valkyrie grunted. "What was your second suggestion?"

"Based on what I know about curses and such, I said there's probably some place, perhaps some object, from which the evil afflicting Vanaheim originates. If we could destroy the source, that would end our problems. Ysolt agrees, but her magic hasn't identified the spot. I told Lord Frey that, traveling swiftly on Golden Mane and using the sight of Mimir, I hoped I could do better. He gave me leave to try. I'm going to start with the blighted areas we saw from the air."

"Well... that part is reasonable, anyway."

"Will you keep an eye on things here until my return? I'm

sure my father's guards are able, and now they have Frey's warriors reinforcing them, but you truly are the comrade I know and trust."

"Of course. I'll do all I can to keep your mother and father and their karls safe from harm."

Twelve

The Brightblade in one hand, shield in the other, a wood-and-rawhide lantern hanging on her arm, Uschi stalked among the trees of the benighted apple orchard. His hands similarly occupied, only with one of the rune blades, her partner, one of Lord Frey's warriors, a gruff fellow named Rhain, prowled along beside her. At other points in the orchard and the rest of the farmstead beyond, more of the god's warriors and Rodric's were likewise searching for draugr. The tallow candles in their own lanterns glowed like fireflies.

So far, the preventions Heimdall had discovered in old books coupled with cremation of the dead, had kept most of those who perished of the sickness from returning as corpse-things. Unfortunately, more of the creatures kept showing up anyway, including those that had supposedly appeared on this farm, prompting the karls to flee to the castle for help. If in fact they existed and weren't just the product of someone's fearful imagination, the new draugr had possibly dug their way out from some forgotten burial site, where time had turned them to dust but the curse had reformed them to trouble the living.

Uschi wondered how Heimdall, who'd departed at dawn, was faring on his search to find the source of the curse. Peering about for signs of the enemy, worried that at any moment she might find herself battling one of the ravening dead, she wished it were her friend beside her now. Although Rhain seemed about as steady as any of them did in suspense of facing the ever-worsening threat of the draugr.

Her mistrust lingered even though no one in the castle had given her any further reason for suspicion. Everyone seemed focused on eliminating the draugr and the sickness. Such being the case, when she'd learned a band of warriors was heading for the farm to investigate a report of new draugr, she'd felt obliged to lend a hand. She had, after all, promised her friend she'd do all she could to deal with any threats until he returned.

A shadow appeared in the darkness ahead. Uschi and Rhain jerked to a halt and raised their broadswords. The Valkyrie's mouth went dry. The vague shape before her was too small and low to the ground to be a draug in manlike form, but it could be one that had disguised itself as an animal.

The two warriors edged closer, until the soft yellow lantern-light revealed an elkhound. The silver-gray, deep-chested dog looked at them, bared its fangs, and growled. Such animals were generally good-natured, and they'd given this one no reason to think they meant it ill.

"It's not what it appears to be," Uschi said.

"I'm not so sure about that," Rhain replied. "Maybe it saw the draugr, and now it's spooked about everything." He crouched, and his voice became a reassuring croon. "Hey, boy. Did you have a scare? It's all right now. If you lead us to the bad things, we'll kill–"

The elkhound charged him.

Told you, Uschi thought. She looked for the moment of transformation and poised herself to cut at the creature's neck. To her surprise, the dog didn't change. Maybe Rhain was waiting for the same thing. As the animal came at him, he hacked down at it at the last possible moment but missed.

The elkhound lunged in under his shield, reared up, and caught his forearm in its jaws. Snarling, it held on and gnawed even when Rhain tried to shake it free.

Uschi went to help Rhain, but there was no need. It was awkward to use a broadsword at such close quarters, but he managed. He pulled the rune blade back and stabbed repeatedly. The dog fell to earth and lay whimpering. A final thrust dispatched it.

"Are you all right?" Uschi asked.

Panting, Rhain inspected his forearm. From the elbow down, his byrnie didn't cover the limb, but the thick wool tunic he wore beneath it did. "I think so," he said at length. "I'll have bruises, but the bite didn't draw blood. What ailed the dog, I wonder? Was a draug controlling it?"

"Or being near draugr drove it mad," Uschi said. Heimdall had warned her the draugr kept coming up with new tricks. She hoped that if insanity was one of them, it wasn't a madness that affected human beings as well.

As she finished speaking, the stench of decay filled the air. A second shadow, this one massive and tall as a brown bear lumbering on its hind legs, shambled around the trunk of an apple tree. Unfortunately, it was a tree within easy reach of Rhain.

Lord Frey's warrior spun to face the new threat but was

too slow. In the lantern light, the draug was fish-belly pale except for the darker spots of putrescence. It swung its arm in a backhand blow. Uschi heard a *crack* as the attack connected. Rhain collapsed, leaving her to face the draug alone. Across the orchard, warriors shouted battle cries and warnings to one another as their own foes came out of the night.

Growling like a beast, black spittle flying and drooling from its mouth, the draug threw one powerful blow after another. Uschi caught them on her shield, which soon started splintering. She retreated lest she be knocked or pushed off balance and only at the last instant realized the corpse-thing was backing her up against a tree. Narrowly avoiding the swipe of a fist like a rotting ham, she dodged away from the tree and onto the creature's flank.

At last, she saw an opening to attack in turn. She cut at the draug's neck, and it was like cutting at granite.

The fight aboard the fishing boats had prepared her for the draugr to be resistant to ordinary weapons, but not like this. Over the course of the next several moments, she scored twice more, but as far as she could tell by the uncertain light of the lantern swinging wildly from her arm, the Brightblade was at most only scratching the creature's pallid skin.

Her heart pounding, feeling increasingly desperate, she struck at the rotting parts in the hope they'd prove more vulnerable. They didn't. Judging from the shouts and the racket of attacks striking shields that pounded through the orchard, her comrades were still busy with their own fights. Presumably that was why no one was rushing to her aid.

Uschi thrust at the draug's bloated, snarling face. Surely, she thought, if her aim was true, her point could put out an eye.

And maybe it could have, but the corpse-thing brushed the sword aside with its forearm, stepped in, and punched at her over the rim of her shield.

She dodged quickly, but the blow still grazed her cheek and jaw, and that was enough to fling her back and stun her for an instant. When, head ringing, she came to her senses, she was on her back, her sword was no longer in her hand, and, stooping, arms outstretched, the dead thing was coming after her.

Gasping, she scrambled up and away, and saw the Brightblade where it had fallen in the grass. She *might* be able to recover it without the draug landing another attack, but in the current battle, it wasn't doing her any good anyway.

She faked a first step toward it, and the corpse-thing turned to assail her as she tried to snatch it up. She then dodged in the other direction, darted around her flummoxed foe, and dashed on toward the fallen Rhain.

The candle in his lantern had gone out when he hit the ground, and at first she could only see him and not the rune sword. The draug's feet thumped the ground as it raced after her. She felt a pang of fear that the dead man would catch up with her before she found the blade.

But, no, there it was, revealed at last by the glow of her own lantern. She bent down, grabbed it, spun around, and cut.

The draug was only a stride behind her, and the rune blade sheared through his neck. The head fell away.

Panting, her heart pounding, Uschi knelt beside Rhain. She could do nothing for him. The corpse-thing's initial attack had broken his neck and slain him. Which meant, she realized, he wouldn't be reclaiming his enchanted sword. She mourned his loss, but it left her free to put his weapon to good use.

She retrieved the Brightblade as well. As far as she was concerned, it was still one of her family's treasures, even if her father thought she'd ruined it by squandering the magic. Though it had lost its flame, it had seen her through many a battle in the years since. But it was the rune sword she carried in her hand as she ran to help the other warriors slay the remaining draugr.

The struggles that followed left her bruised and drenched in sweat. It was apparent, though, that fighting the draugr with a rune blade in hand was easier than trying to destroy them with some other weapon. She wondered if she'd have to argue with her comrades to retain possession of the enchanted weapon, but none of the survivors sought to take it from her. Maybe they felt she'd earned it, or that the question of who merited a rune sword and who did not was a matter for Lord Frey or Lord Rodric to adjudicate. At any rate, she still had it later in the stables as she lay down on a bench in front of Avalanche's stall to pass the night.

Even with a folded blanket covering the hard wood, the makeshift bed she'd created wasn't comfortable. Among other deficiencies, it was too short for her unless she stayed curled up or let her long legs hang off the edges. But she'd slept on worse, and it wasn't the discomfort that kept her wakeful and tense. She supposed it was the leftover excitement and fear from the fight earlier that night.

Or maybe it was worry about fights yet to come. Because there were still sick people in the castle, and any one of them could die and rise as a draug. True, someone was supposed to watch over them to ensure that didn't happen, but how likely was it that the weary karl would remain vigilant every moment through the night? For that matter, Heimdall himself had confided that the precautionary measures he'd found, even if applied quickly, might not prevent every horrific resurrection.

Uschi imagined a draug entering the stables in search of prey. She assumed the horses would raise a commotion and wake her, but there wouldn't be time to don the mail she'd left hanging on the railing of Avalanche's stall alongside his tack. She might not even have time to grab her shield.

She could be sure of having her new rune blade, though, if she kept it to hand. Indeed, she felt a keen desire to sleep with it actually *in* her hand, a fear that she'd come to harm if she didn't. Her common sense told her that was nonsense. On the short, narrow bench, she had no hope of sleeping while clutching the hilt. She could, however, leave the unsheathed weapon on the straw-strewn floor directly underneath, where she could snatch it up in an instant, and that was what she did.

Afterward, she finally felt a measure of security. Her muscles relaxed, her breathing slowed, and her eyelids drooped.

The next thing she knew, she was looking over a battlefield. The raven banners flying above one army revealed it was made up of the Aesir while the golden-boar standards of the opposing force indicated the warriors were Vanir. After another moment, she made out Odin and Frey themselves commanding their respective legions. The All-Father bore his three-pronged Uru spear Gungnir, rode his eight-legged steed Sleipnir, and had the enormous wolves Geri and Freki prowling around the horse's feet. Frey sat astride Gullinbursti with the sword Laevateinn floating in the air before him and a second blade in hand.

Uschi was a warrior to the core who never flinched from the prospect of battle. She also realized she was witnessing something that had happened long ago, and there was no changing it. Still, both factions of those who had come to be called Asgardians were her people, and she called out in an effort to forestall the slaughter to come. In this place, however, she was a silent phantom. No one heeded her. Odin brandished his spear to command a charge, and, howling, his followers hurled themselves at the shield walls of the Vanir.

In a matter of moments, or so it seemed, the Aesir had routed their foes and were hunting those who'd fled and summarily slaughtering others who sprawled wounded on the field or who'd laid down their weapons and surrendered. To Uschi's shock and horror, the All-Father gloated over the massacre. He and the other Aesir demonstrated that same cruelty in the weeks that followed. They butchered karls who had no part in the war and set their farmsteads ablaze. They used sorcery to break the walls and spires of Vanaheim's surrendered cities, reducing them to ruins and the inhabitants to homelessness and poverty in the course of a single day.

Eventually the Vanir had to bend the knee lest Odin bring about the extermination of all their kind. Humbled, they then set about the arduous task of rebuilding the Realm the Aesir had laid to waste, work that took centuries to complete.

To Uschi's relief, at first King Odin was content to let the Vanir toil and enjoy the benefits of their labor. As Vanaheim healed, however, and she hovered unseen at the All-Father's shoulder, he scowled to see that its bounty and strength had once again come to rival that of Asgard, something that, he'd resolved, must never be. With her trailing along behind him, he rose from his throne, descended to the vaults beneath his castle, and sealed himself away in one devoted to the wicked art of necromancy.

Closeted therein, neither drinking, eating, nor sleeping, oblivious to Uschi's pleas to relent, he cast spells for nine days. When he resumed his throne, Hugin and Munin, the ravens that flew throughout the Realms gathering information for him, informed him a plague of draugr had come to Vanaheim. Whereupon the All-Father laughed.

His joy at his subjects' plight was ghastly, but more than that, Uschi realized with a surge of denial, it was *wrong*. She was no skald or sage, but what she'd witnessed didn't match what she knew of history.

Motivated by a desire to unite the Aesir and Vanir into one Asgardian people with himself as monarch, Odin had indeed been the aggressor in the war between the two Realms. But so far as she knew, he hadn't prosecuted the campaign with unnecessary savagery. Frey, commanding the other side, had made his own questionable decisions, notably the disastrous one to ally with the fire giant Surtur of Muspelheim.

Even more to the point, perhaps, Odin had been a just ruler to both the Aesir and the Vanir in the years since the war ended, aiding both and favoring neither over the other. It was inconceivable that for all that time, he'd nurtured a secret hatred of Vanaheim in his heart.

This vision – or whatever it was – had in a sense come to a halt. Seated on his throne in his great hall, one raven perched on his wrist and the other atop the back of the chair, Odin still laughed that mad, vicious laughter. With all her strength of will, Uschi insisted that the tableau before her was a lie, and it disappeared, perhaps falling like a tapestry dislodged from its moorings, perhaps shredding to pieces, maybe doing both. It happened so fast, she couldn't be sure, but she was certain of what she beheld behind it.

In the unlit gulf before her loomed a hairless, four-armed giant so huge it dwarfed even the ice giants she and Heimdall had battled together, so enormous there was no missing its purple-black form even in the darkness, so titanic she felt a jolt of terror, and it was as if the shock had the effect of making her corporeal in this awful place. Hitherto, she'd witnessed the war and what followed as a mere phantasmal point of view. Now, however, she stood before the giant without weapons or armor but ensconced in her body once again, complete with hammering heart and trembling limbs.

She cried for help. Her father, Lord Frey, and several of the god's elite warriors stood around her with swords in hand. Then, however, they sneered, turned away, and abandoned her to her fate. In an instant, they vanished into the gloom.

The creature reached for her with a hand easily capable of engulfing and crushing her. She recoiled, and as she did, her thoughts changed, the images of Odin's cruelty flooding back, her conviction that it hadn't really been that way warping into doubt. Struggling to cling to what she held to be true, she realized the giant was actually reaching for her *mind*.

That was even more terrifying than standing weaponless before a hostile colossus. Scrambling back, she insisted the giant couldn't have her, couldn't have her, and then she was flailing and gasping on the floor of the stables. She realized her convulsions must have rolled her off the bench.

Even then, her ordeal wasn't over. Some portion of the

four-armed giant's power pursued her from nightmare into wakefulness. Mental pictures of the All-Father's supposed viciousness and gleeful betrayal of Vanaheim persisted while her skepticism and particularly any recollection of the purple-black colossus sought to squirm away. She pounded her fist on the floor as she fought to hold on to the latter. She succeeded, and after a few more heartbeats, the psychic assault ended.

She rose unsteadily and noticed Avalanche regarding her with puzzlement but not agitation. The other horses in the stalls were similarly calm. Whatever had just happened had affected only her. More importantly, she told herself, the attack was over and done with, and she'd resisted.

But would she have prevailed, she wondered, if the oddities of the past couple of days hadn't already disposed her to question and doubt? Perhaps even more to the point, would she have done so if she'd slept with the rune sword actually in her hand as she'd so wished to do? As would surely have been the case had the confines of the bench not made it impractical.

She imagined Lord Frey, his jarls, and their finest warriors all gnawed night after night by the same anxiety that had beset her as she sought her rest, and all dealing with it by sleeping with their hands on the weapons. And all, accordingly, now convinced their king was a monster who'd sent the draugr to torment the Vanir and lay them low.

If it was true, maybe it explained why so many had treated Heimdall and her so peculiarly. The travelers were Vanir born, but they were also thanes sworn to Odin's service. In particular, did it explain why everyone was so adamant that the All-Father's warriors shouldn't return to Asgard to ask for aid?

Were they worried that Heimdall and Uschi might have figured out they knew the king was responsible for their troubles, and they didn't want Odin to know they understood?

Had Heimdall been affected by his presence around these swords?

Uschi frowned. She felt a certain confidence that her guesses were correct but also a nagging worry they didn't go far enough. There was more she had yet to understand.

Maybe it would all come clear in time. Meanwhile, she shifted the rune sword well away from the bench before lying back down. Removed from what she took to be its influence, she slept poorly and suffered bad dreams. The dreams, however, were of fighting the draugr, not lies about the All-Father given life.

Thirteen

As Golden Mane soared on the cool morning wind, Heimdall instructed himself not to be impatient. The blight had taken hold of areas throughout Vanaheim, and even for the rider of a winged steed, it was going to take time to check them all.

But he was finding it impossible to feel any other way when he didn't know what was going on back in his parents' castle. Had more draugr appeared with fearsome and unforeseen abilities? Was the sickness spreading? Had people succumbed to hysteria and turned on one another?

Surely, he insisted to himself, the situation couldn't be as dire as his grim imaginings. Uschi was there to contend with new developments. By the Tree, Frey himself, a true god and the overlord of all Vanaheim, was there. If they couldn't manage the situation, who could?

Even so, as Heimdall and his mount hurtled toward the next brown and yellow patch marring Vanaheim's carpet of greens, worry gnawed at him. He flicked the reins to command a quicker pace. Golden Mane's wings beat faster.

Much of the Realm was forest, and Heimdall's current destination was no exception. It was not, however, virgin forest. In a previous age, the Vanir had built and subsequently abandoned cities, whereupon Nature set about erasing them. He was approaching the site of one such. At first glance, all that remained were tumbles of stone amid the spruce, pine, and junipers, but on closer inspection, the broken tops of several towers peeked above the treetops.

Heimdall peered with the sight of Mimir, and everything that had previously blurred together or been too small to make out at all exploded into clarity. He could discern each withered leaf clinging to every twisted, suppurating branch, every pock and chip in crumbling, failing masonry, and, just visible through the tree limbs blocking much of the view at ground level, an unnatural sheen. In the light of day, even his eyes had trouble discerning foxfire as such, but there was unquestionably a kind of seething glow crawling in the air.

He felt a certain wariness as he did in the presence of any manifestation of the curse-afflicted Vanaheim. But that caution was undercut by excitement. Maybe he truly had found the solution to his homeland's troubles!

Swooping lower, he discovered that the distortion emanated from the entrance to a dilapidated keep. The battlements and most of the upper reaches of the keep had fallen away. Vines covered much of the stonework. The doors that had once sealed the entryway had presumably rotted off their hinges, thus permitting a trace of the foxfire to escape.

The ruined keep was adjacent to a plaza that had kept its form better than most of the city around it. Here and there, saplings and young trees had grown up between the flagstones and forced them out of true, but there was enough clear space left for Golden Mane to set down without undue risk of breaking a wing or a leg.

Once they were on the ground, Heimdall regarded the flickering in the air from the saddle. From that vantage point, and to his frustration, he still couldn't determine the exact source of the emanation. It filled the entirety of all he could see of the structure's interior, which otherwise looked like what he imagined the remains of any once-proud but long-forsaken edifice might resemble.

He felt the urge to investigate further. After all, for all he knew, he could find the source of the draugr curse, destroy it, and end the evil immediately. If so, that would be a more expeditious remedy than going back to his parents' lands and returning with a company of warriors. It would save lives that would otherwise surely be lost in the interim.

He started to swing himself out of the saddle, and Golden Mane raised his head and snorted. At the same time, in some vague way that even the eyes of Mimir couldn't define precisely, the darkness inside the keep thickened and the flicker became more energetic, as if the power within was gathering itself to strike.

Heimdall felt a chill of fear ooze up his spine. He wasn't sure if his horse had truly tried to warn him, if he'd actually seen the darkness stirring, or if it had exerted some subtle influence to lure him in. Maybe he'd only imagined those things as his good sense belatedly caught up to his curiosity. Either way, annoyed that his better judgment had momentarily deserted him, he now realized it would be folly to venture into the keep alone. The curse was raising menaces across the length and breadth of Vanaheim. How likely was it, then, that it had created no defenses for itself?

He patted Golden Mane's neck. "It's all right, my friend. We're getting out of here." He turned the stallion toward a stretch of plaza long and unobstructed enough, he judged, for the steed to break into a gallop, lash his wings, and climb into the air.

Just as he did, though, three draugr, one ashy pale, the others bruise-blue, burst from around the sides of the doorway. They chased after the retreating Valkyrie steed. Their bloated rottenness and crooked limbs made their progress look flailing and clumsy but paradoxically didn't prevent them from coming on as fast as any man could run.

His pulse racing, fearful they'd catch up before Golden Mane took flight, Heimdall wondered if he should turn to fight them. But who knew how many draugr would end up emerging to mob him if he did? His imagination conjured a gruesome dozen of the creatures tearing him and his steed to gory pieces.

Getting news of his discovery to Frey was what mattered. His heart racing, and with bellowing encouragement, he urged the stallion forward.

Glancing over his shoulder, he saw with a surge of dread that the draugr had nearly closed the distance. The pale one just missed catching hold of the stallion's streaming tail. Then, however, a wingbeat carried Golden Mane into the air. Balked, the draugr could only look up after their quarry with glazed and sunken eyes. Heimdall laughed with relief.

Moments later, though, joy gave way to a fresh surge of alarm as he realized the curse hadn't finished trying to stop him.

Columns of shadow swirled up from the ground like cyclones. They didn't create furious winds like he'd once encountered when attempting to enter Jotunheim, but over the course of several heartbeats they expanded to become a single darkness, engulfed him, and rose above his head to blot out the sun. Now it was as if he was flying through starless, moonless night.

The phenomenon was uncanny, but, he thought, breathing deeply to steady himself, for a warrior who could see in the dark, not truly a hindrance. He continued to climb, making sure to avoid trees and the broken remains of ruined buildings as he did, and Golden Mane, who trusted his rider even in the worst of conditions, didn't balk even when the flimsy tip of a branch he hadn't known was there brushed or snapped against his body.

After another dozen heartbeats, they were still in the unnatural darkness but above the trees and the derelict buildings. Hoping he'd finally escaped the curse's power to harm him, Heimdall turned Golden Mane north, toward his parents' lands and the sea.

More swirling masses rose from the blighted forest. Had he not invoked the sight of Mimir, he wouldn't be able to see them in the blackness although he suspected he would still have heard the fluttering. As it was, he could discern they were made up of hundreds of birds – eagles, kites, hawks, vultures, shrikes, and even grouse, doves, and swifts – all rushing in pursuit. Evidently the malignancy originating in the keep had control of them.

Already, the creatures were converging on him from all directions. His sword and Golden Mane's natural weaponry would avail him nothing. He and his steed could kill one or two birds at a time, but meanwhile, dozens more would rip at them with beak and talon.

For a moment, he couldn't think of anything to do, and then he remembered the Gjallarhorn. He hastily raised the trumpet to his lips and blew. To his relief – indeed, in that moment, to his savage satisfaction – the blare sent stunned or slain birds plummeting and cleared the section of sky before him.

The other birds might still overtake him, though. To forestall that, he twisted and bent in the saddle and sounded the horn in all directions. The possessed creatures hurtled like rain, clattering the tree limbs below as they slammed against them.

You see? Heimdall silently told the curse. I have my own tricks, and my comrades and I will be back for you. As if to affirm this declaration of defiance, after another moment, Golden Mane burst from the cloud of darkness into the light.

Heimdall was eager to share that he'd found the source of the curse as soon as possible, and he coaxed Golden Mane to fly fast through the rest of the morning and part of the afternoon. When he reached his parents' holdings, he judged he'd been right to hurry.

In half a dozen places, black, foul-smelling smoke was drifting up from the remains of pyres, proof that despite all precautions, new draugr continued to rise. One such was right outside the castle walls. Apparently, not even those who resided within were safe.

Well, Heimdall promised himself, they will be soon. He set Golden Mane down in the courtyard and dismounted. When a groom hurried up to take charge of his steed, he was too full of his good news not to share it even though, according to protocol, Lord Frey ought to hear it first. "I've found the source of our troubles!" he said. "Everything's going to be all right."

The karl hesitated as if uncertain how to respond. "That's... good, captain."

Puzzled at the other man's lack of enthusiasm, Heimdall frowned. "What is it? What's happened?"

"There was another wave of people falling sick. Those the draug gave the evil eye to, mainly. And Lady Estrid was one of them."

For an instant, it was as if Heimdall's heart stopped in his chest. Then he dashed for the keep and his parents' chambers.

Fourteen

Uschi had made her way to the kitchen to forage for leftover lamb and oatcakes. She wanted a meal and a nap to fortify her before sunset. She was glumly anticipating another long night of patrolling and fighting any draugr that might appear.

When, still chewing a last bite of oatcake, she came out into the light of day, a groom was leading Golden Mane toward the stables. Heimdall had returned.

Her own worries and frustrations vanished, eclipsed by eagerness to hear what her friend might have to report. She also felt a comparable urgency to share what she herself had learned along with concern for Heimdall's reaction to what had befallen Lady Estrid. She turned to the karl. "Does Captain Heimdall know about his mother?"

"I told him," the groom replied. "Should I not have?"

If Heimdall knew Lady Estrid had caught the sickness, he was surely headed for her quarters. Uschi ran to find him.

She lost her way inside the keep – she hadn't spent enough time inside to learn all the twists and turns – and wandered, seething with frustration, in the wrong direction until a servant set her right. Maybe the delay was beneficial. By the time she approached the jarl's apartments, she'd realized that, her impatience notwithstanding, respect mandated that she couldn't just grab Heimdall and start jabbering at him. Not when he was standing at his mother's sickbed.

Despite her sense of urgency, she stopped beside the doorway to the Lord Rodric and Lady Estrid's bedchamber. Hushed voices sounded from within.

"What are her chances?" Heimdall asked. Apparently, he saw no reason not to speak bluntly. Uschi reckoned he must think his mother was too profoundly unconscious or lost to delirium to hear the conversation, and she felt a pang of pity on his behalf.

"I'll do all I can," Ysolt replied. As Uschi understood it, the other woman's witchcraft encompassed some knowledge of healing, and, like Nile, she was tending the sick. As there was no one else to do it, the Valkyrie was doing her best to believe Ysolt's ministrations were a good thing although she herself still didn't trust the sorceress.

"That doesn't answer my question," Heimdall snapped.

Ysolt sighed. "If you have to hear it straight out, so be it. Spells and medicines have kept some of the sick clinging to life longer than they would otherwise. But so far, no one has recovered, and there's no reason to think Lady Estrid will be the first."

Heimdall was silent. Uschi's heart ached to imagine him standing there devastated, perhaps even with tears running down his face. But when her friend finally spoke, his voice was firm with resolve, just as she'd often heard it when they'd found themselves in one tight spot or another.

"But there is something we can do," Heimdall said, "and I'm an idiot to stand here agonizing at her bedside when I should be doing it. I beg you, keep her alive a couple more days and all will be well." He strode out of the room and stopped short when he found Uschi waiting for him. He smelled of sweat and was dirty and disheveled from his journey. More than that, Uschi could see the desperation in his eyes. He might have insisted to Ysolt that all would be well, but he was by no means certain that was the case, or at least that he could set matters right in time to save Lady Estrid's life.

"I'm sorry about your mother," Uschi said. The words felt weak and useless coming out of her mouth.

"We can save her," Heimdall said. Uschi had a feeling his insistence was for his own benefit as much as her own. "It's a magical sickness. Kill the curse and you end the disease, and I found the source. It's not even that far away. It's in one of the abandoned cities, and on the flight back, I saw that one of the old roads that served the place runs nearly all the way from there to here. If I talk to Lord Frey, maybe the expedition can even leave this afternoon and make a few miles before nightfall. Come on." He took a first stride toward the staircase and, presumably, the God of the Harvest's present location.

"Wait!" she said. "Things have been happening here as well. Things you ought to know about."

Frowning, he looked back. "I know there have been more draugr. I saw the remains of the pyres flying in. I'm sure Lord Frey and my father will leave enough warriors here to suppress them for a couple more days. The source of the curse is inside an old building. There are only so many warriors who could fit inside anyway."

"It's not that," she said. "I've learned something as well. Or at least I think I have." She told him about her nightmare and her guess that the dream had come from the rune sword.

When she'd finished, he said, "That's... troubling. But are you sure it wasn't merely a nightmare? I don't see how you can be certain it came from the blade."

"I admit," she replied, "at this point, I can't be *absolutely* sure. But if it was only a nightmare, it was a very targeted, specific kind of nightmare. Imagine that everyone who carries a rune blade feels the same sort of anxiety I felt when lying down to rest. The same urge to sleep with the sword in hand. And then the blade fills the warrior's head with that same dream, or a variation on it. Except that the other sleepers never fight their way through to the four-armed giant like I did, only the parts they're meant to see. Over time, they'd come to regard the dream as some sort of, I don't know, mystical revelation of Odin's treachery. That would explain why they all view the All-Father and us two thanes of Asgard with suspicion."

Heimdall took a moment to ponder what she'd told him. Then he said, "Maybe you're right. There must be something wrong with the rune swords. But the catch is, they're still our best weapons against the draugr."

"I know," she said wryly. "You'll notice I'm still carrying mine in addition to the Brightblade."

"And the draugr are an immediate threat to all Vanaheim. We have to solve that problem first. I've promised you that afterward, we'll look into every worrisome thing you've encountered, and that now includes the rune blades. If you think they're tainted, I take that seriously."

Uschi realized that with his mother succumbing to the

sickness, Heimdall could scarcely view the situation any other way. She considered asking him if he'd felt different being around the rune blades but decided against such an action. And for all she knew, his perspective was correct. The draugr *were* a ghastly menace. Maybe it did make sense to deal with them first and then delve into the matter of the rune swords and all the rest of it.

"All right," she said. "We'll do it your way. We'll keep my suspicions between ourselves for now – no point distracting or confusing anyone – and take them up when we've laid the curse to rest."

Fifteen

Heimdall set down Golden Mane on the old road and waited the few moments necessary for the column of riders to catch up to him. The existence of the roadway made it unlikely that he and his comrades would lose their way, but some scouting from the air was still a sound idea.

Lord Frey was at the head of the column mounted on his magical metal boar. "What did you see?" he asked.

"We've nearly reached the blighted area," Heimdall replied. He was aware the journey had taken a remarkably short time. It was only late morning of the day after their afternoon departure. Though it was a subtle magic, undetectable from moment to moment, Frey must have used some power to shorten the journey just as he'd sailed from Peadar's holdings to Rodric's in only a morning. But though it had been short, it had *felt* excruciatingly long with his mother lying sick unto death back in his parents' castle. "No columns of darkness or armies of killer birds rose into the sky at my approach. Mind you, I didn't actually fly into the blight."

"I wouldn't have wanted you to," the god replied, his war

gear shining in the sunlight, even more resplendent with gold and silver than that of his followers. "When we reach the verge, I may be able to do something to clear any such nuisances from our path."

Frey's manner was as affable as it had been ever since Heimdall had found him in the castle and told him he'd found the source of the curse. Whatever the reason for the deity's initial coldness, it had ended now that the two of them and the rest of their company were riding out to fight the evil together, and thank the Fates for that. Mutual trust could only help them end the curse in time to save his mother's life. Afterward, if the God of the Harvest reverted to his former attitude when Heimdall and Uschi suggested that the rune blades bore their own subtle malediction, well, they'd deal with that when the time came.

The company rode on, a war band fifty strong in all, their mail clinking and their mounts' hooves clopping on the ancient stonework. Golden Mane sighed and rustled his feathery wings repeatedly, expressing his discontent at being held to the ground like the common steeds. Whenever possible, he preferred to fly, but Heimdall judged that the time had passed for separating from the rest of the company.

Before long, they spied the yellow and brown of the blighted zone. Oozing cankers mottled the tree trunks, and only dead curling leaves and needles still clung to the branches. The rotting carcasses of birds lay scattered on the ground, and though it had been necessary, Heimdall felt a fleeting twinge of regret at the harm he'd wrought with the Gjallarhorn.

Frey raised his hand to signal a halt. "Now, let's see." He closed his bright blue eyes and touched his fingertips to his temples. New bark sealed over some of the sores weeping sap on a few of the tree trunks, and fresh growth sprouted along the branches. Some of the riders behind him murmured in wonder. Though perhaps more familiar than they with exercises of godly power, Heimdall felt something of the same himself.

Frey opened his eyes and frowned at what he'd wrought. "I couldn't entirely cure the forest," he said. "I'm the God of the Harvest, not the woodland. But the power of the curse has pulled back, presumably to conserve its strength for when we reach the keep you told me of. We should be able to pass through the trees without hindrance."

That proved to be the case except for the natural hindrances the forest afforded once they reached the point where time had obliterated the road. The riders pressed on and in due course reached the plaza and the ruined structure that loomed on the far side of it. As before, when Heimdall invoked the sight of Mimir, the gaping doorway flickered with malevolent power, and the darkness felt coiled and ready to pounce. He felt a renewed sense of foreboding, but his determination was stronger still.

Frey swung himself off the big golden boar. "Gullinbursti and the Valkyrie steeds will guard the rest of the mounts," he said to Heimdall, "along with two of my warriors." He drew the Sword of Destiny and released it to float in the air before him, where it would fight independently and protect its master as needed, then unsheathed his rune blade to hold in his hand.

Heimdall drew a long, steadying breath and pulled his own two-handed sword from its scabbard. He'd considered entering the keep with rune blade and shield in hand like his companions but in the end decided his greater skill with the larger weapon was apt to matter more than the magic in the symbols. Still, it was good to know he'd have allies armed with rune swords just a pace or two away if he encountered a draug that was utterly impervious to common steel.

Once dismounted, the other warriors formed up behind Frey and himself. His father and Uschi were in the second rank. Both looked grimly intent on the business at hand.

Frey turned to Heimdall. "Lead on," the deity said.

Heimdall did, meanwhile using the hearing of Mimir to seek the chamber ahead. He heard nothing but knew better than to drop his guard. If he'd been contending with living foes, that would have assured him no one and nothing was guarding the entryway. But the hearts of corpse-things didn't beat, nor did breath whisper in and out of their nostrils, and as he and Frey stepped over the threshold, the creatures lunged from hiding places that had been out of his sight until that moment. Their nauseating stench swept over him.

There was a solid line of draugr with more behind: some with claws, some armed only with their own prodigious strength, the ones that could reach their living foes scratching and raking or pounding and battering according to their natures. Heimdall dodged, ducked, hacked, and sent putrescent heads tumbling off bodies. Frey's flying sword fought while the god himself sheltered and shifted behind it, letting it create openings for him to slash and thrust with the rune blade.

Despite their prowess, Heimdall feared the weight of numbers would overwhelm Frey and him. The only way to prevent it was to create room for the comrades behind them to enter the fray. Shouting battle cries, he struck and pushed forward with all the reckless aggression at his command and claimed a precious stride or two of ground. Frey must have succeeded in driving forward as well, for a moment later, Uschi, Rodric, and others were fighting beside them. Their sigils glowing like hot coals, the enchanted swords cut and stabbed, and the draugr fell.

If Heimdall's friend and father were afraid, no one could have told it from the ferocity with which they assailed the dead things. When the pressure of his own foes relented, he was proud of his bonds with them.

After the fight, while warriors tended to wounded comrades and the couple who, their rune swords notwithstanding, had perished, Heimdall scanned the entry hall with its rotten faded tapestries, crumbling carvings, and other sad remnants of past grandeur. Here, out of the sun, he could see the foxfire as actual light, a dim greenish phosphorescence clinging to or arising from certain decaying surfaces. Moreover, he could see how it grew gradually, infinitesimally brighter as it receded away from him and toward, he assumed, the source of the curse.

Wiping putrescence from her rune sword, the sigils still shining red to Heimdall's eyes even out of combat, Uschi came to stand beside him. "I doubt that was all of it," she said. "The defenses, I mean."

"We'll remain vigilant," said Frey. Face tight with disgust, he flicked away a bit of rotten flesh that had stuck to one tip of his long white-blond mustache. "Can you see the way to what we're looking for?"

"Yes," Heimdall said. "To my sight, changes in the brightness of the foxfire point the way." The way into further clashes with the dead, quite possibly, but daunting as that prospect was, with so many lives at stake including his own mother's, he and his comrades would just have to cope.

"Will you still be able to see the gradations if we kindle some lights?" asked Frey.

"I expect so."

The god turned to the rest of the company. "Lights!" Firesteels scratched, sparks flew, and rote invocations of Thor sounded as some of the warriors kindled the lanterns with which they'd been entrusted. The company then pressed on, now forty-one strong minus the slain and those too badly hurt to continue.

Heimdall noticed that, by chance presumably, Uschi and Peadar ended up walking side by side. Evidently neither was willing to make a show of pushing through the throng in an obvious effort for distance, because they stayed that way. But unlike the many comrades who'd chosen to advance together, they didn't whisper back and forth or even look at one another. It now seemed plain as could be that Heimdall had been wrong to persuade Uschi to return to her childhood home, and he vowed to apologize again after they survived the battle.

The warriors stalked through what had once been the ground floor of some great jarl's palace: through an audience hall, lesser council chambers, and humbler utilitarian rooms where house karls had once toiled to meet the needs of the lordly. Every surviving piece of furniture or other article was decaying, corroded, or rusted and covered in nose-tickling dust. There were shambling, uneven footprints in the grime on the floor, but nothing to be heard except for the intruders' own steps, the drumming of their hearts, and their nervous muttering to one another.

In due course, they came to an arched doorway and the steps leading downward beyond it. "This way?" asked Frey.

"Yes." Heimdall took a long breath. Since being lost, lightless and alone in the troll-infested Realm Below, he wasn't especially fond of unfamiliar and perilous spaces underground. But the trail led where it led, and he and his companions would have to follow.

As they started down, it occurred to him to say, "This place was magnificent in its day. Did *you* perhaps dwell here when the Vanir chose to live in cities?" If so, Frey might recall some useful information.

The God of the Harvest shook his head. "This was one of Njord's cities, but as far as I know, even he never actually lived here. Too far from the sea for his liking." Njord, Heimdall knew, was the God of the Sea, who'd mostly led a reclusive life since his people the Vanir lost their war with the Aesir. "His followers looked after it all."

At the place where the stairs ended, passages ran off in multiple directions. A few ranks back and thus a few steps up, Lord Peadar said, "If we split up, we can search more quickly."

Frey shook his head. "Splitting up, my lord, is both unwise and unnecessary. Captain Heimdall can see the path."

Let's hope, Heimdall thought. He had no tangible reason to doubt it, but here in the heart of the malevolence, he'd often been surprised and deceived since the rising of the dead. He felt a little less certain than he had before.

Glinting in the yellow lantern light, Frey's sword Laevateinn floated before the company as they made their way through what proved to be a maze of tunnels. Peering into the mouths of branching passages, Heimdall could see a block of dungeon cells, a wine cellar, storerooms, and other spaces whose original function was lost to time. There was nothing stirring in the dark, but he remained convinced that it couldn't be this easy. He and his allies hadn't already smashed through every barrier the curse would place in their way.

The subtly brightening foxfire sheen led to another archway with another forbiddance carved into the top. This one had a gate made of rust-furred iron bars blocking the way, but, obedient to Frey's unspoken will, the Sword of Destiny leaped and struck the obstacle down with a single cut, a reminder that, if the tales were true, it could slash through anything. The clangor of the broken bars falling to the floor echoed away into silence.

The corridor beyond was both wider and more ornate, the walls decorated with dingy faded paintings of ships, the sea, and whales, krakens, and other oceanic creatures, all presumably to suit the tastes of the God of the Sea. Heimdall wondered if any of his companions could even make the pictures out but decided not to bother asking. The ancient images presumably had nothing to do with the task at hand.

Behind him, partway down the line of warriors now strung out along the corridor, someone screamed. Other Vanir cried out in shock and alarm.

Startled, Heimdall spun around and shifted frantically this way and that to see past the warriors who were obstructing the view. He had no idea how, but somehow, draugr had appeared in the midst of the living. Caught by surprise, warriors were falling in horrific ways.

Frey sent Laevateinn hurtling over the heads of the nearer warriors to aid those under attack. A heartbeat later, he came under threat himself. A draug with a seeping, sagging face like a melting candle stepped through the solid stone of the wall just behind him and reached for him with its claws. Heimdall glimpsed the corpse-thing from the corner of his eye, spun, and cut its head from its shoulders an instant before it could rip open the god's throat.

By that time, more draugr were stepping out of the wall. Heimdall cut down another, and then one dropped from the ceiling. It slammed down on top of him and bore him beneath it. He had no hope of bringing his sword to bear and for a terrifying instant was sure the dead thing was about to kill him, but then it stopped moving. When he rolled it off his body, he saw that Uschi had slain it with her rune sword. Another draug heaved itself out of the floor and reached for her leg. She beheaded it, leaving the upper body exposed and the rest still buried.

As, heart thumping, Heimdall scrambled to his feet, Uschi said, "You thought the draugr might show us more tricks before we were through."

"I wish I'd been wrong," he replied.

"Forward!" Frey shouted. "We can't stay here!"

Heimdall realized the deity was right. The warriors – those who were left – now understood the draugr could emerge from anywhere, but no one individual could watch in every direction at once. The confines of the passageway prevented them from supporting one another to best effect or taking advantage of the longer reach their swords would otherwise have afforded. Lunging out of the walls or occasionally even the ceiling and floor, the corpse-things came within striking distance of their foes in an instant.

The warriors fought their way forward, those toward the rear stumbling over the bodies of their fallen comrades and the draugr they'd dispatched. To Heimdall's profound relief – if he and his fellows had had to press on much longer, he doubted they would have made it – he and Frey soon came to a doorway.

The chamber on the other side had once been a sanctum where warlocks worked the style of magic their patron Njord favored. Along with rune stones, mystic symbols carved into the walls, and moldering books and scrolls, the shelves and worktable held seashells, a conch, a spear whose shaft was studded with pearls all the way down its length, and the skull of an enormous fish – all, to Heimdall's sight, faintly glowing with a blue sheen akin to the fiercer crimson light of the enchanted swords.

But at the moment he didn't care about any of that, only that the conjuration chamber was spacious enough to negate some of the draugr's tactical advantage. Frey clearly realized the same thing. "Inside!" he bellowed. "A square! Shield walls! Fast!"

Everyone rushed inside to create the formation their leader commanded. The rows of shields still didn't block foes dropping from over the warriors' heads or rising from beneath their feet, but for the most part, the improved circumstances protected them until the attackers stopped appearing.

Heimdall looked around. Thirty-two of his companions remained, including Frey, Uschi, his father, and the Valkyries. Though there was still no sign of cordiality between them, to Heimdall's surprise, Uschi and Lord Peadar had taken up positions side by side in the formation. Perhaps the frenzy and random chances of the struggle had obliged them to do so.

Breathing heavily, both his rune sword and the blade that

had returned to float before him now filthy and dripping with decay, Frey turned to Heimdall and said, "I don't suppose this space is the end of the trail."

"No," Heimdall said. "The foxfire keeps glowing brighter farther down the passage."

"Then we have to keep following," said the god. "But that's certain death unless we can do *something* to improve our situation at least a little."

Thrusting fear and fatigue aside, Heimdall thought about it. Even the sight of Mimir couldn't penetrate the walls, ceilings, and floors around them to locate the draugr lurking within. That left his preternaturally keen hearing. "Everyone," he called, "be as quiet as you possibly can!"

Even after his companions did their best to comply, there was still sound, the thumping of their hearts and the moans of some unfortunate wounded soul they'd mistakenly left for dead in the corridor outside. Heimdall strained to listen past all that, to ignore it, erase it from his awareness, and hear whatever noise remained.

After a moment, he caught it, a liquid, rippling sound. "I hear them," he said. "I hear the draugr moving through the stonework – it's a swishing sound like swimming – and if everyone stays quiet when we move on, I should be able to point out where one is about to burst into the open a moment before it does."

When they resumed their progress, he bellowed, "Right wall, partway back!" Or, "Ceiling, rear!" Or, "Left wall, front!" as required. The advance down the passage was still a horror, and more warriors fell, but step by step and sword stroke by sword stroke, they forced their way along.

Finally, the foxfire led to a spacious tomb Heimdall assumed to be occupied by a lord who'd once ruled the ruined city on Njord's behalf. Surrounding a stone sarcophagus were the grave goods, weapons, jewelry, and even a longship that had presumably never known the sea.

The dim phosphorescence shone on many a surface with no further gradations in its brightness. Heimdall inferred that meant he'd reached the source of the curse, or nearly so, but from where *exactly* did it emanate? Frustratingly, he couldn't tell. From within the sarcophagus, perhaps, or behind the gunwales of the longship? He took a stride toward the latter. The shadow deepened inside the crypt. The tallow candles inside the lanterns didn't fail entirely, but they now only illuminated the immediate vicinities of those who carried them. At the same moment, there came a fluid, swishing sound from above, below, and on every side.

"The draugr are coming!" Heimdall shouted. From the ubiquity of the noise, he suspected the curse was about to throw all its remaining servants at the intruders. If so, that suggested he and his comrades had indeed reached the source of the evil magic, but that wouldn't do them any good if the corpse-things slaughtered them before they could identify and destroy it.

"Get on the ship!" Frey called. "Shield walls there!"

The company rushed to scramble aboard. Twenty-eight warriors remained. Uschi was covered in slime and the blood of fallen comrades. Heimdall's father still clung to a scrap of shield that bashing blows and raking claws had reduced to near uselessness. Peadar had lost his helmet. The left half of his face was red with the blood flowing from a gash at the hairline.

Uschi had yet to clamber aboard when a first draug lunged out of the darkness and grabbed her from behind. Already standing on the deck, Heimdall was only a few strides away, but amid the press and the confusion, it might as well have been a mile. Unable to help his friend, all but certain the corpse-thing was about to kill her, he cried out.

Uschi wrenched free of the draug's grip and twisted around to face it. Screaming a war cry, she shoved it away with her shield, and that gave her the distance required to drive her rune sword into its torso. The dead thing fell, and she heaved herself onto the longship. Heimdall sighed in relief.

Fumbling and bumping into one another in the gloom, the warriors sought to form their battle lines. They barely managed before more draugr came charging out of the walls to assail them.

The moments that followed were frenzied and desperate indeed. Straining to put dread and fury aside to see and think, Heimdall judged that, for a little while at least, his comrades could hold their own. The rows of old shields hanging above the longship's oar ports protected their lower legs. Their position aboard afforded a modest height advantage against all but the draugr that occasionally dropped through the ceiling. No more rose from immediately below. Maybe the double surface of the ship's hull and the floor beneath somehow prevented it.

Lacking a shield, Heimdall couldn't stand in one of the shield walls. Instead, he stood behind them, thrusting his long blade between two of his comrades when opportunity offered and darting this way and that to dispatch the occasional corpse-thing that jumped down into the longship from above. Mostly, though, he peered about seeking the heart of the curse. He had to locate it fast before his allies were overwhelmed.

It didn't appear to be in the bottom of the ship. Was it then inside the sarcophagus? Maybe, but could he reach the stone coffin, shift away the heavy lid, and investigate the contents with the draugr striking and ripping at him every step of the way? He studied the grave goods arrayed on shelves or hanging on the walls. They still didn't appear magical, but when he peered with the sharpness of the sight of Mimir, he finally spotted the infinitesimal cracks outlining a hidden door.

He didn't know if the source of the curse was behind the door, but he judged it the likeliest possibility. Readying himself, he breathed deeply and waited for the moment when no corpse-things were attacking a part of the shield wall facing the hidden door. When that instant arrived, he shoved between a pair of his comrades, leaped back onto the floor of the crypt, and ran.

Draugr turned to strike at him. He beheaded one, hacked the leg out from under another, and then reached the concealed door. A moment's scrutiny revealed the catch. He lunged through, out of the roaring chaos of the battle, and slammed it shut behind him. That wouldn't stop creatures that could swim through walls, but perhaps with luck they hadn't seen where he'd gone.

He hated leaving his companions behind to fight without him. But, if his guess was correct, he was doing the only thing that might possibly save their lives.

SIXTEEN

Turning, Heimdall found himself in another crypt. Unlike the preceding one, the chamber lacked a longship, but otherwise those who'd prepared the occupant for his final rest had crammed it full of grave goods, and those items were plainly costlier than the last set. The hilts and scabbards of the swords were encrusted with amber, jet, carnelian, almandine, and gold and silver inlay. The rings, brooches, bracelets, and necklaces were superbly fashioned into the shapes of dolphins, fish, snakes, and other animals. Heimdall inferred that while someone might actually be interred in the vault outside, it had also served as a sort of decoy to prevent thieves from finding the place where the true jarl of the city had been laid to rest.

Once, the display must have been magnificent. In a way, it still was, but some upheaval had broken shelves and spilled the items they'd contained to the floor and brought dirt and dust down from the ceiling to dull their luster. It had even crumbled the floor in one corner and opened a sort of pit. Heimdall reckoned that only an unnatural power – like the magic that had originated the curse – could have created such a powerful convulsion without the effect likewise shaking the spaces beyond these walls.

The source of the curse, he judged, was now unmistakable. A marble bier stood in the center of the crypt. Sculpted ships and breaching whales adorned the sides, but runes now split and defaced the carvings, and from the scars bled green light that seemed a fiercer cousin to the foxfire.

The same light burned from the symbols cut into the flesh of the draug that had once laid on the pedestal, and from its eyes and snarling mouth as well. Swollen, rotting hands poised to seize and batter, it lurched forward in the seemingly clumsy but quick manner of its kind and interposed itself between Heimdall and the bier.

All right, he thought coldly, taking a fresh grip on his two-handed sword. If I have to put down one more of you things, so be it. At least he was only facing a single draug after already destroying several of them. He just had to do so fast. With his preternatural hearing, he could hear the battle raging on the other side of the wall, a constant reminder that Uschi, his father, and all the others needed him to bring an end to the fray.

He advanced to meet the draug and cut at the creature's neck with all his strength.

To his dismay, the blade clanged and rebounded without leaving so much as a scratch. He leaped back to avoid the draug's return blow – a sweeping backhand that, he suspected, would have broken ribs.

In the exchanges that followed, he tried cutting at the dead thing's eyes and then the luminous fissures the curse itself had made in its putrescent flesh. To his horror, nothing worked, and meanwhile the hulking monstrosity pressed him hard. He doubted he could stay out of its clutches much longer and reflected grimly that he should have laid claim to an enchanted sword after all.

As if the thought were magic, a wish being granted, Laevateinn flew into his field of vision and cut at the draug's back. Frey, Heimdall thought with a surge of relief, must have noticed him leave the longship, elected to follow, and done so closely enough to find his way through the hidden door.

An instant later, a lantern swinging from his shield arm, the god himself closed with the corpse-thing. As the Sword of Destiny hitched back for a second cut, Frey swung his rune blade at the draug's neck.

Heimdall expected the two magic weapons hacking in concert would surely end the fight. He was thus surprised and alarmed when, unharmed and not even deigning to turn around, seemingly intent on disposing of its current target before attacking another, the draug kept rushing him. He scuttled backward and realized to his horror that he was moving too slowly.

The draug didn't catch him, though. It hesitated and then advanced more deliberately, as if it had reason to be wary of something. Heimdall realized that his last chance, his comrades' last chance, his mother's, depended on figuring out what that something was. He risked a glance backward, saw his retreat had brought him within a few paces of the bier, and then an idea came to him. It was little more than a guess, but the only possibility left.

He drew breath to ask Frey for help with what he had in mind as five other draugr came oozing through the wall. His plan couldn't possibly succeed if more of the corpse-things swarmed on him.

"Hold the rest of them back!" he called to Frey. "Keep them off me!"

To his relief, the God of the Harvest didn't question. He wheeled and sent Laevateinn leaping at the creature in the lead.

Meanwhile, Heimdall circled, and, with a silver ring blackened by tarnish sunk deep in its swollen throat like a strangler's cord, the king draug pivoted with him. When he had its back to the bier, he lifted his sword as though he could think of no better tactic than another futile cut at his adversary's neck or head. Then he dropped the sword, stretched out his arms, and charged.

The move caught the dead man by surprise, and the shove, with all of Heimdall's weight behind it, rocked it back a couple of steps. Even if his guess was right, though, that wasn't far enough, and so he kept driving the corpse-thing onward. The draug grabbed hold of him and dug its fingers into his body with crushing force. Gasping, Heimdall bore the pain as best he could. He had to if he was to keep it stumbling backward. He had to do it to save Uschi's life and his parents', too.

The draug was stronger than he was and would feel nothing of pain. Its rotting body was slimy, hard to hold onto, and the stink of it was all but choking him. Heimdall's one desperate hope was that training and experience had made him the better wrestler.

He hooked the draug's leg with his own, drove forward, and sent it teetering back again. The creature held onto him as tightly as before. The swollen fingers of one hand dug into his shoulder, the pain keen enough that it was as if he were wearing no armor at all. The other lifted to slap his helmet away and squeeze his head. That pressure was *truly* agonizing. It would likely have broken his skull if the creature didn't keep shifting its grip in an effort to reach and gouge his eye.

In desperation, Heimdall stopped pushing forward, hitched back, grabbed the arm that was seeking to put out his eye, and pulled. The sudden reversal toppled the king draug off balance again, only forward this time, and it fumbled its grip on him. Heaving with all his strength, he spun the creature around his body and released it to send it staggering back once more in the direction he needed it to go.

At last, he saw with a surge of hope that he'd driven it nearly far enough. Before it could recover its equilibrium, he slammed a push kick into the center of its chest. The impact knocked it a final step backward. The edge of the bier caught the back of its knees. It fell onto the stone pedestal.

Heimdall dove on top of it and straddled its chest. He then hammered punches at the draug's face. He knew his blows wouldn't damage the corpse-thing, but maybe they'd distract it for the moment necessary for something to happen. Please, please, he thought, for everyone's sake, let that something happen!

The king draug bucked beneath him and flailed at him with bruising, punishing blows – even if their relative positions kept it from using the full measure of its strength. Heimdall somehow kept his seat through it all, and then the green fire in its eyes flared brighter. Heimdall wanted to look away but somehow couldn't. His head swam, and he felt as sick and feeble as he had when he met the gaze of the burning corpse-thing on the fire.

Still, he had to keep the draug pinned atop the bier! Because he must be right that this was the way to end it! Why else was it assailing him with a power it hadn't deigned to manifest hitherto?

He strained to hold the draug down for a few more heartbeats. Then the creature stopped moving, and the green light shining through its eyes, mouth, and the runes cut into its body guttered out. So, too, did the glow from the symbols carved into the pedestal itself.

Meanwhile, Heimdall panted and trembled. He hoped the effects of the king draug's evil eye were passing, but that still left the ache of his bruises, the exhaustion occasioned by his exertions since entering the keep, and the nausea that came from breathing the corpse-things' stink. It almost felt like too much effort to look around and check on the rest of the battle, but it was necessary to determine what he'd actually accomplished.

As it turned out, all he'd intended. The draugr Frey had been fighting sprawled inert, and Heimdall could hear that the battle in the vault with the longship had stopped as well. Warriors exclaimed in wonder and joy that their foes had abruptly collapsed.

Heimdall could hear Uschi's voice, and his father's, and Lord Peadar's. They'd all survived. In that moment of triumph and relief, he felt certain his mother would now be all right as well. Winded and weak as he was, he laughed in elation.

Frey gave Heimdall a smile nearly as wide as his extravagant mustache. "You did it!"

Heimdall returned the smile, meanwhile realizing that, his weariness notwithstanding, he didn't want to be in proximity to the putrid corpse beneath him a moment longer. He clambered unsteadily off the bier and moved to pick up his sword. "We all did it," he replied.

With a flick of the rune blade in his hand, the god waved Heimdall's modesty away. "The skalds will sing about *you*, captain. I'll see to it personally. You'll be remembered as long as there are Vanir. But *how* did you do it?"

"A lucky guess," Heimdall said. "I noticed the creature and the bier had the same glowing runes carved into them and that the corpse-thing was careful about coming near the pedestal. What, I wondered, if the draug wasn't just the guardian of the curse? What if it and the slab together embodied the curse, and the way to quell the magic was to force the dead lord back onto its proper resting place? That's the way a warrior of Midgard disposed of a draug in one of the mortals' sagas."

Frey shook his head. "You risked a great deal on your hunches."

"When even your swords failed to wound the king draug, I didn't see any other option. Shall we rejoin the rest of the company?"

Frey sighed. With Laevateinn hovering before him, he positioned himself between Heimdall and the door. "I regret this more than I can say. Especially after what you've done for Vanaheim. But it seems the time has come."

Heimdall felt a chill ooze up his back. "What are you talking about, my lord?"

"From the moment I learned you'd arrived, it was plain I couldn't allow you to return to Asgard to report to Odin. But I couldn't just kill you openly. Your parents are important folk. I didn't want to alienate them. Then, later, I realized I should likewise stay my hand because you could provide invaluable assistance with putting an end to the curse."

After the moment of praise and camaraderie, this abrupt reversal felt as unexpected as any vileness the draugr had perpetrated. Heimdall strained to shake off the shock of it and think of something to say that would convince Lord Frey to relent. "Everyone who fought alongside us today knows I helped end it. What will they say if you murder me?"

"Nothing, because they'll never know. Fate has been kind. You and I are alone in a room with a concealed door. The draugr's darkness ensured that no one saw us enter. Even if you somehow let our comrades know you're in danger and your approximate location, they'd never find the door and figure out how to open it in time to intervene. The world will believe you died battling the walking corpses. It's unfortunate your song will end with an untruth, but poets often get the details wrong."

"What good is killing me when Uschi will still be alive?" Now that it was too late, how he wished he hadn't put off addressing her concerns!

"My followers," Frey said, "will deal with her as soon as they can catch her alone. A final tragedy: she couldn't bear to go on living with her best friend slain. It won't be as tidy as your death, but then I don't expect her parents to ask nearly as many questions as yours would."

How, Heimdall thought, could this be happening? Mere moments ago, he and Frey had been comrades battling the curse together. He'd saved the god's life when they were fighting their way down the corridor. Still, he could tell Frey was in deadly earnest, and he strained to think what more he could say to sway the god from his purpose. Only Uschi's conjectures seemed to offer even the slimmest hope.

"My lord," he said, "you've been deceived. You think the dreams you've been having, the ones that show Odin conjuring the curse, are true. They're not. The rune swords have cast a glamour on you and all those to whom you've given them."

Frey shook his head. "That isn't so. The dreams come from the soul of Vanaheim herself seeking to warn her children."

"Even if that were true, the curse is gone. Surely now there's time to investigate the matter. Just talk to Odin! You'll see he doesn't hate the Vanir!"

"The time for talk is over," the God of the Harvest declared. "The time for talking to you is over." The Sword of Destiny flew forward.

Even if he'd recovered the full measure of his strength and stamina, Heimdall wouldn't have been eager to duel the supposedly invincible blade that fought all by itself. In his current condition, the odds were even worse. He grabbed the Gjallarhorn and blew it.

The blade slammed Frey back against the wall. It knocked Laevateinn back as well, but less than an arm's length and only for an instant. The sword flashed forward once again. Heimdall dropped the trumpet to dangle at his hip and gripped the hilt of his own blade barely in time to parry an initial cut. He would have struck back, too, but there was nothing to strike *at* except the enchanted weapon itself, and so he could only defend and retreat as repeated clanging sword strokes pushed him around the crypt. Always, Laevateinn hovered between him and the exit.

He remembered the Sword of Destiny could supposedly cut through anything and accordingly did his best to parry without letting his own weapon receive the full force of a cut. That only worked for a few heartbeats, though, and then, despite his efforts, an attack snapped his blade in two so that only the bottom half remained. The pointed piece clinked as it hit the floor.

Thanks to his preternatural hearing, Heimdall caught voices clamoring in the other vault. People had heard the Gjallarhorn, and that afforded him an instant of hope. Then, parsing the excited jabber, he realized no one had yet located the hidden door, let alone determined how to open it. Which meant he was still on his own.

And, making Heimdall's plight seem even more hopeless, Frey had already recovered from the stunning force of the Gjallarhorn's call. The god came stalking up behind the flying sword, using it to fight his present foe just as he'd combatted the draugr, keeping out of range of his adversary's stab or a blade until he saw the right moment to advance and strike. Heimdall faked shifts one way and then sought to lunge the other to flummox Laevateinn and reach its master, but the legendary weapon was never fooled. Heimdall never had a moment to let the Gjallarhorn call again.

A heartbeat later, Laevateinn cut what remained of his blade even shorter. At the same time, Frey stepped in and slashed Heimdall's flank with the rune sword.

The stroke sheared through Heimdall's mail to the man inside. He felt the initial shock of wounding and reeled backward. In that instant, he felt a flare of anger that, with his flying sword to battle for him and protect him, his godly adversary wasn't fighting fair. That initial emotion had likely been his mind's stubborn effort to feel something other than dread and despair. For now that he was wounded, it was plain he'd lost the duel.

His two foes stalked after him, the Sword of Destiny once more floating in the lead, the God of the Harvest sheltering behind it. Panting, ever more unsteady on his feet, feeling the blood welling from his gashed side, Heimdall was certain that if he didn't somehow escape this confrontation within the next few heartbeats, he was going to die. Laevateinn and Frey were still blocking the path to the door. Glancing desperately around, he realized his retreats had backed him toward the pit in the corner of the crypt. He whirled, sprinted to the edge of it, and leaped.

He fell a long way and landed hard, half-wedged in a shaft that narrowed like a spearpoint at the bottom. Only Asgardian hardiness, he judged, had kept the fall from killing him outright, and for all he knew, it hadn't protected him from injury altogether. There was no time to check for that, though, or to investigate the cut in his side, either. Using his enhanced vision to pierce the darkness, he peered up at the opening high above.

Laevateinn flew into view and poised itself blade downward. It then descended into the shaft in a side-to-side seeking sort of way like a hound trying to pick up a scent.

The searching only lasted a couple of moments, and then the sword evidently detected Heimdall with whatever sense or senses it possessed. Having done so, it plunged downward to finish him off.

Galvanized by fear and instinct, Heimdall sought to protect

himself by the only means still at his disposal. He fumbled the Gjallarhorn to his lips and blew.

The blast of sound dislodged dirt and pebbles to stream down the side of the pit. Heimdall just had time to think he'd killed himself and saved Laevateinn the trouble when something hit his head and plunged him into a darkness even the sight of Mimir couldn't penetrate.

SEVENTEEN

Uschi had made sure Golden Mane and Avalanche had adjacent stalls. She hoped that, bereft of his rider, the black steed would obtain some solace from the company of the white one.

She wouldn't have wagered on it, though. She herself hadn't found any comfort in the time since Heimdall's death. Her sorrow was like a lump of lead in her chest. Along with it was a feeling of unreality. She'd known that, like any warrior, her best friend could die. But, deep down, she hadn't believed it would truly happen.

Like all those who'd perished inside the ruined keep, their bodies entombed there forever, Heimdall had received full funeral honors after the company returned to his parents' castle. But a feast of rejoicing followed that very night, for, after all, the warriors had ended the draugr curse and the plague the dead things created. To Uschi, the singing and sounds of celebration that reached the stables felt like a mockery of her sadness and filled her with a seething resentment even though she knew her reaction was unfair. Accordingly, she'd absented herself from Lord Rodric's hall as she'd previously shunned that of her parents. Which only left her free of distractions to relive the terrible moments when she learned of Heimdall's death over and over again.

It had seemed a miraculous reprieve when the horde of draugr collapsed before the shield walls on the longship, and the lanterns shone brighter as the unnatural dark gave way. Relief turned to dismay, however, when someone exclaimed that Frey and Heimdall were gone, a dismay that intensified when the Gjallarhorn sounded once and then, not long afterward, again, from some nearby space. She and her fellow warriors searched frantically but couldn't locate the hidden door until Frey came through from the other side. Frey and only Frey.

The god then explained that the company's efforts had indeed broken the curse, but, sadly, at the cost of one last life. Heimdall had dueled and defeated the mighty draug that was the source of the malediction, but with the last of its strength, the creature had used the evil eye to burn its vanquisher to nothing. Not even a wisp of ash remained.

Rodric sought to hide his devastation at the loss, to conceal it behind a mask of stoic pride that his son had died as the hero who ended the curse. Undeceived, the warriors who knew him best gathered around to give him their condolences.

No one offered the same comfort to Uschi. For a moment, Peadar looked like he meant to approach her, but then, evidently remembering his grievances, he frowned and turned away.

Left to her own devices, she sought to feel some trace of the gladness many of her comrades were feeling. She had, after all, lost friends in battle before and managed to take some satisfaction in victory even so. This time, however, was different. She dreaded seeing how grief-stricken Sif would be when Uschi had to deliver the news her brother was dead.

As soon as the survivors all collected themselves, Frey ordered a swift departure from the keep. The warriors had accomplished their task, they now had the wounded to care for, and they could do that better in the sunlight and fresh air. No one objected. Everyone was eager to escape the dark and the stink of the putrid remains of the draugr.

When they'd bandaged claw marks and splinted broken limbs as required, and the company was ready to depart the ruined city entirely, Golden Mane balked. The stallion had been looking around in vain for his master and didn't want to leave without him. His reluctance gave Uschi yet another pang of anguish, but she shoved the emotion down to take the steed in hand. She was a Valkyrie, knew the signals and commands her sisterhood used to manage their mounts, and, after a final anxious neigh, Golden Mane suffered her to lead him out of the plaza.

On the journey back, travel once again hastened by Frey's subtle magic, it occurred to her that she could now leave the procession, soar into the sky, and return forthwith to Asgard. She and Heimdall had agreed that, once the draugr were no more, they'd address the other matters that concerned her, but with her friend dead, she no longer felt much drive for the task. She'd fulfill her obligations with a report to Odin. The King of the Gods could then sort out the mystery of the rune swords and all the rest of it.

But in the end she decided against it. Intuition whispered that Frey might object to her leaving, and then what? It would be wiser to do it later and less conspicuously. Besides, Golden Mane still wasn't resigned to Heimdall's absence, and she couldn't have a lead line on a winged horse in the air. What if the black steed insisted on turning back toward the abandoned city? Most of all, perhaps, what deterred her was the thought of Lady Estrid lying sick unto death in her chambers. It seemed to Uschi that before she left, she owed it to her fallen comrade to make sure the curse had ended in all its aspects and his mother was recovering.

She'd later seen Estrid well again with her own eyes although, given the choice, the grieving woman – ashen and silent except when spoken to, then giving only the briefest of monotone replies – would plainly rather have died herself than have her son perish saving her. Her despondency made Uschi feel shame, as though she should have been able to save her friend. She insisted to herself it wasn't so. Uschi supposed that at this point there truly was nothing to hold her in Vanaheim.

Or rather, nothing but weariness. After all she'd been through, she was exhausted and eager to sleep. The horses were tired too. So why not rest for the remainder of the night and fly out at first light? She lay down on a bench that was a bit longer but otherwise no more comfortable than the one she'd slept on in her own parents' stables. The discomfort didn't keep her from eventually passing into slumber.

She dozed fitfully, and then something shook her. She flailed at the shaker, or perhaps at the last fleeting vestiges of whatever unhappy thing she'd been dreaming, and then discerned it was her mother who'd awakened her. Juliska was only a shadow in the gloom, but to someone who'd known her all her life, her dumpling silhouette with the beehive shape on top was unmistakable.

"Mother," Uschi groaned, "what is it?" She felt a jolt of alarm and sat up quickly. "Are the draugr back?" Was it possible that despite Heimdall giving his life to stop the corpse-things, the horror *wasn't* over?

"It's not that," Juliska answered. "But you should go and go now."

"Why?"

"I'm afraid someone might be coming to hurt you."

"Truly? Why?" Uschi certainly remembered Ysolt's late-night spellcasting in her own parents' stables. It was why she'd slept in proximity to Avalanche ever since. But she'd never proved the sorceress meant her steed any harm, and a great deal had happened in the days after. Despite the disquieting truths she'd discovered about the rune swords and the lying dreams they brought, with the draugr gone, partly through her own efforts, it had seemed less likely that Frey or his followers still intended her stallion any ill and unlikelier still they intended harm to her person. Yet, even so, the urgency in Juliska's voice and manner persuaded Uschi to thrust aside her grief, put her on her feet, and made her reach for the byrnie she'd left hanging over the railing of Avalanche's stall.

Juliska took a long breath as though mustering the strength to do something difficult. "Your father would be furious if I told you this. But... he, Lord Frey, and the other jarls are convinced Odin raised the draugr to humble Vanaheim. The idea came to them in their dreams."

"That much I knew." Uschi pulled her clinking mail shirt over her head.

"I had the same dream sometimes," Juliska continued, "but I wasn't completely convinced it showed the truth. Your father was."

"Because he actually slept with his hand on the hilt of his rune sword. You were close to it, but not touching it. There's the difference." Uschi momentarily considered leaving her own enchanted but tainted weapon behind now that she didn't need it to slay draugr anymore, but the All-Father might want to examine it. She strapped it on along with the Brightblade.

"Is that it?" Juliska said. "Anyway, I'm terrified that Frey and the others won't let you go back to Asgard to report on anything you've seen here. They'll stop you however they can."

Uschi lifted Avalanche's saddle off the stand provided for it. "Why does it matter so much?" she asked. "Wherever they came from, the draugr are no more."

"That's what I would have said as well," Juliska replied, "until this afternoon. But after your father returned, he was jubilant with victory and tired, too. The combination loosened his tongue, and he finally told me *everything* Frey and the jarls have planned."

Uschi felt a pang of apprehension. Tightening the girth of the saddle, she said, "Tell me."

"Before anything else, they had to rid Vanaheim of the walking corpses and the disease. They couldn't allow the curse to threaten all those who aren't warriors longer than necessary. But now that that's done, the fighters will assemble at various points across the land, and when everyone has gathered, mages like Ysolt will transport them all to Asgard. Odin will face a hostile army that suddenly appeared out of nowhere."

Shocked, Uschi grabbed her steed's bridle. "A second war

between Vanir and Aesir," she said, "only this time fought on the All-Father's home ground." She smiled a crooked, humorless smile. "And of course, they couldn't let me go back to Asgard to warn Odin about what's coming. Except that until this moment, I didn't know. But I guess Frey couldn't afford to take any chances."

"I just know that during the ceremony honoring the fallen, he looked at you coldly when your back was turned and whispered to Ysolt and one of his thanes. It made me afraid for you."

"I think you were right to be." Uschi led Avalanche out of his stall, put her foot in the stirrup, and then realized it wouldn't do to leave Golden Mane behind. The winged steed deserved better. Specifically, he deserved the company of his own kind and a return to the Valkyries now that Heimdall was gone. As she moved to bring the black horse out of his stall, she added, "Thank you. It's a pleasant surprise to find out I at least have one parent who cares about me."

"We both care about you!" her mother said. "I don't know if your father even understands that Frey means to take action against you. If he does, surely he imagines you're only to be locked up until the war is over. But I'm not convinced that's all Frey intends. There's a madness brewing in all of them now. I sense it. And even if the others do mean to treat you gently, I know that anything can happen if they come for you and you resist."

Uschi scowled. "Even now, you're still making excuses for Father. Insisting I should think better of him than he deserves."

"I only ever wanted to make peace between the two of you," Juliska said. "And if I leaned more to your father's side, well, you had your mind set on leaving and chasing what you wanted no matter what anyone said. He was going to be left behind with his disappointment. So who was more in need of sympathy?"

Uschi experienced a pang of guilt and pushed it away. There was no time for such feelings at present. "I have to go," she said, swinging herself onto Avalanche's back. "Go back to your apartments, and don't let anyone see you. You don't want anybody suspecting you warned me."

"I'll be careful," Juliska said.

Uschi rode Avalanche out into the courtyard with Golden Mane following behind. No one waited in the dark to interfere with her, not yet, but she still didn't doubt her mother's warning. She urged her mount into a gallop, then upward, and the white stallion lashed his wings and soared into the air. The black one followed. A sentry on the battlements exclaimed in surprise, perhaps because he spied them fleeing in the dark, maybe because he merely heard the rustle of feathery pinions in the air, and then they were clear of the castle.

Now, she thought, it was time to carry word to Asgard. On her command, Avalanche would open the way to the void where Yggdrasil towered, and Golden Mane would surely follow. Nothing stood in the way... except, she realized abruptly, uncertainty about what had truly become of Heimdall. The thought came to her with the shocking unexpectedness of a hammer blow from behind.

She only had Frey's report of Heimdall's fate. However noble he might once have been, the God of the Harvest was currently a magic-crazed deceiver and traitor to the throne. She felt like an imbecile for taking his words at face value.

In all likelihood, she thought, Heimdall had died *somehow*, or why hadn't he, too, come back through the secret door? Still, Uschi had to go and see for herself. To do otherwise would feel like failing her friend all over again. She wheeled Avalanche toward the abandoned city, and as before, Golden Mane flew after her.

EIGHTEEN

Heimdall awoke to darkness. His first muddled thought was that the sight of Mimir had forsaken him and in so doing left him with no vision at all.

Then he noticed how hard it was to breathe. A trace of stale, gritty air was present, but not enough. Inhaling it was a struggle and made him want to cough.

After that came the throb of pains all over his body and the realization of smothering weight atop and all around him. It pressed him down and hindered the movement of his limbs like fetters.

Struggling not to give way to panic, to think and remember, he gradually put together what had happened to him. Frey had cut him, and he'd jumped into the pit in the hope of escaping the duel he manifestly couldn't win. Laevateinn had flown down after him to deliver the killing stroke, and in a final attempt at defense, he'd blown the Gjallarhorn. The blast had brought down earth and stone from the sides of the shaft. A rock had bashed him in the head and rendered him unconscious, and the downpouring had evidently buried him.

That was the reason for his blindness, his difficulty breathing, the heavy mass binding him all around.

His best guess was that his interment had created a shield that kept the Sword of Destiny from reaching him, but it seemed all too likely that the ultimate result had merely been to trade a swift death for a slow one. For an instant, he felt a fear not far short of despair, but then he shoved those emotions down. He couldn't give up, couldn't let it end like this, couldn't allow his duty to Asgard to go undone and Frey – that faithless traitor! – to defeat him. Not entirely sure he even knew which way was up but energized by anger at the god's treachery, clinging to that fury to fuel his resolve, he began the struggle to dig himself out.

At first, he could only shift his limbs minutely. A finger curled or a foot pushed outward an iota. Even that effort made the pains in his body throb and flare worse. His head began to swim, a warning that he was using up what little air was left to him faster than before. But while it might bring death sooner if he continued, it would unquestionably be death to stop, and so he kept trying.

Gradually his struggles made hollows around his arms and legs, and he could dig to greater effect. Or at least he hoped it was to some useful effect, hoped there wasn't such a thickness of dirt and rock covering him that extricating himself was impossible. He felt a tearing in his side, realized his efforts had reopened the wound there, and knew he couldn't allow that to stop him either.

The moment came, however, when there simply wasn't another breath to be had. On the brink of passing out, he scrabbled and then felt emptiness around his hands. Frantic, clutching and clawing, he dragged himself upward, and his head slowly emerged from dirt and rock into air. He gasped repeatedly until the inhalations set off a violent round of coughing, then gasped some more after it ran its course.

When he felt able – although *able* seemed too grand a term for the sore, enfeebled thing he'd become – Heimdall finished pulling himself from the clog of earth and rocks. Then, the gifts of Mimir intact after all, his preternatural sight piercing what otherwise would be impenetrable darkness, he regarded the shaft still rising above him.

Though the pit had seemed deeper when he was falling down it, he now judged that about ten vertical yards of it separated him from the vault above. That, he insisted to himself, wasn't too difficult a climb. It had better not be, because he could hear nothing stirring within the keep, no draugr, but not his erstwhile companions either. No doubt following Frey's commands, they'd left him. That meant he was going to have to escape the shaft by himself.

Searching for protruding rocks for handholds, raking at the walls to make his own when necessary, he tried three times. The first, dirt to which he was clinging broke away and sent him falling back down the shaft. The second and third, his strength simply failed as he strained to haul himself upward, and he fell then, too.

He sought to bestir himself a fourth time, but now, truly, he had nothing left. He slipped into oblivion again.

Nineteen

Her impatience mounting, Uschi pushed and poked as she sought the catch that opened the secret door. She'd nearly decided to abandon her efforts, find a war hammer among the grave goods in the vault, and beat the panel down when she finally found the cunningly concealed piece that slid aside to reveal a handle. A person had to release it just so. She picked up the lantern she'd set on the floor, and, watching out for any evil things that might still be lurking about, stepped into the next chamber.

When she looked around, what she saw heightened her vague suspicions. This crypt was full of genuine treasures even if many lay scattered in the dust. It seemed odd that Frey had hurried his surviving warriors out of the keep and away from the abandoned city without permitting them so much as a glimpse of the riches, let alone the chance to carry away wealth that, surely, was no more than a just reward for their valor. Under normal circumstances, it was what any other warlord would have done.

Of course, she realized they hadn't *been* in normal circumstances. The battle had been uniquely horrific, won at great cost, and perhaps anyone could be forgiven for caring only about escaping into the light of day. Now that she was considering the matter, Uschi supposed Frey could even have had other reasons for acting as he had. Respect for the dead, or fear that someone would inadvertently do something that started the malignant magic working again.

But when she stepped deeper into the room, she spied articles that were not precious grave goods. They were, she was all but certain, the broken pieces of Heimdall's two-handed sword. She was sure Lord Rodric would have wanted them for keepsakes, and it seemed inexcusable that Frey, in his haste to herd everyone away from his secret vault, hadn't provided for their recovery.

Though Uschi was now all but certain the God of the Harvest was hiding something, she had yet to find proof he'd lied about Heimdall's fate. Frey had claimed that with the last of its strength, the ultimate guardian of the curse had obliterated every trace of her friend. She didn't have to venture close to see that the reeking, rune-carved corpse on the bier wasn't him. Heimdall's body was nowhere to be found.

She realized that, once she'd decided to return here, some part of her had embraced the hope that her friend might still be alive. Now that she'd seen otherwise, grief slammed down on her once more.

She heaved a sigh, turned to take her leave, and belatedly realized there was one place that had thus far remained beyond her view. She had no particular reason to think Heimdall was there – Frey, after all, had claimed the king draug burned him away to nothing – but she wouldn't depart without making sure.

She strode to the crumbling edge of the pit and peered downward. The yellow glow of the lantern was just strong enough to reveal the form of a lanky man lying motionless at the bottom. Even while covered in dirt, she could make out the trumpet he wore hanging from his shoulder and the empty scabbard of a two-handed sword strapped across his back.

The hope she'd imagined lost for good came surging back, accompanied by an equally profound fear that she'd simply found her friend's corpse. "Heimdall!" she called. "Heimdall!"

He didn't stir.

He likely was dead, then. Perhaps Frey had embellished his death to indicate a more glorious end. But, she thought stubbornly, she still wasn't *absolutely* sure he was dead. She wouldn't leave this place unless she knew for sure. She had the rope that had provided the lead line for Golden Mane among her gear along with a water bottle and even a satchel of supplies for tending the wounded. Heedless now of the possibility that something might come out of the gloom to attack her, she dashed back aboveground, retrieved the items she wanted, and ran back into the keep. The black stallion neighed after her as though urging her on.

Back in the secret crypt, she could see nothing that looked solid enough to anchor the line except the bier where the dead lord lay. With the runes defacing it and the bloated corpse atop it, it seemed an uncanny thing, but she didn't let that deter her. She looped the rope around the base of the pedestal, tied it off, and dropped the rest of it down the shaft. Leaving her shield on the floor, she then descended hand over hand.

When she reached Heimdall, she saw that the majority of the darkness covering him was dirt, as if he'd been buried alive and dug his way out. But there was plenty of blood, too. It had flowed from a gash in his side.

Moving awkwardly in the narrow space at the bottom of the shaft, she kneeled beside him and held her fingers under his nostrils. Breath was rapidly passing in and out. She touched the artery in the side of his neck and found a quick thready pulse.

She rejoiced to find him still alive but was also grimly aware that without help he might not stay that way much longer. His respiration and heartbeat told her he'd lost a lot of blood. She pushed aside all she was feeling to consider how best to aid him.

It would be difficult to tend to him here in the cramped confines at the bottom of the pit. She tied the rope under his arms, climbed the line back up to the floor of the vault herself, and then, exerting the strength of an Asgardian warrior, hauled him up. She winced every time he bumped against the wall of the pit, but that was unavoidable.

So was the roughness when she laid him on the floor and dragged off his mail shirt to better inspect his wound. The cut was indeed seeping fresh blood, maybe because of the jostling coming up out of the shaft. Using the contents of her satchel, reciting an invocation of Eir, Goddess of Healing, that Valkyries learned as part of their training, she cleaned the cut, sutured it with a needle and silk thread, and smeared it with an ointment that smelled of the garlic and wine that were two of its main components. Though still unconscious, Heimdall jerked as the salty mixture came into contact with raw flesh. Uschi then wrapped bandages around his torso.

With that much accomplished, she held her leather water bottle to his lips and poured a trickle of liquid into his mouth. He reflexively swallowed and then retched out the rest to run down his chin and wash a bit of the dirt out of his beard. Afterward, his eyelids fluttered open. "Uschi?" he croaked.

"Yes," she told him, her own gentle tone reflecting little of the fierce surge of happiness that came from hearing him speak. "I'm here. It's all right now. I want you to drink some more. Slowly." He did, and after that she brought out an ivory vial of an elixir. "Now, have this. With luck, it'll give you sufficient strength for long enough to walk out of here."

Unfortunately, as it turned out, the stimulant didn't do as much as she'd hoped. Once she helped him to his feet, he stayed there and even walked after a fashion, but only because she looped his arm around her shoulders and supported him as he shuffled along. She didn't truly mind the burden, though. She would have carried him from one end of Vanaheim to the other if that was what it took to see him safe.

At one point, he groaned, "My mother?"

"She's well," Uschi said, "thanks to you. Everything is well."

With a Vanir rebellion still brewing, the latter statement was a considerable exaggeration, but Heimdall didn't need to fret about the problem in his current condition. With a twinge of sardonic humor, Uschi reflected that one of the satisfactions of having him well again would be telling him that she'd been right: the rune swords were a matter of grave concern, and they shouldn't have deferred addressing the issue, despite their value against the draugr.

They made it out of the keep and back into the sunlit plaza.

The two winged horses trotted forward to greet them, and Golden Mane nickered in delight to be reunited with his rider. The black stallion nuzzled Heimdall and would have knocked the wounded man over if Uschi hadn't been supporting him.

Eyelids drooping, mumbling like a person talking in his sleep, Heimdall half-extended his free arm in the black steed's general direction. "Help me onto his back."

"That's not what's going to happen," Uschi told him. In her haste to leave Lord Rodric's castle, she hadn't saddled Golden Mane. Even if she had, she wouldn't have trusted Heimdall not to slip off the horse and fall to his death, not in his weak and groggy state. "Avalanche will carry double." And she'd tie her friend's body to her own.

Once they were in flight, with Golden Mane following them across the sky, Heimdall stopped responding to her comments. His weight shifted with every turn and dip as if he had no more control than a sack of meal. Which, if he'd passed out again, was the case. Happily, expert rider that she was, Uschi had little trouble keeping her seat as the man tied behind flopped back and forth.

Even so, she worried that the flight couldn't be good for Heimdall. It might even start his wound bleeding again, and she had no idea how a person in such a weakened condition would fare if taken across the cosmic void where Yggdrasil stood. She needed to set down as soon as possible right here in Vanaheim, somewhere there was plenty of food and water and a bed, somewhere she could resume giving her comrade care as expeditiously as possible. The question was, where could she find such a refuge in a world where thanes of Asgard had become the enemy?

Well, she thought, word of Odin's alleged perfidy and Frey's call to arms likely hadn't reached *every* set of ears in Vanaheim. The god would have made certain it came to every jarl's stronghold, everywhere warriors congregated, but the same yearning to live close to Nature that had long ago prompted the Vanir to abandon their cities today inclined some karls to dwell far from the fortress of any lord. She guided Avalanche over a forest until she spied a small, cleared field of barley, a communal garden, and three huts with thatched roofs in the midst of the spruce and pine trees.

She set Avalanche down near the huts, and Golden Mane thumped down behind her. She hadn't drawn either of her swords lest the inhabitants think she'd arrived with hostile intent, but she was poised to do so in an instant if she'd guessed wrong.

A woman with a baby in her arms emerged from the huts. Several adults and a dozen children came running. Everyone was staring and exclaiming in wonder at the fabled winged steeds of the Valkyries, magical animals that, until this moment, they'd likely never seen. In no one's face or manner did Uschi detect hostility or suspicion.

Reassured, she said, "Please, my friend needs help and needs it quickly!"

Twenty

Heimdall rose from the cot one of the karl families had provided for him, and, careful not to wake those still sleeping around him, crept out of the crowded hut into the first light of dawn. As he stretched, the cool morning air was bracing on his skin.

Bare-chested and barefoot, he then hiked to the murmuring nearby stream from which, he'd learned, the forest village drew its water. He stripped off his trousers, removed his bandages, and waded in. The stream was colder than the air, but he ducked down into it and gave himself a thorough scrubbing anyway. This wasn't his first bath since emerging from the ruined keep three days ago, and it was unlikely any of the dirt from his accidental burial still clung to him, but he still experienced a need to make sure.

Once he felt clean, he took a good long look at the parts of his body he could see. Yellow bruises covered his limbs, but they were fading, and any soreness or swelling had gone away. The gash Frey had cut in his side was well on its way to becoming merely a scar. He supposed he was lucky it was the rune sword and not Laevateinn, the weapon that could reportedly slash through anything, that had wounded him. His byrnie hadn't stopped the rune blade, but maybe it had prevented it from cutting deep.

He knew he was lucky as well to be an Asgardian. His people recovered quickly from wounds and injuries. If he'd been, say, a mortal of Midgard, his recuperation would have taken considerably longer.

Or at least he believed he'd recuperated. He felt like it, but it occurred to him that the only way to be sure was to test his capabilities.

He stood knee deep and motionless in the chilly water until an unwary brown trout swam within reach. He snatched, and his fingers closed around the speckled fish. He smiled as he let the squirming creature go. There was nothing wrong with his quickness or coordination.

He climbed out of the stream, pulled his trousers back on, and found a length of fallen tree branch. It was too light but would otherwise do for a practice sword. He broke away the secondary branches that had grown out of it, assumed a fighting stance, and launched himself into one of the pivoting, striking combat exercises his father had taught him when he was small.

After he'd completed several, he took stock. His wound hadn't bled, nor was he breathing hard. His stamina, too, was as it should be. He smiled.

Satisfied, he returned to the tiny village to find everyone else having a breakfast of porridge and barley buns. He pulled on his tunic and boots and ate his share, and afterward he and Uschi walked out to the pasture to see how their steeds were faring.

"You seem to be in good humor," she said.

"Being hale again will do that." After a moment's hesitation, he added, "Earlier, I was reflecting on how lucky I am, and the greatest piece of luck of all was that you came back for me. Thank you."

Uschi grunted. "We're comrades. You would have done the same for me."

"I hope so. But since I didn't take your concerns seriously enough, maybe I would have believed Frey when he said the king draug had burned you away to nothing. Maybe I *wouldn't* have checked for myself. In this situation, you were shrewder than I was."

"Remember that," the Valkyrie said as they neared the meadow where the two winged steeds were grazing like ordinary horses, coats and plumage gleaming in the morning sun. "You may be clever, you may have the eyes of Mimir, but you don't always know better or see clearer than your comrades." Her lips quirked upward. "Especially when the comrade is me."

"Believe me, I'll bear it in mind as we decide what to do next."

Uschi cocked her head. "That's obvious, surely. It's our duty to carry word of a rebellion to Odin. I should have done so already, but I wasn't going to leave until I knew you'd be all right."

"You realize, the rebels include our parents and pretty much everyone we knew growing up."

"Even so."

"You realize, too, because you've seen it firsthand, that while the All-Father is generally a good king, he has a harsh way with challenges to his authority. I'm afraid of what he'll do when he receives the news."

"It's our task to bring the warning. We don't get to decide how the king responds to it."

"Maybe," Heimdall said, "it's our duty to stop the insurrection before it starts and keep anybody from suffering ugly consequences."

"I don't see that. It seems to me that if we tried what I think you're suggesting, we'd be making a decision that's well above our station."

Heimdall grimaced. "I know. We would. But do you know the story of Aesheim?"

"No. I've never even heard of Aesheim."

"I'm not surprised. It all happened long before either of us was born, and it's not a story the skalds ever tell in the halls of Asgard. But if you read certain old books and ask the questions of certain scholars, you can stumble across the basics."

"As I gather you have. Tell me, then," Uschi said.

"After Bor died, Cul the Serpent proclaimed himself King of Asgard. Odin led a rebellion against him and ultimately overthrew him."

"That much I do know. But I've never heard of this place, Aesheim."

"It was more than a place. It was an entire Realm perched on a branch of Yggdrasil, and Cul had ensorcelled its countless inhabitants to be loyal to him. To feel secure on his throne and remove any memory of Cul, Odin slaughtered every single one of them. He destroyed Aesheim itself, and created another world in its place, the one we know as Midgard today."

"But that was when he was young. He wouldn't be so merciless today."

"Are you sure? To this day, he's quick to anger and to punish. I've heard him say so himself."

"He wouldn't treat the Vanir so if he understood they weren't in their right minds."

"He knew the people of Aesheim weren't in their right minds either, and it didn't stop him from exterminating them. Even if you're right that Odin would be merciful in victory, it could still be a long, hard road getting there. The All-Father would field an army of his own against the Vanir. There's no other way to deal with a rebellion. Then people would die on the battlefield. People you and I care about."

Uschi scowled. "Curse you. Mere moments ago, you said you wouldn't go thinking you know better than everyone else, me in particular, and here you go again."

"I'm aware of the irony," Heimdall said. He paused, feeling guilt swell within him once more. "Truly, I'm sorry for pushing you to visit your family. I'm sorry for all the rest of it."

The Valkyrie's scowl softened. "Well, you weren't right that we needed to deal with the draugr before all else, but you weren't entirely wrong, either. And I understand how you couldn't think of anything else once your mother fell ill. In the present situation, though… if you don't want to warn Odin a rebellion is coming, couldn't one of us at least warn somebody else? Frigga, perhaps, or Thor?"

"Is there anyone you trust not to pass the word to the All-Father prematurely? Just a moment ago, you were telling me you were convinced it was *our* duty to warn him right away."

"Well… maybe not."

"Besides, it's likely to take both of us to unravel this problem, restore sanity to Frey and the others, and stop a rebellion from happening in the first place. I'd certainly rather attempt it with you beside me."

"Let's say we did bend our oaths of service to the breaking point to try to do that. How would we go about it? How would we mend a quarrel between two gods?"

Heimdall sighed. "I don't know yet."

"There you are then!" Uschi took a deep breath. "Look, maybe the All-Father regrets what he did to Aesheim. Maybe, this time around, he'll show mercy to folk who are only fighting him because they're under a spell. I do have one of the rune swords to show him as proof."

Heimdall felt a surge of excitement. "That could be it! The rune swords! If we could stop the evil magic coming through them that's filling the jarls with fear and giving them nightmares about Odin, surely then they'd come to their senses, just as the sick got well when we broke the curse of the draugr."

"And how would we do that?" Uschi asked.

"What do we know about the rune blades?"

"They're good for slaying draugr. Other than that, nothing." Uschi's mouth thinned in thought. "Except… I saw the box Lord Frey was carrying them around in to give them out to jarls. It was made of some gray metal with a black hammer on the lid."

Heimdall grinned. "I know that emblem from my reading. The Blackhammer clan of Nidavellir are some of the best weapon smiths in all the Nine Worlds. Frey must be getting the swords from them. And maybe if we find out how and why the dwarves are forging them as they do, we'll know how to break the curse they carry!"

Uschi frowned as if considering the idea against her better judgment. "Well," she said slowly, "Avalanche and Golden Mane can certainly carry us to Nidavellir. But do you truly think we can get to the bottom of it all in time to stop Lord Frey from invading Asgard? Remember, now that I've fled your parents' castle, he has to assume I've already carried word to Odin. He and the jarls must be rushing to prepare for invasion. Ymir's beard, for all we know, they're in Asgard even now!"

"I don't think so," Heimdall said. "Remember that all across Vanaheim, warriors have just finished contending with the draugr. After such a struggle, folk need time to regroup. The leaders will need time to muster their fighters anew. Consider, too, that Frey surely wants his forces to arrive all at once, as one mighty army, not piecemeal. That will require messages traveling back and forth to ensure that everyone is ready, and all the warlocks and witches cast their spells of world-crossing at the same time. For certain, we're in a race, but there's reason to hope we can win it."

"If we don't, we'll be responsible for the rebels taking Asgard by surprise."

"But if we do, we'll prevent a great deal of suffering, perhaps more than we can even comprehend. Please, Uschi. I know I haven't been all that shrewd of late, but I beg you to trust me. The futures of our families and of two worlds are at stake. Imagine Asgard and Vanaheim laid waste, the two peoples hating each other for centuries to come. Do you think the Jotuns will ignore the opportunities that presents?"

Uschi pondered for several moments. Finally, she growled, "Very well. We can go to Nidavellir. But I'll fly back to Asgard and Odin if I think your search is taking too long or isn't getting anywhere."

"Thank you!"

"I suppose you can manage riding Golden Mane bareback even when we're crossing the void?"

"I won't have to. I know where to reequip. You should probably do the same. We want to present a splendid appearance."

Twenty-One

Searching among the grave goods in the hidden tomb, Heimdall had found new tack for Golden Mane and figured out how to alter it to fit a winged horse. His own new trappings – mail shirt, helmet, and two-handed sword – flashing in the sunlight, he heaved the saddle onto his stallion's back.

Looking on, Uschi thought her friend looked ridiculous. In her view, there might be a place for all that precious metal and ornamentation, but if so, it was for an honor guard standing watch in a palace, not for warriors in the field. Which somehow hadn't prevented Heimdall from persuading her to equip herself in similar style. Of the gear she'd carried back to the abandoned city, only the Brightblade and the rune sword remained.

She was, she thought, letting Heimdall talk her into way too much of late. Her duty to report to Odin had been clear before her friend tangled her up in his arguments. It was *still* clear. Except…

As a veteran thane of the Valkyries, she had indeed had ample opportunity to see how the All-Father reacted to those who defied his authority. The God of Wisdom he might be, but that didn't stop him from responding precipitously, wrathfully, and even vengefully. Maybe it was because he'd ascended to his present eminence through force of arms, killing his grandfather Ymir and defeating both Cul and Frey. The bloody climb to the throne of two worlds had left him aware that, as he'd overthrown others, somebody could one day overthrow him. And to what she'd observed firsthand, she must now add the grim tale of the destruction of Aesheim and its inhabitants.

So, yes. She *could* imagine Odin summarily stripping the jarls of Vanaheim of their wealth and lands, imprisoning them, or even sending them to the headsman's block. She could imagine such things happening to her own parents, and though she tried to convince herself they'd forfeited any claim on her concern, it was an ugly prospect, nonetheless. She could imagine the All-Father installing Aesir lords to govern the Vanir or demanding ruinous tribute, poisoning relations between Vanaheim and Asgard forever after.

Thus, she could see why Heimdall believed the two of them should stop the rebellion now, by themselves, before Odin ever learned of it or it reached the point of open war. She let go of the thought that the rune blades had poisoned his thinking – now, she saw Heimdall as a young man desperate to defend his homeland and torn between allegiances.

So, though it made her feel angry at her companion, herself, and the whole wretched situation, she supposed she truly was going along.

"Ready?" Heimdall asked.

"Yes," she said. They mounted their steeds, and the winged

horses carried them up from the ruined plaza and over the forest into the sky.

Golden Mane's innate magic opened a circle flickering with soft rainbow colors in front of him, which closed back in on itself and vanished a moment after horse and rider passed through. Heimdall had gone into the void between worlds, and it was time for Uschi to do likewise. "Yggdrasil!" she called.

Avalanche hurtled forward, but no portal opened in front of him. Instead, for a moment, Uschi felt a sort of hot jaggedness at play in the air around them. It didn't blister or cut her, but the sensation was unpleasant. It was also shockingly unexpected. Avalanche gave a high-pitched neigh, distressed by the momentary discomfort and his inability to do as his rider had commanded.

She stubbornly tried to enter the void twice more, and, still game, Avalanche did his best. To her dismay, he still couldn't open the way, however, and then her friend and his stallion reappeared before her. "What's wrong?" Heimdall called.

"Avalanche can't cross over," she replied.

Heimdall frowned. "Can you show me?" She did, and the results were the same as before. Afterward, he said, "With the sight of Mimir, I can see an enchantment dancing around you and Avalanche when you try that."

Uschi spat in disgust. "Ysolt. I knew she was doing something bad to Avalanche."

"Frey didn't want to have you killed until he could do the same to me. Word of your death might have alerted me to his treachery, so he ordered the witch to make sure that, whatever you learned, you couldn't carry the information back to Odin."

"I see all that," Uschi said impatiently. "Can *you* see how to break the spell?"

"Unfortunately, no. I can often see magic going about its work, but that doesn't make me a sorcerer. You'll have to leave Avalanche behind. We'll ride double as we did before."

Uschi scowled at what she felt to the core of her being was an unacceptable suggestion. "Not a chance. A Valkyrie doesn't abandon her steed."

"I don't see an alternative unless you're telling me to go on to Nidavellir alone."

That was equally unacceptable. She strained to think of a third alternative, and to her relief, a possibility occurred to her. "Ysolt didn't finish her spellcasting. I interrupted her. Maybe that means Avalanche *can* reach the void if we're following close behind you when you cross over."

Heimdall nodded. "It's worth a try."

He sent his black steed winging across the sky. She urged her white one after him. He glanced back, making sure she and Avalanche were positioned as they should be, raised his arm for a moment, and then swept it down. She took from that that he was giving the command and she should do the same. "Yggdrasil!" she cried.

The heat and the scratching sensation assailed her. Meanwhile, another scintillating round opened in the air in front of Golden Mane. Steed and rider passed through, and thankfully, the circle didn't instantly disappear. It did, however, contract.

Uschi pictured it closing on her and Avalanche when they were only partway through, shearing them in half, leaving the hind portions to plummet to the earth of Vanaheim and the rest to tumble through cosmic emptiness forever. But she couldn't let her imaginings deter her. She had to trust her idea and trust, too, in Avalanche's swiftness. She exhorted the white stallion to put on a final burst of speed.

Avalanche's outspread wings came within a finger's width of touching the edge of the shrinking circle as they plunged through into the space where the World Tree loomed. The Nine Realms were suspended on its branches with stars and nebulae growing behind. The sensation enveloping her changed from heat and sharpness to an impression of brittleness, which in another instant broke into tiny pieces and fell away.

She felt a surge of elation, and of pride and affection for her mount. If Avalanche had been even a fraction slower, or if fear had made him balk even briefly, they wouldn't have made it. Fortunately, he was, she felt certain, as fast and brave as any Valkyrie steed that ever was.

Heimdall had wheeled Golden Mane to watch the spot where she'd emerge if, in fact, she did. "You're all right?" he called.

She smiled. "Better than all right. I think that crossing over in spite of the enchantment tore it away." She remembered the urgency of their errand, her uncertainty that it was even a good idea, and her exhilaration curdled. "If we're doing this, let's get on with it."

As they approached Yggdrasil, they also flew downward. They'd entered this place near the top of the colossal ash tree, where Vanaheim, Asgard, and Alfheim perched. Nidavellir was down among the roots. As the horses descended, a glowing silvery path like moonlight appeared beneath their hooves, to guide them and somehow compress distance in the way Frey's magic could shorten journeys in more mundane spaces.

Regarding the worlds on their separate branches, Uschi reflected it was fortunate that the conjunction that, in ordinary reality, periodically made the Realms lie adjacent to one another in normal space wasn't currently in progress. Had it been, Frey's army could have invaded Asgard more quickly and easily. She reflected sourly that that was about the only piece of luck she and Heimdall had enjoyed so far.

The vastness of the void ate at the periphery of her mind. It would have eroded an ordinary person's intellect and personality to nothing, but thanks to the training and rituals of the Valkyries, she withstood it without difficulty and knew the gifts of Mimir enabled Heimdall to do the same.

Soon, they neared Nidavellir. Heimdall and Golden Mane vanished as they crossed over. Avalanche accomplished the same without difficulty, appearing above the realm of the dwarves an instant later. It was only what she'd expected, but it was still a relief to have confirmation that her steed had shed the effect of Ysolt's spellcasting for good.

After Uschi's sojourn among the verdant natural glories of Vanaheim, Nidavellir made an immediate contrast. It wasn't sinister or menacing but nonetheless appeared a more somber and less welcoming place. The sunlight seemed dimmer, the sky a deeper blue, and the forests comprised of darker greens. The terrain was more mountainous with foliage sparse or nonexistent among the higher reaches.

Nidavellir differed from Vanaheim, too, in its lack of visible signs of habitation. The Vanir chose to live close to nature, but a person didn't have to fly too high or far to spy a jarl's stronghold standing here and there, a road connecting one settlement to another, or boats on the rivers and seas. There was none of that in Nidavellir because, as Uschi understood it, dwarves lived almost entirely underground, traveling on subterranean highways and even growing crops and catching fish in their caverns. Only their loggers, hunters, and trappers came out into the light of day in search of timber or deer, boar, and other game unavailable below.

To Uschi, the lack of discernible towns and such meant a frustrating lack of landmarks. She called to Heimdall, "Do you know the way to the Blackhammers?"

"I think so," he replied. "I remember a map I saw in a book."

She smiled a grudging smile. "Of course you do."

They flew on for perhaps three daymarks. Then he led her down to a forest clearing with a mountain looming beyond the edge of the woods. None of the blight that had affected Vanaheim was evident, and she knew the draugr plight did not reach here.

Swinging himself off Golden Mane, Heimdall said, "We'll have to walk from here."

"Why?" she asked. Even though Avalanche seemed fine now, she felt reluctant to part company with him so soon after discovering the effect of Ysolt's meddling. Besides, a Valkyrie was a rider, not a foot soldier.

"We don't know to what degree the Blackhammers are complicit in Frey's conspiracy," Heimdall replied. "If they realize he intends a revolt against Odin and support it, we can't be seen on steeds that proclaim our allegiance to Asgard." He began to unsaddle Golden Mane and addressed the winged horses as he did so. "We need the two of you to stay out of sight till we get back."

Golden Mane sighed as though bored that his rider had stated the obvious.

The hike up the mountainside wasn't as difficult as Uschi had thought it might be. Perhaps, using the gifts of Mimir, Heimdall found the path the hunters presumably used, and not long thereafter, the Asgardians came to tall gates of steel standing open in the rock, each leaf emblazoned with a black hammer. A dwarf sentry stationed at the entryway bore the same device on the oval brooch securing his rust-colored cloak.

Like all his kind, the bearded dwarf spearman was only about half as tall as the average Asgardian, but his burly form hinted at his strength. By all accounts, his people's warriors were deadly fighters. He squinted in surprise at the new arrivals, and Uschi waited tensely to see if surprise would turn to suspicion or hostility.

To her relief, it didn't. Heimdall proceeded onward as if it had never occurred to him that they might receive anything other than a cordial welcome. She did her best to copy his manner. She was, after all, a warrior by nature and training, not a player or a spy.

"Hello," Heimdall said. "We're emissaries from Lord Frey here to see the lord of Clan Blackhammer."

Heimdall was, Uschi knew, hoping the ornate gear looted from the hidden vault would help them pass for a pair of the rebel god's resplendently equipped elite guards, and maybe it did. The sentry rang a bell, the note echoing away down the passage on the other side of the gates, and in due course, a thane arrived. Once he'd heard Heimdall's lie, he conducted the newcomers down the tunnel. Still keenly aware that if this impersonation went wrong, understanding her surroundings could mean the difference between life and death, Uschi studied the unfamiliar sights.

At intervals, ruddy crystals glowed from iron sconces in the granite walls. The illumination was dimmer than she would have liked but sufficed to reveal defenses equal to those of the gates of the city of Asgard. Multiple portcullises were poised to drop, and murder holes gaped to rain down death from the high arched ceiling. If this errand went awry, she doubted she and Heimdall would be able to flee the same way they were coming in.

The passage debouched in a huge open space with ranks of habitations climbing up the walls, pathways rising and twisting among them, and smaller tunnels running off into darkness. Once, she thought, this place must have been a natural cavern. It was so big, it was hard to imagine it being otherwise. But through the ages, the Blackhammers had so shaped it to suit their purposes and carved the stone with so much ornamentation that only its size and the stalactites still hanging from the lofty unworked ceiling spoke of the untamed vault it had once been.

Dwarves, she knew, had a somewhat paradoxical reputation, dour but rowdy too, and she might have expected the latter humor to predominate in their own city. But somewhat to her surprise, people were going about their business with little conversation. She could hear no laughter or music anywhere. A number of folk wore dark clothing with no ornaments about their persons, and she wondered if it was a sign of mourning.

Their guide ultimately led them to the grandest of the structures cut from the living rock, a citadel of sorts with its own fortifications and sentries walking the battlements. He then bade them wait in an antechamber. The wait was protracted enough to make her nervously wonder if someone had penetrated their masquerade and things were about to go badly wrong. Finally, though, he returned and ushered them into an audience hall. Though not as large as Odin's, the chamber was impressive enough, decorated as it was with fine examples of dwarven weapon- and armor-making and enormous glittering gemstones miners had presumably found during their excavations.

The dwarf thane announced them with the false names they'd supplied, and Maarav, the lord of the clan, greeted them with a hearty welcoming tone that didn't match the speculative look in his narrowed eyes. Seated on the high-backed chair before them, he had massive shoulders and shaggy black brows that almost seemed to be trying to compensate for the thinning hair on his pate. Various advisors hovered to do his bidding, some close at hand, others farther back in the corners and shadows.

Once everyone was done exchanging pleasantries, Heimdall said, "My lord, our own master Frey sent us to ask when more rune swords will be ready. He's anxious to receive them. They've served the Vanir well so far, and we come bearing payment to encourage haste." He opened his belt pouch and brought out a handful of black polished stones that glittered even in the dim reddish light.

In addition to other treasure, the hidden vault had yielded a cache of high-quality jet. As the precious substance was generally found near saltwater, Heimdall hoped it was one gemstone the mountain-dwelling Blackhammers couldn't extract from their own mines. To Uschi's dismay, Maarav failed to react with the enthusiasm the two Asgardians had anticipated. Rather, he winced and said, "Truly? Another batch?"

Heimdall appeared as nonplussed as Uschi felt but masked the reaction quickly. "Yes, my lord. If you please."

One of the counselors approached Maarav's seat and whispered in his ear. Uschi couldn't hear what he said but was confident Heimdall did. She felt impatient for the moment when they were alone, and he could share it with her. Assuming, of course, that they emerged from this audience alive.

After the advisor finished whispering, the Blackhammer lord looked resigned and said, "You'll have the swords as soon as we can make them. Go back to Vanaheim and tell Frey they're coming."

"My lord," Uschi said, "our instructions are to accompany the new swords back to Vanaheim. Anyway, we're not mages. We can't transport ourselves back and don't want to put your warlocks to extra bother. May we not, then, remain as your guests until the blades are ready?"

Maarav's glum expression darkened, but he answered as the customs of hospitality bade him. "Of course. Eluf there will find quarters for you. After you refresh yourselves, there'll be a feast in your honor."

Their quarters proved to be a suite of rooms with furniture covered in yellowish dappled leather – the hide, Uschi suspected, of some subterranean beast. As soon as Eluf closed the door and she heard his receding footsteps, she asked Heimdall, "What did the counselor whisper?"

"'We have no choice, my lord.' The dwarves don't want to forge the rune swords. They feel coerced."

Puzzled, Uschi asked, "By Frey? I know he's a god, but what could he do to them? Threaten an invasion? Is he mad enough to plan attacks on Nidavellir and Asgard both?" She flipped an impatient hand to brush such speculations away. "Never mind. That doesn't make sense anyway. Not if we're assuming he didn't go mad until he *got* a rune sword."

Heimdall nodded. "Exactly. Our task is to find out what the Blackhammers are really afraid of."

"And I suppose I know how we do that. By poking our noses into places we aren't supposed to go and asking questions no one wants to answer."

Twenty-Two

It had come as something of a pleasant surprise to Heimdall that, even cut off from the sun and moon, the Blackhammers nonetheless lived in accordance with the familiar rhythm of day and night, awake during the former and seeking their beds during the latter. "Maybe," he murmured to Uschi as they strolled out of the citadel gate, supposedly simply to see the sights of the city, "in a time so long ago no one remembers, dwarves lived aboveground. Or maybe observing day and night makes the city run more smoothly."

"And maybe," Uschi replied, her handsome new mail, helmet, and shield left behind in their quarters as one would expect of peaceful visitors but the rune sword on her back and the Brightblade swinging at her hip, "none of that has anything to do with our mission."

Heimdall realized the reproof was justified. "You're right. I'll keep my mind on what's important." Suiting actions to words, using the sight of Mimir to pierce the ambient gloom, he scrutinized the city at large.

It seemed much the same this morning as it had when he and Uschi first entered late the previous afternoon. There was still a feeling of head-hanging, trudging despondency to the place, and he told her as much.

"Do you think the mood has something to do with the rune swords?" she asked.

"Maybe," he said. "Given that Maarav didn't truly want to make more, even for a substantial payment, it seems as if it could be true. We should keep the possibility in mind as we look around."

"Yes. Let's do that. But first, let's explore down those side passages." She gestured to tunnels opening in the walls of the primary vault.

"I think we might learn more wandering around in the city proper."

"Maybe. But if there's a second way out of the mountain, it would be nice to know what it is in case Maarav or one of his people see through our masquerade."

Heimdall smiled. "When you put it that way, I see the wisdom."

The first tunnel led to more homes and workshops, a spillover from the greater metropolis just as the city of Asgard had grown beyond its walls. The second, however, echoed with clinking tools and the scrape and thud of displaced rock. Following the sound, Heimdall and Uschi came to a spot where a work crew was swinging pickaxes and digging with shovels to clear the stones that had fallen from the ceiling to clog the passage. They loaded the rubble in carts to be hauled away.

One of the dwarves spotted Heimdall and Uschi taking in

the scene and tramped over to them. "You shouldn't be here," he said. "It isn't safe if you don't know what you're doing."

"Sorry," Heimdall said. "Of course, we'll turn around. But what happened?"

"The mine caved in," the Blackhammer said. "Now go."

"That's terrible," Heimdall said. "Was anyone hurt?"

For a moment, the dwarf looked as though he meant to retort that whatever had happened was no business of the Asgardians. Then, however, something – the travelers' sympathetic air, perhaps, or simply the tardy realization that it wouldn't do to be rude to Lord Maarav's guests – softened his gruffness. "Nineteen, here," he said.

"We are truly sorry," Uschi said. "How did it happen?"

The dwarf hesitated before replying, "No one knows. Sadly, cave-ins do happen from time to time." Heimdall had the feeling there was something the miner might have said but decided it was more prudent to keep it to himself. "Now, I really do need for you two to turn around."

On the hike back, Uschi said, "I might not be surprised if the mine of some other folk caved in. But dwarf miners are supposed to be experts."

Heimdall nodded. "Yes, they are. And did you notice the dwarf said, 'Nineteen, *here*'?"

"Implying there have been other cave-ins. We both had the impression the whole city was grieving. If scores of miners have died, everybody has lost someone close to grieve *for*."

"And everyone has cause to worry about what awful thing will happen next," Heimdall grunted. "But we're speculating. We need to verify that there have been more collapses."

As it turned out, that wasn't difficult to establish. As they explored the maze of branching passages leading away from the central city, they eventually came upon the site of another mining calamity, and then another after that.

"Well," Heimdall said, "sadly, here's our proof."

"But is there truly a link to our own errand?" Uschi asked. "These events are tragic, but what have they got to do with the rune swords?"

Fingering his beard, Heimdall considered the question. "What if," he said slowly, "the Blackhammers now believe there's only one way to prevent further collapses, and that's to forge more swords even though they'd rather not? Why else would they feel pressured to forge so many swords for Frey?"

"Why would they believe that?"

"For expert miners, an increase in sudden cave-ins might smack of bad luck like the evil eye. Then Frey's warriors arrive, asking for many blades. The way they acquiesced to forging the swords indicates they're doing it against their will – probably what they consider protecting the greater good." Heimdall sighed. "Truly, I don't know. I'm merely guessing. I think we'll have to snoop around in the city to find out. Let's head back."

Uschi frowned. "We haven't found a second way out of the mountain yet."

"You're right. We should still do that." Heimdall paused. It all suddenly seemed overwhelming.

"Yet we are in a race to prevent a war, after all," Uschi said, and her tone softened as if she sensed his feelings. "Perhaps backup plans can wait."

"And I hope that if we solve the Blackhammers' problem for them, we won't need to flee for our lives," Heimdall said, latching onto her giving him an out.

The Valkyrie smiled a crooked smile. "So now we're solving somebody else's problem? Asgard and Vanaheim aren't enough for you?"

"Not if it's all connected. We end the threat to the dwarves, and Maarav will order his mages or sword smiths to end the evil influence the rune blades cast. He'll want to. You could tell he's ashamed of what they're doing. And with the spell broken, Frey and the Vanir jarls will come to their senses."

"Well," Uschi said in a somewhat grudging tone, "it's one way to come at the problem. But we'd have to know a good deal more than we know – or think we know – so far."

"With luck, the answers are waiting in the city."

Twenty-Three

Once they reemerged into the huge cavern containing the Blackhammer city, Uschi looked at Heimdall. "All right," she said, "do what you do."

He gave her an inquiring look. "Meaning?"

"You can hear every word everybody in the city is saying, right?" If he used his unique abilities, the investigation they needed to undertake might not prove so daunting after all.

"In a way," Heimdall said. "Lately, I keep coming up against the limits of Mimir's gifts, and here's another. I need to narrow my focus to make sense of one particular conversation out of so many. Someone would have to be saying something this very moment that's relevant to our search. He or she would have to be saying it in a way that snagged my attention. I am going to use my hearing and sight as best I can, but basically, it would take an extraordinary amount of luck for me to open my ears and then the information we need to instantly reveal itself."

Uschi sighed in disappointment. "So, we have to do it the

hard way. We poke around and ask uncomfortable questions like I said." She told herself they could do it in time to prevent the coming war. They'd accomplished equally unlikely feats in their time even if, at this moment, it didn't feel like it. "That being the case, we can cover more ground if we split up."

Her companion frowned. "Is that wise?"

"Here in the heart of the city where we're Lord Maarav's honored guests? It should be safe enough. I'll see you back at the citadel in time for supper." With that, she set off on her own, down a street where some dwarves eyed her curiously but then became lost in their own glumness to take much of an interest.

For all her sense of urgency and resolute intentions to uncover whatever was going on, she soon felt a bit flummoxed in this unfamiliar environment. But in her experience performing tasks for Odin and Frigga across Asgard and elsewhere, there was one sort of place where tongues might loosen and confide rumors and gossip an outsider wasn't supposed to hear. She walked on until she came to a tavern, identifiable by the carving of merry roistering dwarves quaffing flagons of ale on the wall outside. She ducked to pass through a doorway that was too low for her and entered.

The ceiling inside was a little higher, but not so high that she could straighten up. Having long ago developed the habit of paying attention to such things, she noted that stooping would put her at a disadvantage if she had to fight.

Not that she thought a fight was likely. Murals executed more crudely but similar in subject matter to the carving outside decorated the interior, and in Uschi's experience, whether the drinkers were dwarves or Asgardian warriors, alcohol and boisterous celebration often led to a brawl or two. But this tavern was mostly empty.

She cast about for someone from whom, if she was subtle about it, she might be able to extract information. One fellow with a tawny triple-braided beard was sitting by himself. Maybe he'd welcome company if she approached him in a way that didn't rouse his suspicions. The fact that he appeared to be a miner made him an even more appealing prospect. He was as grubby as she might have expected after finishing a shift in the mines, and he had a pick sitting on the bar.

She sat down a couple of stools away from him, close enough for conversation but not so near as to make it obvious she was particularly interested in speaking with him. Trying to look as if it had only occurred to her to address him, she turned and asked, "What's good?"

The miner snorted, expressing the superiority that old hands often felt when newcomers asked foolish questions. "They've only got the one kind of ale."

"That's what I'll have, then." When her drink arrived in a stoneware tankard, she raised it in the miner's direction. "To the poor folk who died in the cave-ins."

The tawny-bearded Blackhammer studied her for a moment and then lifted his own ale to share in the toast. "To them."

When she took her first drink, the ale was strong and bitter with a slight metallic aftertaste. "Did you lose friends in the collapses?" she asked.

Once again, the miner hesitated. "Some."

"I'm sorry for your loss. Has anyone figured out why the cave-ins happened?"

He drained his ale, took hold of his pick, and stood up. "I

have to go." He strode out without giving her a chance to reply. Plainly, he didn't want to answer her questions.

Uschi watched him depart with a pang of frustration. She'd obviously pushed too hard, but how was she supposed to obtain information if she didn't steer conversations in a useful direction? She rarely, if ever, felt inadequate as a warrior or a scout, but it came home to her again that she wasn't, either by temperament or training, a spy.

Still, she could only do her best. It seemed obvious that she shouldn't immediately approach another patrol or group of patrons. Bouncing without pause from one to the next would rouse suspicions for certain. For now, it would be better to sit where she was, sip her ale, and eavesdrop. With the hearing of Mimir, Heimdall might have done it more easily, but she knew he'd be roaming the city and looking for information at a faster rate than she could. This was how she could help with their mission.

Four dwarf warriors – more of Maarav's, judging from their weapons, Blackhammer badges, and rust-colored cloaks – occupied a nearby table, their manner seeming as sullen and morose as the rest of the city. They spoke in low tones, but if Uschi concentrated, she could make out much of what they were saying.

"All I mean," grumbled one of the warriors, a fellow whose bristling russet beard and general hairiness made him look as furry as a bear, "is that we could kill it if we tried. Think about all the foes we Blackhammers have fought and beaten in our time. Why should this Spirit of the Forge be any different?" As if already anticipating such a battle, he touched the leather-wrapped haft of the battle-axe sitting on the table beside his ale.

"Because," said one of his companions, a dwarf who had at some point endured a blade stroke that severed half his left ear and left him with a puckered diagonal scar on his cheek, "rumors say no one can hurt or even touch the thing. The phantom probably won't even seem to notice you. Not then. Later, though, something terrible will happen. It has every time. But if the smiths keep making the swords–" He stopped abruptly, possibly because it had occurred to him that he was saying more than was prudent.

"I still say–" the hairy warrior said, and then another comrade elbowed him in the ribs. When the victim jerked around to glare, the dwarf who'd interrupted gave a small nudge of his head in Uschi's direction. It was plain the first Blackhammer warrior still disliked being silenced, but instead of finishing his remark, he merely scowled, picked up his flagon, and took a long drink. Foam clung to his mustache as he set it down again. He wiped the suds away with the back of his hand.

Only a moment ago, Uschi had resolved to listen quietly. Now, though, she was too excited. Luck had favored her with a conversation that might well be relevant and was unquestionably interesting. It was plain she wouldn't hear any more unless she forced the issue. Perhaps her status as a veteran warrior would induce the dwarves to talk to her.

She rose, carried her tankard over to the table, and said her hellos, ending with, "I'm a warrior in Lord Frey's service."

"We know who you are," said the Blackhammer with the scar. "The whole city has heard of your arrival."

As no one had invited her to take a seat, Uschi simply pulled out a chair, and, as it was too low for her, sat down a bit awkwardly. "I couldn't help overhearing what you were saying.

Fighting battles on Lord Frey's behalf, I've come up against all sorts of uncanny things. If you're having trouble with some sort of ghost or demon, maybe I can advise you. Maybe I could even fight alongside you. It would be more interesting than simply sitting around waiting for the smiths to make the new swords."

"Well–" the hairy warrior began.

"Shut up!" snarled the one with the scar.

"It's not honorable–"

"Honor is doing what the head of our clan has commanded us to do." The scarred dwarf turned to Uschi. "Everything is fine, my lady. You don't have to trouble yourself. And now my friends and I have to go." Like the miner before them, the four warriors rose and headed for the door.

It wasn't lost on the tavernkeeper that Uschi apparently wasn't able to attempt a conversation with any of his regular patrons without driving them out into the street. He eyed her with a thinly veiled dislike that made her feel sheepish.

She judged it was time to move on. She doubted there was any more to be learned here – she'd been lucky to pick up as much as she had – and for certain, the proprietor would be glad to see the back of her. As she finished her ale, she pondered what she'd discovered.

Her every instinct told her she'd stumbled onto something relevant to her own problem, but what was the relationship exactly? There was a "Spirit of the Forge" coercing the dwarves to create the rune blades, but how? The only possible connection she could see was if this apparition had caused the cave-ins, and its price for not causing any more was that the sword smiths make the weapons.

Could that conceivably be it? Even if it was, there were still pieces missing. Maybe when she spoke again to Heimdall, he'd be able to figure out what still remained unclear. And what the two of them ought to do about it.

Twenty-Four

Having made himself as presentable as possible for a second supper with Maarav and those close to him – the silver brooch, neck ring, armbands, and gold finger rings he'd looted from the secret crypt in the abandoned city helped – Heimdall paced around the sitting room of the suite the Blackhammer lord had provided for his visitors' use. He was listening, listening, listening, but even when he limited his eavesdropping to the citadel, he couldn't ferret out anything germane to the tainted rune swords. If anyone was discussing the topic at all, it wasn't in a way he could identify.

He told himself to be patient, even though, with the armed rebellion looming, patience was something he could ill afford. The brisk click of footsteps coming down the corridor outside roused him from the effort. Moments later, Uschi pushed through the door. From her expression, she'd learned something she was eager to share, and that made him eager to hear it. "What have you got?" he asked.

"The Blackhammers are afraid of something," she said, "and I know what." In a few sentences, she told him of an encounter with four dwarf warriors in a tavern and what she'd overheard. Afterward, she added, "Listen to the city again. Listen for someone talking about the Spirit of the Forge."

"That conversation still might not be easy to find. Not in this whole great echoing cavern. But it was Maarav's warriors you overheard before, so let me start with the castle barracks." He closed his eyes, exerted his extraordinary hearing to the fullest, and started to sort through the countless sounds rising from the citadel – footsteps, heartbeats, breathing, the swish of a broom, two sweethearts kissing and pledging their undying love, the crackle of hearth fires in the kitchen, bubbling pots in the same location, senior karls instructing underlings – to find the conversation he wanted.

To his disappointment, none of the guards seemed to be having such a talk, not in the barracks and not on the battlements or elsewhere in the fortress. Yet, having begun, Heimdall wasn't willing to abandon the search just yet. He kept trying, meanwhile sensing Uschi's growing impatience as she watched him. At last, he thought he might have found what he was seeking, and it was at that exact moment she spoke.

"Is there–"

"Hush!" he said. "Let me concentrate!" In truth, it probably wasn't necessary. He had little reason to doubt he could ignore her voice and miss nothing of what he wanted to hear. Still, he had no intention of losing the only fish he'd managed to hook.

Or the only two fish, depending on how you looked at it, for he'd caught the conversation of what he took to be a little girl and boy. Along with their high-pitched voices came rhythmic rubbing sounds that alternated with liquid noises that made him think of something being dipped in water and then some of the water dribbling away when the object was lifted out again. Unless he missed his guess, some adult had set the children the task of scrubbing something with brushes and pails.

"It's stupid!" declared the girl. "Why is everyone so scared of a shadow that doesn't even do anything?"

"It does things," said the boy. "It made the cave-ins in the mines."

"Says who?"

The boy hesitated. "Everyone knows."

"I still say," said the girl, "the grown-ups shouldn't do things just because they're afraid."

"They aren't! Blackhammers don't knuckle under to anyone!"

"They are! They did! Kelda's uncle is a sword smith, and she listened when he was talking to her father. He said they're doing bad things in the forge and making bad swords."

"They are not!" said the boy, and then, "Someone's coming!" Heimdall could hear the approaching footsteps as well. "So shut up! We aren't allowed to talk about this, and I don't want to get in trouble."

Heimdall reined in his senses and opened his eyes to find Uschi staring at him. "What have *you* got?" she asked.

"A little more," he said. "Finally. The children I overheard didn't mention the Spirit of the Forge by name, not while I was listening, but I think that's what they were talking about." He told Uschi what he'd gleaned from the conversation.

When he finished, she said, "My guess was right. The Blackhammers do believe they have to make the rune swords to placate this Spirit of the Forge. And they won't admit as much because they have some sense they're being coerced into doing something wicked and giving in seems dishonorable."

"So it would seem."

"I was thinking on the way back. The Spirit of the Forge and the thing I saw in my nightmare have to be the same creature, don't they?"

Frowning, Heimdall took a moment to consider. "I don't know," he said at length, "do they? The thing you saw was a four-armed giant that rushed to attack you and influenced you against Odin. The dwarves have no such driving force that I can see, or they would be more strongly allied with Frey and not so reluctant to work with us. They seem to be under direct threat of the Spirit. There's not enough evidence to say for certain that they are the same entity."

Uschi grunted. "All right, maybe. But they're both working toward the same ends."

"That, I don't doubt."

"So, what's our next move? Do we go Spirit hunting in the mines? Try to destroy the thing and hope the grateful Blackhammers will then suck the evil magic back out of the rune swords?"

Heimdall sighed. "That may be our only option. But we don't know the mines, and there's a fair chance that if any dwarves spot us, they'll want to shoo us out. Then there's the difficulty that while I can hear all sorts of things, I can't hear a phantom walking if its body doesn't have any solidity at all."

"Plus," Uschi said, "if the dwarves' weapons can't hurt the thing, why would our swords do any better?" She hesitated. "I know you don't want to break off what we're doing. It would anger me, too, considering what we're uncovering. But we've already been in Nidavellir for two days. If there's no hope of doing what we came to do in time to prevent the rebellion, maybe it's time to fly back to Asgard and report."

Maybe, he thought, she was right, but before he could open his mouth to say so, a notion came to him. "Or maybe we can take a different approach. Based on what we've gleaned so far, the Spirit of the Forge doesn't talk. How, then, did it reveal its price for stopping the cave-ins? How did it instruct the sword smiths as to exactly how they were to make the rune swords?"

Uschi grinned a fierce grin as the realization dawned. "It must have someone speaking for it."

Heimdall nodded. "That's what I think too. Possibly even somebody on its side. And who could plausibly explain a ghost or demon's demands without appearing to be in league with it? A warlock."

"So, we have to start looking at mystics all around the city? And hope that when we find the right one, we can shake some useful information about the Spirit of the Forge out of him?"

"Maybe not all around the city. For the most part, dwarf magic involves the creation of enchanted articles like the rune swords or Odin's spear. Warlocks who can work other sorts of spells are rare, and surely Maarav has recruited any such into his inner circle."

"That makes sense," Uschi said. "By Audhumla's milk, the sorcerer in question almost has to be someone who has Maarav's ear, doesn't it? Someone we're likely dining with this evening. The question is, how to spot him if there's more than one mage in attendance."

"There will be," Heimdall said. "From the amulets and such

I noticed, he has three warlocks among his counselors. As for how to identify the right one, I suppose we keep on poking around."

The Valkyrie shook her head. "No. We can't afford to waste time creeping about and spying when Frey's already assembling his rebel army. We now know enough to poke *at* the traitor and provoke him into revealing himself."

Heimdall mulled that over and after a moment said, "You have a point. Any thoughts on how to go about it?"

Uschi shrugged the rune sword off her back and reached to unbuckle the Brightblade. "It starts with our dinner conversation."

Twenty-Five

As honored guests at a feast, Heimdall and Uschi were sitting near Maarav at the head table on the dais. No one was sitting on the other side of it with his or her back to the warriors and other karls dining at the tables running down the length of the hall. Lesser folk didn't want their view of the jarls and thanes obstructed, or at least, Uschi reflected sardonically, that was what the jarls and thanes of all peoples and places seemed to assume.

The seating made it more difficult to study the trio of mages Maarav counted among his counselors. Still, leaning forward a bit as she ate venison, garlic mushrooms, and other dishes slathered in thick sauces and gravies that seemed to be the hallmark of Blackhammer cooking, the drone of conversation all but drowning out the musician gamely puffing away on a boxwood panpipe, she watched the three as best she could.

Bergljot was an apple-cheeked sorceress who laughed often, and judging from the mirth of those around her, was keeping them entertained with a steady stream of jokes and humorous sallies. She reminded Uschi of her own mother, or rather, Juliska as she'd been before her daughter's willfulness brought strife into the family.

Gulbrand was thin by dwarf standards, and a tattooed blue pattern covered his shaven scalp. His long beard had iron and silver trinkets knotted in it and dyed blue and yellow streaks in the midst of the natural brown and gray. He scowled and picked at the succession of dishes set before him as though he wished he were anywhere else, and, evidently realizing he wouldn't appreciate the attention, those seated around him made little attempt to draw him into their conversations.

In terms of demeanor, Ailpein represented a midpoint between the other two. Looking too youthful for the position he enjoyed, boyish behind the wispy whiskers he possibly hoped made him appear older, he wasn't full of merriment like Bergljot but wasn't standoffish like Gulbrand, either. He chatted with others readily enough.

They all had what Uschi took to be talismans and mystic symbols about their persons, but no emblems she associated with Jotunheim, Muspelheim, or any other enemies of Asgard and Vanaheim. Nor were any of the three obliging enough to leap onto the table and declare affiliation with the Spirit of the Forge.

It was possible that Heimdall with the gifts of Mimir and the learning acquired from his books and over the course of his travels discerned something Uschi didn't, but she suspected not. It was a good thing, then, that the two of them weren't going to limit themselves to mere observation.

Eventually Maarav provided an opening for them to steer conversation in the direction they needed it to go. "I understand you were walking about the city today. Did you enjoy your excursion?"

"Most of it," Heimdall replied with the slightest of edges in his voice. He was, Uschi thought, trying to portray annoyance covered over with tact.

Maarav's frown indicated he'd picked up on the underlying feeling. "What was it that displeased you?"

Heimdall hesitated as though he regretted bringing up the subject. "I sought to visit the hall where the master sword smiths practice their craft. Of course I trust you, my lord, but I still felt a responsibility to Lord Frey to see for myself that the work on the new rune blades is proceeding apace. I couldn't get in, though. A guard at the entrance turned me away even though I explained I was your guest, and the smiths were forging the very swords I myself commissioned."

This much, Uschi knew, was true, give or take. After they separated, her friend had sought admission to the workshop of the finest sword smiths and been denied.

After a moment of awkward silence, Maarav said, "I apologize for that and ask for your understanding. The secrets of our craft are the foundation of our wealth. We have to guard them zealously."

Heimdall smiled as though the explanation had mollified him. "When you put it that way, I understand. Although you'd have nothing to worry about where I'm concerned. I know little about weapon-making and nothing at all about magic. I wouldn't glean anything about your secrets even if I was looking right at them. It's my friend here you'd really want to keep out."

It was Bergljot's turn to hitch forward for a better look at Uschi. "Really? And why is that?"

"My mother is a sorceress," Uschi said, taking up the thread of the ruse that Heimdall had begun. "She did her best to prepare me to follow in her footsteps, but I lacked the knack for spellcasting. The lore, though, I absorbed before she gave up on me. Thus, I'd be very curious to see how the rune swords are enchanted. You have my word, I'll never tell another soul."

This part was altogether a lie. Juliska was no witch, and Uschi knew only the few rote charms every Valkyrie learned. But she hoped it was a plausible falsehood. Mages were rare in every Realm, but Vanaheim produced a few more than most. Other folk with limited knowledge of the place tended to imagine it was full to bursting with sorceresses and enchanters.

Maarav spread his hands and smiled an apologetic smile. "It grieves me to refuse guests a second time, but the weapon makers would have my head if I let you in. Please, ask for any other boon."

Uschi smiled back. "I completely understand. To be honest, the refusal surprised me because I've always thought of dwarves as, well, a bit mundane and matter-of-fact. But, sojourning here, I'm already discovering your people are as rich in magic and lore as the Vanir or anybody else. You have the profound mystical knowledge that goes into the shaping of the rune swords. And you have a wealth of tales and legends just like any other folk. This Spirit of the Smiths, for example. Spirit of the Smiths? No, that wasn't it. Spirit of the Forge."

This time, the silence that fell was more prolonged. Eventually, forcing back the smile that had briefly fled his face, the lord of the Blackhammers said, "I'm sorry, I don't know what you mean."

"That's strange," Uschi said. "I overheard more than one

person murmuring that name as I drifted around the city. Some sort of specter or something?" She looked to the three mages. "Maybe one of you knows. This is the kind of thing witches and warlocks understand."

"Well, yes," the youthful Ailpein said, "but only when the apparitions are real. I've never heard of the Spirit of the Forge. Which makes me think this is some new story – one without any basis in fact – that some clever storyteller has concocted to please the crowd in a tavern or on a street corner."

"I'm sure you're right," Uschi said. "It's just that people seemed so serious as they spoke of it. If everybody understands it's only a story–"

Heimdall turned to her. "Please, enough. Our friends have explained, and this is getting boring."

She'd been waiting for him to intervene. Their scheme called for him to intervene to avoid offending their hosts and be seen as the emissary focused on simply getting their business done, and for her to be seen as the visitor likely to follow a dangerous curiosity wherever it led. She inclined her head in acquiescence and permitted the conversation to turn to innocuous matters.

After several more courses, supper ended. Pleading tiredness, she and Heimdall took their leave of the talk, drinking, songs, arm wrestling, and knife-throwing games that followed as soon as courtesy allowed. Once they were out of the banquet hall, she asked, "Did those eyes of yours see which of the mages is the enemy?"

"No," Heimdall said. "There was nothing to point to one as opposed to another."

"Not even a feeling?"

"I imagine you'd agree that Gulbrand was the least

congenial. But that doesn't mean he's in league with the Spirit of the Forge or even that he's the conduit through which the phantom speaks."

"Well," she said, "if there's nothing yet to point us to one as opposed to the others, I suppose we go ahead with the plan."

Which depended on her having created the impression that she might be curious enough to slip into the hall of the master sword smiths and snoop around. If she'd failed, nothing would happen. If she'd succeeded, however, maybe the mage who was in communication with the Spirit of the Forge would be worried enough to monitor the vault via scrying or some other occult technique. Maybe he or she would want to keep her from bearing witness to something she wasn't meant to see and try to take action to prevent her.

"Just remember," Heimdall said, "if a sorcerer chooses to strike at you from a distance, the sending may not be anything you can fight with a sword. If the Spirit of the Forge shows up, it definitely won't be. In which case, get out of there."

Uschi snorted. "Yes, Mother. And you remember, your job is to pick out the right sorcerer and stop him before he finishes his death spell or whatever it is. Now, let's get moving."

Twenty-six

Uschi looked this way and that as Heimdall knelt and sought to pick the lock securing the iron doors leading to the armorers' halls. As far as she could tell, no one was abroad in the night to see them breaking in, but that didn't mean somebody wouldn't come along. Even if that didn't happen, if Heimdall couldn't get the cursed lock open, their plan would fail before it had fairly started.

After another moment, though, her friend said, "There!" and she heard the sliding internal bolt and spring mechanism give a tiny click. He rose, stuffed his tools back in his belt pouch, and cracked the door open wide enough to peek through. When he pushed both doors all the way open, she knew he hadn't detected anybody waiting on the other side.

As they slipped inside, he whispered, "I knew learning about locks would come in handy someday."

Uschi didn't bother responding. She was too busy peering ahead into gloomy spaces lit by the ubiquitous glowing ruddy crystal lamps for any signs of movement. She knew that with the gifts of Mimir, Heimdall could see – and hear – far better than she could, but her instincts and training required no less.

He led her on through an exhibition where especially finely crafted weapons and mail were on display along with workshops equipped with forges, troughs for quenching blades, hammers, tongs, stacked iron ingots, bundles of ash shafts for spears, and stacks of spruce and pine boards for the shield makers. The place was something of a maze, but Heimdall knew where he was going. He'd explained that this part of the complex was open to the public, and he'd explored, being turned away from the innermost chamber.

In time, he raised his hand to signal a stop. She knew why. The sentry guarding the vault of the master sword smiths wasn't far ahead, and further progress would be dangerous. As she and Heimdall had agreed she should, she found a hiding place behind an anvil atop a block of stone. The anvil was at a comfortable height for a dwarf, not an adult Vanir like herself, so she had to crouch low for it to conceal her. Meanwhile, Heimdall turned and trotted silently back the way they'd come.

Before long, the sound of crashing metal echoed through the stony spaces. As the two of them had decided he should, Heimdall was raising a commotion.

The noise continued until a Blackhammer spearman ran by Uschi's hiding place to investigate. He might conceivably have orders to guard his post no matter what, but even if so, the ongoing racket had lured him forth. For all he knew, some lunatic was destroying the masterpieces the smiths took such pride in, and he didn't want to be the warrior who stood and did nothing while the treasures were vandalized.

The crashing ended shortly thereafter, presumably because Heimdall had heard the warrior coming and taken cover. The plan called for him to lunge out of hiding and strike the guard unconscious when his back was turned, then race back to Maarav's citadel.

Trusting that all that had indeed happened, Uschi crept on toward the arched entryway leading into the hall of the master sword makers, not relaxing her guard an iota until she saw with her own eyes that, in fact, no second sentry remained to bar the path. She hurried inside and took her first look around.

In many respects, the vault resembled those she'd already passed through – the ones where less illustrious smiths practiced their craft. At this late hour, the fires of the forges had burned down to a few embers. The difference was the glyphs and symbols graven on anvils, tools, and even the floor and walls.

Though she wasn't sure – she'd been too busy looking for Heimdall to pay them much attention at the time – a few of the runes reminded Uschi of the ones carved on the bier in the secret tomb and the rotting corpse that was the king draug. Others resembled the ones etched down the length of the enchanted sword she carried, and she wondered if, given sight like Heimdall's, she'd see them agleam with phosphorescence. As she hadn't observed these particular runes elsewhere, perhaps this was the only room where they were utilized. It might be a way of keeping the evil of the rune swords away from other creations.

At any rate, the symbols made her feel uneasy and reinforced her belief that there was something wrong with the way the rune blades were being manufactured. And that at least some of the Blackhammers understood that very well.

Beyond the correspondences she'd noted, however, she had no idea what the esoteric runes signified. She unrolled the several sheets of parchment she carried and with a piece of charcoal set about copying them just as if she did. As if, with time and study, she could unravel their secrets.

Meanwhile, her heart thumping, she listened and watched from the corners of her eyes for any emerging threat. For a four-armed purple-black giant springing or a shadowy wraith gliding out of nowhere, or even a warning rumble and cracks opening and zigzagging across the ceiling.

Yet change, when it came, was so subtle and seemingly innocuous that she almost missed it. In the dimly lit chamber, she'd had to squint and peer intently to accurately reproduce the runes, and then, eventually, she realized seeing them had become easier. The hall was brighter than it had been before.

Alarmed but still not behaving as though she suspected anything was amiss – in her role as bait, she wanted to give Heimdall as much time as possible to identify their quarry even if it increased the danger to herself – she turned to a different set of runes, two lines of five symbols each etched on one of the anvils.

No one had laid fresh split hardwood and bone on the fires, nor had anybody stirred the embers or blown fresh air into them. But coals that had been almost entirely gray were glowing orange now, and little tongues of blue and yellow flame were dancing over them.

"Heimdall," she breathed, confident that her friend heard her, "the attack is starting. Hurry up, pick out the right mage, and stop the death spell." She then returned to her copying, meanwhile peering from the corners of her eyes and straining to listen to detect whatever would happen next.

Twenty-Seven

Heimdall received a couple of inquisitive looks, but the guards didn't stop or question him as he strode back through the gate leading into Maarav's citadel after parting company with Uschi and rendering the guard unconscious in the halls of the weapon makers. He was a guest of the head of the clan, with no restrictions on his movements other than the prohibition against entering the vault of the master sword smiths. If he wanted to take late-night strolls around the city, that was up to him.

Once inside, he hurried on toward the apartments where the three mages lived and cast their spells. When he'd scouted the area previously, it hadn't surprised him that they occupied their own separate area within the fortress complex. These spaces, opening into the wall of the enormous cavern, were set apart from everything else. In his experience, ordinary folk liked to put a little distance between themselves and the uncanny no matter how benign it supposedly was, and apparently the Blackhammers were no different.

As he took up a position in a shadowy corner where, he

judged, his loitering was apt to go unnoticed, he couldn't help thinking of all the ways the present plan could go awry. As of yet, he had no absolute proof that some sinister presence had terrorized the dwarves into giving Frey tainted rune swords, but it certainly seemed that way. It likewise seemed a reasonable inference that one of Maarav's three mages had played a secret, treacherous role in the terrorizing.

But that didn't necessarily mean the warlock was monitoring the forge where the swords were made. Nor was it a given that he or she would strike at Uschi when the Valkyrie was alone inside. The mage could just go running to Maarav and have him dispatch more warriors to arrest the trespasser.

But Heimdall didn't think that likely. Back in Vanaheim, the four-armed giant – and it seemed overwhelmingly likely that there was a connection between the entity from Uschi's dream and the Spirit of the Forge – had chosen to act through pawns who were already completely under its control and to do so in such a way as to avoid destroying the trust between Frey and his parents, or between the god and Uschi's. Here in Nidavellir, surely it would prefer that Uschi die or, better still, disappear mysteriously, so as not to disrupt the reluctant relationship between the Blackhammers and the Vanir rebels.

Heimdall was more worried that unmasking the sorcerer who might attempt murder on Uschi wouldn't be enough to convince Maarav to confess his clan's ignoble dealings and act to set things right. What if the mage wasn't a traitor per se? What if he did everything with the full knowledge and acquiescence of his lord?

But Heimdall's instincts told him that wasn't likely, either. The Blackhammers had the reputation of being a fundamentally honorable folk, and that was his sense of them as well. Surely, there had to be some limit to what they would abide, even with a terrifying specter killing their miners by the score.

And in any case, Heimdall thought, Uschi was correct. With the Vanir invasion of Asgard imminent, the two of them had to try *something* to move things along.

Exerting the gifts of Mimir, he listened for Uschi's voice and heard it. "Heimdall," she whispered, "the attack is starting. Hurry up, pick out the right mage, and stop the death spell."

Heimdall took what comfort he could in the fact that she still sounded calm. Whatever was going on, it didn't have her fighting or running for her life yet, and his task was to make sure it never would. Accordingly, he focused his preternatural hearing on each of the mages' quarters in turn. The witch or warlock seeking to kill Uschi was presumably reciting an incantation. Heimdall might not fully understand it, but he was confident of understanding enough to recognize it for what it was.

As it turned out, though, nobody was saying anything. From Bergljot's apartments buzzed a snore. Inside Gulbrand's, paper whispered at regular intervals as though the dyspeptic sorcerer was reading and periodically turning the pages of his book. Liquid gurgled as, guessing from the sound of it, the boyish Ailpein poured himself a drink. Apparently, the plentiful ale, beer, and wine flowing at the feast earlier hadn't been enough to slake his thirst.

Maybe, Heimdall thought, one of these innocuous-sounding noises was a mask of sorts. Perhaps the traitor mage knew a way to strike at Uschi without speaking words of power aloud. There was still no reason to panic. He could identify the enemy by the flickers of magical light escaping under his or her door. The ironbound wooden doors were well made, well fitted in their frames, but they still had tiny gaps around them. For the sight of Mimir, that should be enough.

No matter how hard he looked, however, he could only discern the steady red light of the crystals that provided illumination everywhere in the city leaking out. Was there a kind of sorcery, he wondered, so subtle it revealed itself neither to the ear nor the eye? Or had he and Uschi been making false assumptions and inferences the whole time? Was she in danger not because one of Lord Maarav's mystics was striking at her but for some different reason altogether?

With an effort, he pushed that fear away. He had to assume that he and the Valkyrie had been right at least to some degree, that one of the three mages was responsible for her current danger. Because if that wasn't so, Heimdall had no way of helping her.

He listened and stared at the three doors once more. It didn't help.

Twenty-Eight

Uschi waited as the fires burned gradually higher and hotter. Heimdall was supposed to break the spell, at which point the flames would presumably die down.

He was taking his time about it.

He'd warned her that the magical sending might not turn out to be anything a warrior could fight. Still, she was poised to draw the Brightblade in an instant if some hostile entity emerged from the flames. Her journeys on Asgard's behalf had never taken her to Muspelheim, but she suspected the magic targeting her might ultimately spawn a killer akin to one of that Realm's fire demons.

That never happened, though. Instead, the hall gradually filled with smoke. Whatever measures existed to draw the smoke out were rendered inoperative by the hostile spell. It stung her eyes and after another few moments made her cough.

Soon, tears welled from her eyes to blur the runes she was copying, never abandoning her ruse. She broke out in coughing fits that became more frequent, painful, and prolonged. Even then, she continued to play the part of bait too stupid to realize she was in trouble. She hoped Heimdall's heightened senses had by now identified the mage responsible.

The pretense lasted until she coughed so long and hard that she emptied her burning lungs, her head swam, and it felt as if there was no clean, wholesome air to be had. At that point, her stubborn resolve gave way to anxiety... or perhaps an assertion of her own good sense. Heimdall, she decided, had failed to stop the spell in time, and she was going to suffocate if she didn't escape the hall. Dropping the parchments and stick of charcoal, she took a first running stride toward the exit.

The flames leaped higher and put forth greater quantities of choking gray smoke than before. The mage, she judged, must have discerned her intent to flee and empowered the enchantment to overcome her.

But, she thought with fierce satisfaction, his effort was too feeble and came too late. Though the veils of smoke before her concealed the doorway, she knew in which direction it lay. After a moment, her outstretched hands bumped against the wall. Now she need only grope her way along till she found the opening.

She sidled left, and, as she coughed, her fumbling hands discovered a corner. All right, she told herself, that meant the exit was in the opposite direction. She need only reverse course and she couldn't possibly miss it.

She did, though. She found only solid stone wall for what, as she struggled to breathe, seemed a long time, and then at last another corner.

Her heart pounding, she was truly frightened now. Had being starved for air so addled her that she'd missed the way out? It was remotely conceivable, but she trusted her instincts too much to believe it. She thought it more likely that her enemy's sorcery had sealed the exit or hidden it so well she'd never find it before the smoke finished smothering her.

If that was the case, Heimdall was her only hope. But why hadn't he intervened already? Maybe he'd tried, and the warlock had struck him insensible.

She refused to believe that, though. Her friend would save her just as they'd saved one another's lives so many times before. She just had to do whatever was necessary to survive until he did.

Her mentor in the Valkyries, she recalled, had once told her that if caught in smoke, she should drop down low because that was where the good air was. Accordingly, she lay down on the floor and gasped for breath.

The air at floor level wasn't entirely free of smoke – her frantic inhalation set her coughing yet again – but the air truly was a little cleaner. When the coughing passed, she knuckled her teary, smarting eyes and peered back into the hall.

Thick as the smoke now was, she could make out patches of yellow glow that gave away the locations of the fires. She crawled to the first, pushed one of the quenching troughs full of water up next to it, rose, and drew the Brightblade. She used the sword to rake the burning coals from the forge into the container. They hissed as they came into contact with the water.

She dropped to the floor once more, crawled to the next forge, and pushed its embers into its trough. Then, hacking, she moved on to each in turn until she extinguished every fire.

It had occurred to her that her efforts might possibly break the spell and that everything it had created would vanish, but in that desperate hope she was disappointed. The air was still thick with smoke. She was grimly sure that even if she mustered the strength to drag herself back to the far wall, she still wouldn't be able to find the exit.

Putting out the flames had won her some time, but if she didn't get fresh air to breathe soon, she was still going to die. As she struggled for one more breath, she found herself thinking of how she'd left things with her parents. Even though she insisted that the estrangement was all their fault, still she couldn't help feeling regret.

Twenty-Nine

Heimdall shifted his attention from the quarters of the three mages to the halls of the armorers. Uschi was coughing and wheezing. Her distress was unmistakable.

He considered racing back across the Blackhammer city to help her but feared he wouldn't arrive in time. Instead, telling himself there had to be *some* telltale sign to reveal which warlock or sorceress was attacking the Valkyrie, he used the gifts of Mimir to once again investigate what lay beyond the three doorways. There was still nothing revelatory to hear, and no eerie flickering leaking out into the night, either.

He decided that with time running out, he'd simply have to choose at random. If he chose incorrectly, he had to hope he didn't run afoul of an innocent spellcaster's potent magical defense. Assuming that didn't happen, he'd persuade or force the Blackhammer to tell him who really interpreted the wishes of the Spirit of the Forge.

A part of him jeered at his intent. By nature, he was a thinker, a planner, and didn't like surrendering himself to the whims of pure chance. But with his best friend in dire peril, depending on him to succor her, there was no help for it now. He drew his two-handed sword, strode to Ailpein's door, and gave it a booming kick.

The door remained closed. He winced at the noise that might bring guards running and had surely alerted the boyish warlock that someone was breaking in. He booted it once more, and with the second impact, Asgardian strength prevailed. The door flew open and banged against the wall. Heimdall charged through.

The space in which he found himself resembled the quarters Maarav had provided for his and Uschi's use. It was full of furniture covered in speckled yellowish leather, a hearth, and shields and tapestries depicting Blackhammer smith craft, mining, and warfare decorating the sculpted and polished stone walls – the difference being that everything was sized and positioned for a person half as tall as he was. Beyond an arch was a warlock's conjuration chamber with shelves of books and scrolls and a sorcerer's circle inlaid in silver on the floor, but that wasn't where Ailpein was.

If the goblet and stoneware bottle on a table beside the most comfortable-looking chair and footstool were any indication, Ailpein, the fine clothes and ornaments he'd worn to the feast exchanged for a ratty old robe, had been relaxing with a cup of wine mere moments ago. Now, alarmed by the violent intrusion, he'd jumped out of his seat, scrambled across the room, thrown open a box, and was bringing out an intricately carved ivory wand.

Heimdall was now certain he'd accosted the wrong mage. He was also sure he shouldn't give Ailpein the chance to point the wand at him. The ceiling just high enough to accommodate his lanky frame, he charged across the intervening space, swung his sword, and knocked the magical implement out of the warlock's grasp with the flat of the blade. Ailpein yelped as he lost his hold on it. Heimdall then aimed his weapon's point at the Blackhammer's chest.

For an instant, it made him feel like a bully to threaten someone so much smaller than himself. Ailpein's youthful appearance didn't help. Behind his patchy excuse for a beard, he was like a brave child scowling with fierce Blackhammer defiance. But Heimdall reminded himself that, given the opportunity, Ailpein might well strike him down with wizardry, reminded himself, too, that Uschi was in deadly danger, and his moment of shame gave way to resolve.

"Which of the other two mages speaks for the Spirit of the Forge?" he asked.

Ailpein blinked. "What now?"

"Whichever one it is, Bergljot or Gulbrand, is cursing my friend to death at this very moment. So, I don't have time for you to play stupid. Tell me or I swear I'll cut you down."

The Blackhammer mage peered up at Heimdall, eyes narrowed, plainly considering. His pallor suggested the intruder's threat had frightened him, but not to the point of blurting out something he would consider traitorous or dishonorable. Heimdall was about to knock him unconscious and move on when he finally spoke, his voice quavering just a little.

"None of us three interprets the wishes of the Spirit."

"That can't be," Heimdall replied, although his instincts told him Ailpein was speaking the truth. With a surge of dread, he wondered again if his inferences had led him utterly astray, if he truly had no idea about what was happening in the Blackhammer enclave and Uschi was going to pay for his faulty reasoning with her life. "Somebody has to."

"Someone does," Ailpein said. "But it's not one of us sorcerers. It's Cormag the seer. Among dwarves, warlocks and seers are different. My kind cast spells. Seers reveal what's hidden. Cormag came to us with the Spirit's demands and when we refused, the angered entity caused cave-ins throughout the mines. Once we began manufacturing its swords with the prescribed magic, the catastrophes stopped."

Heimdall remembered the other counselors he'd seen when Maarav first received him and later at the feast. He'd paid them scant attention, focusing instead on the lord of Clan Blackhammer himself and the three mages. If he could believe Ailpein – and he thought he could – that had been a mistake, one that Uschi might pay for with her life.

But maybe it still wasn't too late to prevent that. "Do seers cast spells of their own?" he asked.

Ailpein shook his head. "Not really. We have our skills, and they have theirs."

"What if some powerful being helped him?"

"Well, then... possibly. In our various fashions, we're all accessing the same occult forces."

"Does Cormag live here in the citadel?"

"Yes."

"Take me to him now!"

Ailpein swallowed. "So you can do him harm? No, I won't. Not even if you kill me instead."

"I swear by the Tree, I don't want to hurt or kill anyone. But at this very moment, Cormag is killing my friend. Besides, I believe there's more to this Spirit of the Forge business than anyone but the seer understands, secrets he needs to disclose for the good of your people and mine."

"What kind of secrets?"

"There isn't time to explain." Heimdall picked up the fallen wand and proffered it to Ailpein. "Take this back. If I try to do anything I shouldn't, cast a spell on me."

The sorcerer accepted the arcane implement and gave a nod to convey he had decided to cooperate. "Just let me put on my shoes. I'll run faster."

The pair dashed out of the mage's quarters and set off running across the citadel. Although, with his shabby robe flapping out behind him, Ailpein was pounding along as fast as he could, Heimdall knew that he with his longer legs could sprint faster. With Uschi coughing her life away, if she wasn't dead already, he begrudged the need to let the dwarf take the lead. But, he judged, there was no real choice. Ailpein was the one who knew where they were going.

Thus, Heimdall held back as they wound their way around buildings and through the stretches of open courtyard until he spied a round structure with a conical roof rising above the battlements. The turret occupied a position just shy of the point where the castle became one with the immense cavern wall rising behind and eventually arching over it. Sculpted stairs extended upward, connecting the turret to the ground.

Like the quarters of the mages, the turret seemed somewhat set off from the common comings and goings of the fortress. When Heimdall took an instant to look at it with the sight of Mimir, purplish light of the uncanny type he'd sought previously shimmered around the edges of the door. Now certain the little tower was his and Ailpein's objective, he dashed past his companion and bounded up the steps.

When he was most of the way up but still short of the turret, the door leading into it opened and another dwarf – Cormag, presumably – glared down. The sage was a hunched fellow with a twitching face haloed by grizzled snaky hair and with food stains down the front of his tunic. The silver chain of a pendant set with a deep purple amethyst dangled from his upraised hand.

Deciding he should have anticipated a seer would sense him coming, Heimdall strained to put on a final burst of speed and close to striking distance. His best wasn't fast enough. The swinging amethyst flashed with arcane power. The stone stairs beneath him shattered to rubble. With nothing under his boots, he fell.

He let go of his sword to snatch at the stubby remnants of the stairs. He managed to seize something solid with his left hand and hold on, the arrested drop jolting his body and rough edges of stone cutting into his fingers. He looked for a hold for his right hand. Once he was hanging from both, he meant to haul himself upward, but just as he started searching, Cormag loomed above him on the section of stairs that remained intact. The seer stamped on Heimdall's left hand. The Asgardian lost his grip and dropped again, toward the pile of broken stonework waiting below.

He didn't slam down on top of it, though. Something stopped his fall in midair. The abrupt halt gave him a second jolt but didn't actually hurt him. It was gentler than dropping into the tumble of rocks would have been.

Below him sounded rhyming words. He glanced down to

see Ailpein reciting the incantation while pointing the ivory wand at him. The warlock's youthful face was intent with concentration. Ripples of golden phosphorescence crawled on the implement in his hand.

Peering down, Heimdall also saw that chunks of stone had fallen on the splendid sword he'd dropped and broken it. Though he'd assured Ailpein he wouldn't hurt Cormag, it was still a daunting prospect to face mystical power without a weapon, but he was simply going to have to cope. With Uschi's life in jeopardy, there was scarcely time to go and find another.

Ailpein slowly inclined the wand higher. In response to its power, Heimdall floated upward.

Drops of spit flying from his mouth, Cormag snarled like a cornered animal and scuttled back up the remaining stairs and from there into the turret. The castle wall-walk curved around the structure to form a sort of landing at the top of the steps. Ailpein's sorcery deposited Heimdall there a moment after the seer slammed the door. The Asgardian kicked it, and with a *crack*, it flew open again.

The inside of the turret was smaller than Ailpein's quarters. Still, Heimdall had expected something comparable, a pleasant, comfortable domicile appropriate for a prosperous lord's valued counselor. Thus, he felt a flash of surprise when he discovered the reality.

Stacks of jumbled items towered precariously to either side. Some were pieces of furniture rendered useless by the articles heaped atop them or by the fact that they themselves were jammed in partway up the stacks. Others were garments, so many it seemed impossible Cormag could ever have worn them all, some looking new and fine, others dirty and coming apart at the seams like the castoffs of a common laborer. There was a hodgepodge of pots, pans, tools, and other things as well, too many for Heimdall to regard them all in that first moment except to register that many of them also looked like trash, as if the dwarf was in the habit of scavenging what others considered useless. The whole tangle stank of mice, a sign that anything that hadn't been ruined when Cormag brought it in was in danger of becoming so.

The turret had only one clear space left, an aisle running down the center to a bed. Once, Cormag might have slept there, but eventually he'd piled his clutter on top of it as well. Now, apparently, he made do with the rumpled blankets on the patch of floor in front of it, and it was to that position he'd retreated. Glad to have his quarry cornered, Heimdall started toward him.

Cormag brandished the pendant, and the amethyst flashed. Clattering and creaking, the piles to either side began to topple inward, to batter Heimdall and block the path before him. He'd expected it to be easy to close with the seer, but now that was far from the case.

Hands raised to protect his head, he floundered and stumbled onward. Dislodged from their burrows and nests, mice squealed and chittered. One leaped onto Heimdall's shoulder, clung for a moment, and then jumped off again.

Bruised, bleeding from a cut on his cheek where something with a sharp edge had grazed him as it fell, Heimdall pushed forward with all his strength and emerged from the spilling trash that had done its best to bury him. Cormag cringed backward to see the Asgardian still coming. His rump bumped the edge of the bed, and the items heaped atop it swayed, threatening a final unintended collapse. The Blackhammer raised the swinging pendant a third time.

Before Cormag could draw any more magic from it, Heimdall lunged and caught him by the throat. "Stop what you're doing!" the Asgardian said. "Stop what you're doing to my friend in the hall of the smiths! Or I'll kill you!" He meant it, too, the need to extract information from the seer and his promise to Ailpein notwithstanding. At this moment, Uschi's life took priority over any other concerns.

The jewel in the pendant glimmered. "It's stopped!" the Blackhammer whined. He was trembling, and his bloodshot eyes were wide with fear.

Heimdall invoked the hearing of Mimir. To his relief, he could still hear Uschi wheezing and coughing, her heart still pumping. He snatched away the talisman.

A moment later, scraping and rattling sounded at his back, followed by banging and crashing in the courtyard below. Eventually he could see that, seemingly of their own accord, pieces of the jumble behind him were sliding out the doorway and off the landing to fall to the ground. Once it opened a path all the way across the turret chamber, the cascade stopped. Gripping him by the collar, Heimdall marched Cormag into the open air and wasn't surprised to find Ailpein there with a last trace of amber glow fading on his wand.

"Were you in time?" the sorcerer asked.

"Thanks to you," Heimdall replied, "she's still alive. I need to go to her. Get her to a healer if she needs it."

Ailpein snorted. "I've gone along with you until now, but that doesn't mean I'll let you wander off on your own to flee the city. You just assaulted one of Lord Maarav's advisors, and, may my ancestors protect me, I helped you. Now we have to surrender ourselves for judgment."

"I promise you," Heimdall said, "I will. My friend and I have sought to bring hidden truths out into the open, into the sight of Lord Maarav, you counselors, and everyone. But someone really should see to my comrade without delay. Come with me if you don't trust me to go on my own. Or roust out some warriors and send me under guard. Or keep me here and just send them. It doesn't matter as long as someone goes and Cormag here remains under supervision."

"I believe we'll send the warriors," Ailpein said, "to see to your companion while you bide with me. What is that pendant?"

"The source of the magic that shatters stone staircases and topples piles of trash. My hunch is that the Spirit of the Forge gave it to Cormag. It's the link between them."

"Whatever it is, you need to hand it over." Ailpein looked grave.

Heimdall did so. Ailpein then dispatched several warriors to the halls of the weapon makers as promised.

Heimdall knew Uschi wasn't dead. Even so, anxiety gnawed at him until the dwarf guards returned with her and he beheld her walking under her own power.

Once they were reunited, she asked, "Did you catch the renegade mage? If my escorts knew, they wouldn't tell me." Her voice rasped, and her body smelled of smoke.

"It turns out he's not exactly a mage," Heimdall replied, "but yes. Are you all right?"

She had to stop and cough before giving her reply. "I'd like to drink lots of cold water, followed by lots of ale, followed by a bath and sleep, but I'll live. Why in the name of the Tree did this take so long?"

"Because despite all my reading, I didn't know everything there is to know about magic, dwarf magic in particular. If one of the warlocks hadn't decided to help me, we might not be talking now."

"When I get my ale, I'll drink a toast to him."

"I hope you'll have the chance. Because this isn't over."

Thirty

Uschi stood before Maarav, Bergljot, and Gulbrand, both her swords currently confiscated. Heimdall, Ailpein, and Cormag stood around her, all of them like prisoners facing a tribunal, which, she suspected, wasn't far from being the case. She drew what encouragement she could from the fact that the seer was shooting glances all around as though looking for somewhere to run. Surely, she told herself, his guilty demeanor would count against him.

Something needed to. Heimdall presumably thought astute reasoning had brought them this far. Uschi was more inclined to attribute their progress to guesswork and luck, but either way, what would happen next was uncertain. Would the Blackhammers even listen to what she and her friend had to tell them? Could Cormag be induced to reveal the secrets he presumably knew? Even if the information was all that the two Vanir hoped it would be, would Lord Maarav react with gratitude and contrition? It all remained to be seen.

Looking sour about the whole situation – or maybe just at having his slumber interrupted – balding, shaggy-browed

Maarav glowered from the high-backed seat in the center of the dais at the four people arrayed before him. "According to what you revealed to Ailpein," he said to Heimdall and Uschi, "you two are not who you pretended to be."

"No, my lord," Heimdall replied. He gave their real names. "Uschi is a thane of the Valkyries; I, too, am a thane of Asgard, and Lord Frey didn't send us. We came of our own accord."

"And having passed yourself off as something you're not," the head of Clan Blackhammer said, "you then broke into the halls of the armorers and choked one of my warriors unconscious to trespass in the chamber of the master sword smiths. After that, you somehow enlisted Ailpein in your schemes and attacked my seer."

"Yes," shrieked Cormag, "they did! The man laid hands on me! Kill them, my lord, before they do worse!"

"The strangers can't harm anyone here," Maarav said. "We've taken their weapons, and there are guards all around. What's more, everyone will get a chance to speak, including you." In his reply, Uschi caught the soothing tone healers used to calm those addled by a head injury or some other derangement.

The seer didn't look mollified, but, shivering, managed to hold his tongue. Perhaps as frightened and even demented though he might be, experience had taught him Maarav's patience had its limits.

The Blackhammer lord turned back to Heimdall and Uschi. "Why," he asked, "did you do the things you have?"

"It's a long tale," Heimdall said. "We'll shorten it as best we can. First, back in Vanaheim, Uschi detected there was something strange about the rune swords. Then we figured out your clan was the source and came to look into the matter.

From there, we determined the smiths were making the blades as they are because the Spirit of the Forge had collapsed several mines and threatened further harm if you didn't do its bidding, delivering its message through Cormag here."

Maarav sat silently for a few moments. At length, he said, "I could wish you didn't know all that. Such… capitulation is scarcely a matter for Blackhammer pride, is it? But your discoveries don't explain or excuse what you did next."

"We believed," Heimdall said, "there were things about the Spirit and the rune swords you didn't understand, things honorable folk like the Blackhammers should know even if there was a threat to their own people. We hoped that if we forced those matters out into the open, you and yours would help us avert a catastrophe."

"What catastrophe?"

"Maybe," Uschi said, "you have some awareness that the rune swords aren't *only* weapons for slaying draugr. A supernatural influence can reach through them to touch the minds of those who bear them. But I don't believe you know what that influence wants. It's trying to foment a second war between Asgard and Vanaheim. It's close to succeeding."

"Lies!" Cormag spat.

"They're not," Uschi said. "You've seen that I possessed one of the rune blades. I've dreamed one of the evil dreams myself. A dream that Odin hates his Vanir subjects and sent the draugr to plague them."

Gulbrand fingered his dye-streaked beard. "If that's so," he said slowly, "then we did Lord Frey a kindness by providing the means by which he learned the truth."

"But it's *not* the truth!" Uschi said. "Heimdall and I serve the All-Father and have for a long while. We know him. He doesn't hate his Vanir subjects and wouldn't do evil to them for no reason." She glanced at Heimdall, knowing the fate of Aesheim was on both of their minds, but continued, "The dream begins with visions of the ancient war between the Vanir and the Aesir that plainly differ from what we know of history. There's your proof it fills the mind of the dreamer with lies!"

Maarav looked to Gulbrand and Bergljot, the former appearing as grim as he had at the feast and the latter considerably more serious. "Could the swords influence the mind to such a degree? Even the mind of Frey, a true god of the Vanir?"

"It's possible," Gulbrand said.

"I agree," Bergljot said. "Truly, we've suspected all along that the rune swords had some capability to shape a person's thoughts, but as long as we didn't know to what end, and as long as Lord Frey professed himself well pleased with the blades, we could tell ourselves it didn't matter. But this…"

Maarav looked troubled. Still, he said, "It shames me to say this, but even if these two impostors are speaking only the truth, maybe it doesn't matter. We're not responsible for what happens in Asgard or Vanaheim. We *are* responsible for the wellbeing of our own folk, and as far as I can tell, nothing has changed where we're concerned." He gazed at Heimdall and Uschi, and it seemed to her that his eyes held a pleading for understanding or even forgiveness. "If the mines continue to collapse, the prosperity of the Blackhammers collapses with them. And what if that isn't even the end of the matter? If the Spirit of the Forge can bring down the ceilings of the excavations, who's to say it can't do the same to this entire city?"

And if that's how you truly feel, Uschi thought, why wouldn't you – oh so regretfully, I'm sure – kill Heimdall and me to protect your guilty secrets? Despite the all-but-impossible odds, she might have tried to fight her way out of the chamber if the Blackhammers hadn't disarmed her. As it was, she was tempted to try to wrest a weapon away from one of Maarav's warriors. At least she could die fighting as a Valkyrie should.

But her death here would do nothing to stave off the disaster threatening two Realms. Judging from Heimdall's air of composure, he hadn't abandoned all hope of persuading Maarav to help them. And so, at least for now, she'd stay as she was, a peaceful supplicant before the clan leader's dais.

"No one can blame you," Heimdall said to Maarav, "for putting the interests of your own people first. Any jarl worthy of the title would do the same. But we drove Cormag into the open, exposed him as someone who would murder one of your guests with magic without your consent or even your knowledge, to compel this very conversation. To help us, all of us together, uncover the secrets I believe the seer is hiding. If we can convince him to provide new information about the Spirit of the Forge, information that reveals how to eliminate the threat to the miners or even shows it's been removed already, *then* would the honor of the Blackhammers oblige you to help Uschi and me prevent the coming war?"

Maarav frowned. "What sort of revelations are you expecting?"

"Well," Heimdall said, "plainly we can't know the full extent of them as yet, but they've already begun materializing. It's clear now that, thanks to the amethyst talisman, Cormag wielded arcane abilities a dwarf seer doesn't ordinarily possess. Where did he get the pendant, Lord Maarav, and why did you, his jarl, know nothing of it? I think the Spirit of the Forge gave it to him. If so, that means he isn't merely the oracle who divines the phantom's intentions. He's an actual accomplice."

"Lies!" Cormag repeated. "Everyone who trades in magic, seers and sorcerers alike, have sources of arcane power revealed to no one else."

"But honest seers," Bergljot said, "rarely if ever possess sources that let them mimic what a sorcerer might do."

Maarav scowled. "If Cormag is actually in league with the Spirit of the Forge, that's despicable. But even discovering that wouldn't automatically remove the threat to my people."

And therefore, Uschi suspected, the dwarf jarl was still giving serious thought to having her and Heimdall killed. A lunge to snatch the nearest guard's spear was becoming an increasingly enticing option.

Heimdall, however, still appeared encouraged by Maarav's dubious attitude. "Perhaps," he said, "I can persuade you that the threat is at least diminished. Ailpein will confirm that the power of the amethyst shattered the stone stairs leading up to Cormag's turret."

"That's true," said the boyish mage. "I saw it."

Maarav grunted. "I'm still waiting to be convinced that your judgment is all it should be. But leaving that aside, let's say the steps did break. So what?"

"Simply this," Heimdall said. "A talisman that can break one piece of stone can presumably break another. Including the ceiling of a mine. I now suspect your Spirit of the Forge wasn't causing the cave-ins. Not directly. Rather, Cormag was doing it, and now that we've confiscated the pendant, the immediate threat at least is over."

Maarav turned back to Gulbrand and Bergljot. "I had Ailpein give you the talisman to examine. Could Cormag have used it to cause the cave-ins?"

"Yes," the sorceress said. "It holds sufficient power."

"But I didn't!" Cormag wailed.

"Even if he did," said Maarav to Heimdall, "it doesn't mean the threat is truly past." By now, Uschi was all but certain that no matter what her friend adduced, it was never going to be enough to satisfy the Blackhammer lord.

But, even now hiding any trace of impatience or discouragement, Heimdall pressed on. "That, my lord, is why we need honest answers from Cormag. To determine the true parameters of the situation. To know where we actually stand and what should be done about it."

"I've *been* honest!" Cormag cried. "And you can't make me say anything that isn't!"

"Do you think the seer could be removed from the hall for just a moment," Heimdall asked. "I'd like to speak to you without him overhearing."

"So you can traduce me without me having the chance to deny it?" Cormag snarled. "Refuse him, my lord, please!"

Maarav rubbed his hand over his balding crown. "I can't imagine what Captain Heimdall could accuse you of that he hasn't already. At any rate, I promise you'll have ample opportunity to defend yourself against anything he says. I'm only granting his request in the hope of moving this inquiry along." He looked to a pair of his warriors. "Guards, take Cormag into the antechamber. With all courtesy, of course."

Once the warriors removed the still-protesting seer, Uschi said, "Thank you, my lord. To be honest, that was unexpected. I thought you were leaning the other way."

Maarav snorted. "I'm not a fool. I may not like it, but I see that the facts support your version of events. From the start, it was beyond peculiar that the Spirit of the Forge should want rune swords manufactured to its exact specifications and then offered to Lord Frey. After which, Cormag apparently did try to kill you. My warriors found the chamber of the master smiths still mostly full of smoke, and you lying just outside reeking of it and coughing so hard you could barely breathe.

"Cormag acted without my knowledge, let alone my permission," the dwarf lord continued, "using a talisman I didn't know he possessed even though he had a clear duty to tell me, a talisman that can cause a cave-in. But with all that said, be warned that I still don't know what I'm going to do about the situation. It truly does depend on what more we can learn."

"Have there been signs," Heimdall asked, "that Cormag was wicked by nature?"

Maarav shook his head. "Up until now, I've accounted him a loyal counselor. A loyal Blackhammer."

"In that case," Heimdall said, "my guess is that he's serving the Spirit of the Forge out of fear. Fear's been the common thread running through this entire affair. And getting him to tell us what he knows might require making him even more afraid of us."

Maarav and his counselors eyed one another, and Uschi

sensed their shared reluctance. After a moment, Bergljot said, "If the poor fellow is half mad and was only acting out of fear, is it right to terrorize him any further?"

"Believe me," Maarav said, "I dislike the prospect as much as any of you. I've always considered Cormag a friend. I should have done more to look after him. I sensed his mind was failing, but I prized his service too much to order his retirement. Still, through his complicity, the Spirit of the Forge has killed many of our people. If we can extract information that will keep it from killing any more, we have to do that."

"And for what it's worth," Gulbrand said, "we won't really hurt him, just throw a scare into him."

"The question is how?" Heimdall said. "What do we know about seers in general and Cormag in particular?"

"Dwarf seers turn to stone in the sunlight," Gulbrand said. "It's a price of their power. I never knew one who wasn't afraid of it."

"Maybe," Heimdall said, "as Cormag's reason faltered, he came to be *very* afraid of it. That would explain the trash lining the walls in his turret. In his mind, it was additional layers of protection against the sun."

Gulbrand gave a brusque nod. "We can use that. Leave it to me."

Maarav looked to another of his warriors. "Have Cormag brought back in."

While they waited, the warlock with the tattooed scalp and dyed patches in his beard stepped into a corner by himself and murmured incantations. His arms moved throughout, presumably making mystical gestures, although, since his back was turned, Uschi couldn't make out what they were.

When Cormag and his escorts returned, she felt a moment of pity for the dwarf standing defenseless before so many captors, most of them long-time friends and associates now regarding him with cold, suspicious faces. Then she remembered what he'd done to both his own people and the Vanir and how he'd nearly killed her. Despite his madness and his dread, her compassion largely faded.

"Tell us everything you know about the Spirit of the Forge," Maarav said.

"I already have!" Cormag said.

"I don't think so," said Bergljot, holding up the amethyst pendant. "The Spirit gave you this and taught you to use it, isn't that right? And use it you did, to cause the cave-ins."

"No! All I did was tell you what the Spirit wanted you to know! Its price for leaving us alone!"

"We've known each other a long time," Maarav told the seer, "and up until now, you've been a true friend. So I'm giving you one last chance to speak of your own free will. Tell me all you can about your new master."

"I did!" Cormag wailed. "It's the two Asgardians lying! Lying, lying, lying!"

It seemed clear to Uschi that the seer would never say anything different of his own volition. Maarav must have decided the same, because he looked over his shoulder at Gulbrand still waiting in the corner. "It's your time."

The warlock turned slowly, with a theatricality Uschi hadn't expected, and as he did, he brought out the hand he'd held tucked away inside his cloak. The extremity glowed with a light so bright it dazzled her to look at it straight on. Even at a distance, she could feel the warmth it shed. With a cruel sneer that looked entirely at home on his underlit countenance, Gulbrand advanced.

Uschi noticed that no one else wore the same expression. Maarav and Ailpein expressed regret and distaste. Bergljot kept turning her face slightly away and then forcing herself to look squarely at the prisoner once again. It was plain that, by nature, the Blackhammers truly were no more inclined to terrorize or torture helpless captives than Asgardians were.

Cormag thrashed in the grip of the guards. "Keep it away from me!" he begged.

"That's up to you," Maarav said, and while his expression might convey regret, his voice was as stony as the walls of the chamber.

"The creature said it would do horrible things to me if I didn't obey!"

"And what is it that's happening to you now?" Maarav asked.

Glowing hand outstretched, Gulbrand paced slowly, deliberately closer. Gray streaks ran through the visible portions of the seer's skin. The limbs concealed by his clothing stopped their struggling as though the petrification there was even more advanced. Alarmed on Cormag's behalf even if he had tried to murder her, Uschi wondered if this could be merely the scare that had been promised.

"Please!" Cormag screamed. "I'll tell! I'll tell!"

Maarav raised his hand to signal Gulbrand to stop. The warlock stuck his glowing fingers back inside his cloak and stepped back a pace.

The Blackhammer lord drew breath when Heimdall spoke first. "You said 'the creature'. Not the Spirit of the Forge, 'the creature'. Why?"

Cormag sighed. Now that he was done asserting his innocence and no longer feared petrification, he seemed somewhat calmer and more lucid than before. "There's no such thing as the Spirit of the Forge."

Uschi felt a pang of surprise, and judging from the wide-eyed expressions of many others, she was far from alone.

"The being that came to me is a four-armed giant. It told me to tell you there was a Spirit. That way, I wouldn't be talking about it, and its schemes and doings would remain all the more secret."

"That's the same creature I saw in my dream!" Uschi said.

"Then you know how terrifying it is," Cormag said softly.

"What more do you know about it?" Heimdall asked.

"A little. It's called the Lurking Unknown. Or just the Lurker or the Unknown. It didn't want me to know, but I *am* a seer." Despite his current disgrace, Cormag said that last with a hint of pride.

The three mages exchanged puzzled glances, after which Heimdall took it upon himself to speak for all the learned people in the chamber. "None of us has ever heard of it."

"Because it doesn't come from any of the Nine Worlds," Cormag said. "It's from outside!"

"'Outside?'" Maarav repeated.

"Mystical lore teaches there are universes beyond what Yggdrasil encompasses," Ailpein said, "and that Midgard is a sort of nexus that exists in more than one universe at the same time. I can imagine a creature from outside possessed of sufficient power and knowledge entering the mortal Realm and from there traveling on to one of our other worlds."

"So it's here," Uschi said brusquely, hoping to keep the

interrogation from bogging down in metaphysics. She and Heimdall still had an urgent mission to complete. "What is it and what does it want?"

"It's a being called a Fear Lord," Cormag said. "It draws strength from fear, and its nature is to conquer, kill, and torment. It's laid waste to countless worlds beyond the ones we know, and now it's here to do the same to Asgard and Vanaheim. Then, for all I know, the other seven Realms as well."

"So, its opening move," Heimdall said, "is to create a draugr plague in Vanaheim and give Frey tainted rune swords to deal with it? All in the service of instigating a second war between Vanir and Aesir?"

"Yes," Cormag said. "The Lurker is cunning. It knows Vanaheim and Asgard are defended by mighty warriors and mages. But after the two Realms batter away at one another, it won't be that way anymore. They'll be weak, and it can take them."

"No," Uschi said, "that will never happen."

"Whether it could or not," Heimdall said, "our goal is to keep the war from ever starting in the first place. To do that, we need the Blackhammer mages to lift the curse on the rune swords. Then Frey and the other Vanir lords will come to their senses and realize they don't need to attack Asgard after all."

"The difficulty," Maarav said, "is that even though we now know more than we did before, we still can't be certain this Lurker won't mount more attacks against the Blackhammers, either directly or through another agent like Cormag."

"Ymir's bones!" Uschi shouted. "Will nothing satisfy you? You have the pendant in your possession and the traitor in custody. It's clear the Lurking Unknown is directing its attention to Asgard and Vanaheim. You Blackhammers were only ever a means to an end. For now, at least, the threat is over. If it comes back, you'll at least know where to aim your swords. If you *still* won't help us, then everything I've ever heard about dwarf courage and dwarf honor is as great a lie as any Cormag ever told!"

After she finished, the chamber was silent. Presumably the dwarves were shocked if not outraged at her effrontery. Then, however, Maarav gave her a crooked smile.

"You Asgardians don't lack for boldness," he said, "but you're right. I needed a moment to mull the situation over." He turned to the mages. "Do as Captain Heimdall asked. Lift the curse."

The trio just looked back at their lord for a moment. Finally, Ailpein said, "I don't think we can."

"What?" Heimdall said.

"Maybe we could stop the Lurker from sending any more nightmares through the swords," the youthful warlock said, "but that wouldn't free Frey and the other Vanir from the influence the creature has already exerted. It would have to do that itself."

"Then we'll have to force it to do exactly that." Heimdall turned back to Cormag. "Where do we find it?"

"I don't know," said the seer, "truly, I don't. I divined many things about it, but not where it stayed when it wasn't appearing to me."

Uschi felt a surge of mingled rage and despair. She and Heimdall had come so very far. Yet even so, it seemed the Unknown had thwarted them at the last, and now there was no alternative but to report back to Odin as she'd proposed in the first place. And then bear witness to all the horrors of the war that would almost certainly follow, conceivably even to the All-Father obliterating Vanaheim as he'd once destroyed Aesheim.

But Heimdall wasn't done with the questioning yet. "In your visions of the Lurker, did you see anything that might give us a clue as to where it is?"

"Well..." Cormag's eyes narrowed as though he was straining to remember. "I think there were big boulders behind it. Only they were shiny. Almost like diamonds."

Uschi's anguish gave way to a thrill of excitement. "I know that place! My Valkyrie sisters and I have flown over it!"

Heimdall nodded. "I know it, too, though only from my reading. It's the Crystal Glade of Gundersheim."

Gundersheim was an uninhabited region of Asgard far from the royal city or anyone who might notice a malevolent entity pursuing its machinations there. Uschi reckoned it was a good place for their enemy to hide.

"Thank you," Maarav said to Cormag. "I promise no harm will come to you. Gulbrand?"

The sorcerer pulled his hand from his cloak and blew on his radiant fingers as though puffing out a candle. The light vanished, and at the same moment, the streaks of gray disappeared from Cormag's face. He lurched in the guards' hands as, Uschi realized, the rigidity left his limbs.

Uschi looked to Gulbrand. "The sunlight and the turning to stone were just illusions, then."

The warlock smiled for barely an instant, the first smile Uschi had seen on his generally bitter and forbidding face.

"We're not brutes, captain. We wouldn't do that to a prisoner. Ordinarily, I wouldn't even have pretended to do it, but we were all in desperate need of answers, were we not?"

Maarav addressed the guards. "Lock Cormag up and make sure he's comfortable." He looked to the two Asgardians. "What's next?"

"Uschi and I travel to Gundersheim," Heimdall said.

Maarav frowned. "Not alone. Not to confront a being that claims to have conquered whole worlds. The Blackhammers will accompany you. This situation is our fault, and it's our obligation to set things right."

"Thank you," Heimdall said. "Believe me, we'd welcome your help." He looked to the mages. "But how quickly can you shift a company of warriors from Nidavellir to Asgard?"

"The spell we know," Ailpein said, "requires preparation. Two days, maybe three."

Uschi felt a stab of urgency. "Sadly," she said, "we can't wait that long. When we left Vanaheim, Frey was already mustering his troops, and his warlocks preparing a passage from one world to the other. Which is to say, the time to prevent an invasion is running out. Follow as soon as you can. If it turns out we failed, maybe you can still prevail. But Heimdall and I have to go now."

"How will you do that?" Maarav asked. "Can you take my warriors and me along with you?"

"No, my lord," Heimdall said. "Uschi and I will ride the Valkyrie horses waiting nearby. Even if they could carry so many, your minds might not survive a journey through the void where the World Tree stands. She and I have special defenses. As she said, you must simply follow when your mages are ready. For now, if you can give me a new two-handed sword sized for an Asgardian, that will have to be sufficient. My old one broke when some of the stone from the broken staircase fell on top of it."

The lord of the Blackhammers grunted. "We can do better than a common sword." He rose from his seat. "Come with me back to the halls of the armorers."

Thirty-One

Heimdall stood once more in the chamber where the weapon smiths exhibited their masterworks. All the gleaming treasures, the battle-axes, war hammers, spears, shields, helms, and coats of mail remained whole and pristine. On his previous visit, he'd clanged iron ingots borrowed from a different chamber together to make the guard protecting the vault of the master sword makers fear that some ghastly desecration was under way.

By now it was early morning, and the armorers reporting to their labors had been startled to find their lord, his three mages, four of his guards, and his two Asgardian guests all awaiting them. After some confusion and scurrying about, Nishant, the first master sword smith to arrive, had assumed the task of seeing to the needs of the guests.

Nishant was a black-bearded dwarf as burly as Maarav. Old scars dotted his hands and massive forearms where sparks from the forge had evidently burned him. Heimdall wondered if a long life devoted to his craft had so toughened him that embers couldn't sear him anymore.

At the moment, Nishant was conducting a sort of tour where fine swords sized for Asgardians were on display. Somewhat to Heimdall's surprise, there were quite a few. He supposed it was because trade with other Realms contributed so much to the Blackhammers' wealth.

Nishant proudly discoursed on the virtues of each weapon, excellences produced either by superior workmanship or enchantment. This blade would never need sharpening, and a warrior would never lose his grip on that one. It was all interesting, and Heimdall would have been curious to hear it all had he not been so eager to depart. He could tell from Uschi's sour expression that she was seething with a similar impatience.

He was about to interrupt Nishant and say that truly, any two-handed sword would do, when Maarav forestalled him. The Blackhammer lord said, "Enough of this. Captain Heimdall needs one of the weapons you don't put on display. Bring us Hofund."

Everyone fell silent for a moment. Then Nishant said, "My lord, it took Roksana, the greatest sword smith we ever produced, ten years to make that blade. According to prophecy, it's meant for the hands of a true God of Asgard."

"I'm less impressed with the pronouncements of seers than I used to be," Maarav said. "Besides which, it turns out the clan has done both the Aesir and the Vanir a great wrong. We'll be dishonored forever if we don't do all in our power to set things right. Now, fetch Hofund as I bade you."

Nishant turned and strode off down a hallway. Heimdall drew breath to protest, but this time it was Uschi who spoke first. "Take what Lord Maarav is offering," she said. "Who's to say how powerful the Unknown truly is? We're apt to need every advantage we can get."

Thus counseled, Heimdall held his peace, and in due course Nishant returned carrying a sword considerably longer than he was tall. After a moment of hesitation, he presented it to the Asgardian. Heimdall gripped the weapon's hilt and pulled, and with a faint metallic hiss, the blade slipped from the silver scabbard. At which point he caught his breath in wonder, for the composition of what he beheld was unmistakable. It had a duller sheen than steel, akin to but different from the appearance of poorly wrought iron.

"Yes," Nishant said, "it's made of Uru." Now that Heimdall was actually holding the sword, the smith appeared to have accepted the relinquishing of the weapon and wished to proclaim its virtues. "Metal from the first moon that ever was, found only in Nidavellir. It conveys many of the minor advantages these lesser blades possess." He waved his hand to indicate the swords on public display. "It's perfectly balanced and will never lose its edge, for example. But it has greater virtues as well. It can disguise you as anyone you like. Grip the hilt tightly and picture that person's face."

As Heimdall buckled on the baldric to get it and the scabbard out of his way, it was the image of his father that came to mind, Lord Rodric with his powerful frame, square face, and fringe of graying beard. His poor father who was surely heartbroken believing his son to be dead. As Heimdall squeezed Hofund's silver wire-wrapped hilt, he swore to himself his parents would find out he yet lived, and sooner rather than later.

When his companions' eyes widened in wonder, he realized

his appearance truly had changed. When he relaxed his grip on the sword, let go, too, of the image of his father he'd concentrated on, their reaction let him know everyone saw him as himself again.

"That might come in handy," he said.

"That's not the extent of Hofund's abilities," Nishant said. "When you need it to, it can strike harder and cut deeper than even your strength and its keenness would normally permit. But perhaps its greatest power… well, that's best learned outside."

Accordingly, he, Heimdall, and all their companions trooped back outdoors. By now, the streets of the city were filling with Blackhammers beginning their daily routines, At Maarav's command, his attendant warriors cleared the street of pedestrians for half a block in one direction. The pedestrians lingered to see the reason why.

"Stand here," said the master sword maker to Heimdall, who obediently did as he'd been told. "Everyone else, stand behind him."

"What now?" Heimdall asked.

"Imagine some mighty foe is before you," Nishant said, "but out of striking distance."

Heimdall did his best to visualize the four-armed horror from Uschi's dream. "Got it."

"Now, will Hofund to smite it."

Heimdall did so while making a cut at the air. Blue flame exploded from the Uru blade to engulf the space in front of him to a distance, he thought, of about ten paces. He recoiled a step in surprise and felt lightheaded for an instant. He swayed and caught his balance.

"The fire of the stars themselves," Maarav said, "or so I'm told."

"As you've just discovered," Nishant said, "invoking Hofund's special powers takes a toll on your own strength. You'll grow used to it in time."

"The blade is a gift beyond price," Heimdall said. "Thank you."

Indeed, now that he knew the full range of Hofund's powers, the words seemed woefully inadequate. He could see why Nishant had believed the weapon was destined for a true God of Asgard. Once, he might have tried again to decline it had he not reckoned that Uschi was right. If the Lurking Unknown was a conqueror of worlds, he would need such a sword to prevail against it.

"The blade's not a gift," Maarav said. "Call it wergild for the evil done your people."

As Heimdall slid Hofund into the scabbard, he noticed Uschi and thought he detected a sardonic cast to her expression. He then saw himself as he imagined she was seeing him, armed with both the sword and the Gjallarhorn while she bore no enchanted items at all save for the tainted rune blade that only possessed extraordinary properties versus draugr.

In a sense, he knew, that was his fault. She'd exhausted the Brightblade's fiery magic saving his life during the war with the frost giants. His survival had proved essential to the subsequent Asgardian victory, and she'd never said anything to so much as hint that she regretted her action. Still, he always carried a bit of guilt that she'd needed to make the sacrifice, the more so when he learned the weapon was a family heirloom.

He looked to Nishant. "What can you do for my friend?"

"Less than I've done for you," the sword smith replied. "Hofund is one of a kind. But we can certainly do something." He turned to Uschi. "You saw the weapons we put on display. Was there anything that caught your eye?"

"Thank you," the Valkyrie said, "but I've always managed to win my battles with this." She tapped the pommel of the Brightblade hanging at her side. She probably hoped her refusal would allow for a courteous departure without further delay.

Whatever she was thinking, Nishant's reaction was not what she expected. He peered at the weapon, and his eyes widened in surprise. "May I examine the sword?" he asked.

Uschi frowned, drew the Brightblade, and handed it over. "Please be quick."

Nishant squinted at the weapon. "This is the work of Demir of the Deep Delver Clan, a renowned sword smith who lived and forged his masterworks centuries ago. It, too, is a treasure, but it appears to have lost its chief enchantment, worn thin by time, I suspect, and then perhaps depleted utterly when called upon to perform a feat at the very limits of its strength. Fortunately, I can renew the magic. It won't even take long."

"Thank you," Uschi said, "but the sword is fine as it is."

Heimdall was surprised at her response. "Take what our friends are offering," he said. "Who's to say how powerful the Unknown truly is? We're apt to need every advantage we can get."

Uschi scowled to have her own words quoted back to her

verbatim, but she also gave a stiff nod and said, "Very well, then. If you can do it fast."

With that, they all trooped back into the halls of the armorers and from there into the chamber where the Valkyrie had nearly perished the night before. Taking a position at one of the anvils, Nishant crooned to the sword and punctuated each line of the song with a clinking tap of a little hammer on the blade. Ailpein, Bergljot, and Gulbrand looked on curiously. The smith wasn't performing their kind of sorcery, but he was working magic, nonetheless.

Watching likewise, Heimdall murmured to Uschi standing at his side. "I apologize for prodding you."

"No need this time," she said, "you were right. I knew it in the moment, too. It was just..."

"What?" he asked.

"My father reproached me for losing the Brightblade's magic. Assuming I ever see him again, I don't want him to think I rekindled it in an effort to make amends. To Ginnungagap with him and what would please him!"

Heimdall sighed. "I think I understand. But the magic truly may make the difference between victory and defeat."

Uschi glowered. "I already conceded you were right. Don't push it."

He raised his hands in a conciliatory gesture. "Of course not."

Nishant finished his song and raised the Brightblade high. Yellow flame erupted from point to cross guard and blazed there, turning the broadsword into a torch as well. Despite Uschi's previous grudging attitude, her perverse impulse to refuse the sword's renewal, she gasped and grinned to see the enchantment restored.

The smith willed the fire out and extended Brightblade to Uschi hilt first. "Your sword, captain."

"Thank you," she said, her brown eyes shining.

"And now," Heimdall said, "we truly do have to go."

Thirty-Two

Initially, there was no sign of Avalanche and Golden Mane when Uschi and Heimdall returned to the forest clearing where they'd left them. Yet when her companion blew a long, deep note from the Gjallarhorn, they trotted out of the surrounding pines.

The winged steeds looked none the worse for their time away from their riders, and that was as she'd expected. They were war horses capable of defending themselves against most any wild beast that sought to prey on them on the ground, and should they find themselves overmatched, they could always retreat into the sky.

Still, Uschi felt relieved to see Avalanche alive and well. She supposed she'd been a bit wary on his behalf after the difficulty he'd had shifting from the skies of Vanaheim to the void where the World Tree loomed. His distress had reminded her that he was a staunch comrade and how much she cared about him, and perhaps, despite Heimdall's assurances, she hadn't been certain the stallion had shed *every* trace of Ysolt's magic.

Wrapped in the ground cloth where she and Heimdall had left it, their tack was in good shape as well. They saddled the horses, mounted up, urged them into a gallop, and soared into the air. The steeds barely avoided the fragrant deep green branches waiting to batter them, but barely was good enough. Once above the forest, the riders each said, "Yggdrasil," and the Valkyrie horses opened opalescent gateways to the void where the World Tree towered.

The stallions' wings lashing, legs galloping for all that, at first, they had only emptiness beneath them, the riders flew toward Asgard. Before long, a winding path shimmered into existence under the steeds' hooves to guide the travelers along the shortest way.

Though she tried always to appear as confident as befitted a thane of her warrior sisterhood, inwardly, Uschi wondered if the gossamer trail was speeding them to their deaths. Thanks to the generosity of the Blackhammers, she and Heimdall bore weapons infused with potent enchantments, but that didn't necessarily mean they were ready to contend with a foe that had conquered worlds. She pictured the raging giant from her nightmare, and her mouth went dry. The thought returned that perhaps, now that she and her friend were about to re-enter Asgard, it would indeed be wiser to return to the royal city, report to Odin, and let the All-Father decide what should happen next.

After a moment, she pushed the idea away, because Heimdall, curse him, was right. For all his wisdom, Odin was all too likely to react ferociously, just as he had when confronted with the intransigence of Aesheim. Even learning of the Lurking Unknown might not deflect his wrath, and neither the Vanir nor the Aesir deserved the war and suffering that would result. Certainly, her mother didn't.

Onward, then! She and Heimdall had beaten terrible adversaries before. All they needed, she silently implored the Fates, was a fair chance. *Don't let us return to Asgard too late. Don't let the invasion already be under way.*

When the riders flew forth into the clear blue sky of the Realm Eternal, she found reason to hope the Three Gray Sisters had granted her plea. She and Heimdall emerged over one of Asgard's many sparsely inhabited stretches, a region mostly of forest and lakes with only a few scattered farmsteads, but as far as she could tell, there were no armies marching across the face of the land and no great columns of smoke rising to foul the air.

Of course, Heimdall could see better than she could, and so she called to him, "Are Frey and the Vanir here?"

Heimdall grinned. "No! We made it back in time! Come on! The Crystal Glade is this way!" He wheeled Golden Mane and headed south, in the opposite direction from the royal city. With a last half-rueful thought of the choice they might have made instead, Uschi followed.

For all their extraordinary abilities, when traveling between Realms, Valkyrie horses couldn't reliably create portals that opened at the precise destinations the riders intended to reach. Fortunately, their speed in the air generally kept this from being a matter of great concern, and now the landscape of Asgard streaked by below. Before long, the travelers neared one of the vast forests of Gundersheim. She could even make out a glittering in the middle, where the tallest of the enormous crystalline rock formations were catching the sun.

She peered in the hope of catching a first glimpse of the

Lurking Unknown. Instead, she spotted shimmering rainbow colors on a ridge just shy of the place where the Glade proper began. It was a doorway between worlds, but for her to see it at this distance, it must be larger than any portal Avalanche had ever opened. She took it to mean the Vanir were arriving.

"No!" she snarled. "Curse it, no!"

"Fly higher!" Heimdall called. "Maybe they won't see us!"

She realized it was a good idea. If they could soar over Frey and the Vanir warriors undetected, maybe they could still engage the Lurker within the Glade, force it to lift the spell it had cast, and halt the rebellion short of an actual battle. It felt like a slim hope, but at this point, it was the only one remaining.

The two riders took their steeds higher, where, despite the bright sunlight of Asgard's perpetual summer, the air was crisp and cold. From this altitude, she had a better view of the gleaming, faceted boulders of the Glade but could no longer discern the arriving Vanir at all. She had no doubt, however, that they were still there, and probably more and more by the moment. Warriors would all too soon be bearing arms against their Aesir brothers and sisters if she and Heimdall failed to intervene.

The pair flew onward. Until Avalanche screamed and convulsed, pinions suddenly flailing out of time with one another. The white stallion plummeted. Golden Mane shrieked an instant later. At the upper edge of Uschi's vision, the black horse dropped, too.

For a moment, she didn't understand what was happening, but then the truth became clear. Despite their altitude, Frey's troops had somehow discerned them, and, by even worse luck, Ysolt must have been in the vanguard. Her witchcraft was cursing the horses, only in a more vicious and obvious way than she'd afflicted Avalanche before.

Uschi leaned out over Avalanche's neck and said, "Just get us down to the ground safely! I know you can do it!" Astride Golden Mane, Heimdall was no doubt saying much the same.

Avalanche sought to spread his wings and simply glide down, but it was far from a smooth descent. Recurring spasms made the pinions jerk, and when they did, the stallion lurched and dropped until, straining against the pain, he managed to assume the proper attitude again. The forest below was coming up too fast, and as far as Uschi could see, there was no clear space in which the Valkyrie horse could set down. It was taking all he had just to keep from plummeting to earth like a stone. In this moment, his rider could do nothing to help him. All she could do was wait, stiff with apprehension, to see if they'd live or die.

After another moment, she and Avalanche plunged into the crisscrossing boughs of the canopy. The tree limbs whipped and battered her and snapped when bent too far. The punishment half-stunned her, but even so, she had the anguished realization that the animal beneath her was taking the worst of it. Somewhere off to the left, a similar snapping and crashing revealed that Heimdall and Golden Mane were falling through the trees as well.

A final branch or set of branches gave way beneath Avalanche, and then he and his rider slammed to the ground. The impact nearly jolted Uschi off the stallion's back, but her stirrups and the trained reflexes of a Valkyrie held her in place. Dazed, she raised her shaking hand to touch a spot on her jaw where pine needles had scraped her. Her fingertips came away bloody. Then, her thoughts snapping back into focus, she leaped from the saddle for a proper look at her steed.

The white horse was scratched and bloodied all over. Worse, one wing was crumpled and bent at a place where it shouldn't, and he stood so as to avoid putting weight on the right foreleg. She was horrified at the harm he'd endured, furious that Ysolt had struck at him in such a fashion, but most of all relieved that none of his injuries had killed him or was likely to. Valkyrie stallions were more resilient than ordinary horses, and the karls who tended them could work wonders. Avalanche would recover if only he and his rider survived the day.

As she rubbed the white steed's neck and told him what a good brave boy he was, she heard footsteps behind her. She turned, and Heimdall emerged from the trees. His bruised, disheveled appearance made it obvious he'd endured the same sort of drubbing she had, but it didn't appear to have done him any serious harm.

"How's Golden Mane?" she asked.

"He'll live," Heimdall said, "but he won't fight or fly any more today. I see Avalanche is in the same condition. We'll have to continue on foot."

"Is there a point?" Uschi didn't like the sound of the words coming out of her mouth but feared they were sensible, nonetheless. "You know I'm not one to give up, but if Frey's whole army has already come through or is coming through, and they're between the Lurker and us–"

"But the whole army *isn't* here," Heimdall said. "I kept an eye on the enemy as Golden Mane and I were falling to earth.

There are only twenty or thereabouts, and the portal has closed. Ysolt brought a small force across, I suppose to scout out the lay of the land before everyone else arrives. With luck, we can slip by them into the Glade and confront the Lurking Unknown as intended."

Uschi nodded. "It's worth a try." She loosened the Brightblade in its scabbard. "Lead on, then."

Thirty-Three

As Heimdall and Uschi stalked south through the trees, he invoked the gifts of Mimir. The ranks of pines and spruces made even his preternatural sight of limited use at ground level, but his hearing, he trusted, would prove more so. He sifted through the myriad forest sounds – the sighing of the breeze, the flutter of a bird's wings, the rapid clicking of claws on a branch as a squirrel scurried along – for noises the enemy might make. Eventually, to his disappointment though not his surprise, he caught the murmur of voices, the creak of leather, and the clink of mail.

"Apparently Ysolt sensed we didn't die when we fell," he whispered to Uschi, "or else the enemy means to make sure. I hear them advancing through the forest."

"But you can also tell where they are and how to avoid them before they spot us," the Valkyrie replied.

"That's the idea," he said. "For now, we should swing to the right."

The course he'd chosen took them by a stand of lavender and under a birch where hungry chicks cheeped in a jay's nest perched high overhead. He used his extraordinary hearing again and then frowned in surprise and dismay.

"What's wrong?" Uschi asked.

"Frey's warriors sound closer than before. I think that when we swung to the right, they compensated."

"How did they know to do that?" his friend replied. "They aren't you. They can't have heard or sighted us yet."

"They also aren't dwarves," he said. "Ysolt is of the Vanir and may be both a sorceress and something of a seer. She didn't have much trouble spotting and targeting us no matter how high we flew. She may be tracking us and guiding the warriors to us now."

"So, what do we do about that?" Uschi asked.

Heimdall shook his head. "I don't know. Keep trying to evade and hope her talent isn't infallible. Fight if we must."

Uschi flashed a wry smile. "Pretty much the usual."

"Just remember, if we do have to fight, our foes are fellow Vanir acting under the coercion of a spell. Don't kill anyone unless you have to."

"Right. Because otherwise, this would be too easy."

Changing course again, they crept onward, through patches of shadow and bright spots where rays of sunlight fell unimpeded through gaps in the canopy, the air tinged with the sharp scent of the conifers growing all around. A red deer raised her head at the Asgardians' approach and led her faun bounding away.

In short, the forest seemed quiet and peaceful. Even when the periodic exercise of the gifts of Mimir revealed the presence of foes still heading in his and Uschi's general direction, that feeling of serenity gradually insinuated itself into Heimdall's attitude, and, once ensconced there, placidity gave rise to drowsiness. He kept trudging forward but called on his extraordinary hearing and vision less and less frequently. It was difficult to remember that he should.

Until the moment came when he failed to notice a stone on the ground, his shuffling foot caught it, and he tripped. He stumbled into the pale gray trunk of an aspen, and the collision jarred him fully awake. He looked around in startled confusion and discovered Uschi was no longer at his side.

He couldn't imagine why she would have allowed herself to be separated from him unless they'd both fallen half-asleep, and it was difficult to imagine how that might have happened. They'd gone without sleep the night before, but a single night without rest was no great matter for hardy Asgardian warriors. He'd experimented with the powers of his new sword, and it was just barely conceivable the exercise had taken a greater toll on his strength than it seemed to at the time, but Uschi hadn't attempted anything comparable.

As the last of the muddled feeling gave way to a flash of alarm, it came to him that if he and Uschi had both gotten drowsy and drifted obliviously away from one another, it was likely because Ysolt had cursed them with her witchcraft. If she could afflict the horses soaring high in the heavens, why couldn't she do something comparable to a pair of Asgardians prowling through the forest?

He put his hand on the Gjallarhorn hanging at his hip. If he sounded it, the note might rouse his friend and guide her back to him.

But the tone could easily draw the enemy to him as well. It would be wiser to first exercise the gifts of Mimir. Maybe he could locate Uschi and go to her instead.

It was only then that he spotted four Vanir archers standing with arrows nocked and drawn. Despite the gaudy silver and gold mail with which Frey had equipped them, they'd done a good job of staying hidden in the thicket ahead as they sneaked up on their prey and took aim to shoot him dead.

Heimdall threw himself prone just as they loosed their shafts. The arrows whizzed over him. It was plain that had he not dropped, they would have found their mark. As the next ones surely would if he stayed in the open.

Fast as he could, he crawled toward the base of a towering pine several paces away. He felt a thump high on his back, heard a metallic ting, and realized an arrow had struck Hofund's hilt or the sword's scabbard and glanced away. An instant later, another pine shaft, with eagle-feather flights and iron wire wrapped beneath the head, suddenly appeared in the ground a finger-length in front of his head and stood there quivering. He yanked it out of the earth and out of his way, kept scuttling, and reached cover a moment later.

The pine was old, its trunk broad, but when, standing up again, he listened with the hearing of Mimir, it was plain that it wouldn't provide cover for long. His foes were advancing to flank him.

His pulse thundered, less from exertion than the acute awareness that his life depended on what he did next. He sought to clear his mind and think and judged that unless some had moved, the archers at least were close enough together that a single blast from the Gjallarhorn might incapacitate them. As he drew breath and raised the trumpet to his lips, he recalled how he'd cautioned Uschi not to kill anyone unnecessarily. With so many warriors now trying to butcher him, that didn't feel like such an important consideration anymore, but the instrument still seemed like the best weapon for the task at hand.

He peeked around the right side of the pine and spied the archers with yew bows drawn and ready, waiting for their quarry to reveal himself. They shot and he blew the Gjallarhorn at the same instant.

The blaring note caught the arrows in flight, sent them tumbling off course, and slammed three of the bowmen backward, crashing one into a tree trunk and knocking the others down. The fourth one only caught the fringe of the blast. That was still enough to spin him around and make him stagger and fall. With luck, it even incapacitated him in one way or another, but there was no time to watch and see if he'd get back up again because Heimdall heard multiple sets of running footsteps pounding at his back.

He spun back around, and half a dozen warriors were charging him, spread out widely enough that a single blast from the Gjallarhorn couldn't possibly get them all. While he was sounding it to fell one or two of them, the rest would close with him and cut him down with the rune swords in their hands.

He dropped the horn to swing from his shoulder, grabbed Hofund, and snatched out the enchanted blade. He made a sweeping horizontal cut from right to left, and because he willed it so, blue flame exploded from the Uru weapon. He meant for the fire to stop short of the onrushing warriors and hoped he'd judged that correctly. If he had, the flash hadn't horribly burned anyone, but it had dazzled and disconcerted them and balked the charge. Summoning the flame made him feel strain rather like he'd heaved some heavy weight over his head, but the sensation only lasted an instant.

Without more of his concentration to feed it, the fire didn't last either, but he lunged through the final fading haze of heat and glare to confront the flummoxed Vanir on the other side. Stooping low, he cut under one warrior's shield to slash her leg. The limb gave way beneath her, and she fell.

He pivoted, caught a second fighter's rune sword in a bind, and spun the weapon out of his grip and tumbling away. As the disarmed warrior reflexively turned his head to follow the blade's trajectory, Heimdall sprang in close and smashed Hofund's pommel into his adversary's head. Metal bonged as the heavy silver knob struck the steel rim of the other combatant's helmet. The man went down.

Heimdall turned again to discover that another of Lord Frey's rebels had recovered sufficiently from his surprise to aim his sword and swing his shield into the proper attitude for defense. Recalling Hofund's other properties, Heimdall cut while bidding the two-handed sword to lend extra force to the blow. Once again, he felt an instant of extreme effort, but the single stroke sufficed to rip away the top of the sturdy fir shield with its raised iron boss in the center. The rebel gaped in consternation at the loss of his protection. In that moment, Heimdall's follow-up action sliced a deep gash in his forearm. The other man reeled back and dropped his sword to clutch at the wound and try to stanch the gushing blood.

By now, the remaining three warriors had recovered from the shock engendered by the burst of flame. Heimdall retreated, putting the ancient pine at his back so no one could get behind him. His adversaries pursued, still game but warier now that they'd seen how capable a fighter he could be.

In the end, caution didn't help them. He drew on Hofund's

powers again to shear apart one shield after another. Ultimately, he had one foe stretched unconscious on the pine needle-carpeted earth and the other two kneeling or leaning drunkenly against a tree trunk several strides away with incapacitating wounds.

Breathing heavily, he surveyed the scatter of fallen warriors. He smelled the blood he'd spilled, and heard the moans and gritted curses rising here and there, making him hope all the vanquished were merely incapacitated. But if not, well, he'd scarcely had the option to be dainty, nor was there time to help anybody bandage their wounds. He had to find Uschi. The two of them needed to enter the Glade and capture the Lurking Unknown.

He sucked in another deep breath, poised himself to invoke the gifts of Mimir, and at that moment Lord Frey stepped out of the thicket. With his splendid glittering armor, superior smile, and perfectly shaped white-blond goatee and the long mustache curling out beyond the sides of his face, the God of the Harvest presented his usual impeccable appearance. He seemed not at all concerned that Heimdall had accounted for a full ten of his followers. The lord of the Vanir drew Laevateinn, tossed the broadsword into the air, and the weapon floated there. He readied his rune sword as well, and, just as Heimdall was thinking his situation could scarcely get more dire, Gullinbursti, the huge golden boar, pushed out of the rustling brush.

Thirty-Four

Uschi was dimly aware that at some point, she'd started walking through water. It made little splashing sounds as she trudged drowsily along, and the chill of it had soaked through her boots. She also felt mud and smooth round stones beneath her soles.

Peering from under her drooping eyelids, she saw she was walking in a shallow stream winding its way along a low place in the forest floor. She couldn't remember when she'd stepped down into it or why she had, but she didn't care, either. Sleepy as she was, it didn't seem to matter. Nor did the gurgling sound rising from up ahead, a sign, maybe, that she was approaching a place where the water ran faster.

Off to her left, the Gjallarhorn sounded a blaring note. She looked around in confusion. Why, she thought, was Heimdall blowing the trumpet? Why did the tone sound so far away?

The answer to the second question, at least, was readily apparent. Her friend was no longer walking at her side. Somehow, they'd separated without her even realizing. As she mulled over the possibility, the liquid hissing sound grew louder.

In her mind, alarm warred with the reassurance that, despite any appearance to the contrary, everything was all right. That being the case, it would be foolish to cast off the pleasant somnolence she was currently experiencing.

The Gjallarhorn called again, and that tipped the balance. Her eyes popped open wide, and then she gasped in shock at what was rushing at her. Though the stream was only ankle deep around her feet, the water ahead of her had raised itself up and was surging at her like a towering wave on a storm-tossed sea. She could make out some vague semblance of a face – glimmering eyes and a long slash of a mouth – toward the top of the mass of liquid.

Uschi whirled to the side. The mossy bank of the stream – and safety, provided the hostile spirit could only manifest within the confines of the watercourse – was only a couple of strides away. Even so, she wasn't quick enough. The wave slammed into her, bore her off her feet, and carried her along. It dragged her over the creek bottom, bumping and scraping her atop the stones, and then she came to rest.

When she did, her ears ached and the light was dim, as if she was at the bottom of a deep lake or the ocean itself instead of sprawled in an ankle-deep stream. Apparently, the water spirit had shaped its body into a sort of dome arching over her, the thing's malevolent will keeping the mass of water from spilling away despite the absence of tangible barriers to constrain it.

When the wall of water hit her, Uschi had only managed to suck in a shallow breath before her attacker bore her under. To her dismay, she already felt the urge to inhale building and sought to flounder clear of the liquid prison before she drowned. Her shield and weapon arm thrust into air, then her face, and she gasped. She just managed to fill her lungs, and then a grip seized her by the ankle and yanked her back into the center of the stream bed.

Peering, she could make out the crude shape of a hand that had formed to lock around her leg. Untrammeled by the constraints that limited solid matter, her protean assailant was manifesting more hands and reaching to hold her down. Once they immobilized her, she wouldn't defer drowning a second time, not even for a moment. The water spirit evidently knew it, too. Rippling with the motion of its body, now gazing down at her from the top of the arch of liquid, its flat mask of a face looked like it was laughing.

She wondered fleetingly if the water thing could be some strange entity that haunted the environs of the Crystal Glade and had attacked her of its own will, then decided it was far more likely to be another of Ysolt's sendings. Not that it mattered now. Whatever the creature's true nature, she had only the length of time she could hold her breath to slay or at least repel it. If she didn't, she was going to die.

Still in its scabbard, the Brightblade was beneath her. She snatched for the hilt and dragged the weapon from its sheath. Its magic renewed by the craft of the Blackhammers, the broadsword burst into flame even though it, like its wielder, was under cold, glimmering water.

Pushing against the resistance of the liquid, she hacked and stabbed savagely, focusing her efforts on the misshapen hands reaching to grasp her. Her attacker was manifesting too many for her to strike at all of them at once, but she warded herself with her shield and held back the rest. The hands dissolved into the greater mass of water when the Brightblade found them.

When all the hands were gone, she floundered to her feet and kept slashing at the spirit's amorphous body. The bubble of water containing her splashed down and away, leaving her standing gasping and dripping wet in a stream bed where once again, the gentle flow barely came up to her ankles.

The excess water wasn't gone, however. It surged a few paces upstream, gathered itself, and rose above her head once more with the manifest intention of charging her again. The wavering suggestion of a face now wore a snarl.

Uschi, however, had no intention of letting her foe continue to take the initiative. Full of fury, she bellowed, "Asgard!" and rushed the spirit before it could sweep at her.

She cut relentlessly. Now that she was no longer submerged, her burning blade turned water to puffs of steam. The spirit formed arms and smashed at her, but she caught the splashing attacks on her shield. Though they hit hard, they were no worse than blows from a war hammer or battle-axe. She didn't let them push her back or rob her of her balance.

The moment came when she was able to step in and slash deep into the spirit's face, the Brightblade's edge and yellow fire destroying one of the eyes. As before, the creature's body spilled down and apart, but this time it didn't rise anew. As she watched, the water that had constituted its substance sloshed away downstream to merge and become indistinguishable with the natural flow.

As Uschi stood there soaked, blinking away the water that dripped down into her eyes, she felt a fierce satisfaction at her victory. Quickly, she scanned the trees for some sign of Ysolt.

Because on further reflection, she was certain the thing she'd just bested hadn't been a natural being or attacked her of its own accord. The witch had conjured and commanded it.

She could see no sign of Ysolt, but to her anger and dismay, she caught the gleam of gold and silver armor as a number of Lord Frey's warriors advanced through the trees. She had no doubt they meant to succeed where the water spirit had failed, and given the weight of numbers on their side, they well might.

She scrambled up out of the stream and ran at a right angle to her present course, in the direction from which the Gjallarhorn had sounded. If she could find Heimdall, they could make a stand together. If her foes caught up with her first, well, maybe some would have chased her faster than others. With luck, they'd come at her one, two, or three at a time instead of all together.

She peered through the pines and firs ahead but could see no sign of her friend. Meanwhile, racing footsteps thudded behind her, drawing closer, and she realized she was out of time. She turned and came on guard.

As she did, she discerned that her ploy had worked, but only a little. One of her foes was plainly a superior runner and had outdistanced the rest. Some of the others were coming on fast, however, and by the time she dealt with the leader, the rest were likely to be upon her.

Hoping to dispose of the first warrior in an instant, she sprang at him and cut but failed to take him by surprise or provoke him into doing something reckless. He caught her first blazing stroke on his shield and made only a careful, testing riposte with his rune sword. It took three actions before she managed to send him reeling backward with a seared gash down the length of his face, and by then, other foes were spreading out to flank her.

She put her back against an oak so at least no one could cut her down from behind. Controlling her breathing, in part to ensure she didn't look winded, she smiled a fierce, contemptuous smile. She was, after all, a Valkyrie wielding a flaming sword who'd just defeated a terrible monster. Even so, a display of confidence wasn't likely to daunt her adversaries when there were so cursed many of them, but it did no harm to try.

The smile felt frozen and wrong, however, when she spied her father pounding along among the slowest pursuers. Heimdall hadn't wanted her to kill any of the rebels – a scruple that seemed ludicrous now that she was facing so many – but in that moment, she knew she truly didn't want to kill Peadar even if the fight afforded her the opportunity. Whereas he, she thought bitterly, was unlikely to reciprocate the sentiment. He'd gladly be the one to cut her down to avenge the wrongs and betrayals he believed she'd committed against the family.

Glimpsed at the periphery of her vision, sudden movement recalled her from such reflections and back to the business at hand. A warrior lunged in on her right, where her shield didn't cover her. She parried with her broadsword, a defense that, relying on shields to protect them, even some veteran combatants didn't master or expect, and sent her attacker stumbling back with a forearm both slashed and burned.

By then, the warrior on her far left was attacking. He, however, may have expected her to swing her shield around to block his comrade's sword stroke, thus giving him an opening. As she hadn't, it was easy to defend against his head cut and riposte with a slash to the ribs. The mail links of his byrnie split but kept the cut from going deep. Still, the Brightblade set the tunic he wore beneath on fire, and, howling, floundering backward, he threw down his rune sword and shield to slap at the flames.

Uschi laughed, mostly as a further attempt at intimidation but partly out of honest satisfaction, because she was fighting as well as a thane of the Valkyries should. That almost certainly wouldn't be enough to get her out of this situation alive, but, she insisted to herself, anything was possible.

A moment later, however, she saw something that made a mockery of that sentiment and gave her a sick, sinking feeling in the pit of her stomach. Ysolt had emerged from wherever she'd been hiding and advanced close to the fight. Taking up a position behind the rebel warriors, where Uschi had no hope of getting at her, the sharp-featured woman clutched her bone pendants in her left hand. She then raised the right above her head, half-closed her eyes, and began to sway and croon.

Uschi couldn't feel any ill effects from the incantation yet. Ysolt was a powerful spellcaster, but unlike some mages, who could hurl a devastating attack as swiftly as an archer could loose an arrow, her more potent conjurations seemed to require some time. Still, safe behind her line of protectors, she was apt to have all she needed.

Uschi fought grimly on, for there was nothing else to do. She felled another opponent with a chest cut, and after that, the rest fought more defensively. Maybe they'd decided not to risk themselves unnecessarily when they only needed to pin her in place until the burgeoning magic took hold. She wished she didn't think that was true.

As the uneven battle continued, she noticed Peadar was one of a few warriors who had yet to step up and join the front line of her foes. Maybe, she thought, he felt some slight reluctance to help kill his own daughter after all. She judged it more likely, though, that he was simply waiting for a space to open up.

Her shield arm jerked with pain, and despite herself, she cried out. She cut at a man on her right, and a second spasm made the attack clumsy. Her opponent shifted his shield and deflected it easily. Additional pains stabbed up and down her legs and made the muscles clench.

Meanwhile, ragged strands of red-veined shadow coiled around Ysolt's body and upraised arm like serpents. Every breath or two, her left hand squeezed the bone amulets, each squeeze immediately preceding another wave of spasms biting at Uschi's body.

The recurring pains slowed her and made her awkward, and it was more difficult to fend off the opposing swordsmen. Likely perceiving as much, they pressed her harder.

Peadar looked back and forth between the fight and the sorceress. He blinked repeatedly. Distress painted across his face. His mouth opened and closed as though he sensed he should say something, then realized he didn't know what it was.

A sword thrust caused Uschi to make a frantic retreat. She stumbled backward, and her spine bumped into the trunk of the pine. She wanted to step forward again, regain a little precious room to dodge and shift, but more spasms balked her, and then it was too late. The rebel warriors were closing in.

Behind them, Peadar cried, "No!" He jerked around and

threw himself at Ysolt, who gawked at him in open-mouthed surprise.

One of the swordsmen in front of Uschi edged closer and blocked her view of what happened next. When she could see past him again, Ysolt lay on the ground with the coils of shadow dissolving and Peadar standing over her. The debilitating pains and uncontrollable jerks and twitches stopped, leaving the Valkyrie as strong and agile as ever.

With the rune swords reaching for her, though, she had only a final instant to protect herself. She frantically shifted her shield to block one cut and then another, simultaneously swept her sword to parry still more attacks and slash at her assailants. Evidently responding to her desperate need, the flames leaping from her enchanted broadsword flared bright enough to dazzle an opponent, hot enough to ignite a wooden shield at a touch, although neither the glare nor the heat hindered the woman gripping the hilt. At the back of her mind, Uschi realized she'd only ever known the weapon when its magic was already fading. She now held the Brightblade as Demir the sword smith had intended it to be.

Yet even despite her prowess and the broadsword's enchantments, the weight of numbers was so against her that for another couple heartbeats, her opponents might have overwhelmed her, nonetheless. Then, however, a warrior fell even though she hadn't scored on him, and then another after that. Her father was striking them down from behind.

Belatedly realizing a new threat had presented itself, some of Uschi's foes turned to confront it. But the nearest to Peadar was too flummoxed, too slow, and Uschi's father slashed his leg and spilled him to the ground when he was only halfway around.

Uschi grinned. When, back in Vanaheim, her mother had claimed her father truly did love her, she hadn't believed. Yet now it was clear he did, and that seeing her in mortal peril, he'd even thrown off the malign influence of the Lurker to fight on her side. And now that she had an ally, now that their confused foes were caught between the two of them, the odds no longer seemed insurmountable. As she battled on, she was even able to honor Heimdall's insistence that it was better to incapacitate than to kill, though there was a cold warrior part of her that would do whatever was required to survive. Or, she realized suddenly, to protect Peadar.

Happily, though, neither she nor Peadar had to strike another mortal blow. There were no enemy warriors left on their feet. The fire of the Brightblade dying down now that it had done its work, she and her father regarded one another over the warriors they'd strewn across the ground. She didn't know what to say and sensed he didn't either.

"Ten of us warriors attacking the one of you, and magic on our side, too. It was unfair, cowardly, even, and, well..." Peadar drifted off.

And I'm your daughter, Uschi thought, but before she could decide whether she wanted to speak the words aloud, a warrior slumped on the ground nursing a bloody leg croaked, "Traitor!"

Her father winced at the accusation.

Swinging wide around the fallen warriors lest she give one of the less severely wounded a final chance to attack her, she strode to Peadar. "You are *not* a traitor," she told him. "Odin didn't raise the draugr. There shouldn't be a rebellion. The rune swords you're all carrying are cursed. They gave you evil, lying dreams to convince you of things that aren't so."

Peadar removed his helmet and raked his fingers back through his sweaty hair as though trying to clear cobwebs from his mind. "Lord Frey said two thanes of Asgard were carrying word of the rebellion to the All-Father. Ysolt had raised sufficient power to transfer a band of us to Asgard to intercept you. I happened to be there, and I guess he thought I'd be willing to hurt and stop you." His face twisted in shame. "I guess I thought so too. But when I saw you... I couldn't do it."

"You remembered you loved me," Uschi said softly.

"Well... yes." He said it with a certain gruffness. He was often uncomfortable expressing the most tender emotions straight out. It was a trait, Uschi knew, that he'd passed along to her. "Daughter, I don't know how there came to be such hard feelings between us. I'm sorry."

"You should be," Uschi said. "You rejected me when all I ever wanted to do was what was necessary to make me happy. But... you did just save my life. You shook off the influence of a rune sword when even Frey, a God of Asgard, hasn't managed it. Perhaps, when we've done a lot of talking, we can find a way to discover what we used to have, but know that it will not be an easy road."

"That's what I want," Peadar said. "For now, though, what's the actual errand that brought you here, daughter, and how can I help?"

"Heimdall and I journeyed here to defeat the thing that speaks through the rune swords. It wants a senseless war between Asgard and Vanaheim to weaken both Realms so it can then sweep in and conquer them. It's hiding in the Crystal Glade. You and your companions are the protectors it summoned to keep us away from it. I suppose that after Ysolt's magic separated us, Frey led warriors to kill Heimdall as you and these others came after me."

"Yes."

"Then I have to go to his aid. Is Ysolt dead?"

Peadar shook his head. "I know she wields powerful magic, but she wasn't holding a sword or any tangible weapon. It felt wrong to do worse than strike her unconscious."

"I wouldn't have minded seeing her dead for what she did to my horse. But that doesn't matter now. Here's what I need from you. Don't let her cast any more spells or let any of these warriors try to follow me. I suppose you can even bind their wounds if it seems safe and they'll allow it."

"I understand. Daughter, I promise you can count on me."

"Good." She took a fresh grip on her shield and dashed away.

Thirty-Five

Heimdall grabbed the Gjallarhorn, pointed it at Gullinbursti, and blew the most damaging blast he'd learned to produce. It flattened the patch of thicket immediately behind the huge golden boar, but the magical automaton itself only rattled and shivered a little. Its dwarven makers had fitted their creation together too well for the waves of sound to shake it apart.

Heimdall recalled only too well that the Gjallarhorn had failed to stun Frey before, but he had to try *something* to avoid facing a true God of Asgard and his fearsome steed at once. He pivoted and blew a second note at Frey. The God of Harvest stumbled back, and the hovering Sword of Destiny lurched back too, but, just as Heimdall had grimly expected, that was all.

Frey smiled and stroked his long curling mustache with the forefinger of the hand that wasn't holding a rune sword. He seemed to be making sure the blast of sound hadn't buffeted either white-blond end out of its meticulously groomed position. "I'm afraid," he said, "that even the Gjallarhorn has its limitations. Gullinbursti isn't some brittle ice giant to be shaken apart, nor am I a lesser Asgardian to be battered insensible."

Heimdall let the horn fall to his side and raised Hofund with both hands. By his stance, expression, and voice, he sought to project an intimidating confidence he was far from feeling. "Then maybe you're hanging back because of this."

In fact, after his defeat and narrow escape from death back in the hidden crypt, he doubted it. But, he thought, if he could keep Frey talking, maybe he could catch his second wind, and maybe Uschi would show up to help him. Or maybe he could convince the lord of Vanaheim of what was truly happening. Something!

Frey frowned as though somewhat affronted. "I haven't been 'hanging back'. It was the job of those warriors to fight on my behalf, and given the odds, I didn't expect them to have much trouble with you. Is that an Uru blade? Wherever did you get it?"

"Nidavellir." Though still keenly aware that his situation was dire, Heimdall was marginally encouraged that Frey had taken the conversational bait. "The same place I learned that you and those who follow you are deluded. Odin didn't raise the draugr, and there's no need for a rebellion. A being called the Lurking Unknown has influenced your dreams through the rune swords to make you believe what isn't so." So far, he thought, no one but poor demented Cormag the seer had known the name or title or whatever it was, but maybe a true God of Asgard would recognize it.

Alas, Frey's scornful snort made it clear he didn't. "I'm impervious to such tricks."

"You're not," Heimdall said, looking the god in his blue eyes, willing him to believe. "Think about it. How did you even know to come here, to Gundersheim of all places? You just sensed it, didn't you? Because the Unknown perceived Uschi and me and summoned you by whispering through the connection it's established with your mind."

To Heimdall's chagrin, he realized as soon as he'd uttered the words that he'd said too much, or that he shouldn't have framed his point in that way, for now Frey looked truly offended. "I'm no one's puppet," said the god. "I'm Frey, master of Vanaheim, come to avenge the wrongs done my people and cast off a tyrant's yoke." The deity took a long breath. It calmed him somewhat, but his normally fair cheeks were still flushed, his anger still apparent. "And you, Heimdall son of Rodric, are a traitor to those same people. But you've also proved yourself a fighter worthy of my personal attention, and now you'll have it."

With that, Gullinbursti charged. Evidently the golden boar was like Laevateinn in that it would heed Frey's commands without him speaking them aloud.

Heimdall called a blast of azure flame from Hofund. The automaton plunged through it undamaged and undeterred. Its long, pointed tusks were now only a few strides away. Though he could all but feel the boar's strike already rending his body, Heimdall made himself wait until the last possible moment, then dodged aside. As he'd hoped, Gullinbursti was too heavy and coming on too fast to change course.

He hacked at the boar's flank as it plunged by. With a metallic crash, Hofund opened a narrow gash in its golden substance. When the magical automaton rounded on him for another attack, it was clear Heimdall hadn't done it any serious harm.

It charged a second time, and once again he dodged. As it hurtled by, he cut at a hind leg, this time willing Hofund to lend extra force to the blow, grunting at the strain it cost him. The Uru blade cut the leg more deeply and dented the shining gold around the wound, but as before, Gullinbursti's functioning and single-minded intent to rip him apart appeared unchanged. What in the name of the Tree was it going to take to take to cripple the automaton?

Breathing heavily, Heimdall was grimly certain of one thing: he couldn't just sidestep every time. The boar would eventually compensate and tear him from groin to heart. But if he could fell its master, maybe that would stop its assault, and its back-and-forth charges had returned it to where he needed it to be.

Gullinbursti ran at him. As before, Heimdall held himself squarely in front of his attacker until it was about to close, and then, using his Asgardian strength, leaped forward into the air. Much to his relief, he'd timed the action properly and, with a clank, landed on the automaton's back.

Relief, however, only lasted an instant before giving way to desperation. The boar's precipitous forward motion and the bunching of whatever passed for muscles beneath the golden hide immediately threatened to spill him off again. Still, he managed to keep his balance long enough to sprint down the length of its spine and jump off its rump.

In a fair universe, he would then have taken Lord Frey by surprise. But in fact, the lord of the Vanir – or anyway, Laevateinn – was ready for him. As Heimdall landed awkwardly, the Sword of Destiny streaked at him. He recovered his equilibrium just in time to swing Hofund in a frantic parry.

The two blades rang together. He'd stopped Laevateinn's

cut short of his face. He'd hoped Hofund might even snap the other weapon in two as the Sword of Destiny had broken the one he had carried into the abandoned Vanir city, but here, too, he was bitterly disappointed. By the looks of it, Frey's sword wasn't made of Uru, yet even so, its magic apparently preserved it from such a fate.

Worse, Heimdall heard Gullinbursti turning around behind him. Though his risky maneuver might have bewildered the golden boar for a moment, it had now orientated on him anew. Heimdall refused to be caught between the automaton and the flying sword. He darted sideways.

Somewhat to his surprise, Laevateinn didn't pursue. Instead, the weapon shot backward to hover protectively a couple paces in front of its master.

Heimdall didn't believe Frey was a coward. He'd heard tales of his adversary's feats in battle, and the God of the Harvest had dueled him – taking unfair advantage, arguably – in the hidden tomb. Nonetheless, it was apparent that given a choice, the lord of Vanaheim preferred to stay warded and safe while his agents, whether common warriors or weapons animated by enchantment, did the slaying for him.

It was a realization that, until he resisted the emotion, nudged Heimdall even closer to despair. He'd imagined he might prevail in this fight if he could get at Frey himself, but that seemed even less likely than when they'd clashed in the secret crypt. Still, there must be a way! He just had to find one!

Unfortunately, no cunning tactic came to mind. In the current confrontation, Gullinbursti seemed fully capable of harrying Heimdall about the battlefield until he made a mistake or grew tired. Then the boar would rip him apart before he ever got within striking distance of Frey. His only hope was to incapacitate the automaton first, but he had no idea how.

Heimdall scrambled into a spot where the firs grew close together and dodged from one to the next. The obstacles slowed down the massive Gullinbursti as it gave chase. Even so, it was only a matter of time until the golden boar caught up with him.

As he dodged repeatedly to keep ahead of Gullinbursti, Frey laughed at his frantic efforts. Heimdall struggled to remember all that Nishant the sword maker had told him about Hofund's properties. Finally, it came back to him that the Blackhammer had said the sword hurled the fire of the stars themselves. According to one of the tomes he'd read in the library of his parents' castle, the stars were really suns that burned very hot indeed. Maybe that was cause for hope. But only if he could evoke flame hotter than any he'd called from the blade so far.

I know we're new to one another, he silently told Hofund, and I've only barely learned to use your powers. But I need your best.

Gullinbursti rounded a tree. Still retreating before his pursuer, Heimdall cast fire. The attack set the fir and two of its neighbors ablaze, but the boar kept coming as fast and relentlessly as ever.

He blasted the automaton twice more before he was forced to abandon the thick stand of firs. Too many were burning now, and although he seemed to be impervious to the bursts of blue flame he drew from the sword, he felt the fierce heat and could plainly suffer harm from the crackling yellow fires they'd kindled. His repeated efforts, moreover, were taking their toll.

He doubted he could manage many more. If his tactic was going to work, it was now or never.

Gullinbursti trotted forth from the burning stand of trees. Its golden form now glowed red from the repeated applications of Hofund's flame. It lowered its head and charged Heimdall with the same speed and savagery as ever.

Heimdall faked a shift to the right, sprang left instead, and managed to dodge the boar one more time. As it pounded by, he cut at its head with all the might of which he and his sword were capable.

Smiths, he knew, used fire to soften metal and make it easier to work with. He'd hoped Hofund's fire would soften Gullinbursti's body and evidently it had, for the Uru blade plunged halfway through the head. The magical automaton pitched forward onto its belly, made one attempt to raise itself up again, and then lay motionless.

Heimdall's heart pounded and Hofund felt heavy in his hands. He'd won in the only way he could contrive, but repeated use of the Uru sword's extraordinary powers had cost him. He trembled with exertion.

Still speaking from his previous position, Lord Frey snarled, "You broke my boar!" God or not, he sounded like a child on the verge of a tantrum.

Heimdall struggled to control his breathing and keep his answer from coming in a wheeze. "You, your floating sword, and the boar should all have come at me at once. You would have overwhelmed me. But I understand why you and Laevateinn held back. You're afraid of me. Maybe you're afraid of every foe. Maybe that's why you fight in the cowardly way you do."

In reality, he was certain Frey didn't fear him in the least. But if the god was angry at the loss of Gullinbursti, maybe the taunt would make him more so. Angry warriors sometimes made reckless mistakes.

But Heimdall soon realized that in this case, that was unlikely to happen. Frey's blue eyes were indeed alight with rage, and he wasted no more time sending the Sword of Destiny floating forward to strike down the foe who'd insulted him. But he hadn't abandoned his accustomed fighting style. He was still advancing cautiously behind the flying weapon.

Heimdall gave ground and, trying to repress the dread that dried his mouth and threatened to cloud his thinking, struggled to devise a second winning tactic. Laevateinn flew into striking distance before he came up with anything.

The ringing exchanges that followed were similar to those Heimdall had experienced in the secret tomb. Laevateinn cut and thrust at him, and after he parried, he had no vulnerable opponent to attack in return. Frey continued to stay well back, maneuvering and waiting for a moment when he could strike with minimal risk and to maximum effect. The difference was that Heimdall didn't even try to reach the foe behind the hovering sword. He couldn't. Laevateinn was pressing him hard. Repeatedly ducking behind trees as he had to evade Gullinbursti, he needed every iota of his skill simply to defend. Justifying its reputation for invincibility, the Sword of Destiny seemed to fight as cunningly as he did. He feared his defeat was merely a matter of time, and not much more time at that.

But, he told himself, he mustn't lose. Uschi, wherever

she was, might need him. His parents and all of Asgard and Vanaheim needed him, to prevent a needless war that would leave two Realms broken and helpless to resist the Lurker's conquest. There *had* to be a way to win this fight, and as some of the stamina he'd expended trickled back, a notion finally came to him. It was a gamble to say the least but also the only idea he had.

He struck hard and knocked Laevateinn into some thick branches bearing long, dark green needles. It was nowhere near far enough to prevent the Sword of Destiny from protecting Lord Frey, but maybe the obscuring tree limbs kept it from perceiving the Asgardian combatants clearly for an instant. It all depended on what senses the weapon utilized, something Heimdall had no way of knowing.

As soon as he swatted the sword into the branches, he drew a flash of blue fire from Hofund and in that same moment willed the two-handed weapon to mask him in the image of Lord Frey. The two invocations of power made him cry out in pain. He sensed, though, that he had his cloak of illusion even if he didn't yet know if it was going to do him any good. The next moment or two would tell the tale.

He hurled himself at Frey. At the periphery of his vision, Laevateinn leaped back out of the branches... and hesitated as though unable to tell which of the combatants it was supposed to attack and which it should protect.

Surprised, Frey nonetheless made a stop thrust with his rune sword, but simply out of trained reflex, not with any extraordinary display of skill. Heimdall beat the broadsword aside and poised his point at the God of the Harvest's throat. By then, its momentary confusion gone, Laevateinn was streaking at him but, restrained, perhaps, by Frey's unspoken command, it stopped and floated a couple of strides away.

"Drop the rune blade," Heimdall gasped and allowed his disguise to dissolve. He wished the fierce ache in the core of him would vanish with it. It was fading, but not fast enough.

Frey let his secondary weapon fall.

"Now have Laevateinn fly over to that thick old oak on the right and stab itself in all the way up to the cross guard."

The sword did so with one smooth action that showed again that Heimdall had been fortunate indeed to thwart its lethal intentions.

"Now tell it to go to sleep or give whatever command you use to make it stop fighting."

"Done," growled Frey. He was white-faced and trembling, less, Heimdall suspected, out of fear for his life than at anger at this defeat.

Not that Heimdall much cared what Frey was feeling. He was more concerned about whether the god had actually commanded Laevateinn to cease hostilities. He decided he'd have to take the Frey's word for it. All he could tell was that the Sword of Destiny was no longer moving.

"Now turn around," he said.

Frey sneered. "Coward. Can't you look me in the eye when you kill me?"

"I don't want to kill you," Heimdall said. "Just do as I say."

Frey slowly obeyed. "My death won't stop the invasion. My jarls are as set upon it as I am, and they have the sorcerers to shift their forces into Asgard."

Telling himself the God of the Harvest wasn't in his right mind, Heimdall tried not to feel annoyed at Frey's refusal to heed anything he said. He judged, however, that further talk was futile. He bashed the lord of the Vanir over the back of the head with the flat of his blade.

Frey pitched forward to sprawl face down on the ground, unconscious. The back of his head was bleeding freely, but, Heimdall judged, he'd only split the scalp, not broken the skull. An Asgardian could recover from that.

As he stood there sweaty and breathing heavily, the moment felt unreal. How was it possible he'd even defeated Gullinbursti, let alone Lord Frey himself?

More of Nishant's words came back to him. Hofund had been intended for a true God of Asgard. Heimdall wasn't one and had no particular aspirations to ever rise to that exalted status, but it appeared that, with Hofund in his hands, he was nonetheless capable of besting one in combat.

After all the God of the Harvest had put him through, Heimdall felt a fleeting childish desire to roll Frey over and cut short the ends of his stupid mustache. He didn't, though. What he *truly* wanted to do was pause and recover from his exertions, but that wasn't an option either, not when, for all he knew, Uschi might be in desperate need of help. He summoned the gifts of Mimir to locate her, and then, to his relief, she came running out of the pines alive and well.

Uschi grinned, no doubt at finding him not only alive but also victorious, standing among the unconscious Frey, the inert Gullinbursti, and the fallen Vanir warriors. "It looks like you had a bit of a battle," she said.

"I suspect you did too," he replied.

"Yes. Ysolt won't be giving us any more trouble." She hesitated. "My father's keeping watch over her and the warriors who followed her. When he saw me in trouble, he threw off the influence of the rune sword and came over to our side." She'd tried to speak matter-of-factly, even gruffly, but there was a hint of pride in her voice.

Heimdall smiled. "His strength of will – or the strength of his regard for you – is impressive. Of course, I'd hoped the two of you could patch things up."

She scowled at him. "Don't gloat. For now, my father and I have a truce, nothing more. Besides, you've been wrong about plenty of other things since this journey began."

"Fair enough. I'm curious. How did you find me?"

Uschi laughed. "You blew your trumpet and sent up a great plume of smoke. Who *wouldn't* be able to find you? Shall we move on and finish this?"

Heimdall took stock of himself and judged that the stamina he'd expended fighting and using Hofund's powers had returned. "Yes. Frey separated us because he believed we were even more dangerous fighting side by side. Let's show the Lurker just how true that is."

They set off moving southward once again. Some of the warriors Heimdall had wounded croaked taunts and defiance after them, but distance rendered the cries faint until the forest swallowed them entirely.

Thirty-Six

The last trees grew at the top of the slope that ran down into the Crystal Glade of Gundersheim. Heimdall and Uschi paused there to avail themselves of the high ground. Both scanned the landscape below them in the hope of spotting the Lurking Unknown, he with the sight of Mimir, she no doubt with the craft and care a life in the Valkyries had taught her.

He couldn't see the Lurker, and as she hadn't pointed, he knew Uschi hadn't, either. The Glade of Crystals was in truth more of a broad valley where towering faceted boulders gleamed in the sunlight and the winding pathways among them turned the area into something of a maze. At a distance, the stones looked like rough-cut diamonds and gave the impression of transparency, as if an observer should find it possible to peer right through them to locate anything hiding in their midst. When Heimdall looked more closely, however, many of the facets were more like mirrors, the boulders reflecting one another in bewildering recession.

"Well," he said at length, "I suppose we'll just have to go down and prowl around until we find our quarry."

"That suits me," Uschi said and, swords in hand, they headed down the slope.

As they did, the day darkened. Heimdall glanced up and saw thick clouds blowing in to cover the sun. It reminded him unpleasantly of the weather-working giants who'd assailed Asgard during the war with Jotunheim. By the time he and Uschi prowled between the first of the crystalline boulders, it was like they were creeping through twilight.

The gloom didn't stop the irregular planes of the looming stones from reflecting. It did, however, turn the images they captured shadowy and indistinct. Even when peering with the sight of Mimir, Heimdall repeatedly spun and raised Hofund to strike, only then realizing that, at the edge of his vision, he'd glimpsed not a threat but instead his own reflection. Uschi did the same thing, then cursed upon discerning the truth. Her uncharacteristic jumpiness scraped away at his own nerves, and, he thought, he was likely having a similar effect on her.

From there, the worry gradually rose in him that, befuddled as they were by the reflections, he might become separated from Uschi just as he had before. He told himself that was nonsense. His friend was right beside him, and there was no longer a witch turning them into sleepwalkers. Still, his mouth dry, sweating despite the chill the overcast had brought, he checked again and again to make sure he wasn't blundering through the labyrinth of boulders alone.

Though there was still no sign of the Lurking Unknown, he had a growing feeling that the entity was well aware that he and Uschi were here, and that it wasn't caution that had thus far kept it from revealing itself. Rather, it was amused by the newcomers and stretching out and savoring the moments leading up to the savage joy of confrontation.

"We should have reported to Odin," Uschi muttered.

Heimdall couldn't tell if she'd intended him to hear. He only knew that, his breath coming in quick pants, he suspected she was right. What madness had made them imagine themselves a match for a demon that had devastated entire worlds? The powers of Hofund that had seemed so formidable when he'd bested Lord Frey now felt like a pathetic joke measured against the strength the Unknown must command. He tried to push that thought and the defeatism it engendered out of his head.

Eventually he caught a soft sound like a bare foot scuffing the ground. Uschi plainly didn't hear it, and he gestured to stop her advancing. Though the two of them had come to fight, he didn't want to rush into danger until he had a better sense of what they were facing. After another moment, the Lurker reared up from behind a roughly trapezoidal mass of translucent crystal and looked straight in the Asgardians' direction.

The demon was as Uschi had described it after glimpsing it in her nightmare, so Heimdall had imagined he was ready for the sight of it. He wasn't. In the dim light, the creature's purple-black hide was as dark as the heart of some long-sealed barrow. The beady eyes in the hairless head glittered with malevolence, and it gnashed the tombstone teeth in its mouth as though it couldn't wait to chew up its foes and devour them. Its four arms were thick and knotted with muscle, and auras of purplish fire hissed around the hands on the right side.

Heimdall's pulse raced and his limbs quivered. He might

even have made a tiny whimpering sound. He felt more inadequate to this challenge than to any in his life, and ached to turn tail and flee as he never had before.

But duty to his family, his friends, and two Realms demanded he stand and fight. So he struggled to repress his dread and look at the Unknown objectively. It was, he told himself, huge, but not much bigger than the ice giants he'd vanquished at the siege of Asgard, and he hadn't had Hofund then. He *could* defeat it no matter what he was feeling.

He forced himself into motion. When he did, Uschi advanced at his side, and, responding to her will, flame erupted down the length of the Brightblade. Meanwhile, the Lurking Unknown simply held its ground as though certain the Asgardians could do nothing to harm it.

Heimdall assured himself the demon was mistaken about that. Surely, it had to be. Uschi separated from him just shy of the trapezoidal boulder, cutting right when he went left. Though he understood the tactical reason for it – they could come at the Unknown from opposite sides – it still took an effort not to call her back. He didn't want to go on alone.

He rounded the faceted stone, and the Lurker turned to regard him. Heimdall raised the Gjallarhorn. It had shaken apart the ice giants, and, unlike Hofund, it didn't draw on his own vigor to fuel its greatest powers, so it made sense to try it first.

Blowing it, however, proved more difficult than expected. He angled the trumpet up at the giant's head to keep the blast from battering Uschi, but the first time he tried to sound it, only a sad bleat emerged. Dry-mouthed and panting as he was, he hadn't drawn a proper breath. Swallowing and then straining to control his respiration, his second attempt produced the intended blare.

The forceful blast, however, had no more effect than the bleat. It didn't even make the Lurking Unknown wince or blink. The colossus just kept watching him. With derision and contempt, he was all but certain.

He insisted to himself that the fire of the stars would hurt the demon and drew a blue burst of it from the Uru sword to splash against the Lurker's chest. The flame burned and died without drawing any more reaction from the entity than the Gjallarhorn had, nor did it produce even a slight change of color in the creature's purple-black hide.

After the attack ended, however, the Unknown finally saw fit to respond. It raised the uppermost of its two right hands with its corona of violet flame, and Heimdall realized it meant to strike back at him by hurling fire of its own.

He jumped back behind the boulder. Roaring down onto the patch of ground he'd just vacated, the purple fire was so hot that mere proximity made him flinch and gasp in pain. In that moment, he was certain that if even the fringe of the burst had brushed him, it would have ignited his body as if he'd been dipped in oil.

A battle cry – "Asgard!" – split the air. It was Uschi's voice, though shriller than he was accustomed to hearing it. He realized that, now that he'd induced the Lurking Unknown to turn and face him, she'd rushed in to attack the gigantic demon from behind.

Maybe, he thought, she had the right idea. Where a magic trumpet and the fire of the stars had failed, blades and warrior prowess would succeed. An unfamiliar part of him yearned to hang back and retreat, but he made himself lunge around the boulder and dash forward anyway.

The Brightblade blazed as Uschi cut at the Unknown's feet, ankles, and lower legs, but, to all appearances, without causing the giant any distress. When Heimdall joined in, he could tell why. Hofund did cleave the Lurker's flesh, but when he withdrew the Uru blade, the gashes sealed over instantly without bleeding or leaving any sort of mark.

Still, he told himself, there had to be some sort of artery to sever or bone to splinter, some sort of weak spot. He just had to keep cutting and find it.

Looking down, the Lurking Unknown suffered his and Uschi's attentions for several more sword strokes. After that, it started growing, maybe because, now that it had lured its prey in close, it deemed it time to show them what they were actually facing.

Its body swelled until the tallest of the gemlike boulders only came up to its knees. Its bald apish head seemed to brush the gray overcast sealing away the blue of the sky. The fires shrouding its right hands were like two purple suns, and, slashing and stabbing uselessly at its naked feet, Heimdall felt as small as a mosquito.

He'd defeated trolls, Jotuns, ice giants, draugr, and sorcery in his time, but no warrior could devise a way of vanquishing this horror. He scrambled around one enormous foot to reach Uschi. "Run!" he bellowed.

When they fled, the Unknown seemed in no great hurry to stop them, and why should it be when they were helpless against it? Eventually, though, when Heimdall glanced over his shoulder, the colossus was poising both burning hands to cast more fire.

"In here!" he said. He dodged behind the cover of a stone. Uschi scrambled after him.

The torrents of fire turned all the surrounding crystalline boulders purple and for a moment made the air blistering hot and unbreathable. Yet when the attack ended, Heimdall discerned that the stone behind which he and Uschi were cowering had shielded them from the worst of it. They jumped up and scurried on.

Unhurriedly, as though still enjoying toying with its prey, the Lurking Unknown pursued. As Heimdall and Uschi ran, changing course repeatedly in the hope of throwing the enormous entity off their trail, he reckoned that the boulders that came up to its knees were slowing the Lurker down a little. Otherwise, it would likely have caught up to them in a matter of moments, its long steps covering ground much, much faster than the Asgardians could run.

Heimdall's sole remaining hope was that if he and Uschi could make it back out of the Crystal Glade and into the forest, the Unknown might lose track of them. Unfortunately, the need to turn and evade repeatedly kept the borders of the woodland from ever seeming any nearer.

From somewhere behind him came a crunching sound. A moment after, the gloomy day grew darker. He glanced up, and something translucent and barely visible arced through the air overhead. He realized the Lurking Unknown had uprooted one of the gemlike stones and tossed it, apparently in the hope that it would smash down on top of its prey.

Heimdall and Uschi dodged into the narrow aisle between two other boulders. The stone crashed down close by. The impact jolted the ground, making Heimdall jump.

A moment later, he spied the Lurker looming above the nearer boulders. The colossal demon was closer than it had been since he and Uschi left off hacking at its lower extremities. Maybe it was growing bored with its sport and was ready to finish off the Asgardians.

Meanwhile, shaking, nearly weeping with fear, all Heimdall knew to do was press himself up against the stone and hope the Unknown would overlook him. Given the near-transparency of his hiding place and the creature's height enabling it to look down into the gaps between boulders, it seemed a forlorn hope at best.

At first, Uschi looked as frightened as he felt, but she took long, slow breaths, and after several inhalations, panic seemed to give way to resolve. "I'm a Valkyrie," she gritted out to him. "I'm not going to die a coward. Maybe if I distract it, you can make it into the trees."

"Don't," Heimdall said. "It'll kill you in a heartbeat."

Not heeding him, she rose. The Brightblade burned and hissed with yellow flame. She stepped into the open and shouted, "All right! Here I am! Come and kill me if you can!"

Plainly, what she was doing was suicide. Odin might conceivably be a match for the Unknown, but no lesser warrior could be. As it was too late to stop Uschi, Heimdall reckoned that at least he shouldn't let her sacrifice go for naught. It was possible that if he could spur his cringing body into motion and time his bolt from cover correctly, he might make it to the forest.

It was, he thought, the only rational thing to do. Uschi was doomed. If he got away, maybe he could still do something to help his parents, Vanaheim, and Asgard.

Yet rational or not, he realized it wasn't in him. Maybe it was because he and his friend had been through so much together, but he wouldn't abandon her to fight and die alone. He needed to muster courage like hers. He inhaled deeply, rose, took a fresh grip on Hofund, and stepped out into the open beside her.

Now that he'd accepted the inevitability of his own imminent death, something unexpected happened. His terror lost its edge. He was still afraid. How could he not be, considering the monstrosity towering before him? Panic, however, had departed, leaving his limbs steady and his breathing even. Like the friend beside him, he meant to die well.

Uschi shot him a smile that revealed that, despite urging him to flee, she was glad they were fighting their final battle together. Meanwhile, the Lurking Unknown seemed to hesitate. Had he not deemed the notion nonsensical, Heimdall might almost have wondered if it was the giant's turn to feel uncertain and afraid. As it was, he supposed the Lurker was merely surprised its prey had opted to make a stand.

Heimdall nodded, and he and Uschi ran forward like angry ants scuttling at a bear. The Unknown roared, and twin cascades of fire exploded from its two right hands. The purple flames swept down the passage through which the Asgardians were charging.

Heimdall glanced to the sides and found only walls of faceted translucent rock from which his own bearded face peered back at him. This time, there was no gap between boulders within reach, and thus no cover to be had.

Accordingly, expecting only a moment's agony and then

oblivion, he tried to run even faster. If he could pass through the advancing stream of fire quickly enough, it seemed just barely possible he'd survive.

The world turned violet and searing hot. Then to his own surprise, he sprinted out the other side of the fire. He glanced to the side, and Uschi was still charging beside him. Purple flames danced on the face of her shield, and she cast away the protection as she ran.

The Unknown lifted its two right hands to cast another torrent of fire. In the hope of forestalling it, Heimdall hurled Hofund's blue flames at the giant's legs. The Lurker recoiled a step in response to the blast, and then, an instant after the azure flare blinked out of existence, the two Asgardians closed with their foe. They slashed at its bare extremities as they had before, only to greater effect.

The wounds they inflicted still didn't bleed. Apparently, the Lurking Unknown had no blood. But neither did the gashes close without trace the moment Hofund and the blazing Brightblade were withdrawn. They remained as livid mauve splits in the demon's flesh. The damage gave Heimdall a fierce satisfaction even though he was certain another torrent of purple fire would burn down from on high to annihilate Uschi and him in another heartbeat.

But that didn't happen either. Maybe, he thought, because the Unknown wasn't immune to its own conjured fire and couldn't employ it now lest it sear its own lower limbs. Instead, it resorted to stamping and kicking, seeking to squash its opponents flat or pulverize them.

Heimdall grinned. The Lurking Unknown was the biggest giant he'd ever fought but scarcely the first one. He'd encountered such tactics before, learned how to cope with them, and knew that Uschi had too.

When the Lurker lifted a foot high, they dodged out from underneath. When one was on the ground, they took care not to be in front of it. One kick grazed Heimdall anyway and threw him crashing into a boulder, but his byrnie kept him from suffering serious harm. He leaped to his feet and rushed back into the fray.

He didn't expect the fight to continue to go in his and Uschi's favor. No doubt the Lurker, conqueror of whole worlds that it was, would realize in another moment that it need only take a single stride to once again distance itself from its foes. Then more purple fire would pour down, and the Asgardians couldn't endure it forever.

The Unknown did indeed take a staggering step away, but as the demon lurched back around, Heimdall realized the retreat hadn't carried it as far as he'd anticipated. Moreover, the boulders that had formerly barely reached the demon's knees now came up to its waist.

"It's shrinking!" he yelled, and he and Uschi rushed the giant again. As they did, he noticed that the Unknown's upper right hand had lost its halo of violet fire.

As the Asgardians charged, the Lurker cast flame from the hand that still burned. It was, however, a narrower cascade which didn't fill the path between the faceted boulders, and Heimdall and Uschi dodged around it. The column went out as they evaded, and the hand's fiery aura along with it.

The two warriors charged back into striking distance. Their weapons slashed relentlessly, the Brightblade splashing arcs of yellow fire. As the sword strokes opened new wounds, the Lurking Unknown continued to shrink until their blades could threaten its belly, chest, arms, and finally, when it was only a bit taller than its foes, the neck and head. Meanwhile, it bashed and snatched at the Asgardians with prodigious strength, but Heimdall and Uschi either avoided the attacks or met them with stop cuts that made the demon jerk its hands back.

Heimdall wondered fleetingly why his attacks and Uschi's were hurting the creature now when they hadn't before. Cormag, he recalled, had said the Lurker was a Fear Lord. Perhaps, then, when the Asgardians had overcome their terror, had acted in defiance of it, the demon started losing strength.

Eventually Heimdall slipped behind the Unknown while the Valkyrie had its attention and slashed deep into the back of its leg. The demon howled and pitched forward onto one knee. Her face a mask of battle fury, Uschi raised the Brightblade to strike the Lurker's head off.

Heimdall felt the same rage and urge to finish off their adversary, a feeling fueled by his earlier dread and certainty he and his companion were about to perish. But he also remembered something Uschi, caught up in the moment, had evidently forgotten.

"Don't kill it!" he cried. "We need it to break the spell!"

The Brightblade didn't make the decapitating cut, but Uschi's scowl showed she wasn't happy at being balked. "Killing it will break the spell," she said.

"But maybe not," Heimdall said. "My way is surer." He glowered down at the Lurking Unknown. "Do you surrender?"

"Yes," the demon growled. Much of its purple-black body

was crisscrossed with the gashes the Asgardians' swords had made.

"Then you've heard what we need you to do," Heimdall said.

The Unknown hesitated. "That which I've set in motion cannot be undone. But you've proven yourself worthy warriors. Join me. Be my jarls. You can rule Asgard, Vanaheim, and a thousand other worlds as my lieutenants."

"Sorry," Heimdall said, "we're not interested. And if you keep insisting you can't lift your curse, then I will let my friend kill you. We'll see if that helps."

Uschi hefted the Brightblade, and new fire ran down its length. "By all means. I'll truly enjoy it."

"That won't be necessary," the Lurker snarled. It was quiet for a moment, rather like Frey giving silent instructions to Gullinbursti and Laevateinn. At length it said, "I've done it."

"How do we know that?" Uschi asked.

"Look at that blade you wear on your back," the Lurking Unknown replied.

The Valkyrie tried to draw the rune sword and found she was only grasping the hilt. She unbuckled the baldric securing the scabbard and upended the sheath. With a soft hiss, particles of red rust poured out.

"That's a promising sign," Uschi said, "but it isn't proof."

"We'll know for certain when we return to Lord Frey and the others we left in the forest," Heimdall said. "If it turns out they're still deluded and bent on rebellion, cut the creature's head off."

"You may have bested me in battle," the Unknown said, "but surely you aren't such fools as to imagine you can long keep the conqueror of worlds a prisoner."

Heimdall snorted. "Actually, I like our chances. You need the fear of others to feed you strength. But you no longer have the rune swords to spread fear, and Asgardians don't scare easily. When people see you've shrunk to something scarcely bigger than a man, covered in wounds, and with warriors walking behind you ready to strike you down, they're not going to quake in terror. Uschi and I should be able to manage you and march you to where we want you easily enough."

Once they were under way, with the prisoner hobbling along in front of its captors, the Valkyrie said, "You must be right about the creature needing the fear of others to give it power. Shaking off our own fear is what enabled us to win. After all, why would the Lurker summon Frey and his followers to fight for it, thus disrupting the plans for the invasion, if it were truly as mighty as it appeared?"

"Exactly," Heimdall said, "but once we breached its first line of defense, we still had to cope with the fact that it had established the Crystal Glade as its place of power. From the moment we entered, its magic was gnawing at us to make us afraid. It even blotted out the sun to make everything gloomier – something I didn't notice until now." With the demon defeated, the sun was shining again, and though the diamondlike boulders had seemed menacing before, their sparkling beauty was now apparent.

"Fortunately," Uschi said, "even in the Glade, it couldn't daunt us for long." She frowned. "Did you realize all this about the source of the Lurker's power when we were hiding and I was sure we were going to die? Because you might have said something."

Heimdall hesitated, his natural honesty in conflict with the satisfaction he took in his reputation for always being shrewd and cool-headed. In the end, he split the difference and replied, "Well, not *all* of it."

Thirty-Seven

Three days later, Uschi stood in the throne room of Asgard prepared to deliver the long-deferred report to Odin. She'd addressed the king before and even received his praise a time or two, but that didn't keep her from feeling nervous. She did her best to hide her anxiety beneath a warrior's stoicism.

At least, she reflected, she wasn't standing here alone. Heimdall was beside her, not that his presence was likely to diminish the All-Father's wrath if, in fact, what he was about to hear made him angry.

More usefully, perhaps, Lord Frey and a number of Vanir nobles, her own parents and her friend's mother and father among them, were waiting to confess they'd planned to rebel. The destruction of the rune swords had indeed purged them of false beliefs and resentments centered on Odin, and now they were the picture of rueful contrition.

Lord Maarav, Nishant, Bergljot, Gulbrand, and Ailpein were also present to explain their clan's role in the near disaster. The dwarves had arrived in Asgard too late to take any part in the subdual of the Lurking Unknown, but not too late to corroborate a substantial portion of Heimdall and Uschi's story.

Although probably the most important corroboration of all hulked sullenly with two of Odin's guards holding it at spearpoint. Uschi suspected the spears were unnecessary, for though they were healing, the Lurking Unknown still bore the marks of her sword and Heimdall's. It was bound, moreover, with glimmering silver cord. The cord appeared no more substantial than the finest gossamer thread, but enchantment evidently made it considerably stronger than it looked. It might even be akin to Gleipnir, the cord made of a cat's footsteps, the beard of a woman, the breath of a fish, and other mystical components once used to restrain the Fenris Wolf.

Uschi was likewise glad to see Queen Frigga sitting on the dais beside her husband in a high-backed golden throne nearly as ornate as his. She looked thoroughly regal in her golden gown and with her silver-blonde hair swept high atop her head, but considerably less stern than her royal spouse. Born in Vanaheim, Frigga still loved the people among whom she'd grown up and was also the monarch who'd first taken special note of Uschi and Heimdall and commended them to Odin's attention.

For once, it was attention the Valkyrie would just as soon have forgone. The All-Father was a mountain of a god with a shaggy white beard that implied his immense age – he'd been born in a time before the Nine Realms had even come to be – but in no way belied his manifest might. The patch that covered the socket of the eye he'd traded for wisdom was white as well, a contrast to garments predominantly blue. He wore

Draupnir the Odinring around one muscular forearm, held Thrudstock the power scepter in his lap, and glowered at the folk arrayed before him. Clearly, he'd been apprised, at least in broad outline, of what he was about to hear and was less than pleased about it.

As he, too, was a true God of Asgard, Frey took the lead in telling the tale, and while Uschi had yet to warm to the lord who'd wanted her and Heimdall dead, she had to admire his composure. Frey's voice was steady, and he looked Odin in the face as he laid out his aborted plan to start a second war between the Vanir and the Aesir without hesitation or any attempt at equivocation.

The God of the Harvest couldn't tell the entire story, however, because he hadn't been present for all of it. It fell to the Blackhammers, Heimdall, and Uschi to fill in the gaps. As her fellow thane approached the moment when they'd opted to journey to Nidavellir instead of returning to Asgard, she worried that Heimdall would say flat out that they'd feared Odin's reaction to their news, and that such a suggestion would itself provoke the king to fury. To her relief, in Heimdall's retelling, he and his companion had never even considered such an option. It had appeared to them that their duty was clearly to travel to the Realm of the dwarves, and accordingly, that was what they did.

When all the explanations were through, Odin sat silently for a few moments, pondering what he'd learned, apparently, while giving everyone else time to grow tense in anticipation of an explosion. When the All-Father finally did speak, it was to the Lurking Unknown. "Let's start with the easy case." He smiled a scornful smile. "You thought you could conquer my kingdom. Looking at you now, it's hard to imagine you could be such a fool."

Though a helpless prisoner, the demon nonetheless dredged up the wherewithal to answer with a certain arrogance. "You haven't seen me as I am when I bestride a world my schemes have broken and filled with terror. Then I'm a power as mighty as you. You'll see it one day."

"No," Odin said, "I won't. You should never have come to Asgard, and now you must pay the price. Sorcery will bind you for good and you'll come when I call you and do as I bid you like a faithful hound. Properly trammeled, you'll be useful when I see fit to test the courage of one young warrior or another."

The Unknown snarled in outrage. "I am not your dog or your slave! I am a Fear Lord–"

Odin lifted his scepter and gave it a casual flick. The Lurker vanished like a blown-out candle flame.

"And with that," the All-Father said, "we come to the rest of you." He regarded Frey. "Was it truly impossible to remember that I've been a just king to you and yours? To question whether I had reason, or it was even within my nature to lay a curse on all Vanaheim?"

"I can only tell you," Frey replied, "that faced with the horror of the draugr and with the rune swords warping our minds, we found it so."

"Had it been true," Frigga said to her husband, "would it not have been just cause for a rebellion? You took up arms against your brother Cul when he proved cruel and mad."

Odin grunted. "And besides, family is family. Fine. I pardon Frey and all who would have followed him into rebellion." He shifted the gaze of his single cold blue eye. "You Blackhammers, though. You forged the swords that incited the Vanir to rise against me."

"For that," Lord Maarav said, "we are truly sorry. In our defense, I can only say we didn't understand the consequences of our actions."

"And the blades *did* slay draugr," said dour Gulbrand with his dyed multicolored beard and tattooed shaven pate, "and the customer – Lord Frey, there – said he was satisfied with them." Meanwhile, his fellow dwarves stared at him as though they felt he was speaking out of turn and hoped to hush him through the force of their disapproval. Noting their reaction, he scowled back. "It's not an excuse, but it's the truth."

"Were you to retaliate against the Blackhammers," said Frigga, placing her slender hand on Odin's burly arm, "the other clans of Nidavellir might well strike back at Asgard, and then we'd have a different needless war between Realms on our hands."

"And until we won it," said the king sourly, "to whom would I turn when I needed another wondrous item made? Very well. Lord Maarav, you and yours retain my favor. Although Asgard will expect bargain prices moving forward."

The master of Clan Blackhammer inclined his balding, bushy-browed head. "You'll have them, Your Majesty."

Odin then looked down at Uschi and Heimdall. "But now we come to my thanes. The only people in this affair who *can't* claim the magic of the Lurking Unknown affected their thinking. You didn't acknowledge it when you told your story, but I *know* you must have understood that when you realized an insurrection was nigh, it was your duty to come to me and report. Instead, you rushed to Nidavellir, and all Asgard and all Vanaheim might have suffered for your recklessness."

Uschi shot Frigga a glance to implore her help as the queen had previously given it to Frey and the Blackhammers. The look the All-Mother returned conveyed that she'd help if she could but, in this instance, didn't know what to say.

Heimdall, however, had a response, and to Uschi's relief, it didn't involve invoking the memory of Aesheim. She suspected such a reference might have annoyed the king even more. Instead, looking up at Odin as bravely as Frey and Maarav had, her fellow thane said, "Majesty, if you're finding fault with Captain Uschi and me for not telling you of a brewing insurrection, I can only answer, what insurrection? What rebellion? What war? I don't see how we can fairly be blamed for not wasting your time on things that didn't happen and never will."

Odin stared coldly back, and then his severity ended in a snort. "Very well. Except for the Lurking Unknown itself, no one will be punished. But captain, this is twice you've disregarded the wishes of your superiors, once when you and Sif saw fit to break into the vault of the Odinsleep and now again. I recognize, Asgard has benefited from your independent streak. Should you do it again, though, you'd better continue being right."

It was Heimdall's turn to incline his head. "Yes, Majesty," he said.

After the All-Father dismissed them, many of the assembly lingered in the corridor outside the throne room chattering about how relieved they were that the king had forgiven them. Uschi, however, hesitated before approaching her mother and father. The conversation to come wouldn't threaten her rank and liberty like the one with Odin had, but the prospect made her feel tongue-tied and maladroit, nonetheless.

Peadar spoke first as he had when they were looking at each other over the fallen rebels they'd defeated in the woodlands outside the Crystal Glade. "That went better than I thought it might."

"It helped that the Lurker, the true enemy, was there to provide a target for the king's anger." Uschi took a deep breath. "Father… Mother… I'm not sorry for running away. I needed to do it, and I had the right. But maybe it's not too late to mend old quarrels."

"I truly hope not," Peadar said. "For what it's worth, I understand now that you had your heart set on being a Valkyrie and would have been miserable walking any other path. I should have considered other ways to restore the family's fortunes and have an heir. I could have pursued other trading ventures and alliances. Your mother and I could have fostered the child of some other house to raise as our own. But once I conceived the plan to marry you off, I was too stubborn and proud to abandon it. It had to be a grandchild of my actual bloodline someday inheriting my position." He paused and cleared his throat. "I've been such a fool."

"As I said before," Uschi replied, assured more so that their response was genuine, "maybe it's not too late to patch things up."

"Indeed not," Juliska said, smiling through the happy tears flowing from her eyes. "That's the advantage of being long-lived Asgardians. It's not too late at all. Daughter, can we visit the Valkyrie barracks? I'd like to see the place you now call home."

"Of course," Uschi said. She realized she was in danger of shedding tears herself. But she didn't think that would be consonant with her dignity as a warrior and a thane of the Valkyries, so she held them back as best she could. "And afterward, I know a good place for a midday meal." She turned to lead her parents down the passage. By then, the crowd had thinned out, affording her an unobstructed view of Heimdall, Lord Rodric, and Lady Estrid. The three were smiling and engaged in animated discourse with one another.

For once, a reflexive pang of envy upon beholding a happy family didn't rush through her. Her mother was right. Though she would never have guessed it only a week ago, there was still a chance for her parents and her to reestablish ties.

As they approached her friend, Rodric, and Estrid, she overheard what they were talking about. The small, apple-cheeked woman clad in the red clothing she favored beamed up at her son. "I don't think the All-Father was truly cross with you. Or if he was, he'll get over it quickly. Then he'll appreciate that if not for your 'independent streak' – and sharp mind and other talents – Vanaheim and Asgard would be at war."

"With that Lurker brute waiting to conquer us all at the end," Rodric said.

Heimdall smiled. "There were times along the way when those qualities did serve me well. Still, I think I'd grown somewhat prideful and complacent in the years since we beat the Jotuns back. Now I've learned my wits don't always mean I'm right. The gifts of Mimir don't always enable me to see farther than others. Occasionally, my friends understand what I don't, and I'll do well to heed them and follow their lead."

"He's talking about me," Uschi said. "I'm the comrade who was cleverer than he was."

Heimdall turned his head, saw her and her parents approaching, and gave her a grin. "You'll notice," he replied, "I said 'occasionally.'"

EPILOGUE

Hogun was no accomplished spinner of tales – he generally left it to Fandral and Volstagg to provide such entertainment when they were drinking in a feast hall or lounging around a campfire – and it took longer than expected to work through the story of Heimdall, Uschi, the rune swords, and the Lurking Unknown. By the time he finished, he and skinny, blonde little Gunhild had prepared a supper of salted herring, carrots, coarse sourdough bread, and bilberries, eaten it, and washed the dishes afterward.

Meanwhile, full night had fallen outside the comfortable home. He and the child needed the crackling flames in the firepit to push the darkness back into the corners. Most of the smoke went up the smoke hole in the ceiling, but some of it made a pungent, eye-stinging haze in the air, prompting Hogun to reflect in passing that Gunhild's stonemason father ought to take time off from maintaining the mighty walls of Asgard to equip his own dwelling with a chimney.

When Hogun finally reached the end of the story, Gunhild

said, "But what about Avalanche and Golden Mane? Were they really all right?"

Hogun frowned. "After all I told you, that's what you think to ask?"

"I like horses," the little girl replied. "So, were they?"

"Yes," he said. "They recovered from their injuries, and Uschi and Heimdall are still flying around on them today. Most of the bewitched Vanir the two thanes fought in Gundersheim recovered as well, if you care anything about them. Uschi and Heimdall were such skillful fighters that they only killed a couple."

"That's good," Gunhild said, although it was plain the fate of the rebel warriors had concerned her less than the wellbeing of the winged stallions. She sat quietly, her forehead creased in thought. Then: "I liked the story. Truly. But you told it to teach me something, didn't you? What was I to learn?"

Hogun hesitated as he realized he didn't know either. He'd decided to share the tale when he was floundering in his efforts to help her figure out how to prevent her schoolmates from risking their lives in a perilous climb over the edge of the world and do so without informing on them to a teacher or their parents. He still felt Heimdall and Uschi's dilemma as they sought to satisfy their competing responsibilities constituted a comparable situation. But if he'd ever had a tidy moral in mind, he'd lost track of it while narrating desperate battles with draugr.

"What do you think the lesson was?" he replied, hoping an answer would come to one of them.

"Well… Uschi was a great fighter. Heimdall, too. And if I could fight well enough to beat up Leos, I'd be the leader, and if I told the others we weren't going to climb over the edge of old Yonas's land down to the ledge, that would be the end of it. I could stop it without needing to be a tattletale."

Hogun had the feeling that hadn't been the moral he'd been working toward, but he liked it. Now that Gunhild had framed her problem in terms of brawling, he was finally on familiar ground. Although...

Heimdall had learned that his insights and ideas weren't always the wisest. Uschi had discovered the love within families could transcend even bitter quarrels. For a moment, Hogun wondered if he should try to apply one of those lessons to Gunhild's situation but then decided his way was better.

"You told me this Leos is older and bigger than you," he said, "but that's no great matter. I've bested plenty of actual giants in my time. It's all in knowing how. Would you like to learn?"

"Yes!"

"All right, then." He rose from his bench, and she from hers. "Stand facing me. There's good. Now make a fist. No, the thumb goes on the outside. Otherwise, you're apt to break it when you throw a punch."

Acknowledgments

Once again, thanks to my editors Gwendolyn Nix and Charlotte Llewelyn-Wells, and to Marc Gascoigne, Anjuli Smith, Vanessa Jack, and all the great people at Aconyte Books for their help and support.

Humble appreciation as well to all the creators who have worked on the Asgardian part of the Marvel Universe, Stan Lee and Jack Kirby, of course, but also all the gifted writers and artists who came after them. The saga of the Realm Eternal has been running for almost sixty years now and is sure to run for many more, and I hope this novel is a worthy link in the chain.

About the Author

RICHARD LEE BYERS is the author of fifty horror and fantasy books including *This Sword for Hire* and *Blind God's Bluff*, novels for *Marvel Legends of Asgard*, *Forgotten Realms*, and the Impostor series. He's also written scores of short stories, some collected in *The Things That Crawl* and *The Hep Cats of Ulthar*, scripted a graphic novel, and contributed content on tabletop and electronic games. A resident of the Tampa Bay area, he's an RPG enthusiast and a frequent program participant at Florida conventions, Dragon Con, and Gen Con.

twitter.com/rleebyers

# MARVEL LEGENDS OF ASGARD

Defend the honor of Asgard and the Ten Realms in the epic quests of its mightiest heroes.

THE HEAD OF MIMIR
RICHARD LEE BYERS

THE SWORD OF SURTUR
C. L. WERNER

THE REBELS OF VANAHEIM
RICHARD LEE BYERS

THREE SWORDS
C. L. WERNER

MARVEL UNTOLD

MARVEL CRISIS PROTOCOL

- **The Harrowing of Doom** — A prose novel by David Annandale
- **The Patriot List** (The Dark Avengers in) — A prose novel by David Guymer
- **Witches Unleashed** — A prose novel by Carrie Harris
- **Target: Kree** — A prose novel by Stuart Moore

MARVEL HEROINES

- **Domino: Strays** — Tristan Palmgren
- **Rogue: Untouched** — Alisa Kwitney
- **Elsa Bloodstone: Bequest** — Cath Lauria
- **Outlaw: Relentless** — Tristan Palmgren

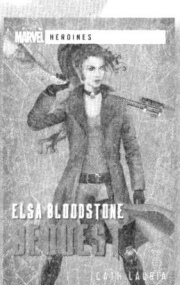

MARVEL XAVIER'S INSTITUTE

- **Liberty & Justice For All** — Carrie Harris
- **First Team** — Robbie MacNiven
- **Triptych** — Jaleigh Johnson
- **School of X** — Edited by Gwendolyn Nix

WORLD EXPANDING FICTION

Do you have them all?

MARVEL CRISIS PROTOCOL
- ☐ *Target: Kree* by Stuart Moore

MARVEL HEROINES
- ☐ *Domino: Strays* by Tristan Palmgren
- ☐ *Rogue: Untouched* by Alisa Kwitney
- ☐ *Elsa Bloodstone: Bequest* by Cath Lauria
- ☐ *Outlaw: Relentless* by Tristan Palmgren
- ☐ *Black Cat: Discord* by Cath Lauria
  (coming soon)

LEGENDS OF ASGARD
- ☐ *The Head of Mimir* by Richard Lee Byers
- ☐ *The Sword of Surtur* by C L Werner
- ☐ *The Serpent and the Dead* by Anna Stephens
- ☑ *The Rebels of Vanaheim* by Richard Lee Byers
- ☐ *Three Swords* by C L Werner *(coming soon)*

MARVEL UNTOLD
- ☐ *The Harrowing of Doom* by David Annandale
- ☐ *Dark Avengers: The Patriot List* by David Guymer
- ☐ *Witches Unleashed* by Carrie Harris
- ☐ *Reign of the Devourer* by David Annandale
  (coming soon)

XAVIER'S INSTITUTE
- ☐ *Liberty & Justice for All* by Carrie Harris
- ☐ *First Team* by Robbie MacNiven
- ☐ *Triptych* by Jaleigh Johnson
- ☐ *School of X* edited by Gwendolyn Nix
  (coming soon)

EXPLORE OUR WORLD EXPANDING FICTION

ACONYTEBOOKS.COM
@ACONYTEBOOKS
ACONYTEBOOKS.COM/NEWSLETTER